Paul Toolan was born in Yorkshire but is no
rural Somerset. After a long career teaching
Education and Universities he turned to writing, and already has a couple
of Christmas musicals under his belt. This is his first crime novel – and
the second and third are in full swing. Like his protagonist, he enjoys
walking and fishing and the occasional whisky but, unlike him, enjoys
travel – to Greece and Crete in particular.

# A KILLING TREE

Paul Toolan

# A KILLING TREE

*To the real Scramblers,*
*who could walk the legs off folk half their age....*

# PART ONE

*The Tree's Bounty*

# One

Waiting rooms.

Which sadistic sod invented waiting rooms?

Steel boxes, slow torture, clocks ticking backwards.

The toffee-nosed door of the Assistant Chief Constable (Crime) gave Batten another flat-faced sneer. Beyond the triple-glazing, Yeovil's rush-hour traffic had bumbled by in silence, five floors below. Best part of an hour, tapping his toes on this bile-green bloody carpet.

For something to do, he wrote a little speech to the new CID team he still hadn't met.

*I bet you collect coincidences? Dubious ones, I mean?*

The smell of fresh coffee wafted in, from somewhere…

*Me, when I've collected a few, and they refuse to cooperate, I get a sort of tingling in my big plod feet.*

In fact, his feet were a bog-standard size nine, barely big enough to support his gangly body, heavier than it seemed – as crooks occasionally discovered, the hard way. A thousand years ago, all that.

He sneered back at the door, tapped his toes, vibrated his lips like a horse. None of it helped. Why is nothing *happening*?

Ten miles away, clocks were ticking patiently forward. Dubious events began darkly to coincide.

# Two

They approached Burrow Hill from the north, fourteen of them. The climb was more challenging than it looked, even on this cool November morning. Fourteen was an average turnout for the Scramblers - their real name was the South Somerset Senior Citizens Rambling Group, but that was too big a mouthful when they were all out of breath.

All except Stephanie, the group's leader, recruiter, and unelected narrator. Stephanie Broke-Mondelle could walk and talk for England, and to the Scramblers' dismay, she frequently did. They'd heard the Burrow Hill speech before, but were too polite - and too breathless - to ask her to give it a rest.

'Burrow Hill may not be the *biggest* hill,' squeaked Stephanie, 'but I always think of it as a very *likeable* hill, yes? And in the low, flat plain of South Somerset even a *small* hill is welcome, no? Indeed, such a shapely little hill with a single, delightful tree set asymmetrically atop of it - well, how could it possibly be disliked?'

'Because it's a *hill*', they might have said. Instead they struggled up the final soggy paces to the top, leaned on their walking poles, parked their bottoms on the edge of the viewing platform, or simply stood there, breathing.

'Such an *inspiring* view! An all-round, uplifting and thoroughly *memorable* view!' squeaked Stephanie. 'Well worth the trifling climb, don't you agree?'

Grudgingly, they did. It was impossible to stand on the crown of Burrow Hill and ignore the effect of its horizon: handsome stands of poplar trees; deep-green bluffs merging into distant purple moorland; the scattered, haze-dimmed outlines of ancient villages; iron-blue streaks of drains and rines feeding the River Parrett, invisibly flowing through the plain beneath their feet. Beyond the roofs of the cider farm at Pass Vale, the vista was pleasantly blocked by the stout trunk of Stephanie's 'single, delightful tree.'

Big Harry Teign tipped back his thick neck and followed the slow flight of a pair of buzzards searching for prey above the long lines of apple trees.

'Oi think they're sizing you up, Eth,' he said, pointing. 'Good taste, them buzzards.' And he nudged a smile from his walking companion, who pretended to gaze at the chain of church spires emerging like stone silos from the mist below. You could navigate by drawing imaginary lines between the spires, Stephanie said. Often.

With a sigh or two, the Scramblers slowly creaked to their feet, still unaware of another presence on the hill. Propped against the far side of Stephanie's tree, his back to the group, lay a lone walker.

'Tree-huggin', are you?', big Harry asked, without reply. A friendly response was the norm in walkers' circles, but no offence was taken because this walker was fast asleep, boots thrust out ahead of him, broad-brimmed hat covering a head lolling dreamily onto his waterproof shoulder.

'Thisun's a sleep-walker', quipped Harry to Eth as they passed.

'Aarh, with a wet bum, the daaft bugger,' muttered Mick Baines, straightening his canary-yellow cap and giving Stephanie a defiant glance. He always swore in her presence, 'to keep 'er on 'er toes'.

For the Scramblers it was a pleasure to see a walker more exhausted than they were, so they descended the south side of Burrow Hill more quietly than they'd ascended the north. Except, that is, for Stephanie whose personal lexicon lacked the word 'quietly' and whose attitude to solo walkers was one of aggressive enlistment.

As the group meandered towards the cider farm below, it was Stephanie who remained on Burrow hill; it was Stephanie who rummaged in her sage-green backpack for a Scramblers membership card (of her own design); it was Stephanie who walked noisily around that single, delightful tree to aggressively enlist yet another hapless, lonely walker; and it was Stephanie's oft-used recruitment gambit ('*surely* you'd prefer to join the Scr-') that was suddenly cut off in her quiet-for-once throat by the grotesque gargoyle face of the prone walker whose empty eyes and snarling teeth screamed silently at her, but screamed so brutally that the dead scream seemed to enter and fill her whole skull before finding its way to the proxy of her jaw-dropped mouth, emerging in such a bird-scaring, tree-shaking, heart-piercing howl that, on hearing it, the Scramblers instantly ran like greyhounds back up the hill they had struggled to climb only minutes ago.

# Three

Zig Batten, a thirty seven year old pupil on his first day at school, pocketed his notes and once more crossed lanky legs in the faux leather chair. The waiting area carpet tried to bounce him back to his feet, demanding to know what he was doing here. He didn't have much of an answer.

It had been a less than smooth transition - hah! - from north to south. His house was sold, then the buyer pulled out - before pulling back in with a lower offer. Exploratory visits to his new workplace went to the wall when two colleagues threw a sickie in the middle of a serious drugs case. One colleague *was* sick; he'd caught a virus - from the drug-dealer's baseball bat. The other one, well, glad goodbyes.

He should have read the signs. Induction sessions with his new Chief Inspector were efficiently arranged then apologetically postponed. Chief Inspector Jellicoe was 'unexpectedly unavailable', they said. Temporarily, the Assistant Chief Constable (Crime) would for unexplained reasons oversee the new CID squad he was about to join. A rare cock-up, but a cock-up nonetheless.

I bet you, Zig, if this Jellicoe bloke isn't 'expectedly *available*' again, and soon, you'll end up doing *his* job as well as your own! You should be sussing out your new workplace, not toe-tapping this bouncy-castle of a carpet. Should have stayed where you were, shouldn't you? Yes, Zig. But I was short on options, wasn't I?

He did what he always did when confronting the unknown. He massaged his moustache, with his left-hand ringless ring-finger and his thumb.

The fittest Scramblers wished they'd never reached the top of Burrow Hill. Stephanie's jarring screams needed no pause for breath and her arms were clawing at the sky like a pair of masts searching for any signal other than the distress call she was currently receiving. To his credit, Harry Teign's first thought was to reach up and draw her hands gently down to her sides. They automatically sprang up to cover her face. When Harry turned to look at what triggered her anguish, his own hands wanted to do the same. As Eth Buller neared the top he turned her away.

'You don' want to see that, Eth. *I* don' want to see it neither, not twice.'

Distracted by his concern, Harry failed to divert the second wave. Stephanie's cries were multiplied as more Scramblers reached the hilltop's single tree and viewed its bounty. Mick Baines, whose girth made him last to arrive, added an exclamation mark to the long sentence of screams.

'Oh bugger me, Harry. Who's done *thaat* to 'im? Who'd want to do thaat to *anyone*?'

Every magazine in the chrome-steel rack had been in a trouser-press. Batten grabbed the nearest - 'Somerset Life.' *Life, Zig?* The entire building was an echo. The first feature told him that All Saints Day - today, November 1st - celebrates those who have attained a beatific vision of heaven. He stared at the plastic leather and puke-green carpet, and flicked to another page. Million pound houses built from the local honey-coloured hamstone taunted his wallet, reminding him of his own gritstone home in Leeds - once a wreck but now a solid, expansive villa to be proud of. He'd practically built the house around himself. Ten good years. Batten liked houses, even the part-furnished village cottage he had just rented, a few miles up the road, though in which direction he hadn't the faintest idea.

More moustache-stroking conjured Somerset life in the form of Mrs Pinch, the Assistant Chief Constable's PA. He half-rose in expectation but she merely ferried a buff folder from her office to the ACC's, and toddled back.

Cursing, he flipped to another page - the flooded Somerset Levels, in pictures: a tractor raising a bow-wake down a water-logged road; horses and cattle stranded on islands of sodden grazing land; torrents pouring from pumping stations into already swollen rivers. 'Communities cut off', said the caption. Well, Zig.

The hard steel magazine rack was clearly spring-loaded because when he rammed *Somerset Life* back in, a door clicked open and Mrs Pinch was simultaneously propelled *out*, towards the Assistant Chief Constable's door. She expertly flicked it open with just the point of her long index finger. The gesture looked like a warning. She said he could go in now - in fact she said he *should* go in, and not wishing to miss his turn at the dentist's, he did, ducking his gangly frame under the low door.

Geriatric druids keened a shrill litany of howls over Burrow Hill. Ageing ramblers ruptured the rural peace with strident wails, pumped to the skies by rasping lungs and the wobbles of bingo wings. The Scramblers had never covered so much ground at such a pace, and they were soon joined in tramping the landscape into mush by any rubbernecker who chanced to be in or around the cider farm when Stephanie Broke-Mondelle abruptly fled from the scene of her anguish, rocketing down the slope with a scream that blotted out the birdsong.

Had big Harry Teign not been a retired hospital porter, a panic of Scramblers might have scooped up what was clearly a corpse and carried it in retinue from Burrow Hill to the cider-farm below. What, to revive it with incantations and a slug of cider brandy?

'Step *back*!' Harry shouted. 'Don't touch him! Are you all *blind* as well as daaft? Can't you see he's *dead*?'

No living face looked like that, Harry knew. He'd rolled bodies to the mortuary many a time, but he'd never before seen a corpse as dead as this one. He raised his eyebrows at Mick Baines, whose loud yellow cap nodded back. Yes, he'd called the police. He wasn't to know but so had several others, and called for ambulances too. A few had called for God, but not even the supernatural could breathe life into the silently-screaming head that lay propped against the single, delightful tree on Burrow Hill.

Eth Buller's fingers gently curled into Harry's big fist. He rubbed the other one against the taut muscles of his brow. When he looked up at the sky, even the buzzards had gone.

Though he'd folded his legs into the offered chair, Batten still looked down at Assistant Chief Constable Gribble, a compact man in a spotless uniform, half-hidden behind a giant desk cluttered with compact trophies vainly boosted by large plastic plinths. Beside them, platoons of framed diplomas stood to attention before three smugly smiling children in the large colour photograph that spanned the far wall. The ACC eyed Batten suspiciously, as though he'd seen him before in unpleasant circumstances, but couldn't remember where.

'Er, Inspector Batten, yes. Apologies, on behalf of Chief Inspector Jellicoe, who, er, can't be here to welcome you. To Somerset, to the force, on your first day. So, a welcome from me. In his stead.' After a vocal pause he added, 'though reluctantly in his stead, truth be told.'

'Thank you very much, sir.' Nice to know the score.

'Long way from Yorkshire, mm?'

'As you say, sir.'

'Shan't beat about the bush here, Batten. Couple of things. A second apology, er, first of all.' The ACC paused, to sort out his firsts from his seconds, gave up and carried on. 'Fellow you're sort of replacing, Inspector Chard. Good enough chap in some ways. Tidy desk, and…..humph. In truth, *cricket* was his true passion - any damn form of cricket. More passion for cricket than for police work, Dan Chard.'

ACC Gribble's sharp eyes checked Batten for signs of cricket, but found none.

'Getting to the point: Dan Chard had what's called a sense of humour….' He said this as if senses of humour were akin to toxic radiation, or piles. '….And it was clearly this sense of humour which persuaded him, as a last act, to team you with the Sergeant that….you are now teamed with. Just noticed this myself. Hence the apology.'

'Sir?'

'Sense of humour. The cricket, you see. Was Mrs Pinch who noticed, truth be told. On the staffing roster. Well, there's you. Inspector Batten. And you're teamed with er, with Sergeant Ball. Sort of a joke. Yes?'

Batten's eyebrows said 'no'.

'Batten? Ball? On the roster as Batten/Ball. Cricket, you see. Mrs Pinch says it's old Dan Chard's departing pleasantry. If so, our apologies. I imagine there'll be some light banter at your expense. Could perhaps intervene, at a stretch, if you'd prefer another Sergeant, different name?'

Batten wished he could have stayed in Yorkshire, where cricket was truly a passion.

'If Ball is a good detective sir, good at his job, then I see no reason to change things.'

'Sergeant Ball is stout. He's local. And his mind's on policing. Do for you?'

Batten nodded. Entirely in hope.

When the call came in, PC Jon Lee tightened his seat-belt, checked his over-young face in the driver's mirror and switched on the siren, pleased to interrupt his search for two sacks of onions nicked from an allotment near East Lambrook.

At the same time, Detective Constable Eddie Hick swept food debris from his driver's seat before doing much the same, though from the opposite direction and without bothering to check his appearance in the mirror. Glad of the excuse to flee the scene of yet another tractor theft, at Westport this time, he stamped his foot on the accelerator pedal as if he'd fallen out with it. An unexplained death? A *death*! He was powerless to keep the thought at bay: Eddie, with luck it might be a murder!

And with murder in mind he gunned his car up the narrow snake of a lane at the foot of Burrow Hill - just as PC Jon Lee did the same from the opposite direction. The two police cars slewed to a noisy, grudging halt, their bonnets barely half a yard apart. Hick's neck was the first to jab out of the driver's window.

'You *pratt*! Are you *deaf*? What's the point of a siren if you take no notice?'

'Pratt yourself! And I've got *mine* on, haven't I? *You* didn't hear *mine*, did you?'

Hick resisted the temptation to start a plainclothes\uniform war. He despatched Lee to the cider farm at the foot of the hill while he grabbed a roll of Police-Line-Do-Not-Cross tape and ran jaggedly up the surprisingly steep bump to secure what little was left of the scene. When he confronted the screaming dead face, he wished he'd stayed at Westport. If murder looks like this, Eddie, stick with stolen tractors.

'You said 'a couple of things', sir?'

'I did. Second thing, er, Batten: Somerset.' The ACC paused, as if about to reveal long-concealed secrets buried in the vaults of Police HQ. 'Don't wish to be uncivil, but this move of yours, from Yorkshire. Well, Yorkshire. God's own country, mm?'

'Some people call it that, sir.'

'Indeed. But, for me, others like me, *Somerset* is God's own country. Best country - county, that is - in the world.'

'Sir?'

'My point, Batten, is you *were* in Yorkshire, but you are in Somerset now. And appropriate allegiance is expected - to the *modern* Somerset. Erase from your mind all images of caravans on the A303, jolly ploughboys, and village idiots chewing straw in turnip fields - forget, forget.'

Batten worked so hard at forgetting he forgot to speak.

'That clear?'

'Absolutely, sir.'

'In you, Batten, we have taken in a Yorkshire refugee. Taken a risk, done a favour. We do expect allegiance in return.'

'Sorry, sir? *Done a favour?*'

'Oh, you know how these things work, a northern favour for a southern favour. Bit of mutual back-scratching, force to force.'

'Sir, I really don't -'

'No need for the high horse, Batten. No need for any horse at all. If you were bent, bad, bovine or plain bloody useless you wouldn't be standing here now. Your competence is not in question. After Dan Chard, it's more than welcome, truth be told. But I repeat, we are not village idiots with empty cider barrels for brains. You've said goodbye to the feisty fireworks of an urban crime squad, and whispered hello to the damper squib of a mostly rural force, yes?'

It's *This Is Your Life*, Zig.

'And you moved from Inspector grade to Inspector grade. No promotion involved?'

'Correct. Sir.'

'Well. Hardly a surprise if an eyebrow or two is raised at your appointment? Hence my comment about allegiance.'

'I don't think you're questioning my allegiance, sir. I think you're wondering if I've come here to *skive*.'

The ACC's face turned as red as a cider apple but his retort was forestalled by the appropriate grr-grr, grr-grr of his desk phone, which he glared at, then ignored.

11

'The best I can say, Inspector, is that your Yorkshire 'directness' lends you clarity. Were it to rub off on me I suppose I should reply, '*Well? Have* you?"

'Most definitely *not*. Sir'. Batten's voice became an angry hiss. 'I have *never* skived. Skiving is not in my genes.'

More unwise words formed in his mouth but a peremptory knock on the door and the tight bun of Mrs Pinch's head kept them there.

'I am advised that you should take this call, sir', was all she muttered before the bun disappeared.

There's a lot of 'should' round here, thought Batten as the ACC grabbed the phone, listened, grunted, listened, and grunted again.

'Well. A chance to prove your 'allegiance' on your very first day, Batten. Hoped we might have a lull, truth be told. Give you time to knock the new squad into shape, over at Parminster. But in the absence of Chief Inspector Jellicoe, I'm afraid the burden falls on you....'

See, Zig?

'An unexplained death, on your new patch. Place called Burrow Hill. Worry not, the good Sergeant Ball is on his way. To show you where Burrow Hill *is*.'

Batten silently groaned. If he had a pound for every hour he'd wasted on 'unexplained deaths' that turned out to be heart attacks....

'We'll do our job, sir.'

'You will. And you'll report back to me temporarily - until Chief Inspector Jellicoe...'

The ACC failed to tell what Jellicoe might or might not do. Neither did he to tell Batten his transfer had involved very little mutual back-scratching. Gribble had wanted a training-minded, results-oriented, experienced detective for the new team - in case Jellicoe 'went wrong'. And Jellicoe had. Gribble doubted now that Batten was all those things, but at least he was *here*.

'I hope you've got some gumboots,' he said, as hard marbles of rain rattled the window, 'because the finest weather in God's own county is saying 'welcome, Inspector."

He *does* have a sense of humour, Zig. And, no, he didn't have any 'gumboots'. They were still in Yorkshire, with his friends, his books and CDs, his fishing gear, his sold-subject-to-contract house, his ex, and most of his experience. He began to wonder if he 'should' be there too.

# Four

Inspector Batten and Sergeant Ball barely shook hands before Ball swept the car across the Yeovil traffic and aimed it - Batten could only wince and hope - towards Burrow Hill.

Batten quietly appraised his new Sergeant: he was short, squat, and looked like an upturned jug. A sandy, cheerful face led quickly down to a pair of stubby, steel-hard arms that shouted rugby football. He's certainly no cricket man, Zig, so 'Batten/Ball' shouldn't be a problem - not that Ball showed any sign of getting the 'joke'.

Removing his glove to shake hands, Ball had unwrapped two pounds of sausage. Now, four pounds of bangers expertly gripped the steering wheel of Batten's Ford Focus. Drives it better than you do, Zig.

Ball's strong Somerset burr was more difficult to size up. Was he putting it on, in some kind of initiation rite, to remind this Northern incomer where he stood? Did Ball call other senior staff 'zor'?

'Not from these parts then, zor?'

'Razor sharp, eh, your skills of detection.' Batten added a smile, nudging the sarcasm towards camaraderie.

'Lancashire, is it, zor?' Ball added a smile of his own.

'*Yorkshire*, Sergeant. Or uniformed constable, if you'd prefer?'

'Yorkshire it is, then, zor.'

'Sergeant it is, then, Sergeant.'

This time they both smiled. Well, Zig, we can do playful. Can we do anything else?

'You're a long way from Yorkshire, zor.'

Batten gave Ball a sideways stare. Has the Assistant Chief Constable doled out a script to this lot? I'll be buggered if I'm sitting through a second lecture on *Somerset* being 'God's own county'.

'I am. And I expect you folk are wondering why?'

'Not me personally, zor. Happy as a pip in an apple, just the way things are.'

Batten read the code. Ball hadn't coveted the vacant Inspector role for himself.

'What about the *un*happy pips, Sergeant?'

Ball dipped his big head to one side. Playful, but careful too.

'Oh, you know folk, zor. If they wonder why, and the answer's unforthcoming, they invent stuff. They were inventing stuff about Chief Inspector Jellicoe till you came along.'

'And now they're inventing stuff about me?'

'Shocking thought, isn't it, zor, gossip in the Police Force?'

Batten chuckled. He sensed that Ball would do. He dropped the 'Sergeant'.

'Well, there's just you and me and a Ford Focus, Ball, so feel free.'

'Oh, zor, *you* could make up what that lot are making up, and a darn sight better, I imagine. Since you presumably know the facts?'

Yes, I do. Too soon to tell, though.

'*That lot?*'

'Let's just say one or two lads who haven't yet passed their Sergeant's exams, zor. And likely never will.'

Batten wondered if Ball's 'one or two lads' were part of his new CID team. It's not a team yet, Zig. Teams take time. He wondered how much time they'd give him. He turned instead to the sketchy notes he'd jotted down while getting the bum's rush from ACC Gribble's over-shiny office. The corridor had still smelled of fresh coffee - though not a thimbleful came *his* way. 'Male', the notes said....'discovered by local walking group....crown of Burrow Hill....alone....presumably deceased.'

'Not much further, zor,' Ball said, as he whizzed the car just a tad too quickly now down a series of narrower, sludgy back roads. Batten was in no hurry to investigate a heart attack on a hill he'd never heard of.

'Tell me about Burrow Hill.'

'*Tell* you about Burrow Hill, zor?'

'Ball, are you going to repeat everything I say?'

'Sorry, zor. Well. It's a hill.'

'Oh bugger, is it? I was going to bring charges under the Trade Descriptions Act.'

'Sorry, zor, what I mean is you're on the edge of the Somerset Moors and Levels now, zor, and single hills stick out. Stick up, that is. Plenty of clumps of bumps, but not a great number of obvious hills round here, you see, zor.'

'Rabbit country is it, then?'

'Rabbit country, zor?'

Even with eyes firmly on the road, Ball felt the sharp end of Batten's eyebrows.

'Sorry, zor. What do you mean, zor?'

'Well, *Burrow* Hill? Rabbits?'

'Oh, I see, zor. Don't know about that. It's more beef and dairy, horses, sheep and spuds round these parts. And cider apples a-plenty, of course. I expect there's rabbits too. Lots of rabbits in Somerset. Stacks of 'em. Don't suppose there's ever a shortage of rabbits at Burrow Hill.'

Batten wondered if a deep, philosophical conversation would ever take place between Ball and himself. Glancing across at the self-contained mass of his new Sergeant, in his nondescript jacket and vague tie, he was simply unsure. Is he solid, or stolid? Maybe he's thinking much the same about me? Time, Zig. Time.

Ball was hardly thinking about Batten at all. Inspectors were all much of a muchness to him. A sergeant's job is a sergeant's job, and he liked his work. Batten had a sense of humour and maybe a bit of depth to him, as far as he could tell. Bloody funny accent, though.

In the narrow lane at the base of Burrow Hill, Batten swapped his good shoes for the ancient pair of walking boots he kept in the car. They leaked a bit and were hardly 'gumboots', but they would have to do.

While the rain had ceased, the chaos clearly had not. A scruffy young detective constable was rushing around like a demented sheepdog, failing to herd the melee of wet walkers, oglers from adjacent cottages, farmhands, apple-pickers, customers from the cider shop, and miscellaneous ghoulish busybodies.

'Who the hell's this plonker?' asked Batten.

'Ah, bless him, zor, that's DC Eddie Hick. Not the sharpest dresser, and not the sharpest knife, but he has his good points - even if behind his back they call him Loft.'

'*Loft?*'

'Are you going to repeat everything I say, zor?'

Batten chuckled. 'OK, why 'Loft'? He's barely five foot nine.'

'Five foot nine, zor, yes, and full of crap.'

Batten was growing to like Sergeant Ball. His estimation firmed up when, to quieten the frenzied babbling of the mad mob buzzing around the base of Burrow Hill, the stocky sergeant's full-of-command voice yelled, 'QUOYYYYYYYYYETTTTTT!!!! '

A mass of faces gaped in bemused silence. Immediately, there was the sound of birdsong, though Batten couldn't locate the source of the distinctive trill and twit. Striding past, Ball pointed up at the trees bordering the road.

'Nuthatch, zor. There, see? Sign of a warm winter, some say.'

Batten failed to spot even a sparrow, but did spot DC Hick wiping an 'oh, so *you're* the incomer' look off his face.

'Who are all these people, lad?'

'This lot? Wish I knew! Can't get sense out of any of 'em. There's an army of wrinklies from some walking group, there's cider-farm staff, there's any number of idle passers-by and nosy-parkers, and a coach party just arrived from Taunton 'cos they're doing tours of the crime scene now! Only person who *hasn't* turned up is the Doc, 'cos he's in a tailback on the A303. I was joking about the coach party.'

'Well, don't,' replied Batten. 'And if the doctor hasn't seen the body yet, don't assume it *is* a crime scene. Just do your job, and with a bit of respect for the dead, eh, lad?'

'Sir.'

'Now, who found the body?'

'Ohh sir, everybody found the body! The scene of crime blokes - well, *someone* sent 'em and they arrived, but the doc didn't, so up the hill they went - they're doing their nuts! That walking group's done a clog-dance up there!'

'Hick, foot off the throttle, eh? Now, who found the body *first*?'

'If it were that simple, sir.'

If only, Zig.

'It's mad. There's two of everything,' Hick spluttered.

'But just one body I hope?'

'So far, sir, yes, only one. Some of this lot have come close though, trying my patience.'

Sergeant Ball cut in. 'Well *someone* must have found the body first, Hickie, so stop trying ours, OK?'

'Sorry Sarge. But I'm still establishing who had the privilege. It was either her or her,' and he pointed in two barely different directions. 'Likely candidate seems to be a Ms Farley, first name Debbie. She's jabbered a pile of claptrap so far and she keeps jabbering. I can't make sense of her nor shut her up. There's a flock of birds flying out of her gob. Mad.'

'Or in shock perhaps?' asked Batten. 'Having discovered a dead body? And not being a completely de-sensitised human being?' *Like you.*

'Suppose, sir.'

'And the other 'her'?'

'Oh, she's from hell this one. Ms Posh. First name 'Very'.'

Hick winced as Batten gave him an eyebrow.

'Er, Ms Broke-Mondelle, first name Stephanie. You couldn't dent her accent with a diamond drill. 'If you please,' she says, 'it's Broke pronounced to rhyme with 'look,' and it's Mondelle with the emphasis on the second syllable'. Or was it syll*able*, I forget.'

'Don't *forget*, Hickie. Write the stuff down,' Ball advised.

Hick wanted to say 'stick a pair of tweezers up my arse and I'll comb the crime scene as well'. He settled for 'Yes, Sarge.'

'OK lad, you've got a lot on your plate I know, but you have set up a temporary post?' asked Batten.

'I did, sir. It's the office in the cider farm here, just across the road. I've had to put Debbie Farley in there for now. The Broke-Mondelle woman, she's the next room along, little staff kitchen. PC Lee's with them, poor sod. The first one can't shut up and the second one, well, she squeaked like a posh pig for ten minutes, then suddenly, whoomph, the brakes came on and she stopped talking altogether - don't ask me why. What a bloody day!'

'You wouldn't know this, zor, but this is Hick's first body. I remember my first. Behaved much the same as Hickie, if I'm honest.'

Batten nodded his understanding. Yes. He remembered his first body too. And wished he didn't.

As they stepped into the cider farm's office, two paramedics who were obscuring the prone frame of Debbie Farley waved them politely away. She wasn't jabbering now. Batten inhaled the sharp smell of fresh vomit.

17

Next door, in a low-beamed store-room that clearly served as an impromptu staff canteen, Stephanie Broke-Mondelle was sitting at a rickety table, still, in her walking gear, amidst the dregs and discards of somebody's lunch, staring at a cup of cold tea, and shaking. She didn't know how much longer she could keep quiet - it hardly came naturally to her - but by also pretending to shake she had, so far, encouraged the young police constable to keep his distance. She *was* genuinely in shock and saddened to the bone, but coming from a family of military surgeons she was better equipped than most to deal with dead bodies and the living mind's reaction to them. What she really needed wasn't sweet tea but time, time to think. Contrary to external impressions, she was normally capable of deep, incisive thought. But normality had absconded. And so the deliberate shaking went on, in the hope they would leave her alone.

Telling the police exactly what she had found on Burrow Hill, how and when - this would not be a problem. But admitting she knew exactly *who* she had found, once she'd clumsily dislodged the hat from his poor, stricken face? Oh my heart, could she admit exactly *how* she knew him? And reveal what he had entrusted to her? Word would seep out, surely? 'They', whoever they were, might…. She shuddered, not daring to imagine who 'they' were. Or what they might do.

Two slightly soggy males, policemen presumably, one tall and one stocky like a fork and a spoon, she thought, peered at her from the doorway and triggered more false shaking and sobbing. They withdrew, and she heard them whispering with the young constable before the tall one with the moustache said 'up the hill, then.'

'Oh dear, Stephanie,' she said to herself. 'This must stop. What did Daddy always say? 'Never, never run from the enemy, girl!' But if you don't know who the enemy *is*….?'

18

# Five

At a very inconvenient moment, the phone rang in Lady Wake's de luxe hotel suite in southern Spain.

'I'm very sorry to disturb you, m'lady, but there's no sign of Lawrence anywhere and the Estate can't run itself. What should I do? I know it's his morning off but he's always back from his walk by now - '

Lady Wake breathed a testy, long-distance sigh into the phone, rolled over in her late-morning bed, and removed her hairy companion's hand from the inside of her naked thigh. She'd told Rhona to ring her only if a *serious* matter arose at Wake Hall.

'Well, Rhona, perhaps his car's broken down or he's run out of petrol, or something equally obvious, no?'

'But he's neither phoned, m'lady, nor answered his mobile. That's not at all like him. And it was more the pressure on the rest of the staff I was calling about. If I could ring the staffing agency…?'

'Mm, let's see how people cope first, Rhona, shall we? Just for today? If there's a problem tomorrow we'll address it then, mm?'

Rhona knew from experience when a conversation with Lady Wake was over. She put down the phone, at the very moment that the muscled hand of Lady Wake's bed-mate pulled firmly on the leather bridle strapped round her slender neck, drawing her smooth, eager and very naked body as close to his as it was possible to get.

'It's fine for *her*,' moaned Rhona Fiske. 'She's not one of the people having to cope!' In Lawrence's absence she'd already pulled a surly Jake Tuttle, the one remaining full-time gardener, off the ride-on mower and onto the Wake Hall office telephone, coerced Allie Chant out of the stables and into the post-room, and signed off the till-rolls in the Estate's retail outlets on her own flimsy authority. Now she was dealing with deliveries of animal feed, IT equipment orders, tractor repairs - ridiculous! She was at least comforted that her job description as Wake Hall's Head Housekeeper wasn't the only one expanding daily. Lawrence's Estate Manager role was clearly stretching too.

'It's the recession, Rhona. Money is temporarily less fluid than of late. It's a test of our willingness to adapt,' was all Lady Wake had said in response to Rhona's previous complaints. Huh! She means 'find another job if you can, Rhona dear, or stop whingeing.' She would have liked to give Lady Wake a piece of her mind, but it was safer to take it out on the cook instead. Alas, the cook was another one who hadn't turned up for her shift. Thank god Lady Muck's abroad, Rhona thought, or *I'd* end up making lunch for her and her current muscle-bound bed-warmer. Olly! What kind of a name is *Olly* for a mammoth like him? Would he last any longer than Lady Wake's previous sexy bad boys? Who cares? With relief, she slammed the kitchen door. She hadn't a clue what pampered beauties and hairy gorillas ate these days.

Having brought a semblance of organisation to the chaos at the foot of Burrow Hill, Batten and Ball ducked under the police tape and slogged up the deceptively steep incline to the top. Half-way there, Ball's phone rang. After a few rich, burry grunts he popped it back in the pocket of his battered blue waterproof.

'That was the doc, zor. Traffic's clearing on the A303, be here soon.'

'He'll arrive in a foul mood and treat us like cretins - the ones I've met usually do', sighed Batten.

'Seemed calm enough, zor. He was listening to a bit of Bach.'

Batten's jaw dropped. Ball could identify the background strains of Bach? Down a mobile phone? *Ball*? How very singular.

'Hadn't got you down as a classical music buff,' said Batten, still amazed at the hidden depths of his stubby red colleague.

'M'not, zor. Doc Danvers, he always listens to Bach in his car. Says it calms him down. Don't understand it myself. He says it's to do with the counter-something. Counterpane, is it?'

Batten prayed that Bach's use of musical counterpoint would sooth Doc Danvers. A dose of Bach in a traffic queue on the A303 could just as easily make his mindset too Baroque to be helpful.

Despite the new surroundings, his thoughts drifted back to Dr Jubbe, the most recent police surgeon he'd had dealings with, and to the last murder scene they'd attended, two years ago, in an overgrown copse behind a lay-by on the Leeds-Bradford Road. Doc Jubbe had been a piece of work.

'You want me to be more definite, do you, Inspector? Well, bully for you. All I will say is that, from a medical viewpoint, the body is definitely dead. Though from the viewpoint of philosophy, can we ever *know*?'

Pointing down at the definitely dead, definitely naked body, with its meat and two veg definitely on display, Batten had asked, tongue plonked deeply in his cheek, 'but he is definitely *male*?'

Jubbe had followed Batten's finger, shrugged, and replied 'oh, those. Well, I'll first have to check that George here is the original owner. We could be looking at Georgina, plus the surgeon's art, couldn't we? Good-day.'

As soon as Batten saw the now-tented body he envied Doc Jubbe's sense of detachment. Not a tent, but a chamber of horrors. Did he and Ball silently collude in a swift exit? He reminded himself that the dead body had been a living man – though nameless, as yet.

Equally swift was their survey of the pulverised crime scene - if crime scene it was. The police photographer's face was a collage of frowns as he struggled to locate anything worth removing the lens-cap for.

'Pile o' mud, zor, and sod all else,' Ball said.

And what was the dead man *doing* here, other than taking in the view? Everyone gotta be somewhere, Zig, even exiled northern Inspectors from the CID .

A frustrated Batten inspected the rest of Burrow Hill. Hurry up, Doc Danvers, whoever you are! Pronounce 'Heart Attack', and loudly, so I can shut down here and open up at Parminster. Wherever Parminster *is*.

Policing, he knew, was action swamped by interruptions and by aeons of waiting. Waiting was the worst. He'd never been a man who could keep still for long, without a fishing rod in his hand. He tried to deflect his thoughts from the muscle-tightened rictus on the dead man's face by disliking a police surgeon he'd never met. Failed. Even from several feet, the face was a horror show. To die like that, alone, slumped against the rough bark of a nameless tree.... For a moment, he was back in ACC Gribble's waiting room, reading *Somerset Life*. All Saints Day had not gone well for this particular soul, whoever he was. Saint or sinner, his final vision was hardly beatific. Batten pushed the image away. Had he bothered to read the rest of the feature, he would have noted that tomorrow,

November 2nd, was All Souls Day. When the dead are remembered.

Shuddering, he stared at unknown fields, fields that must be second nature to the weird walking group who found the body. This is your workplace now, Zig. When will its landmarks become second nature to *you*? And who will your friends be, here? Despite his vantage point, he could identify nothing remotely recognisable in the landscape. He felt as solitary as the body, propped up by nothing more than an isolated tree.

Thankfully, the murk began to lift, and shots of sunlight poked at the abating clouds. He plodded to the gentler slope on the north side of the hill, the side that the Scramblers had first scrambled up this very morning. Having taken a look at them, as arthritic a bunch of old wrinklies as he'd ever seen, he found it hard to believe they had minutes later scrambled back up the steeper southern side in response to what the chubby bugger with the daft yellow hat called 'the deathly scream of a how-und from hell!'

As Batten looked down the slope, the sun outstripped its smear of cloud and the vista to the north of the hill came to life, exploding into such a tapestry of contours and colours that even a jaundiced northern policeman was impressed. Burrow Hill certainly had an all-round view. What struck him most was the pointillist panorama of apples, thousands on thousands of apples, on tree after tree, or in multi-coloured mounds where the apple-gatherers had heaped them. Was it apples he could smell? Penetrating dots of red, deep green, mottled shades of yellow and pale-brown sang out from the biggest, the most kaleidoscopic orchard he'd ever encountered, each tiny dot in its perfect place, each dot adding to the triumph of the whole.

And the dot that is you, Zig, where does it fit? What is it doing here? In Yorkshire they eat apples; in Somerset they *drink* them. Which will it be for you?

Momentarily, it was Yorkshire. He had fended off Ball's gentle questions but could not fend off his own. Glad to deflect the dead man's face, he drifted back, to Leeds a few short months ago, visiting Aunt Daze, who had brought him up from the age of two, his mother in all but name, his living roots. Aunt Daze had returned to her little house one afternoon to discover she'd been burgled. Without fuss, she called the local police who sent a beat bobby to take a look. PC Kerr duly arrived, said yes to tea, examined the locks, and followed the burglar's trail through the ransacked rooms.

'It worra mess but 'e took 'is time, I'll give 'im that', Aunt Daze told Batten afterwards. ''E give me a number, you know, to send t'insurance. Did 'a want a locksmith? Nay, 'a said. Dimi'll come round and fix me lock. 'E's 'andy like that.'

Dimi was Zig's younger brother. Zig stopped himself thinking that Dimi might have done the burglary himself. Not even Dimi would steal from Aunt Daze. It was the one bit of decency left in him, and while it remained, Zig lived in hope. He hadn't asked Aunt Daze why she thought Dimi was good at locks, though.

'S' funny, Zig, but when 'a walked in and saw t'mess, first thing 'a did was check me 'iding place, you know, where 'a keep my fortune.' She gave the warm giggle he'd been hearing for thirty seven years. Her hiding place was behind a loose piece of tongue and groove by the airing cupboard. 'Anyroad, it were all still there, they'd missed it, the blind buggers,' and she giggled again.

He'd given her the obvious advice, but she'd never trusted banks. Aunt Daze's hidey-hole contained a wad of rainy-day cash and some old curiosities, including a wartime ration book and a Toby Jug. But her sister's wedding ring was there too, and one of a pair of gold lockets - he had the other - holding a curl of her sister's hair. Her sister. His mother. Aunt Daze giggled on, till it was no longer a giggle he was hearing. He sat down next to her on the old sofa, put a long arm round her shoulder as her tears came.

'It were all there when 'a checked. Every piece, Zig. I don't want to say it, but it must have been '*im*. It were after 'e'd rooted round, that policeman, Kerr. When '*e'd* gone, *they'd* gone!'

He believed her. Aunt Daze might drop an aitch or two, but she was full of marbles. Abuses of the uniform did happen - a rogue PC checks out a burglary, pockets whatever small objects the burglars failed to find. If something's missing, well, the burglars took it. He'd be having strong words with PC Kerr....

'Zor? *Zor*?'

Batten was still gazing in silence at the view to the north, internal and external, and barely heard Sergeant Ball, barely noticed his jabbing finger.

'Doc's here, zor,' said Ball, indicating a little apple of a man at the foot of Burrow Hill. Had the 'Doc' been closer, Batten would have seen the deep frown of dismay on the face of Dr Benjamin Danvers. But then, if the Doc had been closer, he would already have climbed Burrow Hill, the prospect of which was causing the frown in the first place.

'He generally avoids physical exertion, zor,' explained Ball. 'Says being a doctor, he knows how bad it can be for the human body'. Anticipating Batten's reply he added 'I know, zor, I know. But he has his funny ways, the doc.'

Batten was about to remind Ball that funny ways were the norm around here when, to prove it, Ball gave one of his out-of-nowhere yells.

'HICKIE!!! BRING THE DOC'S BAG UP HERE! SHARPISH!'

'And don't let him roll back down again,' Batten muttered. Not till he's said 'heart attack.' *Then* he can bugger off. Then we can *all* bugger off.'

A red-faced man of about forty frowned his way to the top of Burrow Hill. Dr Danvers was wearing a natty blue pinstripe suit, set off nicely by a cream shirt and a silk tie with some sort of motif on it. As he approached, Batten saw it was a tiny stethoscope. What sort of gobbledygook will you get from this one, Zig? Will he be more forthcoming if you hum a bloody Brandenburg Concerto? At least he hasn't brought the press and media with him. Yet.

Danvers quickly recovered his breath and manners and took Batten's hand in a firm handshake.

'We haven't met before, have we, Inspector? No, I thought not. Quite a deceptive little bump, isn't it, Burrow Hill? Now then, where's my bag got to?'

DC Hick was ascending the hill for the umpteenth time that day, so it was no surprise that even the Doc had beaten him to the top. Hick's randomly-jointed frame twitched and jerked into view, the square bulk of the heavy medical bag dragging him to a breathless halt at the now tented body. Before Batten could give Hick a 'well done, lad', the Doc was donning crime scene gear and rattling on.

'Inspector, this is how I work: quickly, carefully, and with close observation of everything in, on or adjacent to the body. I shall tell you all I can today, in situ, and more later, naturally, in my report, which will be in poshed-up medical lingo and as such largely incomprehensible to mere mortals. I shall broadly translate, fear not.'

'Doc - '

'Yes, I do realise what your needs are today, Inspector. I shall offer reasoned speculation - where evidence allows. Since later analysis may modify my pensees, I offer them on the strict understanding that you will *under no circumstances* treat them as factual at this stage. Agreed?'

Batten was so shocked to meet a police surgeon whose policy was avowedly helpful - even if his language was not - that he barely managed a nod of assent.

'Do forgive my forward nature, but I must emphasise: I shall be viscerally miffed if it is later brought to my attention that Inspector....remind me?'

'Batten.'

'Thank you. That Inspector Batten has interpreted my speculation as hard fact or, worse still, was *acting* on the assumption that it was.'

Christ, Zig, if this is after Bach, what's he like after *Wagner*?

'Seems fair, Doctor', said Batten.

'Good. Then shall I take a peek at Mr Body?'

Doc Danvers scooped up his medical bag, humming classically to himself as he entered the white tent whose sides rippled faintly in the weakening breeze. Batten and Ball knew not to cramp his considerable style.

'Hickie', said Sergeant Ball to the yawning figure of DC Hick, 'rest your bum for a bit, you look exhausted.' Ball indicated the seat around the viewing platform which the sun was now warming, before he and Batten strolled a few paces away to compare notes. Hick did as instructed but when he leaned back and closed his eyes, the dead face of his first body made him instantly open them again.

'Strange way of committing suicide,' Batten said, deliberately leaving the more likely theories to his Sergeant.

'And cider's a penny a pint, zor.'

'Heart attack, then, surely? Big breakfast, loads of caffeine, went up the hill too fast? No foul play involved?'

Ball shrugged noncommittally. 'Bit neat and upright, the body, for a heart attack? Not sure, zor.'

'Well, let's say he wanders over by the tree to take in the view, has a funny turn and ends up slumped against the trunk?'

'Not exactly slumped, though, is he? And according to Hickie, one of the Scramblers said that the....er....'

'Jack,' said Batten. 'We'll call him Jack for now.'

Ball looked puzzled.

'As in 'Jack and Jill went up the hill'? Unless you think it's *Jill* in there?' Batten jabbed a thumb at the white tent, and thought of the pedantic Dr Jubbe.

'Ah, I see, zor. No, no, it's a Jack, right enough. Thing is, the tall bloke from the walking group, he said when they first noticed the....noticed *Jack*, they assumed he was asleep. He had a wide-brimmed hat over his face, as if it'd been tipped down over his eyes, on purpose, you know, like when you're having a doze. But...'

'But it would have fallen off, like as not, if Jack had a heart-attack? Or a convulsion. Or some other kind of death-rattle?'

'S'right, zor. Even if the hat was moved by one of the drongos who've done a clog-dance up here, it seems to have been in place when that Stephanie woman and her Scramblers first made it to the top of the hill.'

Batten was pleased he and Ball were finding a working rhythm. Neither man was keen to broach the visible evidence though. Noblesse oblige, Zig.

'Never seen a heart-attack do *that* to a human face. You?'

Ball shook his head. Or was it a shudder? Batten aired some possibilities.

'One: *somebody* unknown discovered Jack before Stephanie Something-or-other and her bunch of arthritic wrinklies got here -'

'-and that unknown someone popped Jack's hat back on, for some unknown reason,' added Ball.

'Two: Jack was *placed* beneath his greenwood tree and smoothed into shape *post*-mortem. To make passers-by *think* he was asleep.'

'To gain time, get away from the scene?'

'If it *is* a scene.'

'If it is, zor, good luck finding evidence of a body being moved - amongst all this.'

They frowned at the 'crime scene'. Ball was right. It was a pile of mud.

# Six

Southern Spain was mud-free and smelt of oranges - a welcome change from Wake Hall, which to Olly Rutter smelt of old cow. Lady Wake didn't though, nothing old or cow-like about her, stretched across a luxuriously-padded sun-bed, in that bikini, the clothless one, which barely concealed her own luxurious padding.

The only bit of Somerset he missed right now was Baz Ballard, his driver and general dogsbodyguard. He'd usually given Baz a slap or two by now, or at least a sharp tap on the cheek. But a tap on the cheek from Olly Rutter was a discount voucher for a good slap. Olly was good at slapping people. Baz was just for practice.

If he had his big hands on bloody Lawrence he'd give him the biggest slap of all. Except *he* wouldn't. Olly Rutter's mantra never changed: deliberate ignorance at one end, and a cast-iron alibi at the other. He yawned and stretched, crushing the sun-bed further into the sand of the private beach. His Spanish alibi had the bonus of Mediterranean heat. Back in Somerset, where frost was forecast, well-paid minions would slap on his behalf - or sub-contract the job to minions of their own. Not Baz, though. Baz seemed to be going off the boil lately. More fool him.

With the sound of silk on satin, Lady Marianne Wake eased onto her side in search of an even tan, and he admired the smooth violin of her back and thighs, framed by an expensive blue sea. But the view was ruined by the thought of bloody Lawrence - and having to pretend to *like* the old bastard whenever Marianne was around. Olly could spot a crook equally well in a mirror or at five hundred yards, and he'd spotted Lawrence in a flash - the worst kind of crook, the dishonest kind who fools people - her included - into thinking butter wouldn't melt between a greasy finger and a crooked thumb.

But Olly wasn't going to say so. Why upset the finest squeeze he'd ever had? And just as well she was. There needed to be *some* reason for being based in yokel-bloody-Somerset, canoodling in the suspect mud and the noxious rural stink. Bedding up in creaky Wake Hall with Marianne was sex de-luxe; but then you woke to antiques-past-their-sell-by-date and brown bathwater.

'You should be breezing off to make top money in Bristol,' he told himself. 'Or why not London, this time?'

But, yes, he had a soft spot for her Ladyship. 'And a hard spot too,' he chuckled smugly. The problem was her soft spot for old-retainer Lawrence, whose management skills kept her overdrawn country estate on the rails. So watch your step.

'I *know* it's Lawrence. I can *smell* him.'

'What's that, darling?'

'Rumbling stomach. Ready for a bit of lunch?'

'Half an hour, mm? This sun is a *delight*.'

Olly removed his shades, squeezed the tension from his eyes, his hand brushing against the gold-plated memory stick that dangled from a gold chain fastened securely round his big neck. Anyone trying to filch the juicy data it contained would get a bunch of broken fingers. The spare stick, the only other copy, was kept in the safe, in Olly's Fort Knox of an office at Wake Hall, and no-one was going to get in there without an invitation.

But someone had.

'It's that old bastard Lawrence. I *know*. Filched the memory stick and left his scent behind.' And Lawrence had given him that look, that patronising look. Nobody did that to Olly. He searched for someone to slap but Baz was in Somerset, out of range. Clawing a large pebble from the beach, he slapped it into the sea.

'They'd better be getting the job done,' he hissed at the Spanish air. Making the tractors and barns more dangerous, the Estate lakes deeper than before. Wake Hall was overflowing with sharp objects, nasty substances - accidents just waiting to happen. If given a helpful nudge. Olly had a smug chuckle at that.

Lawrence, though, he wouldn't be smiling.


Doc Danvers's pill-shaped head popped out of the white canvas package surrounding the single tree, and his arm beckoned. They peered into the tent, which was a good deal whiffier than before.

'Summary,' said Danvers.

Well, he doesn't mess about, give him that, Zig.

'Your Mr Body here - male, late fifties perhaps. Big chap, around six foot; fifteen stone or thereabouts, I'd estimate. Not overweight, and muscle tone very good for his probable age. On the debit side, a man who likely takes more drink than is - apologies, was - good for him. Kindly disregard any inconclusive link between drink and demise. No obvious wounds, no loss of blood, no signs of invasive trauma. Time of death of Mr Body - mm, complicated by his choosing to sit outdoors to shuffle off the mortal coil, with his derriere on the cold wet ground -'

And just why would he choose to do that, Zig? If he did?

' - so, best I can roughly estimate is mid to late morning.'

'Today, presumably?' asked Batten, tongue firmly in cheek.

'Mais oui, Inspector.'

'We were wondering if it's your bog-standard heart-attack, Doc?' said Ball, ducking beneath the Danvers radar.

'We-ell, till the knives come out, heart does have a place on the podium…..And respiratory failure of course, though that need not imply a pair of brutish hands around the windpipe, as doubtless you're aware….'

Batten was about to ask *his* question but Danvers' radar pinged within a micro-second.

'Your chaps won't have spotted this,' said Danvers a little archly, holding up an evidence bag containing a stainless-steel thermos flask, small enough to fit neatly into a walker's anorak pocket. Batten drooled at the fingerprint possibilities. 'No criticism intended, by the by. It was jammed between your Mr Body's derriere and this very tree.' Danvers patted the rough bark with his latex hand. Batten suddenly couldn't remember if it was possible to fingerprint a tree. He wondered again what kind of tree it was.

'If your chaps *had* found it I'd be giving them a piece of my procedural mind - they'd have had to move the body, tut-tut, to have glimpsed it at all. It's empty by the way -'

'But there must be -'

'Oh yes, a small amount of residue. It's soup, Inspector. Curried parsnip, my informed guess - I'm blessed with a good nose. And since

30

you will have noted what appears to be swelling in Mr Body's oral cavity, evidence of excessive salivation, tightened facial muscles - '

*Tightened facial muscles*? It's a bit bloody worse than *that*!

' - traces of vomit on his lips, his right hand and shirt front, and, only apparent when I turned the body of course, slight evidence of bloody diarrhoea, well, further possibilities make something of an entrance.'

That explains why Jack's got whiffier, thought Batten. And do me a favour, Doc, stop referring to him as 'Mr Body', will you?

'The unfortunate news - from your point of view, Inspector - is that the toxicology results will arrive long after your patience has expired. I recommend t'ai chi to combat this, by the way - '

'Doc', asked the less intimidated Sergeant Ball, 'apologies if I'm getting ahead of myself, but you *are* saying he was poisoned?'

'Have *you* ever been poisoned, Sergeant?'

'Er, had a bit of food-poisoning once. Does that count?'

'It does indeed. And my serious point is this: you have been poisoned - and yet you are still alive!'

Batten could hear Dr Jubbe mumbling 'insofar as we can ever *know*, philosophically speaking.'

'Mr Body here, *may* have been poisoned. The thus-mandatory post-mortem will soon reveal more. But poisoned by what exactly? And, if indeed poisoned - through malice or by accident - did the poison in fact kill him? Or did something else? That too, is as yet unknown.'

'Doc -'

'Suspicious death or not, Inspector, I cannot be more definitive today.'

So, 'suspicious' now, Zig. And guess what's next in the hierarchy? He closed off the thought that 'at least we're not wasting our time.' Please god that a man's death is ever a waste of time.

'Your Mr Body, Inspector, died because his heart and lungs ceased to carry out their support role.' Danvers raised his gloved hands in a theatrical shrug.

Batten looked down at the hands of 'Jack', securely wrapped in two evidence-preserving bags that made them look like a pair of small pale paddles, and then at the pale, thankfully-diffused shape of the now-bagged head. Next to the body, a large evidence box enclosed what Batten

31

assumed was Jack's broad-brimmed hat.

'Was he moved, Doctor, do you think?'

'Ah, I take it you mean 'was Mr Body *placed* here, by friend or foe?' Or did he die in situ?'

Batten nodded in silence. The Doc was already talking for two, the tiny stethoscopes on his tie bobbing up and down in rhythm with his adam's apple.

'Lividity is still at an early stage so one cannot be certain, though there are indicators. Speculation?'

Another nod.

'Here Mr Body died, and here Mr Body stayed. Whichever poor pathologist is called to the slab will doubtless confirm or refute.' He chuckled. 'Oh dear, the poor pathologist may very well be me.'

Batten sighed. Ball shrugged. How quickly theories tumble. If Jack wasn't moved, who popped his hat back on? And why?

'Almost forgot', Danvers chipped in again. 'Mr Body's identity. Likely to be revealed when you examine these.'

'And he held aloft three bags containing a wallet, a mobile phone and various keys, as if he'd conjured them from a hidden pocket, in lieu of a white rabbit.

As the SOCOs did their work, Batten mused that identifying the victim was only one of too many tasks facing his new team, most of whom he'd never met. He hoped they were prepared - not for magic tricks, but for long hours, pressure, and hard work. There'd be no room for skivers, he was sure of that.

While a weary DC Hick creaked from his perch on the viewing platform to shepherd Doc Danvers to the foot of Burrow Hill, Batten carefully opened the dead man's wallet. The cold, rubbery feel of his crime-scene gloves triggered unpleasant echoes from the past - they never go away, do they, Zig, bad memories? He would have drifted further into darkness had Sergeant Ball not interrupted him.

'Anything, zor?'

'Oh, er, sixty quid in folding money....gold credit card, 'Mr L. Vann'. Mean anything to you?' Ball shook his head. Batten drew out a business card. 'Well, Jack is not a Jack, it seems, but a Lawrence. 'Mr Lawrence

Vann'. Estate Manager for some place called Wake Hall. Not that *I'm* any wiser.'

He looked to Ball for comment, but Ball was staring silently into a dark space of his own.

'Sergeant?'

'Oh, sorry, zor. I don't know any Lawrence Vann, zor, no. I'll phone it through, see about next of kin.'

'Wake Hall, though? Ring a bell?'

For a moment, Ball's dark space drew him back.

'Wake Hall. Well, zor, yes. I do know Wake Hall.' He pointed vaguely west, his face still a blank mask. 'Hard to miss it. If you wanted to walk all the way round Wake Hall, you'd need a strong pair o' legs.'

'What the hell is it?' asked Batten. 'A theme park?'

'Hardly that, zor. Big estate. Private. A lot of....land. Was old Lord Wake's 'fore he died. There's a Lady Wake runs it now. The daughter. Inherited, I suppose.'

'What does he manage at Wake Hall, this Lawrence Vann? *Who* does he manage?'

An unsmiling Ball merely shrugged. Batten had no idea what an Estate Manager did, or who he did it with. Could Wake Hall provide some clue to his suspicious death? Or his murder? It was a logical place to start. Once they'd finished at Burrow Hill.

Entering the temporary police command post that was normally the office of The Burrow Hill Cider Company, Batten and Ball were surprised by the now sharper tang of vomit - and by the pin-striped form of Doc Danvers. Yet again, his answer forestalled their question.

'I was waylaid, Inspector. These fine medicos here.' Danvers waved an arm at two worried-looking paramedics. 'And just as well, because there *was* genuine cause for concern.' He indicated the prone form of Debbie Farley, adding 'very poorly but no longer in mortal danger, so fear not for a spike in the death-rate statistics.' Then, with more sleight of hand, he produced an evidence bag containing a stainless steel thermos.

'That's not the one we - ?'

'No, Inspector. This is Miss Farley's flask. Identical twins, perhaps?'

'And it...?'

'It does, Inspector. Soup. Curried parsnip, I'd bet my palate on it.'

Ball cut in. 'Doc, I think Inspector Batten's asking if this flask also contains poi-'

'Ah, Sergeant, we are not certain that *either* flask contains poison -'

'But -'

'- but the indications are growing in number and strength, I agree. This unfortunate lady here is presenting symptoms that *possibly* relate to a yet-to-be-identified poison. If so, we are greatly relieved she imbibed merely a soupcon of her soup.'

Batten groaned at the Doc's sense of humour. And, glancing down at the oxygen-masked and ghostly-pale Debbie Farley, he groaned at his sense of time and place, before realising he was himself admiring the curves of her body. She was a looker, even beneath the mask, and what, thirty-five, forty? He felt his toes tingle. Poison, *twice*, Zig?

Danvers chattered on. 'Please note that her flask is still two thirds full. How wonderful for our toxicologist chums to have such copious material to work with.'

'Wonderful' for Batten too. One possible murder on his first day on the job was bad enough. But two of them? Don't even think about it.

Jake Tuttle the gardener had had enough. The best way to stop Lawrence's phone ringing, he decided, was to unplug it. So he did. Just like pruning honeysuckle, only easier. Sitting indoors, in a Wake Hall *office*, at a Wake Hall *desk*, taking messages and telling a stream of callers that 'Mr Vann will get back to you soon, sir' - huh, waste of time. He didn't give a toss what bossy Rhona Fiske said. Stumping across to his ride-on mower, he popped on a pair of ear defenders, started the engine and resumed taming the grass. *And*, he said to himself, if Rhona bloody Fiske or Lawrence bloody Vann step in front of my mower right now, I'll mow their bloody toes off!

As freshly-cut grass spurted from Jake's mower, Sergeant Ball rang the land-line on Lawrence Vann's business card, without success. He could hardly expect a dead Lawrence Vann to answer his own phone, but it would have been interesting to see who did. They would have to drive over there instead. He knew they would have to anyway. He was just trying to put it off.

Batten was also experiencing a sense of frustration, for different reasons. Before disappearing musically down the A303, Doc Danvers had rightly insisted that Debbie Farley be sped off to hospital. He had also given Stephanie Broke-Mondelle a sedative - which, it seemed to Batten, she was more than pleased to take. Great, Zig. Two prime witnesses, and neither can be interviewed. They interviewed the B-team instead.

Erin Kemp was business manager of the Burrow Hill Cider Company, and according to PC Lee, it was Mrs Kemp who first intercepted the distraught Debbie Farley, as she stumbled into her office.

'I've never seen a face so white, Inspector. And please call me Erin. I hate 'Mrs.' I'm divorced anyway.' She laughed softly, gold leaf on a warm breeze.

He wrote down her name, and shamelessly committed the 'divorced' to memory. No detection skills were needed to see she was a green-eyed, handsome woman, with skin to match her voice. She had put the office furniture back in its proper place but the sharp smell of vomit remained, even with the window at the limit of its hinges. He assured her that Debbie would recover, though it was a hopeful guess.

'I'm so relieved, Inspector. When she stumbled in through the door she was a ghost - well, if ghosts can talk, because the poor thing couldn't stop. It sounded like gibberish, made no sense at all. I would have been concerned for my safety if I hadn't recognised her - she's a regular.'

'I'm sorry, your *safety*?'

'Oh, well, she was behaving like a madwoman - forgive me if I'm being politically incorrect, but like she'd escaped from an asylum. We would have called an ambulance earlier if we - Colin, from the shop, he was here by then - if we'd realised what she was trying to tell us, that there was someone ill up there.' She pointed vaguely at the open window. 'We didn't know that he was….that he was more than just ill, of course.'

'I see. So Ms Farley gave you no indication that it was….a dead body she'd found?'

'Oh, gracious, no. Because as I say, she was gabbling. I offered her sweet tea - she certainly looked as if she needed it - but she had her own hot soup. She was a cook, she said - you know, for a living - and she drank some, from a little flask. It certainly didn't make her feel better. Quite the opposite. And quite a mess.' She wrinkled her attractive nose at the damp yellow stains on the carpet. 'It wasn't until the second lady, the tall one, came screaming in here that we fully appreciated what was....' Again she pointed gingerly at the window. 'I would have gone up there, but the walking group, the Scramblers, they warned me off. 'You don't want to see *that*!' They all said the same.'

Batten nodded as the timeline became clearer. Debbie Farley must have found the body first, and fled down the hill to the cider farm, while Stephanie Broke-Mondelle and her Scramblers were tramping up from the other side.

'*She* saw it though, didn't she? The shock, on her face. *Carved* there, poor thing. Thank god I *didn't* go up there.'

I did, Batten felt like saying. And I wish I hadn't.

# Seven

It was late in the afternoon - and felt later - before the police finished questioning the hubbub of ramblers, cider-farm workers, passers-by and the thankfully small number of residents in this under-populated part of South Somerset. Their grumbles and whinges were louder than their witness statements, and about as useful. Not one single report of anything unusual - or anybody.

Once the throng departed, a silence descended over the hill, though not over the Burrow Hill Cider Company at its foot.

For the first time that day, Batten became aware of the sound of apples bobbling along conveyors and rumbling into the scratter - that's what they said it was called - the machine which chopped the apples into a rough pulp. He became aware, too, of the musky-sweet odour that filled the air. It was November, and Somerset cider-makers were pressing their tons of juice-filled apples. It was lucky he liked the smell, because it pervaded the whole farm, and him too. The invisible and penetrating scent of crushed apples was in his nostrils, on his clothes, in his hair. By the cider-press, a burly man in overalls was perched precariously on the lip of a large bin, shovelling pressed apple waste - pomace he called it - into a trailer. It would be sold off as cattle-feed.

'Somerset beasts, aarrh, they love et!', said the shovelling man. 'An' after they've eaten et, they do what beasts do, so et all ends up back in the tree!'

Batten watched the conveyor belt trundle, felt the vibrations as the scratter did its work, heard a shovel scrape and shift. Nothing stops for death, eh, Zig?

He glanced up at the long lines of crime scene tape that roped off the hill and its approaches. There'd only just been enough. When PC Lee joked about sending a car to Parminster to fetch more tape, Batten realised he had no idea what Parminster was like, why it had been chosen as a last-minute base for the new squad, or indeed how to get there from Burrow Hill. He wasn't completely sure how to get from Burrow Hill to his newly rented cottage, assuming he got home at all tonight. He would rely, again, on Sergeant Ball, who closed his phone and shuffled over.

'That was the Housekeeper at Wake Hall, zor. Rhona Fiske. Sounded a bit Scottish to me.'

'Cuh, all these foreign voices invading Somerset, eh, Sergeant?'

Ball was too wily to bite.

'From what she says, zor, it seems Lawrence Vann and Debbie Farley were a bit of this and that.'

'This and that? Any chance of a few *facts*?'

'Well, zor, they were colleagues, for starters. He was Estate Manager, and she was the Wake Hall cook. Still is, I suppose. If she recovers.'

The sting of poisoned vomit returned to Batten's nostrils.

'And they went walking together, according to this Fiske woman - whenever their mornings-off coincided.'

'Which they did today?' Unfortunately.

'Indeed, zor. Good friends, too. *And* at one time they seem to have been '*very* good friends', if I'm reading the Housekeeper right.'

'Her Scottish accent confused you, did it?'

Ball blithely carried on.

'Seems Ms Farley, being a cook, always made hot soup to take on their walks, this weather anyways. Housekeeper saw her leave with two small thermos flasks around eight this morning, in her walking gear.'

Two small poisoned chalices, as it turned out, Zig.

'And a stroke of luck, zor - well, for us at least. Guess what the Housekeeper had for lunch at Wake Hall today?'

'A fiver each way on soup?'

'Ching! Collect your winnings from the cashier, zor. Curried parsnip. From the same batch that Debbie Farley made yesterday evening. Same soup as went in the flasks. Well, same but different, seeing how the Housekeeper's still walking around 'stead of in an ambulance.'

'Any of it left, the soup?'

'Young Lee's sending it to the lab as we speak, zor,' said Ball, proud of his efficiency.

Batten would put more than a fiver each way on the toxicology report, whenever it arrived: pan of soup - no poison; flasks of soup - full of it. So how did poison fetch up in a pair of innocent, stainless steel thermos flasks? And why? And which devious bastard put it there?

Sergeant Ball had his own way of saying things.

'Suspicious death, zor? And cider's a penny a pint. *He* glugs doctored soup and turns into a Halloween mask. She glugs *hers* and splatters the carpet! It's the 'M' word, zor, and you know it!'

What Batten didn't know was who uses poison these days. He'd seen enough violent death to last him, well, a lifetime. Three deaths from ugly gunshot wounds. Three stabbings, one of them producing enough arterial blood to create a red pond round the armchair where the victim was discovered. A skull fatally colliding with a dirty piece of scaffolding pipe. A strangled child. Never death by poison though, unless it was a barbiturate suicide. Poison? *These days*?

'What's the score down here, Sergeant, as far as tox reports go?'

'Don't be holding your breath, zor. Three weeks's standard. Two's a miracle. Four, five, six if they have to send it away.'

Batten blew out his breath. *Six weeks*? The Doc's warning about jumping to conclusions was all very well, but time is a waterfall. Frazzled or not, they had to get to Wake Hall pronto. And with reinforcements. Wake Hall, Sergeant Ball said, was a very big place indeed.

# Eight

DC Nina Magnus could talk to herself for hours. Lately though, her inner voices were asking awkward questions. *What's happened to your judgement, girl?*

When Steve, her live-in lover and fellow cop, nabbed himself a promotion - and a move - to the Dorset force, she faithfully agreed to follow. *Bad decision, girl - don't tell me different.* A transfer to Yeovil with the Avon and Somerset Force was ideal - just a hop across the border to Dorchester, and to Steve's new flat. *Bad decision again, don't deny it!*

Her next bad decision was to practise her combat training skills on the trollop she'd found exchanging bodily fluids with Steve - in *their* bed - when she came home ill, and too early, from a night shift. That was three weeks ago. She and Steve had exchanged only choice words since - *his* mostly, threatening assault charges against her for unfavourably rearranging the trollop's facial features. *Bad judgement, girl, but soooo worth it!*

After that, Nina Magnus's judgement improved. She rubbed a noxious mixture of engine-oil and used cat litter into every inch of Steve's new Sergeant's uniform - her hands protected by a double skin of latex crime scene gloves – draped it across the duvet and drew a white chalk-line all the way around it. Finally, she loaded a van with everything in the Dorchester flat that legally belonged to her and drove away. *Free again, girl. Cheated on, but free....*

Three weeks on, a return to good judgement hadn't brought a return to good luck. She was living in temporary - and cramped - police accommodation. Her Chief, who they all called Fat Jellicoe, disappeared the day after dragging her from Yeovil to a splodge of a place called Parminster as 'support' officer on a new CID team - which probably meant making lots of cups of tea for mostly men. Bad enough being a black face in largely white Yeovil, but in totally white Parminster? *Girl, they'll think you came in on the banana boat!*

Her final bit of bad luck was called Detective Constable George

Halfpenny, who was driving them both to some place called Wake Hall, to assist with interviews. Halfpenny was a tall and surprisingly fragrant man in a natty, fur-collared coat. When he spoke at all it was about cars and alternative careers, and he didn't give a toss what *she* thought. As for his racist attitude, he didn't give a toss what she thought about that either. *I told you, girl. Should have stayed in Balham!*

While Nina Magnus and George Halfpenny walked themselves and their notebooks across the Wake Hall visitors' car park, Tom Bowditch got up from his hiding place behind a clump of sweet chestnut trees several hundred yards away. He carefully positioned his cap over the remains of his hair. Premature baldness, cruel. He was only twenty six. He wanted to shave off the lot, but Dipstick Dave said it would make him look like a criminal. 'Well, that's what the pair of us *are,*' he'd retorted. 'No need we *show* it', Dave had said, in his pidgin English.

Tom climbed into his old green Land Rover. Should anyone ask, he was a birdwatcher, right down to the the bird book on the passenger seat.

He had quickly realised that neither his hidden presence nor his short career in crime could have caused the arrival of so many police cars full of miscellaneous plods. But why risk it? Whatever had triggered the influx would take its course.

Through binoculars, he had scoured every road, track, building, wall and tree on the big estate, and drawn an accurate plan of all access routes, gates, cattle grids and bottlenecks. Dave said that the new owner had slashed the security budget, more fool her. At night, it was two underpaid guys in a white van - and the place was vast. No match for Tom and Dipstick Dave. Six minutes. That's all they'd need.

The light was fading as he gave Wake Hall a final stare. Not being a fully hardened criminal, he preferred to nick from places he disliked. And it was easy to dislike Wake Hall. Its ornate entrance doors were over-large, top-heavy. The eyebrow-like windows in the wide frontage of the main house seemed to frown down at visitors, in a sneery attempt at intimidation. Nor was the house built from local stone - hamstone or blue lias - but from imported white limestone now dirtied with age. Wake Hall was off-white on a good day, a muddy grey in the murk, and sunlight didn't soften it. Yet give it a good sand-blasting, Tom thought, and the stone-cold whiteness would make it look like a tomb.

Driving away, he scanned the old stable block and its vast new neighbour, scanned the conference rooms, staff cottages, gardens and gravelled roads spidering away from the house's central hub past acres of grazing land towards outlying farm buildings and lakes in the far distance. The place was tractor-heaven. And with a top-of-the-range 'liberated' tractor clearing twenty grand and more, he'd definitely be back, once the cops had gone. Him and Dipstick Dave. And Dave's trailer. Quietly, one night soon.

Rumours were surging down the Wake Hall grapevine: whispers in cowsheds, tractor-borne chitchat or, for the younger staff - if they could get a signal - the digital beeps of texts on mobile phones. Whatever the medium, the upshot was the same: *Lawrence Vann? Dead? OMG!*

'At least oi won't 'ave to look behind me next time oi bend down in the stables', was Allie Chant's view. 'If you have to go to his office, take a cattle-prod.' That's what the other stable girls advised.

Jake Tuttle kept his distance from Lawrence Vann because, being the only full-time gardener, Jake was pretty much his own boss - and liked it that way. Lawrence had only ever ticked him off the once, when Lady Wake complained that the grass on the croquet lawn was too high. Croquet! Invented by some tosser who couldn't spell 'cricket', far as Jake was concerned. Why mess about with little mallets when you could swing a three pound bat and knock a hard red ball out of sight for six - which he frequently did? And as for Lawrence? Well, better the devil you know.

'He kept you on your toes, he certainly did,' was the opinion of June, a cleaner who 'sort-of supervised the other cleaners.' The other cleaners later said, yes, June *tried* to supervise them, but they took no notice. It was Rhona Fiske who told them what to do, and *she* made damn sure they did it.

When formal questioning began, these responses were translated into whatever euphemisms were available to the individuals concerned, or at least those whose shifts had ended. DC Hick very pointedly told his Sergeant that 'this lot work almost as many hours as *we* do.' The polite part of Ball's sullen reply reminded Hick to bloody well get on with rounding up the staff that *were* available and keep his bloody opinions to himself.

'What's up with Crystal?' Hick asked George Halfpenny. 'Don't he like stately homes?'

Jake Tuttle took a minute to recover from DC Halfpenny's aftershave but then said all Lawrence wanted was short green grass where it was supposed to be, scented English roses in the rose garden, and a large vegetable plot to keep the cost of buying-in to the barest minimum. 'And I gave him all that, nine times out of ten, so he left me alone. Mostly.'

Allie Chant spoke for all the stable girls when she said Lawrence knew more about horses than horses knew about themselves, and as long as you minded your p's and q's when the nobs were around, he was easy enough to work with. Young PC Lee raised his eyebrows though, and his pencil, when she added 'y'ad to watch him sometimes, 'cos he went cross-eyed at a tight pair of jodhpurs.'

June explained that, yes, it was true that, technically, she wasn't in charge of the cleaners, but then neither was Lawrence - and that didn't stop him *appearing* whenever a lone cleaner was doing what cleaners do. 'You soon learned to keep a bucket and a wet floor between Lawrence and your boobs and backside. His hands, they sometimes had a life of their own, if you get me.'

DC Nina Magnus got her alright. 'Lawrence the letch', she considered writing, with Steve, her ex, in mind. In the end she took the safe, concise route: 'Victim rather forward with the female staff?'

'Food and drink's coming, zor.'

Batten, punch-drunk, hadn't stopped all day, a day fuelled only by the smell of apples. Real food was welcome. He leaned against the Ford Focus. The Wake Hall Visitors' car park had become the police garage.

'Anything useful on that piece of crap?'

Ball shook his head at the black mobile phone found on Lawrence Vann's body.

'Nothing and useless, zor. Thought it was too good to be true when we cracked the password second go. It's a work phone, bog-standard. All the full-time staff here have 'em. Business calls only - strictly monitored.

Every number's a supplier, a mechanic. Bales of hay. Tractor repairs. Dead end.'

'So where's his personal phone? It's got to be *somewhere!*' Batten knew how much information a smartphone contained. Contacts, photographs, messages. And if it could be tracked....

'According to the Housekeeper, it's a silver i-phone, but no sign yet, zor. I'll get George Halfpenny to chase up the service provider.'

'Silver i-phone? Pricey.'

'Pricey it may be, zor, but it's not switched on.'

So where is it, Zig? They'd recovered Lawrence Vann's parked SUV and it wasn't in the glove box, or anywhere else. The car's contents didn't even run to a discarded chewing-gum wrapper. No expired parking permits, no mud in the boot, not even a coffee ring in the cup-holder. Mr Vann was a meticulously clean motorist. Or he'd been tidying up. Or someone had. Batten didn't expect they'd find any rogue fingerprints. He produced a coin, flipped it.

'Call.'

'Tails, zor.'

'Bad luck, it's heads. You and Hickie get his office, I'll search his home. Who's available?'

'Everyone's on interviews now, zor.'

Batten growled in frustration.

'I did say it was a big place, zor, if you recall?'

Another growl.

'Jess Foreman's on his way - local beat copper, and a good 'un. Either wait for him or it's young PC Lee, zor. Who's half asleep.'

We're all half-asleep, Zig, but needs must.

'Tell young Lee to wake up and fetch the keys. If you find Mr Vann's phone before I do, give me a ring, but - '

'I know, zor. 'Use your own phone."

# Nine

Slumped in his parked Ford Focus, Batten swallowed half of a much needed breakfast sandwich. It was the first food he'd had *since* breakfast. Every previous murder investigation included a moment when he washed down half a sandwich with undrinkable sludge from a plastic cup.

At least the reinforcements meant the first wave could take it in turns to have lunch. It was almost seven-o-clock. The shrill babble of disgruntled Wake Hall workers twitching to leave - and disgruntled press and media folk twitching to get in - had thankfully subsided. Rolling down the window, he realised he was habituated to traffic noise, street lamps, bright shop windows. Here in this vast rural estate it was eerily quiet and bible-black. He got out of the car and stared at the ill-lit blockhouse that blocked the view. Wake Hall was a building designed by a committee that couldn't make up its mind. What will it look like in daylight, Zig? The dirty white stone made him think of urban snow, which turned to grubby slush the instant it fell to earth.

He flopped back into the driver's seat. Where the hell was PC Lee with those keys? Leaning back, he smoothed his moustache with the ring-finger and thumb of his left hand, and closed his eyes, shutting out the images, words and actions of a long, unfinished day. Alas, images, words and actions from the recent past simply elbowed their way into the reclaimed space, thrusting him back to Leeds, to Aunt Daze and to a beat plod who doubled as a thief....

....Once his suspicions were confirmed, Batten should have reported PC Kerr, and let the justice system have its way with him. But what had been stolen from Aunt Daze was personal. A locket containing his dead mother's hair, for god's sake. This was family.

Finding Kerr's home address was easy. Easy to ring the bell of his nondescript Victorian semi. Easy to pre-plan a calm, business-like approach. But the plan is not the experience. When the front door opened, they vaguely recognised each other. It was PC vs. Inspector, straight away. And PC Kerr blustered and denied. Batten explained that all he wanted was his family heirlooms, precious things of memory. If they were returned, the rest of his memory might lapse. The only thing returned was Kerr's sneer.

'Please don't tell me you've melted the stuff down? If you have, I'll...'

'Do what? Are you deaf? I. don't. know. what. you're. *talking*. about. And I'll tell you what else, *Inspector*, I much prefer your back view - so why don't you show it me, as you bugger off?'

Mistake. This toilet flush, Zig, he's taking the piss. As Batten later explained to best-friend Ged, 'we were roughly the same age, roughly the same build. And that's how we settled it. Roughly.'

Kerr's hallway lacked the space for kung-fu kicks. They traded punches instead, Batten taking one in the temple and responding with a vicious jab at the nose which missed but caught Kerr in the throat. He fell against a thin internal door which swung aside, his momentum propelling him backwards into the room, and crashing him against the doors of a large oak cupboard. They shattered open as he bounced off them and landed on the worn carpet, wheezing for breath.

Batten would have preferred to hit him again but there was no need. And his attention was drawn away from his gasping adversary to the inside of the cupboard itself. Floor to ceiling shelves were full to bursting with small items: rings, pearls, necklaces, gold and silver watches, and expensive photo-frames from which smiled the faces of real people, as if they'd never given up hope of being returned to those they loved. PC Kerr had built a shrine, in a cupboard, to the god of theft.

Batten slipped cable-ties round the wrists and ankles of the slowly recovering heap on the floor. For fear of saying evil things, he said nothing at all. Instead, he rang best-pal Ged Morley, asked for his urgent help, and sat down to wait....

He had no memory of picking up the second half of sandwich, but his teeth were definitely chewing it. A swallow of stewed tea washed the worst of it down. You'll give yourself an ulcer, Zig, eating this way. Really, Zig? Cancel the murder, then. Book us all a table at the Ritz.

He must have switched on the engine because hot air from the fan was hypnotising him. All was pitch dark, and the slush-grey stones of Wake Hall had turned to black ice. What the hell am I *doing* here, Zig? He glugged cold tea, yawned, closed his eyes again....

….Zig Batten and Ged Morley had done their basic training together and stayed friends, though Ged's ambition had pushed him along to Chief Inspector. He still managed to moan about it.

'You think you've got problems, Zig. My grade - *Chief* Inspector - it's being phased out. I'm a bloody dinosaur, waiting for the Ice Age! First frost of winter and I tell you, I panic!'

When Ged arrived at PC Kerr's house, all he could say was 'you pillock, Zig. Why didn't you ring for a nice policeman?'

'I did,' Batten replied. 'I rang *you*.'

Ged pondered. Phrases such as 'without a search warrant' came to mind, but here he was.

'Find a bathroom, Zig, wash your face. And don't leave any prints. I'll have a chat with the putrid meat in there.'

Kerr had recovered sufficiently to breathe, but not speak, which suited Ged because dialogue wasn't on offer. He nudged Kerr with his foot, in case he didn't already have his full attention.

'You're going away for a string of pernicious thefts, mush, I think you know that. Oh, and for anything to do with abuse of the uniform. We're talking years, but you know that too, unless you've forgotten the criminal law part of your training as well. When I say 'as well', I'm referring to the other part you've forgotten, where they teach you what a policeman *IS ACTUALLY FOR!*'

Batten heard Ged's raised voice, but knew better than to intervene.

'Wouldn't fancy a long stretch inside, if it was me,' Ged continued. 'Not with all those nice cop-shafting criminals. But perhaps you think 'well, if I grit my teeth' - and your arse-cheeks of course - 'maybe I'll be out soon enough.' Maybe you will - if we drop the additional charges. ABH on a police inspector, for a start, And resisting arrest, naturally. It'll tot up nicely….'

PC Kerr would have kept silent even if he'd been able to talk. From his hogtied position on the floor of his 'trophy room', he could see nothing but shelves of shiny gold evidence against him. When Ged rehearsed the version of events that all three of them must tell, he nodded his head in agreement. He was a crook, not an idiot. He glanced at the shelf of photo-frames. He should have got round to removing the photos, whose identifiable faces smiled vengefully back at him. Perhaps he *was* an idiot, after all.

As Ged rehearsed it, two off-duty policeman were on their way to the pub. While passing this very house, they heard cries of distress. Entering, they saw the back of what they assumed was a burglar running out of the rear exit. They would have given pursuit had they not discovered Mr Kerr on the floor, injured. They went to his assistance, but then noticed what appeared to be a large, suspicious collection of objects stock-piled in his house.

'Or you could tell the judge it wasn't a burglar that escaped out the back, it was Robin Hood, and he left all this gear behind, just for you, you shit......'

The diffident knuckles of PC Jon Lee tapped on the window. Batten jerked into alertness, cursing as cold tea spilled onto the car mat. It's only rubber, Zig. Yes, rubber, like dreams, boomerang dreams, bouncing back at you, unwanted. When he opened the door, the cool air hit him.

'Sir? I've got the keys, sir.'

Lee shook silvery metal at his yawning Inspector, and wished *he* was allowed to sleep on the job.

Jon Lee had only done one proper search in his short police career - a small-scale cannabis factory, little more than a few plants, some aluminium foil and a heater. No little black book, no bags of cash. No guns. He didn't expect to find much in Lawrence Vann's home either. It was tucked away to the side of the main house, amongst other staff cottages, and hidden from Wake Hall's important visitors by a stand of closely-planted yew trees. Lee had discovered that Rhona Fiske, Jake Tuttle the gardener, Allie Chant, Debbie Farley and Lawrence Vann all paid a peppercorn rent for their homes. Allie Chant had reminded him in no uncertain terms that this was hardly a perk. Her salary were so low, she said, that if she couldn't 'live in' cheaply, she'd be pushed to live at all.

Even so, Lawrence's cottage was a more impressive dwelling. Though single storey, the middle part was taller, and it was detached and far more private than the others, whose windowless rear walls made up two sides of the neat gravelled courtyard that led to Lawrence's front door. Lee slid on a pair of disposable gloves and was about to go in when Batten stopped him, with a twitch of his hand. He didn't know what to make of this new Inspector from up t'north, shipped down for whatever reason to Somerset when local folk could do a better job. And in a *Ford Focus*? But when Batten said dance, Lee did the tango.

'Best search the outside first, eh?'

'Sir? Where exactly do you….?'

A hand indicated the matching pair of miniature bay trees in neat terracotta pots straddling the entrance. Lee lifted each pot in turn. Nothing underneath but frantic woodlice. He felt around the base of each tree, tunnelling into the soil with his gloved fingers. 'Nothing, sir'.

Batten made a lifting movement with his fist, and Lee carefully shook the bay trees out of their pots, rummaging in their roots and examining the cavities left behind. 'Zilch, sir.'

'OK. But we didn't know that before we looked, did we?'

Lee moved to enter. Batten's hand again, pointing at the pots.

'Tuck them back in, the bay trees. Their owner's dead, but they've still got life in them, eh?'

Once inside, Lee was determined to show Batten how thorough he was. Under watchful eyes, he scoured each drawer and cupboard in the scrupulously-tidy kitchen/diner, peering into, below and behind every aperture or container he could see. A full-sized door revealed an array of wine racks, stuffed with bottles. Lee whistled with envy. Batten was examining the long shelf of expensive-looking whiskies which ran from one end of the dining area to the other. Lee imagined a Las Vegas TV barman asking 'What's your poison, bud?'

He moved to the adjacent utility room, pushed ladders aside, went through coat pockets, shook scarves, peered into hats, and squeezed the fingers and thumbs of every pair of gloves he discovered. Zilch again, but he felt better when Batten didn't find anything either. Hardly surprising. He wasted half his time looking out the window through first one pair of Lawrence Vann's binoculars, then through another, before suddenly skiving off towards the Hall. For what, a sneaky fag? Just do it yourself, Jon. You'll be an Inspector one day.

Batten put down the second pair in disbelief, rubbed his eyes, raised the binoculars again and stared through them. *Here*? In *Somerset*? *Why*? He refused to accept what the glasses had picked out when the harsh floodlights by the side entrance to Wake Hall clicked on. He jogged over to check. No, he wasn't seeing things. But who and what he saw should be in Leeds, surely, not *here*? For a moment he was boomeranged back, to his old patch this time, before snapping out of it. Carrying the past on your back, Zig, like a tortoise?

PC Lee, by contrast, was moving like a hare. He rattled the handle of Lawrence Vann's bedroom door and entered. The first object he came to was a white wicker laundry basket. Turning it upside down seemed the best way to search its contents, but that half-asleep Northern sod wandered back in and shook his finger again. Must have finished his ciggie.

'If you turn things over before checking them the right way up, you might forget what they're supposed to look like in the first place. Start by taking the lid off….Now what do you see?'

Lee leaned in and wrinkled his nose. 'Smelly socks, sir. Yergh. Maybe that's what poisoned him.'

Batten gave an unfelt smile. 'Best let them air a bit, then, while we see what else there is?'

They searched through wardrobes, drawers, in and under the king-sized bed which sat against a feature-wall painted hot-red. Batten had imagined Lawrence Vann to be subtler than that. They tapped and wiggled anything loose enough to be a hiding place, without success. A bedside cabinet revealed nail scissors, condoms, a gold Rolex, a silver hip flask. Lee opened it, sniffed. 'Whisky, sir.' Batten sniffed it too, because he liked the smell. He didn't mention this to PC Lee.

Next door, the comfortable sitting room was tastefully-furnished and eerily spotless. The square bay window housed a handsome antique desk, whose single drawer revealed nothing unusual to PC Lee. Its polished surface sported the only clue so far of Lawrence Vann the citizen: an HMRC tax return guide lay open on one side of the desk, next to a neat set of pencilled jottings and figures. It felt intrusive, reading the hand-written notes of a dead man, but Batten and Lee converged on them nonetheless. Allie Chant may have complained about Wake Hall salaries but Lawrence Vann didn't seem under-funded at all, offering to pay tax on well over fifty grand of annual income, most of it his Wake Hall salary.

With his peppercorn-rental cottage, petrol and meals thrown in, that was a generous deal. Batten would need to talk to the absent Lady Wake. Did Lawrence do something special for Her Ladyship?

A canny use of deductions and allowances would doubtless keep the tax bill down, but for Lawrence Vann, if not for the police, it was all irrelevant anyway. He would never finish going through the pile of tax-deductible bills poking out of a cardboard box propped against the desk's cabriole leg. George Halfpenny had so far drawn a complete blank on next of kin. If no distant relatives surfaced, and no will was found, the State would get it all.

Batten hoped Sergeant Ball was having better luck in Lawrence's Wake Hall office, because everything seemed aggressively neat in his cottage. One thing was certain: there was no silver i-phone. And no suicide note.

Steering PC Lee back to the bedroom, Batten tapped the open laundry bin with his foot.

'Notice anything about these socks, lad?'

'They stink, sir. You know. Dirty socks.'

'And what do you do with *your* socks, when your feet have had enough of them?'

Lee had had enough of Batten. He tightened his lips, blew air through his nose.

'Well, you can't wear a pair of socks forever, can you, Lee? How do you take them off?'

'*How*? I just… roll them off my feet, I suppose.'

'And they end up, what, as two little balls, in the laundry bin?'

'I expect they do. Sir.'

'So who does the washing in your house, Lee?'

Bloody hell. Fat Jellicoe was bad enough, but this northern git….

'Luce does, Lucy, my girlfriend. She does the washing.' If you *must* know.

'Lucky man. And your Lucy, I bet she has to unroll your smelly socks before she puts them in the washer?'

Despite himself, Lee humphed a smile. 'Well, she does sometimes go on about that. I still forget.' Lee flexed his latex gloves. 'Maybe I should lend her a pair of these.'

'Do you change your socks every day, Lee?'

Cheeky sod. 'Course I do!'

'Just your socks?'

'I'm very *clean*. Sir. Clean underwear, shirt, everything.'

'So on a Monday you drop your dirty socks, your shirt and your pants in the laundry bin?'

'Yes. Sir. Don't you?'

'And on Tuesday, you drop Tuesday's washing on top of Mondays? And on Wednesday, Thursday, same again?'

'I don't know why you're asking, sir. Course I do. Not even Luce does the washing *daily*. Sorry sir, but this is daft, right?'

Batten ignored the question. 'The thing is,' he said, 'Lawrence Vann, he didn't do the same as you and me? You can see that?' And he pointed a long finger at the laundry bin. On top of the randomly mixed pile of shirts, pants, hankies and the like, lay a neat pile of dirty socks, six pairs of them. All had been unrolled and flattened out, and lay more or less side by side, separate from the rest of the laundry, like a garnish.

'So why would the busy Mr Vann bother to do that with his daily discarded socks, do you think?'

PC Lee blew out his lips. Batten allowed silence to descend while Lee mentally re-traced his search of the clinical neatness of the house. He was changing his mind about Batten.

'*He* didn't put his socks in there like that, did he, sir?'

Batten shook his head. 'No, I don't think he did.'

'Then someone's already sneaked in? And searched the place?'

Batten glanced through the window at the tall yew hedge, a thick helpful curtain.

'Looks that way.'

'They weren't looking for cash and kind then, sir. Wouldn't have left a gold Rolex. Got to be worth a grand at least.'

'No, it wasn't Lawrence Vann's watch they were after.'

Batten walked Lee over to the antique desk, slid open its deep drawer, and pulled out from the very back of it a coil of thin black cable with a stubby transformer at one end and a jack connector at the other. He patted the empty space on the surface of the desk, next to the tax guide.

'Oh shit - sorry, sir. His laptop?'

Batten nodded. 'They were quick, whoever they were. And very thorough. Local, like as not.' Batten pointed towards the laundry bin. 'Tell me, Lee, what did 'they' think Lawrence Vann might conceal in a rolled up sock?'

Lee moulded his hand into the size and shape. Diamonds? A key? A phial of poison? A bag of heroin? And a hundred other things.

'Beats me, sir. Anything and everything small enough. Hope they wore gloves, though. These socks. Yergh.'

A glum, worn Sergeant Ball had no better news about the Estate office.

'No i-phone and nothing else of significance, zor, not as I could see. Keys galore though - must have spent half his life making key-fobs. And the Housekeeper - still on duty, covering for Debbie Farley - she has keys for the whole world. All places Mr Vann had access to. We'll need daylight for them, zor, even assuming we know what we're looking for?'

Batten didn't know what they'd be looking for either. Even if they got extended permission from the owner. Lady Wake was 'expected back soon' from some horsey jaunt in Spain.

'We've a lot on our plate, zor, and there's only so much we can do tonight. Wouldn't you say?' Ball realised he was beginning to sound like DC Hick.

'Anyone been in his office? Before you got there, I mean? Anything moved or missing?'

Ball pondered. How was *he* supposed to know? He had no idea what was there in the first place. They'd need to ask the locals, hope they got straight answers.

'No obvious gaps anywhere, if that's what you're asking, zor? Everything ship-shape and Bristol fashion.' He heard himself; re-played the search of the SUV and the militarily neat office space. 'Could be he was a stickler, I suppose….Do we know if he was, zor? A stickler?'

Batten shrugged. All he knew was that persons unidentified had removed Lawrence Vann's laptop - and learnt of his death before the body was cold. If they didn't already know.

There was a lot to do, and they'd need daylight to do it. He arranged for a probably futile watch on Lawrence Vann's cottage and office, and sent his tired troops - and himself - home to bed.

# Ten

Sleep came slowly in his beamed bedroom, then dreams dragged him back to the silent blackness of Wake Hall. He was trapped in his car, eyes closed, *'what am I doing here?'* etched in spidery black letters on the lids. Answers were scrawled in the dirt of the windscreen but the wipers erased the words, then re-wrote them, then erased them again, always a split-second before he was able to make out what they said, all night long, right through to early morning when bip bip bip bip *beep*, bip bip bip bip *beep* drew him back to the waking world.

Zig, *must* you have such a bloody irritating alarm clock? Ged had bought it for him, a sarcastic leaving present.

'No traffic noise in the sticks, where you're going, Zig. Nowt to wake you up in the morning. This little beauty beeps forever till you switch it off. No wimpy snooze buttons - if you stay in bed, your brain explodes. 'Ta very much, Ged,' you're supposed to say. 'What a god amongst men you are."

If Ged walked into Zig's rented cottage right now he'd struggle to walk out again, with the vicious little clock painfuly inserted. Batten opened the curtains and drank in the view across a deep green valley full of orchards and ancient trees and wide fields of soft fruit towards the first stirrings of sunrise over Ham Hill. While absorbing nature's art gallery he realised the alarm clock was still doing what Ged intended. Bip bip bip bip *be*-click. Then silence and sunrise and staring into space, light and affirmation.

He spooned fresh coffee into the battered little espresso machine and set it on the stove. While it brewed he did what he did most mornings - interrogated his past, hoping to find a future. *'What am I doing here?'* refused to go away. Why, Zig, are you - a lifelong urbanite - now waking up in the beeping middle of nowhere? *It's complicated, Zig.* Don't be evasive, Zig. You *decided* to. Didn't you?

Yes and no. External pressure to leave the Yorkshire force could not be denied. It had certainly dampened the joy of waving PC Kerr off to prison - a joy thoroughly soaked when Kerr fell under the protection of the local Mr Big, in return for inside information about police tactics, dirt-dishing on cops large and small, and anything else that would smooth the wheels of criminality. Is there no justice, Zig?

'No, there isn't,' he could hear Ged say, anger in his voice. After dealing morally - but illegally - with Kerr, their weekly night-out in The Victoria, Ged's favourite Leeds pub, had quietly gone to the wall. When finally they met there, the place was packed and they *just* nabbed the last table, near the big mahogany bar. Ged came to the point.

'Zig? You got eighty quid in that hermetically-sealed wallet of yours? To buy something off me?'

'Buy what?'

'Just trust me, yeh?'

After pretending to wave away moths, and pocketing four crisp twenties, Ged handed over a small envelope.

'Eighty's what I paid for them, legit, so we're both honest.'

The envelope contained three lockets. Batten immediately recognised Aunt Daze's amongst them.

'How....?'

'I've been a naughty boy, and you mustn't tell Sir. Sneaked a look at Kerr's receipts - stupid sod spread a few bits round the pawnshops, the cretin. They've all got CCTV. Anyway, three receipts said 'gold locket.' Didn't know which was which, so let's say I arranged to have 'em all redeemed. Eighty snivelling quid....But I'm sorry, Zig, no wedding ring.'

Batten gratefully turned the locket over in his hand. Aunt Daze would at least have that. The curl of hair inside, that was his mother, her alone. The ring had been his mother and his father. Of his father he knew only what Aunt Daze knew.

Ged was still talking.

'Bloody Kerr, cupboard full of booty just lying there. Well, you saw. Didn't need the money. Lives on his own and hardly goes anywhere. Sounds a bit like *you*!'

The downside of true friendship is you understand your friends too well. And Ged's levity, Batten knew, concealed deeper feelings. He said so.

'We've both crossed a line here, Zig. Good reason, yes, but it's not how the law should be done, is it?'

How to respond? His conscience was untroubled. A plod nicking from the people he's supposed to protect? He thought of all the old people in the area, safer now. He said all this to Ged, omitting the truer complications of Aunt Daze, a long-dead mother, and barely-filtered anger at the past.

'Sounds noble, Zig, doesn't it, put like that?'

'But you're saying it's not?'

Ged was silent for a long moment.

'My Chief Super, Zig, he's as sharp as a lemon injection. I've just come from an expert dressing-down in his office….which explains why my glass is empty.'

Batten returned with two more pints. Ged, who could smile at the mere thought of a drink in The Vic, took an unsmiling pull at his beer.

'Your boss is spit-splutteringly keen for you to grace his presence, so I am informed. I bet *your* bollocking's already burnt a hole in the old sod's tongue.'

Batten's mobile lay forlorn on the table, switched off. He flipped a beer mat in the air, caught it, snapped it on top of the phone.

'I don't care.'

They both knew he did.

'He'll say what mine said, Zig. They're glad to see the back of PC Thief. But it's the *how*. Your Super'll ask you what mine asked me: if you cross a line, does it help you cross another, and then one more after that?'

'One line, Ged. One. *Only* one.'

'You sure? I'm not. Which line *won't* I cross? I used to know.'

In the din of the packed pub, they silently drank their beer. Batten didn't share Ged's doubts. For him, it wasn't about crossing lines, it was about defending them. If you fail to look after the few people you can call your own, what are you worth?

It was just as well Batten could answer his own question, because his face value diminished rapidly after PC Kerr's arrest. It was bad for the local force, this sort of thing, Chief Superintendent Farrar told him. 'They', he said, pointing upwards, can't condone such behaviour. Coughing to conceal his embarrassment, Farrar said there'd even been talk of an assault charge and an exit from the force. He leaned closer, lowered his voice. 'If they get rid of cops good as you, Zig, they'll end up with a force full of PC Kerrs, the stupid bastards.'

Batten asked the obvious question.

'A transfer,' Farrar replied. 'And I'm not talking about those stick-on things in cornflake packets. A transfer somewhere else. To another force. I've got a connection or two. You know. Mebbe get yourself out of the smoke for a while? How d'you feel about Somerset?'

Batten felt nothing at all about Somerset. But he didn't feel overmuch about Yorkshire either. It was the people he knew there; they were his bonds, his roots. He said so.

'Come on, Zig, you'll get the usual time off. Free every other weekend, give or take. Somerset's hardly the North Pole, man.'

No, Batten thought, it's closer to the *South* Pole. And I've never been there either.

Ten miles south-west of Batten's cottage, two early-bird voices hissed into untraceable mobile phones.

'Laptop?'

'Yeh, gorrit.'

'And his i-phone?'

'Norra whiff. Must be on *Mars*.'

First voice sighed.

'Then p*lease* tell me you recovered the memory stick?'

'Norra whiff of that neither - and no, we're *not* stupid, before you say we are!'

'Convince me. By searching harder.'

'Oh yeh? Wharrabout the plod? They're *everywhere* now.'

First voice sighed again. 'Remain vigilant,' it said, and rang off.

Second voice knew not to expect a thank-you. He invited the dead phone to go screw itself.

The sharp smell of burnt coffee snapped Batten wide awake. Cursing, he moved the hissing espresso pot off the heat and filled a cafetiere, as self - interrogation continued.

OK, you had to leave Yorkshire, but you could have gone to big-city Midlands, even the Met. Why Somerset? Touch of country bumpkin in your genes, Zig?

Why? Because despite the buzz of city life, something inside him wasn't being….drawn on?...nurtured? For god's sake, Zig, you'll be into psycho-babble next. Just look out the window and say what you see! A view so good - for god's sake, say 'beautiful', it won't kill you! A view so beautiful that something happens to your insides when you look at it, and when you open the window it's not scarily-angry engines that you hear, but silence. And birdsong in the heart-stirring distance.

Before the coffee kicked in, he drifted back to his house in Leeds, dilapidated and unloved - till he'd revived it with sweat and curses. Too many rooms, he couldn't keep up with the garden, the heating struggled to reach the attic floor. Yet now it was all but sold…. It was a fine, gritstone villa, enjoyed despite the road noise and the city smells, and the sirens, day and night, screaming anguished screams of warning and dismay, like the keening from an endless wake. Each time he drove out of his garage opposite the little local park with its graffiti-covered gates, formal flowerbeds - informally weed-choked now – and smog-defiant trees, he felt revived. If the car windows were firmly closed against the smell of dog-shit and the outlet from the brewery.

Somerset birdsong claimed him as the contours of Ham Hill grew sharper. He had reached, what? An epiphany? Come on, Zig, you're not James Joyce. A penny's dropped, for Christ's sake. In Leeds, not being awake to see the sunrise, if he could see it at all, meant he wasn't on the early shift and could have a lie-in. After mere days in his Somerset rental, he was getting up early - even setting that bloody irritating alarm to *get* him up - hoping to see a sunrise out of JMW Turner in all its glory of colour and light and sensation. It made no difference if he was on earlies or not. The murder of Lawrence Vann wasn't why, though it was reason enough. He was doing it because he chose to.

He refilled his cup and sat in the little rear porch overlooking fields brimming with cows. The smell no longer bothered him. When you live next to the gasworks, you soon stop smelling gas. And what's a bit of methane from a cow's arse when it comes with a view like this, framed by a sky like that.

Draining his coffee, he ducked back inside, beneath a low beam sporting a warning picture of a duck. Next to it, for the visually illiterate, someone had scrawled the word 'Duck!' Initially, Batten forgot to, and almost replaced the D with an F. Yet the first time he woke in his eaves bedroom, golden flames of sunrise silenced his curse as head met ceiling. A few days on, he neither ducked nor groused, but dipped and swayed, automatically. The cottage had trained and tested him. And he had passed.

As he washed up, the sunrise glow reminded him to remove the batteries from Ged's alarm clock and shove it in his sock drawer. He'd bring it out again if Ged came to visit - no sense in upsetting a man who was scrupulously fair in buying his round. Instead, he retrieved his old clock-radio from a cardboard box, and tuned it to BBC Radio Somerset. Why not, Zig? It's where you live now. Let local voices wake you. And let the morning light continue to amaze.

# Eleven

Ten miles north-west of Batten's cottage, behind the closed doors of an old barn that served as a very private garage, Dipstick Dave removed the false plates from his whisper-quiet tow-truck, stowed it with the non-existent 'West Country Diesel Repairs' logo, and tidied away the large tarpaulin used to conceal the spoils of last night's theft.

In the adjacent office-cum-kitchen he eased himself onto an old wicker sofa, and waited for the kettle to boil. Though only half-English, he was wholly addicted to tea, and looked forward to choosing one of the several different kinds that sat in airtight caddies on a shelf above the worktop. He drank a different tea each day. So, which one this morning?

Last night, he and Tom Bowditch had suspended their plan to deprive Wake Hall of an expensive Massey Ferguson tractor. Wake Hall was too cop-heavy just now. Instead they liberated a top-of-the-range motor-home from a gated parking area behind a posh stone house north of Somerton. Dave was too canny to be stalled by locked gates and wheel-clamps - guard dogs even less so.

Dave's Pa's method of subduing guard dogs had been basic to a fault - feed the dogs drugged meat, wait till they snore. Pa would hate Dave's modern method, but Pa pre-dated DNA. If a dog sank its teeth into Dave's leg, onto the canine's canines Dave's DNA would go. Cash-strapped Mr Plod *might* not swab the dog's chops, but as Tom kept saying, why take the risk? And Dave would have to finish the mutt, get rid of the carcass. Hassle.

He hated dogs anyway. Like Pa, he tempted them with juicy meat. But instead of soporifics, Dipstick Dave added a large dose of powerful poison, enough to kill a *horse* stone-dead, let alone a dog. He was good at poison, was Dave. Adulterated heroin; banned rat-killer. You could even find lethal stuff online, if you knew how to look. Half the world's poisonous.

Choosing today's tea would be easy. A cool twenty grand for the mobile home, once it and its fake paperwork were in a container-ship bound for Russia, or points east - Dave had useful connections out there. His real name was David Vossialevydipsic, which nobody could pronounce. He hadn't twigged at first when his 'friends' at school renamed him 'Dipstick' - hadn't realised they were taking the piss. Who is clever boy *now?* he asked, as the kettle boiled. With a twist of his mouth that was almost a smile, Dave 'Dipstick' Vossialevydipsic spooned Russian Caravan tea into the warmed pot.

Batten had raised vocal eyebrows on first seeing his team's 'office' at Parminster. His eyebrows screamed this morning when he weaved through half-assembled workstations, empty boxes and plastic packaging. An enclosed cubby-hole in the far corner said 'Chief Inspector Jellicoe' on the door, but needs must. He flopped into Jellicoe's ample swivel chair. There was just enough room to spin all the way round, so he did, coming to rest with his view fixed on the broad back of his new Sergeant, humped over the pile of paper rumoured to conceal a desk. The new paint on the office wall was pale brown, and smelled worse than new paint was supposed to. No-one had asked his opinion anyway.

Without warning, a bemused technician popped up from behind a computer console, dragging behind him a bird's nest of phone and computer wire. He looked like he'd been there all night. He was in good company - the whole team looked that way. But then some of them had.

Batten had managed just five hours sleep. He might have snatched another hour had he known a quick route home from Wake Hall, via the Parminster office, to his rented bed near Ashtree, but his satnav was on the blink and short-cuts take time to learn.

And this morning his car was blocked off for an age in the narrow lane next to his cottage, while a big lorry unloaded dozens of bundles of thatch. He hadn't noticed his neighbour's house was thatched, still less that it needed a new roof. Soon after squeezing by he was lost, and had to stop for directions.

'*Where'd* y'say?' the woman asked....'You don' mean *Pamm'stor*, d'you?'

He allowed himself one more spin in the swivel chair before jamming his knees beneath the desk and sifting through the early transcripts of 'the ongoing investigation' - a phrase he hated - shuffling them into a briefing sharply focused on what Ball dubbed 'a suspicious death by murder, zor.' The new team would love that. If they'd woken up.

Lonny Dalway was more than familiar with the gravel driveway which curved round towards the rear entrance of Wake Hall. He'd driven down it six mornings a week for the last forty years, whistling on most of them. The cause of the whistling was old Lord Wake, who'd stubbornly continued to use The Dalway Dairy for Wake Hall's milk supplies - in shiny glass bottles for preference - long after traditional 'milkmen' disappeared from the landscape. Rural values, local business, looking after things *right* - that was Lord Wake. God bless him, said Lonny, as his whistling van rattled down the drive.

When Lord Wake died, Lonny stopped whistling out of respect, and because he thought by keeping quiet, *the daughter* - which is how he referred to the current incumbent - might not notice he was still rolling up with the milk. Pub wisdom said she was clawing back the overspend of her un-businesslike papa. That Lonny still delivered to almost every enclave of the scattered estate - main house, offices, conference rooms, stables, cottages, fishing lodge - was because nice Mr Vann continued to apply the policies of old Lord Wake - if he could sneak them past *the daughter*, that is.

Lonny hadn't dared offer his services to the brand-new bit of Wake Hall, the big horse-dealing business, because that was *the daughter's* pet project, her and her fancy-man, so they said in the pub. Low profile, Lonny. Try to keep going for another year. But sod it, whistle too, boy. Retirement's just round the corner.

Also round the corner was the raised hand of a super-sized uniformed policeman. Lonny winced as the brakes bit and the van scattered sharp gravel into the shrubs edging the road. The rattles behind him increased almost to bottle-smashing proportions. He had no problem recognising PC Foreman. He delivered his milk.

'Where you to, Lonny?' asked Jess Foreman.

'Up the 'ouse, Jess. With all these drugs.' He pointed a gum-heavy smile at the yoghurt cartons in the back.

'Better pull over first, Lonny,' said Foreman, 'fore we both get high from sniffin' cowjuice.'

Lonny Dalway was just the distraction Jess Foreman needed. A man could go batty with boredom, pulling over non-existent traffic on the back-road to Wake Hall. In ninety slow minutes, only five cars had driven through. And he could have questioned their drivers in the comfort of The Lamb and Flag, since he regularly shared an evening pint with most of them. They added nothing to the sum of knowledge about 'comings and goings' on the day Lawrence Vann lost his life. 'Oy just work 'ere, Jess,' was all they said. Many more people worked here, he recalled, in the old days.

Jess Foreman disliked 'assisting and supporting CID'. Eddie Hick called rural beat cops like him 'the cider fuzz', but fresh air and no writing suited Jess. And he knew his onions. Thirty seconds with Lonny Dalway, and he tagged the milkman as a key witness. Up yours then, Hickie, thought PC Foreman, as he radioed in.

His news was a welcome boost for Zig Batten, who still didn't know where anything *was*. He didn't know where *where* was either, amid this confusing Somerset pottage of small towns, linked by skinny roads to higgledy-piggledy villages - entirely different villages but with entirely similar names. And compared to inner-ring-road-Leeds with its fast multi-lane carriageways - OK, Zig, not at rush hour - the A303 was a footpath.

He knew where his two chief witnesses were though: they were unavailable! Debbie Farley was still hospitalised and 'very poorly'. Stephanie Whatsit-Whatsit was answering neither phone nor doorbell. He knew this because he'd eventually found her front door, *despite* his sat-nav, after discovering that Little Norton, Norton Mill, and Norton-Sub-Hamdon were not the same Norton at all. Unfortunately, he had failed to discover *her*, in all or any of the bloody Nortons.

So it was a relieved Batten who confronted the strange form of Lonny Dalway, still leaning against his van of curdling milk, on the gravelled back-road to Wake Hall, surrounded by autumnal trees and emptiness.

Seconds later, Batten was wondering if he'd driven through a wormhole in Somerset space-time and arrived at a fifth dimension, where alien creatures spoke in strange tongues. Lonny Dalway looked to Batten like a bristled pig, suspended from the grubbiest flat cap in the wormhole-universe. Six inches below the cap, a gum-heavy orifice spat out a rag-bag of what Batten assumed were words.

'Aarh, I do. I knows 'im. Proper gent. 'E look affer us local folk, do Misser Vann.'

Batten had mixed feelings when Lonny fell silent. He wasn't sure Lonny knew Lawrence Vann was dead, until he lowered his voice and deferentially removed his cap.

'Kept me goin', did Misser Vann, bless 'is soul. Just as ole Lord Wake wan' it. Men of 'onour, both on 'em. Aarh.'

'Mr Dalw-'

'- Too late to thank 'im now, Misser Vann. But I did at least wave at 'im, when I was to 'ere, yesserday.'

'So you did see Mr Vann? Yesterday? Here?'

'Aarh. I said. To Jess.'

'To PC Foreman?'

'Aarh.'

'And what time was that, when you saw Mr Vann?'

'Oh, 'bout eight, thereabouts'. 'S when I deliver 'ere. Well, I sees Misser Vann's *car*, anyways, reconnised it. And Debbie Double, she war climbin' in. Offen sees the two on 'em, walkin'.'

'I'm sorry, Mr Dalway - *Debbie Double*?'

'Aarh. Debbie. Debbie Farley. See, she used to play at ours when she war a tot. Moy lass is a Debbie, so when Debbie war playin' with moy Debbie, well, war two Debbies! Like twins they were, so I calls 'er Debbie Double. Two on 'em. Two fine golden girls.'

Lonny Dalway lowered both cap and voice.

''Ers war a poor place. 'Er dad, ole Farley, 'e war a bit, you know….with the young 'uns.'

He made an apologetic, vague groping gesture, which Batten immediately understood. Was sign language the way to go with Lonny?

'I shouldn't say so, you bein' a policeman, but I once give ole Farley a thump with the flat o' my 'and.' He waved a calloused mitt that could have doubled as a brass knocker on a giant's door. 'Beast of a man, ole Farley. Did no good, thumpin' 'im. Nor for Debbie Double neither.'

Lonny Dalway withdrew into his thoughts. Batten wondered if he was regretting not thumping 'Ole Farley' a bit harder. He was changing his mind about Lonny, though. Decency was welcome, whatever its source.

'Mr Dalway? Just to clarify: you said Debbie Dou - Debbie Farley - got into Lawrence's car, here at Wake Hall, at eight yesterday morning?'

'Aarh.'

'And he was in the driver's seat?'

'Musser been. It don' drive it*self*, do it?' A noise similar to laughter oinked out.

'And they w -'

'Saw 'er later too. Nice lass, Debbie Double.'

'I'm sorry?'

'Saw her again, Debbie, 'bout tennish, over at Burrow 'Ill. Deliverin' there, oi was.'

'So you *spoke* to Debbie?'

'Aarh. See, I generally need to go for a, you know, use the….facilities at the cider farm. An' there's only the one….facility, see? She war comin' out as I war tryin' to go *in*.'

'Tennish, or….?'

'War ten-o-clock sharp. They's a clock, 'bove the gates.'

Batten knew. He'd seen it.

'Strikes the 'our. Blummin' loud, too. Louder'n a -'

'- Right, so you spoke to her, to Miss Farley?'

'Aarh. I says, what you been up to, Debbie? She give a laugh, says 'I just come out the toilet, Lonny, what you think I been up to?' Then she says, 'Misser Vann, he's pronked up the hill without me, see the view' - you wanna go up there, Inspeccor. See 'alf the world from Burrow 'Ill.'

Batten saw a twisted dead face, slumped against a tree, screaming.

'Well, Debbie says, 'I've seen that view so offen I could paint it from memry, 'cept I can't paint!' Then she says, 'You seen Misser Vann, Lonny?' No, I says. An' she says, 'I bet 'es still communin' with nature up on that blummin' 'ill.'

Communing with his maker, as it turned out. But the timeline was firming up. Lawrence Vann had not lived much beyond ten-o-clock.

'And that was all, Mr Dalway?'

'She just says, 'I better slog up there an' fetch 'im. Need to be headin' back to Wake 'All. Work t' do.''

'Did you see her go up Burrow Hill?'

Lonny pondered.

'Well, I saw 'er go *toward* Burrow 'Ill, so she musser done. Me, I needed….you know, to *go*. So I just shouted after 'er. There's no shortage o' work, I shouts.'

65

And Lonny gazed meaningfully at his van, and the undelivered milk slowly curdling in the back of it.

# Twelve

Sgt Ball was tired. Of fruitless searches; of sensible questions producing senseless answers; tired of Wake Hall. The team were working flat out – Batten had made sure of that. Right now, Ball wanted a sit down in The Jug and Bottle with a pint of cider, a packet of crisps and a pickled egg. Alas, he was standing up in a draughty, ill-lit shed by a Wake Hall stable yard, failing to interview a wiry, hard-looking man clad in dubiously dirty riding boots and a waterproof coat shiny with wear, and probably with something else.

'Mr McCrory? Am I spelling it right, zor?' asked Ball, showing McCrory the name he'd pencilled in at the top of a blank page in his notebook. McCrory's ratty face peered suspiciously at it, before pouring out a stream of scouse noise.

'Yeh, yeh, but they all call me Manny round here. Me real names Manfred, see. Me grandma was German. Came over here after the war. With granddad. He worra soldier, met her in Berlin. Brought her back to England. Said they left one big bomb-crater behind, and ended up in another - it was called Liverpool, hah-hah.'

Ball intervened before he got an entire family history.

'Lawrence Vann, Mr McCrory. You'll have worked with him, presumably?'

'What do you mean 'presumably'?'

Ball wasn't sure. 'Presumably' was just something the police said.

'Well, he was Estate Manager and you worked on the estate. That kind of 'presumably', zor.'

'Ah. Right. Well, I worked more direct. With her Ladyship. I'm horses, see?'

Ball didn't see, and wondered why a man could tell you his family history without being asked, yet fail to give a straight answer to a simple question.

'You're saying you worked with Lady Wake, zor?'

'Nah. I worked with Mr *Rutter*, and *he* worked with her ladyship.'

The name 'Rutter' rang a bell in Sergeant Ball's head. He'd seen or heard that name, but couldn't remember where.

'So you didn't work at all with Lawrence Vann, zor?'

'*He* was the Estate. *Me*, I'm Wake Hall Horse. 'S'what we're called.' He pointed at the massive sign over the high gates, in case Ball had failed to spot it. 'Company name, official, registered. We're *separate*. Old Lawrence, he never -'

'- managed *you*, zor, yes.'

'See? You got there. Perseverance. 'S what Mr Rutter says. 'Just you persevere, Manny.' With horses, you gorra.'

'Because….?'

'Because they're funny beasts. One day they lick you, next day they kick you. 'N some of them, you never know which it's going to be.'

Same with people, Ball thought.

'So, zor, this Mr *Rutter*, he'd be your manager?'

'Mr *Rutter* was who brought me *in*. Knew him from before, see.'

'From before what, exactly, zor?'

'Er, well, from the ponies. Racetracks. Likes a good bet on a good race, Mr Rutter.'

'So he brought you in as what, some sort of horse dealer?'

'*Horse-dealer*? Nah. Bit more than *that*.'

Ball waited for the 'more' to be defined, and when it wasn't he decided his first instinct about Manny McCrory was correct: Manny wasn't short for Manfred. It was short for Manure. And he was full of it.

'Just say exactly what your role is, would you, zor? And if you came into contact with Lawrence Vann regularly? And on the morning of November 1st in particular? Please?'

'What's this? 'Who Wants To Be A Millionaire?', whinged Manny. 'Can I ask the audience?'

Ball gave Manny a stare.

'Look, horses from the estate, you know, for wedding coaches, weekend trippers, yeh? That's all Lawrence. His instructors. His stables. His girls. Hay. Straw. Everything.'

'So…?'

'So, *my* job is buying horses *in*. A *lot* of horses. Racehorses. Workhorses. Polo ponies. Riding School hacks. You name it. My speciality's bringing them along, and selling them *on*. 'Adding value', Mr

Rutter calls it. A tidy profit, even from the knacker's yard. You should try it.'

A sharper stare.

'*My* horses, they're in transit. Passing through. Separate stables altogether. I run eleven horse-boxes. *Eleven*. Big boxes too, with good engines. None of your clapped out stuff. I send horses all over the country. Even overseas. I'm international, me'.

McCrory was so puffed up with his own importance he forgot to be unresponsive.

'With old Lawrence, it's the daily doings. Hardly call it a business, would you? Me, I'm import and export. Ask Lady Wake. Me and Mr Rutter and Wake Hall Horse, our profits keep her out of the muckheap. Come to think of it, we make a profit from the muckheap too! Hah-hah.'

'So, your horse activities and Lawrence Vann's horse activities were totally separate? You're saying that?'

'Yeh. Nah. Yeh. I mean, he'd try nicking a bit of hay if they were short. And piggyback on Roddy and Neil sometimes.'

'Roddy and Neil?'

'The farriers. Lawrence nabs 'em sometimes, when they're shoeing *my* horses, cheeky sod. Otherwise, separate.'

Ball sighed as a pair of farriers went on his interview list. 'And yesterday morning?'

'Nah,' said Manny. 'Wasn't here. Was in a box.'

Ah, if only, thought Ball.

'I take it you mean a horse-box? Zor.'

'*Yeh*. Was in a box on the motorway heading for Stoke. Look.' McRory's fingers sucked a grubby page-a-day diary from a shelf on the shed's wall. 'Box 1' was scrawled in longhand on its dirty brown cover. The entry said 'Stoke-on-Trent', nothing more.

Ball relieved Manny of the diary, almost having to wrench it from his grasp. A voice in his head said 'now wash your hands.' Box 1's journeys seemed to be designated by place-names, scrawled in block-capitals, and little else.

'What does this mean, zor? B-A-Z?' asked Ball, pointing at the three capital letters scrawled next to some of the journeys. Manny pretended to peer at them.

'Ah, no, that's Baz, see.'

'Baz, zor?'

'Er, yeh. Er, Mr Rutter's Baz.'

'And he is…?'

'Well, he's *Baz*. Baz Ballard. Mr Rutter's chauffeur. But see, Mr Rutter lends me him, now and then, if we're short. Can't do long trips on me own, can I? It's illegal. Thought you'd know that. Hah-hah. Anyway, Baz is a good driver. So he drives while I kip. And vicey-versey.'

'So where your diary says 'Baz', he's your co-driver?'

'Er, yeh. Baz.'

'No other co-drivers in here, zor. So, no witnesses at all yesterday? On your trip to Stoke?'

'Nah, nah, that's where you're wrong. I only put Baz's name in when it's not Bulky. Never put Bulky in, 'cos with Box 1 it's always Bulky, see. Nearly always.'

Give me cider, to get me through this, Ball thought.

'When it's not bulky, zor? When what's not bulky?'

'Nah, *Bulky*. You know, *Bulky*!' Manny raised his hand as high to the sky as it would go. 'Big feller. Bulky Hobshaw. Works with me, here.'

'I see, zor. And this….Bulky was your co-driver yesterday?'

'That's *right*. He *was*.'

He had the sarcasm gene, did Manny.

'And *you*, you *left* when and got back *when*?'

'Left at sevenish, I s'pose, yesterday morning -'

'Seven*ish*, zor? Any chance of being a bit more specific?'

'I dunno, *seven*ish. I mean, we don't clock on and off. We're norra *factory*!'

Looking along the Great Wall of China surrounding Wake Hall Horse, Ball could disagree.

'And you got back at….?'

'*Didn't* get back. Too far. There's a bed above the cab, and a pull-out behind the driver's seat. Got back today. Dropped Bulky off near Bristol. He's driving an empty box back home.'

As McRory spoke, a pair of big muddy horse-boxes chugged into the yard, reversed towards the stable-blocks and cut their engines. The first had the number 3 stencilled onto the driver door, the second a 7. Two bleary-eyed, thickset men in well-worn horse-gear jumped down from the first, then a Goliath emerged more slowly from the other, which seemed to sigh with relief when the ground once more bore the burden of his weight.

'Which stable for these 'orses, Manny?' growled Goliath, thumb jerking at the first box.

'Not now, Bulky. Just bloody wait, can't you?' snapped Manny. Surprisingly annoyed, it seemed to Ball.

'Now'd be better, Manny,' Bulky yelled back, massive hands challengingly planted on hips. 'These lads have had a bloody long trip.'

'Moron', spat Manny, under his breath. 'Work to do, Sergeant,' he said. 'Got your answers now?'

Sergeant Ball nodded and turned away. He had his answers, yes. Except to the question he was silently asking himself. If Manny Manure McCrory had other horse-box staff for 'a bloody long trip', why did he need the help of Baz Ballard, Mr Rutter's personal chauffeur?

While this thought filtered through Ball's ample skull, his Inspector eased his gangly frame into a comfortable-looking armchair in one of Wake Hall's neat staff cottages, and sipped piping hot tea from a china cup. The armchair, though, was lumpy and needed re-upholstering; the china cup's pattern was rubbed and faded; and he'd never liked the smell of Earl Grey tea.

But he needed tea, any tea, to help him recover from the chore of picking through rack after rack of Wake Hall keys, hoping that one of them would open the doors of perception. His head ached from staring in bad light at the scrawled handwriting and small print on dozens of fobs dangling from a weird range of key rings that made the whole key cupboard look like a giant charm bracelet. There were rabbit's feet, gonks, crucifixes, tiny teddy-bears, even a gold ingot which he assumed was fake. The cupboard was in a dark corner of the Housekeeper's cramped office, beneath a mini-neon light whose tube flickered as Batten switched it on, then failed entirely before he could even take stock. Two of the key-fobs sported miniature torches. He flung down the first in frustration - its bulb and lens were smashed - while the second gave out a meagre spindle of light barely enough to see by. And to see what, Zig? If Lawrence Vann

71

had access to all the doors and rooms represented here, it would take the combined efforts of the entire Avon and Somerset Force to search them.

Batten tried to ignore the negative symbols piling up around him: neon tubes that failed as soon as you switched them on; broken bulbs and smashed lenses throwing no light; multiple keys to unknown doors. When you're looking for a needle in a haystack, Zig, at least you know it's a needle you're looking for!

As a small compensation, Batten's current interviewee - he didn't know if she was more or less than that – was much prettier than Lonny Dalway, and her answers arrived on a soft voice with a hint of Edinburgh at the back of it. Rhona Fiske was about his age, well turned out in what he assumed was appropriate dress for the Head Housekeeper of Wake Hall: flat shoes, smart skirt to the knees and an expensive-looking linen blouse, but with the sleeves carefully turned back. An apron and a pair of discarded rubber gloves lay on the table beside her. Head Housekeeping at Wake Hall was more hands-on each day, she said. And while this might be a problem for Rhona Fiske, the staff shortage was good news for Batten. Fewer people to question.

Not that questioning Rhona Fiske was irksome. She had soft brunette hair, and eyes you could get lost in. If you weren't a cop, he reminded himself. Twice, because both eyes sat above a quietly confident, quietly shapely body, kept trim, he imagined, by long hours and hard work rather than time at the gym. She certainly suggested as much when explaining her role.

'Yes, I've only been here the two years. But at Wake Hall,' she said, 'that's the equivalent of three or four.'

'Why exactly - if you don't mind me asking?'

'Not at all. The recession. The size of the place. Its age. Its state of repair. Its increasing costs. Its diminishing staff. Its increasing attempts at money-making. Its diminishing budget. The picture is painted, Inspector?'

In oils, yes. 'You missed out 'its owner' from your list?'

'Its owner is my employer, Inspector, so yes, I did.'

He wondered how deep her loyalty went. On the subject of Lawrence Vann, her responses seemed open and balanced. Rhona Fiske had made her position clear, she said, 'in my very first week at Wake Hall, immediately after he 'accidentally' bumped against my softer parts.' She didn't specify which parts, but the picture was painted.

'You *do* know I am Head Housekeeper, Lawrence?' I told him. 'I have access, therefore, to all the equipment relating to that role. Steam irons; rat-traps; bleach in bulk. If we work together in professional respect, I shall have no cause to use any or all of them on you, with unrestrained vigour.'

Batten imagined Lawrence's leery smile at the thought of Rhona's unrestrained vigour. Then the grotesque gape of the dead Lawrence wiped it away.

'Because he was a highly intelligent man, Inspector, he reflected on the drawback of a hot iron searing his flesh. And desisted.'

There was something steely about Rhona Fiske, Batten thought.

'To his credit', she continued, 'Lawrence simply said 'My dear, you are clearer than sunlight on a cloudless day,' before removing himself. Indeed, he gave a deferential bow as he left.'

'It must have been a shock, then, when you heard he was dead?'

'I don't know if my Scottish ancestors would approve, Inspector, but I take a John Donne view of death. Any death diminishes me, because I am involved in mankind, and that included Lawrence, for all his faults.'

'His faults being numerous, I take it?'

She considered this for several seconds.

'You should understand, Inspector, that Wake Hall is not immune to gossip - and gossip exaggerates. If Lawrence had committed all the lascivious acts you will doubtless be told about, he would never have done a day's work. I would say his faults were characterised more by consistency than number. Ask the stable-girls, for example; the freelance caterers; the conference centre staff - well, the female ones.'

'And Debbie Farley?'

'Debbie too, of course.'

'Of course?'

'Well, Lawrence *was* consistent. I suppose I mean 'predictable'. He liked his women slim and shapely, which Debbie is.'

And so are you.

'His age was no barrier, it seems. He was sixty, but didn't look fifty, and most days he acted like thirty-five.'

'A high success rate then?'

Rhona Fiske flushed. 'Depends what you mean by *success*, Inspector,' she replied sharply.

'Forgive me. I'm trying to ask who....how often....well, how many....'

'....did he actually *bonk*, Inspector?'

'That would about cover it. Yes. Thank you.'

He put down his unfinished Earl Grey tea. She smiled just a little more kindly. Those bloody eyes of hers, Zig. It's like questioning the Mona Lisa.

'I have no knowledge of Lawrence's 'success rate' away from Wake Hall, nor of his *tally* in the years before I arrived. But tittle-tattle aside, on three significant occasions I've temporarily swapped my Housekeeper role for Housemistress-in-charge-of-pastoral care. So I can be categorical. First, the previous head lad, in the stables -'

'- Sorry, head *lad*?'

'Alas, Inspector, male language still dominates, and no less so in the world of horses. 'Head lad' can be male or female. The current head lad is a woman - Allie Chant, who perhaps you've met. Her predecessor was slim and shapely too, Karen Sellers. Barely half Lawrence's age, I would guess. She sat in your very chair, tears pouring down her cheeks, before she resigned.'

'Because of Lawrence?'

'Partly, yes. And partly, I suppose, for making her own faulty decisions about him. For all his faults, Inspector, Lawrence wasn't a *rapist*. Mutual consent was involved.'

'And the other two occasions?'

'The second was Ann Kennedy. She worked for the company that supplies our marquees - for weddings, conferences, that kind of thing. She was older. Too old to have a child, so she thought. In the end she didn't. You can probably fill in the blanks.'

Batten could, but noted down the details. Karen Sellers. Ann Kennedy. How vengeful might these two cast-offs be? More legwork, more questions.

'And the third...?'

'Oh, Debbie of course. She had quite a thing for Lawrence, while it lasted. I won't pretend she's my favourite colleague, but to her credit she bounced him out of her duvet once his passion had cooled. He….quietened down, after that - on the premises, at least. Something changed at any rate - but before you ask, Inspector, I don't know what it was. Debbie didn't change him, of that I *am* certain. He has three times her intelligence. If she thought she did, she's a deluded fool.'

Who ended up with a gutful of poison for her troubles, Batten thought, while wondering about Rhona Fiske's fluctuating levels of human sympathy.

'They're still *friends* though, Inspector. Lawrence and Debbie. *Were* friends.'

'Walking companions too,' added Batten. On bloody Burrow Hill.

'Which says something good about them, don't you think? Able to move on, without bitterness. Unusual, in this bed-hopping age.'

She looked at him with those eyes. He got up to go, more reluctantly than he'd expected.

'And I shall miss Lawrence for himself,' she added. 'Our first confrontation aside, he was a gentleman. And damn good at his job, which helped me be good at mine. I think we worked together rather well, keeping Wake Hall on the rails.'

With a Mona Lisa smile, she enticed her rubber gloves and apron towards her.


In his Yeovil office, Assistant Chief Constable Gribble gave himself two squirts of his special spray for tired eyes. It made no difference. What he now thought of as 'The Jellicoe Problem' was just one more of the new Chief Constable's little tests, another smear of rancid icing on a congealed cake of stress and overwork. He frowned down, past trophies and diplomas, at the oblong folder on his desk: 'Chief Inspector Jellicoe'. He was tempted to scribble 'used to be' all over it. Jellicoe used to be good at his job; used to be self-controlled; used to be physically fit; used to be sober. Now he was a poor policeman, angry, a slob, and a 'secret' drinker. His teams compensated by freshening up his nicknames: Bellicose; Jelly-Belly; Beef-Inspector. His current nickname, Fat Jellicoe, was considerably more concise than he was. But that was no help to ACC Gribble. He was supposed to 'manage' Jellicoe.

Creating a new CID team focusing on rural crime had seemed a sensible idea. Chancing on a disused ex-Fire-Brigade building in under-policed Parminster, he had housed his new team there, winning brownie points from the Chief - low-cost, efficient, an improved community profile - as well as bringing whoops of pre-electoral joy from the law and order representatives on the Local Council. Transferring Jellicoe to the rural hinterland where he just might do some good - or less harm - had been a well-intentioned attempt at rehabilitation. And a gamble. Gribble had even managed to bring in new blood from outside. And early doubts about *some* of his hurried selections had disappeared.

Alas, so had Jellicoe, barely forty eight hours after moving into the Parminster CID Centre. He signed orders for building maintenance, IT, and office decoration, even the painting of white lines in the car-park. His diary was full of appointments. He just didn't carry any of them out. Instead, he went on a giant bender before skidding away in his Golf GTi. The traffic cop who stopped him was still on sick-leave with a broken jaw.

Gribble couldn't decide which was more embarrassing: his bad decision to hide Jellicoe in Parminster, or the fact that a hand-picked cohort of trusted officers had yet to discover Jellicoe's whereabouts. The probability that 'elements within the force' were keeping him hidden till the flames died down - or till he dried out - cut no ice with the Chief. Gribble was still overstretched and *very* reluctantly overseeing Parminster CID.

And now a probable *murder*! At a local beauty spot! Could he be forgiven for wishing it was Fat Jellicoe's dead body slumped against a tree on Burrow Hill? How many calls from the Press had he already dealt with? And now the plain-speaking Inspector Batten! Could he somehow spread him across the large doorstep left by Jellicoe? He dismissed the metaphor - if Batten was butter, he was straight from the fridge. He buzzed Mrs Pinch.

'Send him in, please.'

He gave his tired eyes another squirt, in preparation for a curmudgeonly conversation with the Northern nugget.

# Thirteen

Sergeant Ball's sausage fingers typed 'R.U.T.' into the police computer.

'Soon find out who *you* are, boy,' he said to himself. He added 'T.E.R.', and whacked the 'Enter' key with a stubby digit – at precisely the moment the PC screen bleeped shrilly, flashed derisively, and died. He swore, glared across the Parminster office at every other blank screen and picked up his phone instead. *Dead!* Stomping over to the next desk he grabbed another phone. *Dead too!*

In the blue air, Ball's face became so red that Batten could have warmed his hands on it when he loped in after his 'cross-fertilisation' session with the Assistant Chief Constable.

'In training for the Swearing Olympics, Ballie? Or have I interrupted choir practice?'

'Sorry, zor. Responding to my new environment.'

Both men glared at the dead screens, erratic phones and random loops of half-connected cabling. In the far corner, a potential pyre of waste paper and cardboard had accumulated. Most of the kit for their new office had arrived at once, with the exception of waste-bins and liners which hadn't arrived at all, so the cop-shop carpet was a giant dump. The cleaners were threatening a boycott on Health and Safety grounds, and Batten could hardly blame them.

'I hope you got further in Yeovil than I got here, zor?' Ball threw two hopeless arms at the office chaos.

Batten ushered him into the absent Jellicoe's cubby-hole – tidy because Batten had tidied it.

'I got as far as the 'M' word, Ballie - official now, says the ACC – but that's all.'

Ball shrugged. An *un*official 'suspicious death by murder' was enough for him. And now the team would be dealing with the Murder Squad itself – who would assist, liaise, take over, or add to the chaos, depending on your point of view and/or previous experience.

Batten flipped open the initial toxicology report. It did little more than confirm what they knew: no poison in the batch of soup eaten for lunch by Rhona Fiske - but 'a very high concentration of an unidentified toxin' in the thermos flasks of Lawrence Vann and Debbie Farley. The remaining paragraphs burbled on about 'alkaloids', which for Ball belonged in the category of words that started well and ended badly, like 'alcopops'.

Batten pointed glumly at the final paragraph. 'Extensive screening and analysis is ongoing', it said, 'to ascertain the exact nature and origin of the poison or poisons employed.'

'Yep, they've had to send it away, zor. Don't be holding your breath.'

Batten had already phoned 'the toxics', as he called laboratory folk. They'd said plenty about the 'painstaking' nature of their work, but next to nothing about the poison that killed Lawrence Vann. And nothing at all to help identify the devious bastard who put it there.

'Do they write this stuff to help, Ballie? Or to bugger us about?'

He opened the initial autopsy report for Ball to skim through.

'Seems clear enough, zor. '*Cause of Death*....toxin-induced paralysis of the respiratory muscles....primarily, paralysis of the heart muscles.' It's what we thought.'

'True, Ballie. And if you look further down, see, it even mentions 'extremely high toxin levels, consistent with rapid deterioration of the nervous system'.

'Well, zor, transparent. No?'

Batten flipped the page, jabbed his long finger at the next section headed *Additional factors*. 'According to this, our victim's heart was 'unduly susceptible'. I don't know to *what*, Ballie, but if we believe the witness statements, it certainly wasn't rumpy-pumpy!'

Batten's frustration stemmed from his earlier conversation with Doc Danvers....

'He was either poisoned or he wasn't, Doc, so which is it?'

Danvers' phone voice was warm treacle. And I bet you, Zig, the bugger's got his monogrammed socks on the table.

'Ah, Inspector, you are searching for that slippery ghost - the single-factor explanation. A rarity, in my experience.'

Ooh good, I'll just reassure the Crown Prosecution Service.

'But I shall be bountiful. A very powerful poison - of undefined origin as yet, alas - was certainly the lever of death -'

'Right. He was poisoned, that's all I –'

'Patience, Inspector. Let me phrase it so: it was a case of poison *plus*.'

A Yorkshire silence.

'Your Mr Body had reached something of an impasse, Inspector. Lifestyle issues had caught up with him. Do you see?'

Batten saw a giant wine-rack, a hip flask, and the long shelf of fine whiskies in Lawrence Vann's cottage.

'Not to speak of the exertions preceding ingestion. A long country walk. A fast climb up a steep slope - I've experienced the climb myself, as you'll recall.'

But you're not dead, in your striped suit and fancy tie, slumped against a tree on Burrow Hill, are you?

'Tell me then, Doc. If he hadn't glugged poisoned soup, would he have happily toddled back down again?'

'And there lies the difference between us, Inspector. I am of a scientific bent, but you, I suspect, have poetic tendencies.'

Batten considered turning his question into rhyming couplets. Maybe then the Doc would answer it. To Danvers' credit, he did anyway.

'Stretching myself towards the poetic, Inspector, I should say that, yes, he would have toddled back down again.'

'Right. So the poison did for him.'

'But far more swiftly than it would have 'done for' you, Inspector. It impacted very suddenly, very severely upon his life.'

I just said that, Doc. Diddle I?...


Ball's own frustration didn't cloud his understanding.

'Poison *plus*, zor. That complicates things a tad.'

Batten nodded, pleased that - despite frustrations - they were maintaining a working rhythm. Lawrence Vann *was* murdered, but was murder the intended result? Was he supposed to get a warning, but got more than he – and his killer – bargained for? And why was he being warned? Poison *plus*. As if things weren't complicated enough. He flipped a dismissive finger at the dead desktop computer.

'This useless junk isn't going to help!'

'Tell me about it, zor.'

'What were you looking for, anyway?'

'Looking for? Looking for a bloody *technician*! Sorry, zor....It's a *name*, from when I interviewed that dodgy horse bloke at Wake Hall. A name I've *seen*, flagged up *somewhere*. 'Rutter. The horse bloke said he works for a Mr *Rutter*. Whoever he is!'

Ball waved at the silent technology as if about to throttle it.

'Oh, *Rutter*. That's *Olly* Rutter. Him and me go way back. Alas.'

Ball's red face turned puce. His attention moved from the technology towards Batten's throat.

'Nasty bastard,' continued Batten, unabashed. 'Used to be on my old patch, up north. Greedy. Sadistic. Devious. Take your pick.'

'*Zor*? Why didn't you *say* s-'

'How'm I supposed to know you were looking for Rutter? I'm northern, not *psychic*. Look, this is him.'

Batten flashed the mug-shot he'd brought in for the team briefing. He'd crossed swords with Olly Rutter early in his police career, kept the photo. Not that he needed reminding. Ball's sausage-fingers pulled the glossy sheet toward tired eyes.

'Tough, zor? Or just looks it?'

'Tough - behind the veneer of charm. I thought I'd seen the nasty back of him for good. He vanished - *coincidentally* - just as we got permission for phone taps and a bug.' Batten misread Ball's eyebrows. 'Yes, Ballie. Inside information. We never found out who.'

'No, zor, I mean, why would Rutter turn up *here*? In *Somerset*?'

Like a shadow, Zig.

'I'm as gobsmacked as you. When we searched Lawrence Vann's place I took a butchers out the window through his binoculars. Couldn't believe it! Olly's flashy Jag suddenly slides by, parks itself round the side of Wake Hall! Nearly dropped the binocs.'

'Just a Jaguar?'

'Not *just* a Jaguar. *Olly's* Jaguar. RUT73R - hardly your everyday number plate! Thought the cider fumes at Burrow Hill had addled my brain, so I double-checked. I'm squinting through the hedge when one of Olly's beefcakes, bloke called Baz Ballard, lumps out of the Jag and lopes towards that big stable block round the back. Been in the wars, too.'

Ball remembered the name Baz Ballard. He was 'Mr Rutter's

chauffeur' - and a Manny McCrory co-driver on 'bloody long trips'.

'But you didn't actually *see* this Olly Rutter, zor?'

'Look, where Baz Ballard and the Jag go, there goes Olly Rutter. He turns up at Wake Hall, and before you can say 'thermos flask' Lawrence Vann's glugged a gutful of poison? Wake up, Ballie, your toes are tingling so much the floor's vibrating!'

'If only *these* were,' Ball said, pointing at the dead computers.

Batten nudged him back to life. Across the room, a pair of technicians stood in the doorway, blinking at the chaos. Ball couldn't decide whether to pour them tea, or punch them.

# Fourteen

With his boss still in Spain, Baz Ballard had managed a lie-in for once, till the alarm clock drilled at his cauliflower ear. He normally used *two* clocks, since one alone struggled to wake him. Baz Ballard hated early starts. A night person, him.

He was down to a single alarm clock now. The dead carcass of the other lay dismally on the bedside table, pretty much where it had landed a while ago after leaving Olly Rutter's gorilla hand on its way to Baz's skull.

'Car, Baz. 7am tomorrow, sharp.'

That's what Olly had said, plainly enough. And what Olly Rutter said, you did. But Baz hadn't. At seven he was still sleeping the sleep of the dead, he recalled, until he thought better of the metaphor. At one minute past seven, a mammoth shadow had burst into his room and punctured his dreams with a bedlam of curses, then an arm as big as a leg had smashed Baz's second alarm clock onto Baz's only skull. The result was a Baz too concussed to drive - he didn't need to pretend. A livid Olly roped in Manny McCrory to pilot his Jaguar to some dubious early meeting.

All more or less as Baz had planned it. Well, as Lawrence Vann had planned it, in truth.

They'd waited for Derek Herring to jet off again to his Corfu villa, then it was just a case of getting Olly out of their hair for a few hours. When the cat's away. The part of the plan with the big downside was that, on Olly's return, Baz was flicked against a wall and given the beating he knew to expect. But everything else had gone well, so he thought.

Baz's penny should have dropped, though, after Olly flew to Spain with Lady Wake. He'd known Olly too long. When he had an alibi overseas, bad things happened in England. Baz had taken a rare day off and gone to Cardiff, still pleased with what he and Lawrence had accomplished. When he got back, Lawrence Vann was dead.

Olly had been giving Baz an 'affectionate' clip round the cauliflowers for years. But things had changed. Am I getting softer, or is Olly hitting me harder? He looked at the remains of the alarm-clock-bruise in the shaving mirror. A fair-sized lump, but fading. Lately though, the resentment wasn't.

In the mirror's reflection he saw the homely furniture of his Wake Hall rooms. He liked his rooms. They'd been the butler's rooms. Still were, he mused: a driving-bodyguard-dogsbody-slapsponge of a butler. Old Lord Wake had employed the same butler, Norman, for twenty years, but the daughter gave him the boot barely a day after her father's funeral. She puzzled Baz, did Lady Wake. Why she tolerated Olly, he had no idea. And she was getting shut of all the Wake Hall traditions. With the exception of Lawrence Vann, that is.

He scraped a razor at the wiry stubble on a face past its sell-by date. When police pressure in Leeds forced Olly to move from known urban streets to the unknown rural lanes of Somerset, Baz was quietly grateful. Olly liked the easy pickings, the lack of snooping from the law - till recently - and the posh female flesh that had drawn him south. But Olly couldn't settle into country living. Peace and quiet? Flat champagne! He cursed the mud, the narrow roads, the slower pace of life, the smell. Baz knew, because he got slapped for it. And, yes, a lot harder now.

Baz, though, embraced his new rural surroundings. He learned to enjoy the silence, the greenness, arrays of stars in the night sky, even some of the people - Lawrence Vann included. He liked Lawrence. A gent, a rural gent. And when you've spent your day with a slap-happy mammoth, it was good to chew the fat, now and then, with a human being.

Grudgingly, Baz climbed into his chauffeur suit, thoughts drifting back, not for the first time, to Lawrence Vann.....

'How much do you earn a year, Baz, if you don't mind my asking?'

Lawrence poured whisky into two crystal tumblers. Baz had given up trying to count how many vintage bottles sat on the long shelf above his head.

'Earn? Or get paid?'

'Well, yes, I can imagine. What comes in, then?'

''Bout twenty five grand, take or leave, plus bed and board. 'Bout that.'

'And a Pension Scheme? Expense account? Sick pay? Anything of that nature?'

'Chris' sake, Lawrence, you've *met* Olly. What do *you* think?'

'Well, yes, that *was* what I thought, as a matter of fact. My guess is you're about twenty thousand pounds a year short, yes?'

'And if? Cut to the chase, Lawrence.'

'Certainly, Baz. Well, where one's finances are concerned, a useful test is to project forward to retirement. Have you tried that?'

'I have - *as a matter of fact.*'

'And *is* there a pension pot? Do you know how much would be coming in, how much going out? When *you're* not going out - to work, that is?'

A pension pot? I wish.

'This sudden interest in my welfare, Lawrence. 'S very touching. Gonna talk to Olly on my behalf? Out of the goodness of your heart?'

'No, Baz. I'm going to talk to *you*. On *our* behalf. And out of mutual interest.'

Baz sipped his honey-coloured whisky. Top quality, again.

'*Our* behalf, Lawrence? I take it that's just you and me...?'


In the double-locked office of Wake Hall Horse, Derek Herring signed the secret agreement that lay on his pristine desk. With Lawrence Vann thankfully out of the way, it would be business as usual - once Olly Rutter returned and the police departed.

The agreement's advantageous terms pleased him, even if his signature did not. He disliked his name - and a good deal less when people called him 'Del'. As an overweight schoolboy with a chubby face, it hadn't take the bullies long to think up nasty nicknames for him. He dreaded the constant sniffing sounds they made when the teacher's back was turned. 'Can you smell fish?' they'd ask in mock surprise. 'I'm *sure* I can smell fish. There's a fish in 'ere somewhere, it's an 'erring, an' it *stinks!*'

Although unaware of it at the time, he *did* stink. Of dirty clothes and poor sanitation and cigarette smoke. His mother smoked. She did little else, apart from drink. He got himself to school because it was warm there and they fed him. He paid a high price.

'Mornin' Delly! Morning' Delly-baby!' the bullies sneered. 'Shall we bite Delly-jelly-baby's head off today, or just an arm or a leg?' He cowered in a playground corner, unable to stop them biting off all three.

Early adversity drove him rapidly along the qualification highway and into a successful legal career. The hurt inside remained, unforgotten. There would be compensation for the ills suffered as a boy, he would make sure of that. Young Derek Herring became a sharp, acutely intelligent man - a touch slimmer and less unattractive - though hardly every woman's dream. This too, would require compensation.

Even before he crossed paths with Olly Rutter - successfully defending him against a money-laundering charge - the bullied boy evolved. He despised weak people, dismissing their dependency as an insult to those who took the world by the throat. He desired beautiful women, yet hated them for their beauty. Fortunately for Derek, long-term liaison with Olly's dubious 'business empire' provided weak people to dominate and beautiful women to hate. He frequently indulged himself, on both counts.

The documents on his desk had travelled back with him from the most recent of his regular trips to Corfu, where his private villa was both a personal pleasure and a clandestine base from which to do business with 'certain associates' he had cultivated on Olly's behalf. The shores and waters of the Mediterranean were proving most fruitful. He double-checked the last of the agreements, and duly signed it with his gold-plated, antique fountain pen, meticulously replacing the screw-top before returning it to the silk pocket of his silk suit. The pen was inscribed with a single word, 'Victorious'. He had bought it, expensively, in a London antiques emporium. 'Victorious', they said, had been a ship. To Derek, 'Victorious' was a statement of his daily expectations.

Derek Herring absorbed the rare peace of the office abutting the vast stable blocks of Wake Hall Horse, Olly Rutter's current business 'front'. While Derek admired Olly's guile and toughness, he privately saw himself as the true brains of the operation. And in Olly's absence, Derek was captain for the day.


Cider wasn't available so Sergeant Ball settled for tea from the machine. He swallowed a mouthful as he checked the notes that DC 'Loft' Hick had dropped onto the only clear space on his desk. Hickie still had the capacity to surprise - colour-blind where his choice of clothes was concerned, yet once in a while having x-ray vision. He resented being nudged away from his first murder case and back onto stolen tractors, but soon found a new connection. His notes proved it, if his spelling didn't.

'Recent farm machinary thefts: eight,' said the notes. 'Of these, one from an unsecured garidge. Padlock and chain: three - all snapped with bolt-cutters.' It was the final statistic which made Ball spill his tea. 'Guard dogs: four. All piosoned.' Hick had underlined 'All piosoned', in thick black pencil.

Coincidence? Catch a thief, *ask* a thief. But so far not a sniff. Ball scrawled a note for Batten, anchored it to his cubby-hole desk with a brass fish paperweight.


Lawrence had reached a danger point. If Baz spilled all to Olly, the consequences would be monstrous. But Lawrence was a countryman. Patient cultivation was in his blood - ploughing, feeding, sowing. Reaping. He recognised early on that it wasn't just the chauffeur's hat that didn't suit Baz. Olly Rutter didn't suit him either. Baz was a lost man, a man seeking an escape. And a pension fund.

When next they met, in the privacy of Lawrence's cottage, screened from the eyes and ears of the Hall by a thick yew hedge, Lawrence went further.

'My cards on the table, if I may, Baz?'

Baz had been spending too much time near Lady Wake, and languorously waved his arm in assent.

'If I am correct, Baz, your Mr Rutter has expanded into avenues which are, shall we say, 'darker than usual'?'

Baz began to wave his arm, but stopped. How did Lawrence *know*? It didn't matter. Something was squirming in Baz's lower depths. Something that felt like a conscience. He waved his arm.

'Thank you, Baz. Is it also correct that you are less than comfortable with the risks - indeed the very *nature* of Olly's more recent practices? I'm perfectly happy for you to continue waving your hand to signify agreement', said Lawrence, who was an observant man.

Baz gave a gruff chuckle, waved again.

'What is clear to both of us, I'm sure, is that when Olly's foot plops in the mire, as it doubtless will, the displaced manure will land unpleasantly on many people, not least your good self.' With a smile, Lawrence added, 'that was not a question, but a statement, by the way, Baz, and does not require a wave of assent from your hand or any other part of your anatomy.'

Perhaps because he was warming to Lawrence's style, or because his hand was tired, or because he was tired of his hand, Baz spoke.

'If what you say's true, Lawrence, well, what's an ageing number-cruncher like '*your* good self' gonna do about it? Olly'd squeeze your nuts with one hand and you'd still turn blue.'

'He surely would, I agree. I shudder at the thought.'

'So?'

'So Olly needs to be removed.'

Baz gave another gruff chuckle. Lawrence should do stand-up.

'I mean removed legally, of course.'

The gruff chuckle became a jackal laugh.

'Legally? *Olly*? He was running rings round the law before his balls had dropped. And you seem to have forgotten Del Herring, Olly's get-out-of-jail card. I'm going off 'our little chat', Lawrence.'

'Baz, when I say 'legally removed', it is true that I mean by the police -'

'- Ah, I dial 999, s'that it?'

'No, Baz. You help me to lock Olly in a cage so tight not even Mr Herring will lever him out. Nothing more than that. And very much in mutual interest, of course.'

Baz was thinking what a dodgy phrase 'mutual interest' was.

'Who'd do what,' he asked, 'assuming we ever became 'mutual'?'

# Fifteen

Burrow Hill had become a symbol of Batten's uncertainty in this new West Country landscape. It was a convenient scapegoat, he knew. Whether he was driving or walking, the squitty little mound would suddenly appear, a little speck with a tree on top, an undernourished nipple on the breast of South Somerset. But it *was* a crime scene, and since crime scenes repay a second look, he'd bought a pair of 'gumboots', and here he was on Burrow Hill again.

'I'll come with you if you like, zor,' Sergeant Ball had offered, even Burrow Hill being preferable to the crime-scene of his desk.

'Many trees have given their lives for you,' Batten said, pointing at the confetti of documents. 'Stay, give them a decent burial.'

Batten began to wish he'd stayed too. The new boots rubbed, blisters on both heels already. Police regulation size nine or not, they were too tight. Bit like you, Zig, today. Should have broken them in, the boots, worn them in the office at Parminster, waded through that jungle of rubbish covering the carpets.

He reached the hilltop and got to work, first retracing the route the Scramblers had taken from the north-east towards the viewing point and its nearby tree. Yes, a distracted and ageing walker, in rain-disturbed spectacles, might not spot a corpse propped against the far side of this chunky tree. He walked round it, avoiding the taped-off area, new boots chafing. What tree *was* it? He must ask someone - someone who wouldn't treat him like a useless townie who's never seen a tree before. Leaning across the police tape he touched the rough bark. Communing with the bloody thing, Zig? He pulled his hand away. For now, 'a killing tree' would have to do.

From habit, he talked himself through the imagined final steps of Lawrence Vann.

'He's come up the hill from the cider farm. It's a few minutes before ten. Is he alone? He reaches the top, sits on the bench by the viewing point. He's thirsty, or just greedy, and pours himself a cup of soup from his thermos, drinks it while looking down at half of South Somerset. The flask holds two cups and he downs them both, which means the taste doesn't put him off. Unfortunately.'

Batten paused. A death-in-situ seemed the right call. What reason was there to dump a body here, on top of a prominent hill? A warning? To *whom*? And even if the body *was* placed here, wouldn't a super-strong person be needed, to lump it across open fields and up a steep slope - without leaving doubly-deep footprints in the soft terrain, or any other trace? Mm. Dustbin. Neither was there an access road for a vehicle to use, nor barely a visible track. No tyre marks, no hoof-prints. Nothing.

And teams have to get past the 'nothing' point. Asking, checking, recording, assessing - they would need to do it all again. This kind of police work, Batten knew, whether in Somerset or Siberia, was dull and often inconclusive. 'It's the underpants of the uniform, Zig,' Ged once said. 'Essential, clean and tidy, largely unseen - and producing friction in awkward places.'

A rumbling from the sky proved not to be thunder but one of the helicopters that even in this murk wended their way from the Agusta-Westland factory at Yeovil on daily test flights to nowhere, so it seemed to him. Ah well, problem solved: the body was dropped in by helicopter. Or why not from a UFO? Sure, Zig, the same one that makes the crop circles. He rubbed his moustache.

'Lawrence Vann gets up from the bench - because he sees something? Or somebody? Or just to take in more of the view?'

He didn't have his binoculars with him, Zig, so….

'Whatever, he ends up on the far side of this tree. The ground is wet, so does he lean against the bark to finish his soup? He manages to screw the top back on the flask, so how swiftly does the poison make him nauseous?'

Batten heard Doc Danvers' treacly vocals: 'far more swiftly than it would have done for you, Inspector.'

'At some point Lawrence is sick - but not sick enough, alas. Flecks of vomit stain his clothing. He staggers against the tree, dropping the flask on the ground. Soon, he slumps onto the damp grass, trapping the flask behind him. The tree keeps him upright, supports him, but his heart and lungs don't. He has a phone but doesn't use it. Or more likely can't. His breath gives out, his head falls forward and his wide-brimmed hat falls over his face. Or falls off? It's now maybe ten past ten. At what point exactly does the poison do *that* to every muscle on his face?'

Who killed him, Zig? One of his female cast-offs, for revenge? Perhaps. And what of Debbie Farley? Who would want to poison *her*? Almost every witness pooh-poohed the thought of her *having* an enemy. Batten retraced her steps too.

'She bumps into Lonny Dalway at the cider farm, tells him Lawrence is still on Burrow Hill and they need to be getting back. She climbs up - alone? At the top she sees Lawrence's face. It's enough to make anyone scream, and scream she does, all the way back down to the farm, where she babbles incoherently in Erin Kemp's office before reviving herself with a slug of soup. Soon, she's violently ill. If not for the paramedics and Doc Danvers, she'd be victim number two.'

He relived the poisoned whiteness of her oxygen-masked face; the death-distorted scream on Lawrence Vann's.

Enough of Burrow Hill, Zig. Get out of these boots, out of the rain, and into a whisky.

While Batten was adding his blistering wellies to the pile of Somerset soil in his mired car, Stephanie Broke-Mondelle was in the oak-beamed kitchen of her hamstone farmhouse, box of matches in hand. The phone had rung all morning, but she ignored it. That tall police inspector, the one with the moustache, had even knocked on her door - and rather sharply, she thought. She had watched him, from behind the thick dining-room curtains, but had no intention of answering, had no desire to speak to him or anyone. The irony was not lost on her; she knew she talked too much. Now though, she was incommunicado.

She put a match to a pair of compromising photographs of herself and the recently deceased Lawrence Vann. Their private parts were concealed behind a discreetly-placed and partially unfolded Ordnance Survey map of the Somerset Levels - rather tastefully, she thought. But the fact that no other bodily covering, clothing or otherwise, was visible in the rest of the photograph meant that everything else *was*. Oh, Lawrence, such a persuasive man. So exciting. So...saucy, is that the word? And such a drinker! Why in my excitement did I join in, and drink far more than is good for me? I've always looked after my body, I know. But, for heaven's sake, a Broke-Mondelle, in a Playboy centre-fold! Why, why? And *tipsy*! Mummy and daddy would have raised their disapproving eyebrows to the heavens, and emitted that sighing, synchronised 'tuh!' she remembered so well.

Stephanie knew the reason why. It was because she had rediscovered trust. Trust wasn't something to *analyse*, it was a feeling, and for too long she had given up on such things. Disappointment was the only feeling she recognised some days, even when walking, even when sudden sunlight added diamonds to the landscape. Stephanie had closed her heart, relied on un-felt talk. Till Lawrence.

When he entrusted his i-phone to her, asked her to keep it hidden and on no account to switch it on, she had been surprised - but did not question him. When he asked her to look after his key, that tiny silver key, she immediately concurred. Lawrence trusted her to keep phone and key secret and safe - she did not ask from whom. And she trusted him when he swore the key would open the door to their future.

What was she to do now though, with Lawrence's phone and his silver key, but without Lawrence? *They* were in a safe place. But was Stephanie?

She waved away the fumes of burning celluloid. When the flames died, she ran the tap and flushed the photographic, pornographic ash down the Belfast sink, rubbing with a dishcloth till the porcelain sides were pure white again. What a relief!

Rewarding herself with a dash of Radio 3, she buffed dubbin into her walking boots. Schubert's String Quartet in G minor falsely lulled her into a more relaxed state. Had she managed to creep even a millimetre into the digital age she would have known that the ashes of the glossily-printed photos had a crystal-clear parent image of saucy little pixels, and they were still sleeping peacefully inside Lawrence Vann's laptop. Wherever it was.

Home and dry, Batten sipped a large glass of golden Speyside while Lou Reed sang *Beginning To See The Light*. Prompted, he held the glass up to the window and talked to himself.

*Run through more possibilities, Zig, will you?*

How about murder, followed by the murderer's failed suicide?

*Gribble'd be ecstatic. Just think of the money he'd save.*

But why would Debbie Farley want to kill Lawrence Vann?

*Same reason as his other rejects - the green-eyed monster, jealousy.*

The other rejects got out fast, though. Debbie didn't. She moved on, from lover to walking companion.

*OK, it weakens the theory a bit, but....*

And if Debbie Farley murders Lawrence Vann, why the attempted suicide?

*Obvious again, Zig - remorse and guilt.*

But why not enjoy the triumph, having gone to all that trouble? And to choose such a cack-handed method of topping herself?

*Perhaps she took lessons from Eddie Hick?*

Lou Reed finished *Nowhere At All* and began on *Vicious*. Batten swung his socks onto the sofa.

*You've gone quiet, Zig.*

I was thinking! A third person's involved - who knows about poison.

*So you've got a list of suspects, have you? People with access to the flasks? And the time and opportunity to doctor them? And a reason?*

I've got a long list and a short list, as it happens.

*Sure you have. Any evidence?*

Lou Reed fell silent; Batten too. He hated this point in a murder inquiry - dangerous skills and warped motives still at large within persons unknown. When *Perfect Day* began, he switched it off.

'You *do* realise the level of urgency, Inspector? If the press are to be believed, local sales of soup have *plummeted*!'

He had given Gribble a long stare. His team and the Murder Squad were practically working double shifts. In retaliation, he'd reminded Gribble about the hefty bill for Debbie Farley's police protection at the hospital. If she *was* an intended victim then 'someone' must have a pressing need to be rid of her, and might try again. *But why, Zig?*

He put down his unfinished whisky. Yes, Zig, why?


When next they met, Lawrence felt on safer ground with Baz. They were both big men, but Baz lifted giant weights. He could have knocked Lawrence from one end of his beamed sitting room to the other with a single punch. Instead, they touched heavy crystal glasses. Today it was a

Speyside, rich-tasting and smelling of spice and honey.

'As I see it, Baz, you have the benefit of access. And I have the benefit of knowledge.'

''N' what am I supposed to have access *to*, Lawrence?'

'Well, Baz, to Olly's private business data, of course - in that strongbox of an office. I have the skills to decipher such data, and I'm sure the criminality it contains will bring a happy smile to a policeman's face?'

Neither Baz's voice nor hand could say anything for a while. He had been at many a dark crossroads with Olly before, and had always been persuaded to take turnings that grew darker each time. He had always turned *with* Olly, never *against* him.

'I'm not too hot on computers, Lawrence. 'S'where he keeps it all.'

'Baz, you have eyes, ears, and good judgement. They will be sufficient. I have faith in you.'

Baz liked that Lawrence saw his intelligence. Olly wasn't bright, but by god he was cunning. Lawrence, in contrast, seemed to be both….Baz *did* worry about a pension fund. Apart from a few grand in an ISA, he had bugger all. No house of his own. Even the old car he used was Olly's. If he got the sack tomorrow, he'd have to walk out of Wake Hall. But you didn't get the sack from Olly, you ended up *inside* one. Baz knew he wouldn't be walking anywhere….Could Lawrence be trusted?

'This plan, Lawrence, to gift-wrap Olly for the cops? It's because you're public-spirited, right? Give Wake Hall a shake till the nasties fall out, then we all live happily ever after?'

'You flatter my limited powers, Baz, but paint a desirable picture. I have a range of motives. We live in a complex world, you'll agree?'

Baz brought his consenting arm back into use.

'I would say that my first motive *is* Wake Hall, Baz. Do you know how long I've worked here?'

A shake of the head, a sip of fine whisky.

'Thirty years. *Thirty years*. I came here to work for Lord Wake on the day before my thirtieth birthday. He still had a wife then, and a young daughter - she would have been eight or nine, I suppose - who spent as much time playing hide and seek in my Estate office as she did in the Hall itself. Did you know it was me who taught her to ride? Her father brought her up in a tradition to be proud of - a tradition now in danger of being destroyed by your Mr Rutter.'

Baz almost said 'Olly's not *my* Mr Rutter', but since Olly practically *owned* him....

'Wake Hall is dying, Baz; crushed by a brute with as much relevance to rural values as a double-decker London bus. I would like to wave goodbye to Mr Rutter, before the remaining sense in Lady Wake's head is lost forever. Her salvation is my second motive.'

Do *I* give a toss about Lady Wake's salvation? Don't mind her piggy-backing on the chauffeur duties, because she makes Olly sit beside her in the back, his big hands that much further away. Stuck-up cow, all the same. And what do the dying traditions of Wake Hall have to do with me?

Lawrence was way ahead of him.

'My third motive may be of more direct interest, however, Baz. Applying my finance and IT skills, I can comfortably *reconstitute* a significant portion of Olly's data - once you have purloined it, of course. Divert a touch here, a touch there, yes? Transform it into cash to hold in your hand? Olly launders very large quantities of money, you'll agree?'

And just how did Lawrence *know*?

'Come now, Baz. It is childishly obvious. Lady Wake may be the only person in Somerset who believes Wake Hall Horse is an entirely legitimate business operation.'

No arguing with that, Baz thought. Olly doesn't win his cash on the Premium Bonds.

'Imagine, if you will, a not inconsiderable tranche of all that laundered money, diverted into a pair of safe havens, yours and mine? An overseas account? A safe-deposit box? None of it officially exists, you see. But it is *spendable*. Shall we call it an unofficial police reward?'

Baz didn't know what a tranche was, but he could imagine himself twirling a little silver key to a well-filled box secreted away in a bank vault.

'Our gains will of course be secured - and their evidence trail removed - *before* the police are invited in, Baz. So it may now be appropriate to wave an assenting arm?'

Baz no longer needed to wave anything. Not even a white flag. He drained his whisky.

'I'll tell you what, Lawrence. Why don't you talk to me about *amounts.*'

And Lawrence duly obliged.

# Sixteen

'*Incinerated*? What, *all* of them?'

'"Fraid so, zor.'

Batten knew there was no good reason why four dead guard-dogs should still be lying around for an Inspector to inspect, but it did nothing to ease the blisters on his feet.

'Vet's reports?'

'Hickie tracked 'em down - they just say 'poisoned'. No indication of *what* poison. Dunno about Yorkshire, zor, but dog autopsies aren't exactly common practice down here.'

Batten saw a masked and gowned Doc Danvers, doing a Y-section on a poisoned poodle.

'Have you got that report on licensed poisons at Wake Hall?'

Ball went to rummage, leaving Batten to his thoughts. Poison.... Knowledge *of*. Access *to*. Knowledge *how*. Reason *why*. Whoever poisoned four guard dogs had all of these. And whoever poisoned Lawrence Vann, ditto. Could the two 'whoevers' be connected? Or be the same? And if they were, why would an anonymous tractor thief poison Lawrence Vann and Debbie Farley?

He could make little sense of it.

'No great shakes, zor,' said Ball, returning with the report. 'Rat poison and weed killer - small amounts, strict controls, independent signatures required. And they're all in order. No gaps, no missing quantities.'

The toxics had tested Wake Hall's small stock of poison and ruled it out. Pity they hadn't yet ruled anything *in*. Batten flicked through the report. Jake Tuttle the gardener...Rhona Fiske, the Head Housekeeper with the Mona Lisa eyes...both authorised to sign for small doses of the stuff. They had knowledge and access. And reason - to kill rats and invasive weeds. But Lawrence Vann was neither of those, was he?

'You *do* know what I do for a living?'

'Um, 'wedding marquees' is all it says in my notes.' DC Nina Magnus had successfully tracked down Ann Kennedy, one of Lawrence's more recent rejects, but that was all the success she was having. They were squeezed into Ann Kennedy's tiny office on the mezzanine floor of The Perfect Event, and Magnus was sitting on a chair that was a size and a half too small.

'Marquees, certainly - *and* portable kitchens, sound systems, dance-floors, string quartets - indeed anything and everything to do with events in general and *weddings* in particular.'

Magnus clocked the bitter emphasis on 'weddings'. Lawrence Vann was the spouse that got away.

'The point is, I plan and control their *hire*.' She waved a hand at her desk computer. 'I *rent* them out.'

'Rent' received similar sharp emphasis. Magnus had got the message five minutes ago but Ann Kennedy was still hammering it home like tent pegs round a marquee.

'*Rentals*. I of all people should have known better. That's what women were to *him* - he *rented* the sweets in the sweetshop, sampled them and spat them out. In his quest for the perfect sherbet *dip!*'

And were you just one imperfect sherbet amongst them all? Magnus wondered how best to phrase this, but Ann Kennedy didn't need questions to keep her fire crackling.

'When Lawrence said it was time he settled down, I naturally assumed he meant with *me*! I could not have been more *wrong*! I came off the pill, dammit!'

'Ms Kennedy - '

'If that man had a little more give and a lot less take, we might have....I assume you know we almost had a child together?'

'Er, yes. Can I ask how 'almost' that was?'

Ann Kennedy fell silent. Small mercies, thought Magnus. Interviews usually meant dragging information out of people. Here, she'd barely had chance to look at her notes. She looked at Ann Kennedy instead: slim; attractive; tall; forty. Was this Lawrence's formula, the corner of the sweetshop he focused on?

'I....had....to choose, in the end. Awful. I couldn't....I knew I would be bringing up a child on my own....And paying the *rent* on my own, with little help from *him*!'

'So there was no question that Mr Vann…?'

'What? That he would be honourable? How little you've discovered!'

Magnus glanced at her list of Lawrence's discards. None had been so angry, some very much the opposite. Lawrence the letch was a more complex Casanova than she'd thought.

Ann Kennedy began to sob. Angry, sad, angry, sad, with each heave of her chest. Magnus reached for the small pack of tissues she always carried. She doled them out to male witnesses too, sometimes. But Ann Kennedy was less a witness now, more a general suspect. Or a *specific* suspect, given the axe she was grinding?

Where exactly were you on the morning of November 1$^{st}$, Ms Kennedy? And how much do you know about poisons? In your job, can you *rent* them? Magnus wondered how to phrase all this, once the sobbing stopped.

Detective Constable George Halfpenny finished his second espresso, slipped into his fur-collared coat and made his way from Café Nero to his car. Ball had told him and Magnus to 'work together on Lawrence's women' and given them a list of names going back years. When Ball had gone, George snipped the list in two with his nail scissors, and gave half to Magnus. He'd never worked with a black officer before, and he intended to keep it that way. He told Magnus it would be more efficient if they split the load.

Most of his list was already done and dusted. Interviews were a doddle if you upped the pace, quick questions, quick answers, no messing. And a big stroke of luck had meant time for an extra-long coffee break.

'You haven't been told then, have you?'

'I'm sorry, Mr….er….Hardington, told what?'

'I assumed you'd come….I dunno, to investigate. Not that there's anything suspicious *to* investigate.'

'Suspicious, sir?'.

'About Karen, I mean.'

The name at the top of George's list was Karen Sellers, because she was once head lad at Wake Hall. Since leaving, after her failed fling with Lawrence Vann, she'd flitted around the South West like a butterfly. He finally tracked her down via employment records to a racing stable near

Wincanton. Mr Hardington was the boss.

'About Karen, sir, yes, that's right. Karen Sellers. She *is* the reason I'm here.'

'I can understand why they wouldn't tell you, on the phone. Popular girl, was Karen.'

'Sorry, sir? *Was?*' George Halfpenny cursed. Don't tell me I've got to track the bloody woman down *again*. 'You mean she's gone?'

Mr Hardington's face clouded over.

'Gone? Gone alright. Gone under a horse, a racehorse. Three week ago. We've not had an accident in thirty years, not a fatal one. Till now...'


Lady Wake was back from selecting brood mares in the warmth of Southern Spain, with Olly in tow. Gold-plated alibis, the pair of them. Avril, Lady Wake's maid, ushered Batten into a faded ante-room, an off-white limestone Purgatory jammed between Wake Hall's outer and inner doors. She waved him towards a tired-looking chair, covered in pinkish velvet that had once been red. 'Ma'am' would see him 'presently', she mumbled. He heard Avril drop the latch on the inner door as she passed through, then a long silence began. He would wait all day if need be. Plenty of Jellicoe's paperwork to get on with. And worth waiting, to reacquaint himself with Olly Rutter.

He'd asked Sergeant Ball to 'run the rest of Wake Hall through the colander', and Sergeant Ball was trying his best. But it was no easy task to shorten the list of people with access to a simple pair of thermos flasks on the morning of Lawrence Vann's murder. Even the cool Ms Fiske was ill-tempered, having been through all this before. She'd offered him a seat in the big Wake Hall kitchen - but no tea.

'So, it was just the team leaders that had breakfast together that day? That's what you previously said, I think?'

'Team leaders - hah!' snapped Rhona Fiske. 'When we *had* staff we were team leaders. Now that half the staff have been 'rationalised' we just run around leading ourselves!'

Ball looked a little squashed. She mellowed slightly. 'But yes, Sergeant, we do have an early working breakfast together most days, around 7.30. It helps us to plan and prioritise. Efficiency is pretty much the only thing we have left.'

He could have said it was much the same for the police.

'And before 7.30? Is the kitchen busy?'

'Well, we take turns to do the bacon and eggs, at about twenty past. Before that, other than Debbie, no, there wouldn't be anyone around.'

'And on the day in question, November 1st?'

'I don't need reminding of the date, Sergeant. Lawrence and Debbie were off duty, of course - though Debbie dropped in to pick up the flasks of soup, much as she's done a dozen times before. She was in and around the kitchen for a bit, but I didn't see Lawrence at all. Just heard his car leaving, around eight.'

'But you're sure it was his car?'

'*Pretty* sure. Quite a chunky engine. You get to know the sounds they make, don't you?'

'And what about Ms Farley: did you see her pour soup into the flasks?'

Rhona Fiske pondered. 'They're usually there already when I come in. Yes, on the window-sill, behind the sink. She just reached across, if I recall, picked them up and took them out, presumably to Lawrence's car. She'll have filled them earlier - she usually does. Debbie's always the first up, prowling around 'her' kitchen like a tomcat scenting its patch.'

Ball decided not to delve into the obvious tension between Debbie Farley and Rhona Fiske, but he made a mental note. He also noted that the window-sill in question faced the rear. Towards the walled empire of Wake Hall Horse.

'But before Lawrence and Debbie left, there was you and....?'

'Me, Jake, and Allie. The 'team leaders' with diminishing teams. House, Gardens, Stables. Lawrence is usually there, of course, except on his mornings off - oh dear.' She paused for a moment. 'Anyway, the three of us had breakfast together, planned the day. And Mr Valdano popped in, with Oksana, his assistant. Sorry, I can only say her first name - 'Oksana Unpronounceable', that's what we call her. You've met Vito Valdano, I imagine, from Solo Souls?'

Vito Valdano was already on the radar, but currently overseas. Vito Valdano? Solo Souls? Was someone having a laugh? And now an unpronounceable female assistant? Cursing, Ball added 'Oksana Thing' to his list.

100

'I don't think you mentioned this before? About them popping in?'

'Nor did I mention being a week behind with the demands of my *job*, Sergeant!'

This time she didn't mellow, just looked at her watch.

'So Mr Valdano, and Oksana….' He almost said Thing. 'They popped in for why?'

'To see me and Debbie. They were planning yet another Solo Souls event in our conference suite, 'The Beast Within Your Soul'. Some drippy course on getting in touch with your inner gazelle, I expect. Do pardon my cynicism, Sergeant. They wanted to ensure that the lunch we offered would be genuinely macrobiotic - whatever that means. Debbie said she'd sort it out. Fat chance of that, now. If Vito runs his event and the catering is merely catering, well, do I care?'

Ball checked his notes. 'But nobody else?' he asked, with stubborn optimism.

'Well, the farriers were definitely there - the kitchen's the only room in this part of the Hall with windows to the rear, so you can see a bit of Wake Hall Horse from the back.'

'The farriers - that's….Roddy Cope and Neil Tapworthy? Yes? So they were there too, that morning? You saw them?'

'Smelled them, Sergeant, in the first instance.'

Ball imagined a couple of burly blacksmiths, rank with body odour. '*Smelled* them?'

'Smelled the *horseshoes*. Goodness, Sergeant, you're a countryman aren't you?'

Yes, a tired one.

'The smell, the acrid smell when a hot shoe's put on a hoof - doesn't hurt the horse, but it hurts your nostrils. And it doesn't make bacon and eggs taste better. I remember getting up to close the back windows, and Roddy and Neil were in the yard, with their electric furnace and all their paraphernalia.'

'So they could have gained access to the kitchen?'

'Gained access? You mean 'come in'? Of course! We're only talking about twenty yards. They've been in before, certainly. One of our horsey female team leaders has invited them in for the odd mug of tea.'

Ball sighed inwardly. He would now have to check if Allie Chant had the hots for Roddy Cope or for Neil Tapworthy – or, lord help us, both. He peered through the rear kitchen window at the tall wall surrounding the stable yard, hoping they would never need to search its vastness.

'Could anyone else from Wake Hall Horse have gained access to the kitchen?'

'Goodness, Sergeant, you keep referring to the kitchen as if it's a fortress. It's a kitchen, for heaven's sake. A kitchen with a big table and several chairs - one of the few places where any of us can meet. We're hardly going to replace the kitchen door with a ticket-only turnstile, are we?'

Ball blew out his breath at the thought of reporting back to Batten. Instead of reducing the list of people who could have slipped poison into Lawrence and Debbie's soup, he'd extended it. Rhona Fiske, Allie Chant and Jake Tuttle. The two farriers, Roddy Cope and Neil Tapworthy. Vito Valdano of Solo Souls and an unpronounceable assistant, Oksana Thing. And anyone and everyone from Wake Hall Horse. Derek Herring, Manny McCrory, Bulky Hobshaw, and Baz Ballard at the very least, with any drivers or stable hands that happened to be around - by chance or deliberately.

'Does Lady Wake ever come into the kitchen?'

'Well she knows where it *is*, Sergeant. But no, hardly ever. We go to *her*, quite as you would expect.'

Ball nodded, with diminished optimism. At Wake Hall, he thought, nothing was quite as you would expect.


Olly's return brought to an end Derek Herring's brief stint as captain of Wake Hall Horse, and the dark waters it sailed on.

'Del!' yelled Olly, once he'd double-locked the doors from the inside. 'Get in here, will you?'

Though usually viperish in correcting the abuse of his name, Derek made an exception with Olly. One did not correct Olly Rutter. Derek had tried. Once. In the empathy department, Olly had not so much a gap as a vacuum. Derek Herring had empathy - of sorts - to spare, and was cynically adept at using it to manipulate the 'professional' relationships that took place in what he silently thought of as his private kingdom.

Private, because where Olly was concerned there was room for only one king.

'Del! You a cripple all of a sudden? Can't you walk any faster?'

'No, Olly. I'm built for thoroughness, not speed. Usefully so, perhaps?'

'Useful is what you're for, Del. Remember that.'

Derek noted that Olly's vanity was set on '10' today.

'How'd you get on?' asked Olly, his deliberate vagueness reflecting for once the coded language that Derek had long preferred, ever since a bought informer warned that the Yorkshire police planned to bug Olly's office.

'Corfu is a little wet this time of year, Olly, but the villa can truthfully be described as luxurious now. The renovation has gone as smoothly as these things can.'

Olly nodded impatiently. Del's villa in Corfu could be a shack for all he cared, as long as business got done there. He used the code though.

'Still thinking of an extension, are you?'

'Well, if further expansion *is* required, I have been assured that the relevant permissions will be granted.'

'That'll cost a bob or two, Del?'

'Oh, the costs are more than reasonable, Olly. And with expansion come discounts. A case of double the size at barely half the price, I understand.'

Olly pushed his lips into a thinker's pout, while decoding Derek's news and whizzing numbers through his calculator of a brain. He was good at numbers. And economies of scale. Double the size. Yes. At barely half the original price. And they weren't talking about villas or horses. The extra profit was essential now.

'Well, I'll tell you this, Del,' he said in a lower voice, '*I'm* ready. Manny's ready. Transport's ready. So, it's a no-brainer.' He relaxed his pout and slapped his gorilla hands on the arms of his leather chair.

Derek Herring lowered his voice in turn. 'Might the Lawrence Vann investigation imply a touch of caution, Olly? Given the likelihood of further visits from our friends in the force?'

'Del, are you suggesting I hide in a cave while that plonker Batten chases his own arse?'

'Certainly not, Olly.' Derek Herring paused to select words with the correct nuance. 'But as your legal adviser - and an effective one, I trust - I must consider measures to reduce potential risk, yes?'

Olly pouted again. No thick plod was going to find any proof of *his* complicity, least of all Ziggy Batten. While Lawrence Vann was croaking, I was in sunny Spain. And Wake Hall Horse really did sell horses, at enough of a profit to keep Marianne happy and Wake Hall out of the shit. Bloody hell, they even paid tax!

But Del was rarely wrong - not that Olly was going to tell him. Keep your staff hungry for praise, that was Olly's policy. And neither would he tell Del that *someone* had already deciphered the contents of his stolen memory stick - and siphoned off a small fortune from his offshore accounts. Boosting the profits was now a pressing need. He wasn't going to tell that to Del Herring either.

'Compromise, Del? That what you're looking for?'

Derek Herring rarely heard Olly use such a word.

'It may be the way to proceed, Olly. And what type of compromise had you in mind?'

'What if we keep the daylight deliveries just as they are? OK? And the extra....stuff, we'll load and transfer at night. That do?'

Derek thought it might, given all the other precautions he would quietly put in place. Overnight transport was already common. And between dusk and dawn there were no prying eyes to watch a horse-box being unloaded.

'That's agreed then, Del. I'll have a chinwag with Manny Muckheap. Lunch and a lie down for me. Happy now?'

'Ecstatic, Olly, as always'.

At the compromise, yes. And, since Derek was also good at numbers, at the increase in *his* profits too. Derek Herring's most recent 'overseas business trip' at Olly's behest had brought him into further contact with certain parties who conducted negotiations from the comfort of an ocean-going yacht, moored handily off Corfu Town. And not a yacht with sails. This had engines, a crew, a sun-deck, a plunge-pool, a chef, and plenty of young female bodies on display. The body he'd selected was almost too willing. He preferred a touch of reluctance. Derek had done rather well out of Olly. There was the private villa in Corfu; the offshore account; the Mercedes. He didn't have a yacht though. His hand felt for the inscribed gold pen in his breast pocket. Yes. A yacht. A yacht called 'Victorious'. Soon, then.

# Seventeen

As PC Jess Foreman strolled into the Parminster cop-shop to continue assisting CID, DC Magnus burst out of it, almost knocking him over as she crashed into the ladies loo. He hadn't tagged her as a drama-queen. Good company, was Nina. Two minutes earlier and he would have heard her reasons. She *had* arrived in a huff, after a long day of interviews, but was goaded into anger by George Halfpenny whose feet looked as though they'd been up on his desk for a fortnight.

'Finished my half of the list yonks ago. Yours not done yet?'

Her patient description of a vengefully difficult Ann Kennedy cut no ice with George.

'It's because you let 'em babble on, especially the women. Too much detail. You need to learn to separate *black* from *white*. What's *up*, Magnus? You've gone red in the face - not that it's easy to tell!' He pretended to zip up his mouth, slapping his own hand and muttering 'Whoops, politically incorrect comment. *Naughty* boy, George.'

To stop herself sticking her car keys in his eyes, Magnus stayed in the loo till Sergeant Ball sent Halfpenny over to Martock on a wild goose chase, having first made a mental note to 'have a quiet word' with George, in private.

When finally allowed through the over-sized inner doors of Wake Hall, Batten walked slowly across its antechamber-cum-reception because it was too big to walk across it quickly. It could have doubled as a medium-sized aircraft hangar if not for the polished, ancient floorboards covered by ornately-patterned Persian rugs, some more ancient than the floorboards they adorned. Long high walls were hung with worn tapestries and fussily-framed, cracked portraits of glum, overdressed men and rouged women, young and not so young. The venerable ancestors, Batten assumed. Above an ornate fireplace in the centre of the room three figures in a more modern portrait gazed neutrally down at him. Lord and Lady Wake and their teenage daughter, the current incumbent, he guessed. She was a looker, for sure.

He thought of the Batten family photographs on Aunt Daze's mantle-piece in Leeds, and the few photos of his mother currently in a cardboard box with his other mementos, waiting to be unpacked. Whenever he managed to sell one home so he could buy another.

Wake Hall didn't feel like anyone's home at all. The sofas by the entrance were stained with age and god knows what else. Side tables and escritoires, when he looked closer, were marred by lifting veneer, missing inlay and broken handles. And Wake Hall had a smell. Not the sweet wax polish and faint damp-in-the-background he remembered from visits to National Trust stately homes, but a distinct, deep smell of rot. Wake Hall was clean*ish*; it was warm*ish*; it was stylish, but only in an -*ish* sort of way. He looked down the gloomy hall to where at the far end, three once-grand, old-oak doors were presumably supposed to tickle a visitor's interest in what lay beyond. Batten wasn't tickled. As a cop, he'd been in many a place where you wiped your feet on the way out. Wake Hall, for all its grandiosity, felt little different. Humming 'London Bridge Is Falling Down', he continued his slow walk towards the doors.

Whether she heard his footsteps or deliberately timed her arrival to coincide with '....My Fair Lady', he didn't know. But as he made to knock on the large central door, Lady Wake's embroidered kimono silked its way through it, forcing him to take a step back. Stepping back annoyed him, as did her elocution-lessons voice.

'I imagine this....interaction could have waited, mm, Sergeant?'

'Inspector, as it happens. And *you* are?'

She bristled for a millisecond, till status took over.

'*Inspector*? *Really*? My, my. How the public sector over-promotes. I am Lady Wake, but I think you already know that.'

She didn't offer her hand, but arranged herself across an antique armchair beneath the portrait of an equally well-arranged female ancestor. She didn't invite Batten to sit down, didn't pour him sherry when she poured her own from the antique tantalus that sat smugly on the armoire beside her, but then he didn't tug his forelock. Nil-nil, Zig, so far.

'I'm here to ask you about the death of Lawrence Vann, Lady Wake, but I think you already know that?'

She gave a practised glance of disdain. 'Rhona has informed me, ye-es.

Though why you should need to talk to *me* is still a mystery. What could I possibly have to tell you about a *death,* even a very sad one. I should have thought that you, as a policeman, would be expert enough in such matters. Mm?'

She made 'policeman' sound like 'leper', and Batten was forced to admire how, with a few small words, clever use of syntax and the manipulation of tone, she managed to make it sound as if he'd bumped off Lawrence Vann himself.

'At this early stage of an investigation we talk to everyone who knew the victim, including you, Lady Wake. We can't make an exception.'

'You have *not* made an exception, have you?' she corrected him. And dismissing his reply-at-the-ready with a peremptory wave of her kimono-covered arm, she sighed, 'Oh, ask away.'

And ask away he did, receiving terse, bored answers which added little to what was known about Lawrence Vann and his role as manager of the Wake Hall estate. He'd worked for her father, and when she inherited the Hall on his death she inherited Lawrence too. He was an asset; she valued him; he knew where everything was, how everything worked, who was to be trusted and who not. Without ever using the phrase, she depicted Lawrence as the faithful old retainer. He would need to check what it was that Lawrence retained. And who exactly he was faithful to. From what Batten had already learned, 'old' didn't come into it.

'I understand that, despite his age, Lawrence was a bit of a ladies man?'

'What a quaint phrase. 'A ladies man.' Yes, Lawrence, bless, had a healthy appetite, and very sensibly *fed* it. How old are you, Sergeant?'

Batten raised an eyebrow.

'So very coy. Under forty, I suppose? Well Lawrence was sixty, and as full of vigour as you are now. I assume you do still have vigour?'

'I don't think my vig-'

'Age is not a barrier to one's *vigour*, Sergeant, worry not.' And her face moulded itself into a smile that was half cherub, half brothel-keeper. Batten had interviewed the truly vain before, men and women, and it rarely differed: when you asked them to talk about other people, they could only talk about themselves. You're no exception, Lady Muck, are you? And since I've had had enough of being patronised, why don't I run with the vigour stuff and introduce a new body into the proceedings?

'Presumably Lawrence Vann would have come into contact with your....house guest, if that's the correct description for our Mr Rutter? I assume he still has vigour too?'

Her cold smile faded, to match the worn, greying tapestry behind her. Batten felt a host of disapproving eyebrows collectively cock, arch and frown down from the giant ancestral portraits that clothed the high walls. You're sailing against the social wind, aren't you, Lady Muck? I bet you feel as trapped in this rotting stately home as I do.

'Came as a bit of a surprise, if I'm honest,' noted Batten, 'Olly Rutter shipping up at Wake Hall. Our paths having crossed more than once in the murky past.'

'And not crossed happily, I imagine, Sergeant, mm? Mr Rutter having been, erstwhile, something of a gangster?'

'*Erstwhile*, Lady Wake?'

'No, no. You're supposed to say 'a *gangster*, Lady Wake?'

'I don't have a problem with the 'gangster' part,' said Batten, 'it's the 'erstwhile' I'm struggling with.'

She sipped at her sherry, swirling her cut-glass schooner with a delicacy borne of breeding. Had plenty of practice too, Zig, by the look of it.

'Not a believer in reform, Sergeant? Not a term that appears in your policeman's dictionary?'

'Oh I believe in reform alright. It can happen, it does, and it should. But I also believe in a policeman's instinct. It never qui-'

'You mean you have a crap detector, and it goes off when you point it at Olly?'

'A very Yorkshire way of putting it. Thank you for making me feel at home.'

Lady Wake looked at Batten as if he'd hammered tent-pegs into the Persian rug.

'So, now that it's going off, ringing loudly up there, in your clever attentive ears, what is it telling you, this policeman's-instinct-*crap*-detector of yours?'

'Two things, Lady Wake. Both of them plain as a pikestaff. First, making people disappear - people like Lawrence Vann, for example - is certainly within the warped compass of your Mr Rutter, if he had reason enough. Second, if Olly Rutter's reformed then I'm Chief Constable of Somerset.'

Her sherry schooner tipped back once more.

'You're new to the county, I understand, Sergeant, so I'll forgive the unfortunate cross-dressing aspect of your metaphor. I happen to be on very friendly terms with the Chief Constable, who is in fact a *she*.'

Batten knew this too, but he was enjoying himself.

'Let's just say that if I stick with my metaphor, I'll not need a sex-change operation to make it relevant. Olly's nose was made for swill. It's just a question of finding which trough it's grubbing in these days.'

A tight silence rang out, like a cracked bell.

'Mm. I doubt we shall agree about Mr Rutter. I can accept that you, as a policeman, are 'under oath' to seek out the forbidden, and deal with it in your….policemanly way. Perhaps, up to a point, we have something in common.'

Only if we've both caught bubonic plague from the same rat. 'Oh yes?' he said.

'Because in my own way I, too, have always sought the forbidden.' Hearing this, the ancestors seemed to collectively frown down more ferociously from their perches high on the Wake Hall walls. 'And in seeking the forbidden, I have chanced upon Mr Rutter. Your life is perhaps dull, Inspector, but mine is very exciting indeed.'

She licked a drip of sherry from the side of her glass as if she was nibbling its ear. Don't sit down, Zig, she'll be lap-dancing next.

'Very excited to hear it, Lady Wake.'

'But I imagine you won't be arresting me for seeking excitement, will you?'

'Not if you've done it lawfully, no. Is Mr Rutter about, at all?'

'He is, as a matter of fact. Behind you.'

Batten's pride would not allow him to take the policeman's precaution of moving a pace away from danger before turning to face it, though when he breathed in the sweet cologne that seeped like embalming fluid from the bath-robe-encased frame of Olly Rutter, he wished he had. In the wall behind Batten, a real door was concealed within a trompe l'oeil painting of a false door, and Olly Rutter had slid through, as if on grease.

Perhaps the grease stops Olly absorbing too much of the man-perfume he's been marinated in, Zig?

'Well-bloody-well-bloody-well. Must be my magnetism, is it, brings *you* here, Ziggy?'

Only Batten's friends called him by his first name, and they called him Zig. You're going down, Olly, he said to himself, even if I have to break both your legs to make it happen.

'Olly. Lady of the house informs me you're a reformed man. Pity you still smell like a tart's boudoir.'

Lady Wake shot to her feet and might have slapped Batten, had Olly not stepped between them, bringing his sweet cologne closer still. Instead, she smeared herself across a velvet-covered chaise by the ancient mullioned window, and watched the sport.

'I am strictly a businessman now. Ziggy', said Olly, through expensively-whitened teeth clamped into a ready-to-slap-you smile. 'And having consulted my business diary for today, I see that Ziggy Batten's name seems noticeable only by its absence. If you do wish to conduct business, kindly make an appointment through the appropriate channel.'

'Would that channel be big Baz Ballard, or that vat of fish-oil-on-legs that doubles as your lawyer?'

'Either Baz or Mr Herring will be over the moon to take your call,' retorted Olly. And bringing his sweet cologne and bedroom-breath to the very tip of Batten's nostrils, he added 'they have instructions to be flexible.'

Batten would have jousted a little longer but the cologne overpowered him. And it would do no harm to let Olly sweat. 'That's because they're almost as bent as you are, Olly,' he said, popping his business card onto a marble-topped side-table. It would go in the bin, he knew. 'I'll be back. If that's alright with you, Lady Wake?'

She deigned to brush the air with a vague silk hand, and he left. Isn't it amazing, Batten thought, retracing his steps between threadbare tapestries and frowning portraits, how rich folk can give you the V-sign without moving any of their fingers?

# Eighteen

The Scramblers were worried about Stephanie. Big Harry's nickname for her - 'walkie-talkie' - was almost redundant. 'I shall 'ave to just call her 'walkie' if she goes on loike this!' On the one outing she'd managed since Burrow Hill, Stephanie did what Stephanie had never done before. She shut up. The Scramblers were glad she didn't burble on about flora and fauna, about the history of this, the ecology of that. But they were worried, because her silence was….unheard of.

Mick Baines was reconsidering his policy of swearing in her presence, 'to keep 'er on 'er toes'. She'd stopped responding with a plummy-posh reprimand. She'd stopped noticing.

Every week for over a year Eth Buller had told Stephanie to 'just call me Eth - everyone calls me Eth.' On that first and every other occasion Stephanie had given Eth a look that sternly said 'Stephanie Broke-Mondelle is not '*everyone*!', and scrupulously called her Ethel ever since. But last time, one of the very few words that the strangely taciturn Stephanie uttered, was in fact 'Eth.'

'Thank you, Eth,' Stephanie said when Eth threw out a supporting hand to prevent Stephanie's sudden stumble almost turning into a fall. The collective jaws of the collective Scramblers had doubly dropped. Stephanie never said 'Eth' - and Stephanie never stumbled. Never. So a further statement, 'Stephanie almost *fell*' was unimaginable. Or had been.

And now today, at 9am, in the municipal car-park behind The Pilgrim's Rest, the usual starting point for their walks, Stephanie was nowhere to be seen.

'She might be a pain in the ears', said Mick Baines, 'but she's never bloody late.'

Remembering how often she had waited patiently for *them* to arrive, the Scramblers waited patiently for Stephanie. They rang her land-line, without response. And her mobile. With no response whatsoever.

'Well, oi'm going round t'er place, see what's up,' said Harry Teign. 'Eth, you comin'?'

And they went, leaving Mick Baines to lead the rest of The Scramblers on a walk that was devoid of narrative, of swearwords, and of Stephanie Broke-Mondelle.

Detective Constable Eddie 'Loft' Hick, who valued his stomach, had detected a side-street café barely two minutes walk from Parminster town square. It did a bang-on skinny latte and the best bacon roll he'd ever eaten. His offer to take orders and fetch supplies prompted DC Magnus to wonder if Hick was really a woman, working undercover. She hoped so; she was fed up of being tea-girl, particularly where George Halfpenny was concerned.

Lawrence's face looked down from the centre of the murder board, as if tut-tutting the mess of cardboard cups, discarded wrappers and grease stains that littered the big meeting table. Batten wished 'Lawrence Vann' was the *only* name on the board. There were too many suspects, general and specific, too few significant facts. And no crystal-clear motive at all. He rattled his case notes.

'Further thoughts?' he asked, with more optimism than he felt.

A feet-shuffling Parminster silence - pecking order sensitivities were still getting in the way. Jess Foreman was a doer, not a talker. Hick had worked with Halfpenny only a few times before. Lee knew Hick slightly but Halfpenny not at all. Magnus didn't know any of them. But then, Batten didn't know any of them either. It was Magnus who spoke up.

'So we've definitely dismissed natural causes, sir?'

'We have, if I'm reading the Doc right.'

He could still hear Danvers' treacly voice, gently mocking what he'd referred to as Batten's 'poetics' with a cod touch of his own doggerel - 'a hurt heart, nudged along the road to dusty death by the poisoned contents of a cruel gruel.' The Doc should write for Mills and Boon. Maybe he did. 'His ticker *was* a factor, Nina. And the walk up Burrow Hill too. But without a stiff slug of poison, Mr Vann should be rambling around as we speak.'

'We're sure, though, that *murder* was intended, sir?'

'*Something* was intended. Any opinions, the rest of you?'

The mixed males were still on the back foot. A woman, a black woman, gets in first and doesn't spout bollocks. Halfpenny asserted himself.

'It's not an exact science, is it, sir? Poison, I mean.'

The still-absent toxicology report made Batten scowl. Ball maintained the momentum, reading out the margin comments Batten had scribbled down after ear-bending the Doc.

'In language even a constable can understand….' Boos and groans rang out. Hick topped them with a bacon-flavoured fart sound. Ball continued, immune. 'Poison in high concentration - extremely strong potential to kill' -

'Yes, but -'

'I know, George. Or maybe just to hospitalise whoever drank it.'

Hick spluttered out the last crumbs of his sandwich along with his contribution. 'So which is it, Sarge? Murder or….what?'

'Murder, or a warning, sir?' Magnus returned to her theme.

Batten nodded. He'd been asking the same question for days. Why might Lawrence Vann need to be warned? And by whom? Suspicions - about Olly Rutter, for example - were plentiful, but…. Until they'd interviewed the 'still very poorly' Debbie Farley, even the timeline was unconfirmed.

PC Lee was twitching because he hadn't spoken yet. If you've got nothing to say, don't put your nothing into words, that's what his last Sergeant had advised. But come on, Jon, the others are chipping in.

'If it's a warning, sir, which one was he warning? Or she? I mean, was it him, or was it her?'

Batten worked out what Lee was trying to say.

'Ah well, we don't know for sure, do we, Jonathon? Identical thermos flasks, each full of poison. A warning for Lawrence? For Debbie? Both? Or was blue bloody murder intended for the pair of them?'

Lee was miffed that Batten had called him 'Jonathon', not Jon. 'It's a choirboy name, is Jonathon,' Hick regularly sniped. Lee wanted to ask what kind of name was 'Loft'.

'You can all see where we go now, I suppose?'

They all nodded sagely at Batten; it seemed the safe thing to do.

'Till we unearth a clear motive we might as well play spin-the-bottle. So, even deeper background on these two now, OK? Dig till you hear Australian accents. Every associate you can find, friend or foe, why, where, when. What they've done that they shouldn't have - and what

113

they've not done that they should. Special emphasis on two areas: lover's revenge, and Wake Hall.' He stopped himself before 'fine tooth comb' trundled out. 'Sergeant Ball will divvy up the tasks, with his usual delicacy.'

More hoots, more raspberries. Batten didn't mind. Keep them happy in their work as long as possible. Enthusiasm wanes, soon enough, when a case hits the wall. He headed for the absent Jellicoe's cubby-hole-office, to throttle the now working phone. If the hospital still wouldn't let him question Debbie Farley, he'd try Stephanie Whatsit-Whatsit again. If she didn't answer, he'd put a bomb up the toxics instead.

# Nineteen

Something must have made him leave it there, on his bedside table - as a painful reminder. Time to dump it now, the broken alarm clock, staring back at him uselessly. He hadn't bought a replacement. The remaining one would suffice, now he had no problem waking up. *Now*, the problem was getting to sleep at all. Lawrence would have sorted his head out for him.

Baz Ballard had never been big on decisions, happier just to follow. But following Olly had become too….he wasn't big on words either. Too….painful? He touched the scar tissue above his eye and rubbed his finger across the fading bump on his skull, the bump that would eventually go away.

But how could *he* go away? 'I'm handing in my resignation, Olly.' 'No problem, Baz. Here's an unmarked grave in lieu of a gold watch.' And when the horse-crap hit the fan, it wouldn't just hit Olly - if it hit him at all. At least Baz had money now, thanks to Lawrence who'd conjured ready cash from the electronic numbers Baz could neither trust nor understand, and it was locked away in a shiny safe-deposit box. Not even Lawrence knew where Baz had hidden the key. And vice-versa. Safer that way.

But money is one thing, and a plan is another. Lawrence would have done the planning for him. Baz had spent his morning-off sprawled across his Wake Hall bed in the Somerset gloom, trying to think like Lawrence, persuasive Lawrence, Lawrence the life-changer. What would Lawrence do, if he were here? It was a pity. They had come so far….

Baz had protested that computers weren't his thing, but Lawrence had been, yes, persuasive and had repeatedly shown him - *trained* him - till the basics stuck. He knew how to boot up, how to download data from a memory stick, how to bring up the message that said 'it is safe to remove the external device'.

Safe? He hoped so. But Olly's office felt nothing like safe that day, not for the uninvited. And not when theft is the motive, however Lawrence dressed it up.

'It's merely data, Baz. Inanimate. Virtual. I mean, you can't hold a pixel in your hand, can you?'

No, Lawrence, but you can hold a key. Baz silently unlocked the twin Chubbs with the set of keys he'd copied, one at a time, painstakingly. He'd had to wait over a month. Olly never left his keys lying around. Derek Herring was the same. But thank Christ for Manny McRory, who did, once in a while. Baz was proud of his locksmith skills - the skills Olly never imagined he had. If Olly slapped you into a category, there you sat.

'Model planes, Baz? Cuh, for puffters. Why don't you keep snakes? Or antique guns. *They're* not pufften.'

Because I hate snakes, and guns gives me the sweats, Baz might have said. Except you didn't, to Olly. But Baz's accurate models demanded high levels of dexterity, fine manual skills. As did locks and keys.

Once inside, Baz made his familiar way towards the large oil painting, 'Horse Frightened by a Lion' by Stubbs. Well, a copy of it, part of a job lot jockeying for space on the office walls, in case short-sighted visitors failed to appreciate the overlarge 'Wake Hall Horse' sign above the door. He removed the painting, many pairs of equine eyes staring down at him from the yellowy-brown walls. Whatever inspired the choice of a colour like that? Horses with diarrhoea, horses with the trots?

'Focus please, Baz', Lawrence's voice seemed to whisper, as Baz pulled his gaze away from the walls of eyes. He keyed numbers into the touch pad of the mini-safe hidden behind the painting, numbers he'd covertly and patiently memorised, one at a time. Numbers glimpsed fleetingly, on the few occasions when Olly's broad neck didn't totally obscure the process.

This time, it was Baz who quietly opened it, though not without an automatic glance over his shoulder. He ignored the chunky wads of banknotes and the clear plastic sleeves full of investment bonds. His big hand reached instead for the smallest item in the safe, a tiny four gigabyte memory stick. He heard Lawrence's voice again. 'Treasure, Baz. Treasure.'

The small netbook he produced from the poacher's pocket of his Barbour coat was booted up and ready to go. All that remained was to insert the memory stick into a USB port and download the juicy data it contained. While the large desktop computer was double-password-protected - even burglar-alarmed for all Baz knew - Olly was more than confident that the twin Chubbs, coded wall-safe and sheer fear of Olly would protect any items locked within.

'Hubris, Baz. Hubris. Infected, is Mr Rutter - to our advantage.'

Baz couldn't care less what Olly was infected with, or if he took pills for it. He focused only on the stick. Once he'd copied and replaced it and locked up, he would hand the data to a waiting Lawrence, sneak back to his rooms and prepare for the slapping he knew Olly would gleefully give him this very night, shortly after Manny McRory piloted the big silver Jaguar back into Wake Hall, and an angry mammoth snorted out of it.

In Baz's thick but agile fingers, the memory stick seemed no bigger than a splinter. He began to locate it into the USB port - at precisely the same moment that a key in an unknown hand clicked noisily into the first of the two Chubbs, turning it with a deep mechanical 'kerchung'. The fact that Baz had locked both Chubbs from the inside was some small comfort. But it didn't stop his hands from shaking, hands that had made intricate model planes for thirty years and never shaken before, hands that suddenly became sticky with heat and sweat. He blinked more sweat from his eyes.

Before he could move, and before the second lock clicked open, he heard raised voices beyond the door - Lawrence's voice at first, then in reply the whiny scouse twang of Manny McCrory. What's the little shit doing back so soon? And if *he's* back….The thought of being found here by Olly made Baz nauseous. He tasted his half-digested breakfast. In panic he looked round for a waste bin to throw up in. But the combined raised voices outside became a loud argument. The door remained closed. The nausea began to pass.

Baz put his ear to the door as Lawrence, his voice a thin veneer of politeness, informed McRory that tack had gone missing from the Estate stables and he wondered if it might perchance have turned up 'at this place.' Only Lawrence could say 'this place' as if Wake Hall Horse was a sewer.

His buttons duly pushed, McRory spontaneously combusted, vomiting up a torrent of foul scouse which was met by sneery disdain.

'Nevertheless, if you'll care to step this way,' Lawrence said, 'to the scene of the crime? We have three racks of rather expensive horse-gear.

One rack is entirely empty now, and things have a habit of disappearing whenever *you're* around.'

Manny was not to know that the rack in question had been rapidly emptied and its contents hidden under loose straw by Lawrence, as soon as he heard the Jaguar's engine and saw McRory's coiled-wire frame emerge from the driver's seat on its way to the Wake Hall Horse office, keys in hand. Manny was on a message from Olly: whiz back and fetch my calfskin briefcase from the office - the briefcase that our dozy bastard Baz failed to put in the boot this morning when he also failed to move his dozy arse from his bed to the driver's seat. 'And pronto' was assumed when Olly gave an order. As a result, Manny was under pressure and ill-disposed to be polite to Lawrence - not that he ever was. That posh voice, it got up his nose. And condescension came *down* Lawrence's nose whenever Manny was in earshot.

'If you knew anything at all about horses, McRory, you wouldn't have bought *those*!' That was the last thing Lawrence had said to Manny, two days ago, smarmy bastard. And now the smug sod was accusing him of nicking horse tack!

'If I come over there Lawrence, I'll do more than stare at an empty rack - get my drift?'

Lawrence had got McRory's drift many months ago. He blithely pushed another button.

'You are simply too small to do anything *but* stare, McRory. Actions are for larger men than *you.*'

Ear now jammed against the office door, breath held, Baz heard a key click as the lock snapped shut again, heard angry footsteps fade away, and then only silence. He could not hear the escalating argument between Lawrence and McRory, nor witness the brief but forceful exchange of fisticuffs. He did not see - but would have enjoyed - the swift arc of Manny's wiry frame as it descended from the end of Lawrence's fist and collided with the hard stable floor.

Baz enjoyed none of this because he had instant decisions to make. Did he have time to plug in the memory stick? Download its contents? Eject it? Put it back in the safe? Replace the painting? Quietly double-lock the doors and disappear, unseen?

He didn't think so. He had to get out, fast, while Lawrence's clever diversion was still going on. He jammed the netbook into his poacher's pocket and reluctantly returned the memory stick to the safe.

But his big hand remained on its still-open door. They might never get another chance. Olly's suspicions would be raised the instant Manny reported back. Baz looked ahead, to a frozen life of pensionless slapsponge slavery.

No, he said, to the frozen life. Yes, he said, to the tiny plastic gadget full of money. And he grabbed it once again from the maw of the safe and dropped it into his poacher's pocket. He and Lawrence could download it once Manny was out of the way, and return it before Olly got back. Couldn't they?

He swiftly locked the safe, replaced the Stubbs print and double locked the office doors. His hand no longer shook. In fact, he was rather pleased with himself, as he ghosted round the side of the office, across the Manny-less forecourt, and back to his rooms with his booty.

He'd been wrong to be pleased; he knew that only too well, *now*.

# Twenty

Dave 'Dipstick' Vossialevydipsic allowed a slight grin to creep into his Slavic eyes as he closed the phone. Tom Bowditch knew the score right away, because Dave wasn't a natural smiler. The funniest thing about him was the way he spoke, as if halfway through learning English he'd had a change of heart. Tom made allowances, in view of Dave's other areas of expertise - poison, machines, and thieving.

'We go soon, Tom. The owners are not there. Only one dog, can you believe? Big neon sign over gate -'

'Yeh, Dave, it says 'Rob Me!' Dave said the same thing every time. Not much of a joke repertoire, Dave.

'Well, our lucky night, yes?'

Tom wondered about luck sometimes. Were they lucky? Or good? Dave pulled a large chunk of fresh meat from the grubby fridge, began to rub flavour enhancers into it.

'I poison dog, you fix locks, then each of us we load, yes?'

Tom nodded. Exactly like last time. Not lucky, then. Experienced.

'I bet you, Tom, not more than six minutes, this one, yes? Then I'm tucked in bed before the pixies got their nightgowns on.'

He came out with these weird phrases sometimes, did Dave. It's because he's basically a foreigner, Tom thought - but didn't say. Instead, he unclipped the heavy-duty bolt-cutters from the tool-rack in the rented barn. If you didn't know it was there, in the middle of an unproductive apple orchard, you'd have trouble spotting the barn at all. A pair of quad-bikes tonight should fetch them a tidy sum, though it was the bigger sums that Tom preferred. He hadn't told Dave, but Tom had a figure in mind. When his stash reached two hundred grand, he was getting out.

Dave hadn't told Tom either, but he was staying *in*. It wasn't just the money. He liked crime; liked the thrill, the darkness. Dave wasn't lucky, he was an experienced businessman. A tea-drinking, half-English businessman. The faintest hint of a smile flickered across his face, as he stared through the grimy window at the empty trees, and began to poison the meat.

Batten grabbed the last space in the hospital car-park. A cold wind threw leaves at his face as he slogged to the main building, the afternoon light fading and half a day's work still undone. The media on his back and Gribble's finger in his ribs was bad enough, but much of his burden was paperwork belonging to an absent Chief Inspector Jellicoe. *Fat* Jellicoe? Fat lot of use! Get on with the job, Zig, and get out of here.

What is it about hospitals that gave him the jitters? Pretty nurses in their crisp, see-through uniforms, but *you*, Zig, you wish you were somewhere else! He didn't know why. Rules. White coats. The smell.

The job in question looked almost as pale as last time - the only time - he'd seen her, semi-conscious on a stretcher at the foot of Burrow Hill. At least she was sitting up now, in a blue gown, propped on a pair of pillows on her bright-white hospital bed, and without need of the oxygen mask. Debbie Farley had a pleasant voice, more high-pitched than normal maybe? Death, poison, danger, and now the police. Hardly a recipe for normality, eh, Zig?

When he asked about enemies she could only shake her head in puzzlement. She confirmed the supposed timeline of 'the day in question', but added little to the little they knew. She'd made soup the night before, heated some of it and filled the two little thermos flasks at about seven - she'd always been an early riser - and put them on the windowsill, out of the way.

'Out of the way of what?' he asked. She looked puzzled. 'I mean, is the kitchen busy at seven in the morning?'

'Oh, I see. No. Only me. Habit, I suppose. I'm not a clutter person. I have to have a tidy kitchen.'

'And you didn't notice anything different that morning? Nobody who shouldn't have been there?'

'Different?' She frowned, but the pallor of her cheeks remained. 'Not really, no - well, someone had been smoking. Except I can't say that's *different*. A certain naughty colleague.'

For the first time she gave a small smile, pushing her hair away from her face. He noticed again how attractive she was. Lawrence had an eye.

'Cheeky Allie Chant - she gives up smoking twice a week. Crafty fag in the warm kitchen before her late night check on the four-legged friends. It's no-smoking at the stables, so if it's damp *out*side, she'll happily light up *inside*. I always fling open the windows first thing anyway, rain or shine, give the room an airing. I'd have put a flea in her ear when I got back, except...'

She had talked herself towards the issue of Lawrence Vann, and Batten shamelessly drew her into the policeman's mire, the swamp between soft sympathy and hard information.

'I was wondering, that day, did Lawrence show any signs of illness, tiredness?'

'Oh no, not Lawrence. Just the same as ever, a fast walker, fit. You know, like a butcher's dog.'

Images of a poisoned dogs and stolen tractors flashed into Batten's mind.

'Slow down, Lawrence! Don't you realise I'm younger than you! That's the kind of thing I say to him. He just laughs, says see you back at the cider farm. Then off he goes.'

'Up Burrow hill?'

She couldn't say it. A downward twitch of the head.

'And before that, the walk was uneventful? Not different in any way?'

'A bit damp, cool. But November, you know. You expect that.'

'Hence the soup?'

Debbie Farley had reached her own personal swamp. She seemed to be tasting once again the poison that killed Lawrence and almost killed her too. Batten prayed there wouldn't be tears. All she could say was 'Parsnip'.

'*Curried* parsnip. Wasn't it?'

She nodded. 'Always is, yes, on our winter walks. His favourite, you see. Likes it with a tipple of brandy stirred in, so that's what I do. And it's not curry powder from a jar. I make my own, roast the spices myself. A touch of brown sugar.'

'And you'd drink it when?'

'More a case of *where*. Last time we walked....*that* route, we sat on the wall by the Rose and Crown and warmed ourselves up a bit.'

He had no idea where the Rose and Crown was; he cocked an eyebrow.

'Oh, at East Lambrook. A couple of miles down the road from....We usually cut across, past the apple orchards. But Lawrence went up that blummin' hill again. Drank his by himself.'

Her silence returned. It took several careful questions before she confirmed that the flasks hadn't left their anorak pockets between Wake Hall and Burrow Hill - supporting Batten's assumption that *someone* added deadly poison between seven and seven-twenty in the morning, when the kitchen was empty and the flasks sat innocently on a windowsill.

Then Debbie gave a little start.

'Different. You asked me, didn't you, was it different? And my flask *was*. Too much brandy. Too strong for me. Only reason I touched the blummin' soup at all was because I was stone-cold. I wasn't *hungry*. How could I be hungry after seeing....*that*?'

He could empathise; hoped he would never see such a death-mask again. Instead, he saw the multiple bottles of booze in Lawrence's cottage. His taste for strong spirits would be far more advanced than Debbie Farley's.

'Can we re-wind perhaps? You said there was too much brandy in the soup? By mistake, you mean?'

Even in the alien setting of a hospital bed, Debbie Farley retained her culinary pride.

'By *mistake*? I'm a trained chef! I know the taste of things! That wasn't *my* soup. *Never*.'

Hair fell across her pale face again, but she ignored it. Her raised voice dragged in a bespectacled nurse, eyes like scalpels. Ruth Bain, the name-badge said. Ruth Bain herself said nothing, but loudly removed the uppermost white pillow, and lowered Debbie onto the bed. Sharp-eyes nodded Batten towards the door. Frustrated, he thought of clamping his hands tightly around Nurse Bain's throat and squeezing, squeezing till her eyes bulged and her face turned blue. But one murder was plenty.

He clomped angrily down the plastic stairs and pale-green corridors and across the wind-chilled car park. Another bloody postponement! And now another task: safeguarding Debbie Farley, post-hospital, against a threat they must assume was still out there, though Debbie herself had no idea who or what it was. There'd be a Gribble-grilling about police protection - rationale, objectives, manpower. Cost....

A line of big, nameless trees had dumped a slush of fallen leaves, dirty-yellow and brown, all over his windscreen. Scummy puddles at his feet were black with leaf-rot.

*If Sergeant Ball hasn't tracked down Stephanie Broke-Mondelle, I'll….*

He scraped at the slime of dead leaves that clung to the car like brown snow.

*And if the nattery cow has nothing useful to say, Zig….*

Rather than clearing the screen, his scuffing spread oily brown streaks across the glass. He flung the soiled scraper into the car in frustration.

And is Chief Inspector Jellicoe *ever* going to turn up? So I can stop doing *his* job too? He'd never met Fat Jellicoe. But he was sick to death of him.

# PART TWO

*Bare Branches*

# Twenty One

His conveyancing solicitor did what he could, but Batten's choices were limited: agree to the buyer's demand for an early completion, or put your house in Leeds back on the market. Despite the price being whittled down, it was still a whopping amount for a once-derelict home. Mortgage-free, this side of forty?

'Time is of the essence, Mr Batten,' his solicitor said on the phone. 'Were I in your shoes, I should strike while the iron is hot.'

Despite communicating only in clichés, he was right - house prices were sliding. Batten agreed to the buyer's wishes - which meant clearing out the rest of his belongings a month earlier than planned. In the middle of a murder case.

He left Ball a list of urgent tasks, tracking down Stephanie Broke-Mondelle being top priority. Perhaps she could add heat to the damp log-fire of their investigation. He promised he'd be back within thirty-six hours, hoped he wasn't lying.

Driving north along the M5, he hoped a murder-solving moment might hit him, but by Bristol the only thing to hit him was rain. At dusk, he pulled into a service station on the M42 near Redditch, and rang Merlot Marie - hoping she'd be in Leeds. Four hands are better than two, where clearing a house is concerned, he told himself.

'I've had better offers, Zig, even from *you*, you cheeky sod.'

'There's a bottle of champagne in the fridge. Tempted?'

There wasn't. He would buy one on the way.

'And what's it going to wash down, this champagne?'

'I was thinking crab cake starters, spicy noodles, coconut rice and Thai green curry. Am I getting warm?'

'Clap-cold. You're describing the takeaway at the top of your street. And it'd be a waste of good champagne. A bottle of expensive red, please, and some nice chilled Thai beer to go with the food.'

Cheap at the price. And better than saying a lonely goodbye to ten years of house.

'It'll be knackering, Zig. Where am I going to sleep?'

'Well, the usual place?'

Her silence was vocal. They hadn't been an item for a while but, until now, he wasn't sure she'd found someone else.

'No, Zig. I'm sorry. I'll help, for friendship. Just friendship. Understood?'

He'd met her at a conference - 'Criminal Investigation Across European Borders.' She was there for career reasons; he was just *there*.

'My Chief Super would've gone if it had been Paris but, well, Nottingham - he sent me instead.'

The conference hotel was a long way from Paris. It was a fair way from Nottingham too, being closer to the convenient hub of East Midlands airport than to the city's fleshpots. He'd heard her Northern accent at the bar; she his.

'Don't tell me, pint of Tetley's?' she said.

'Well, I was going to have a glass of Merlot. But, please, let me get them.' She had Merlot too, red as her lips. Her name was Marie. Merlot Marie ever since.

'Look at us. The Northern force, drinking foreign plonk in the name of international cooperation.'

'So, you're from Hull?'

'Definitely not. I'm from *Kingston-upon*-Hull - a different place entirely. No docks, no fishing fleets, just crime-free boulevards and balmy pavement cafes.'

'Barmy?' asked Batten.

'Balmy, Inspector, as well you know, unless these foreign voices have affected your ability to understand plain speaking. You've never been to Kingston-upon-Hull, have you? It's very similar to Paris, as a matter of fact.'

'I've been to both, as a matter of fact,' said Batten, archly.

'Oops,' she said. 'Not like Paris then. But don't get cocky. *I've* been to *Leeds*. You might have a Harvey Nicks and some Victorian arcades, but you've got roads full of traffic and sewers full of - well, they don't run with perfume, do they?'

Batten laughed. He liked her. She was about his age, and all eyes and lips. They touched glasses.

'To smelly sewers everywhere.'

The French delegate on the next table must have overheard, because he stared at them with pity and amazement. They didn't notice him at all.

For Batten, the Conference was far less fascinating than Merlot Marie. Drug-running across the so-called global village, the collapse of the Soviet bloc, the re-defined Balkans, the new Europe - all contributing to criminal mobility and innovation. Batten didn't budge from his ingrained view: cooperation provides better sandbags to stem the flood; but it won't stop the rain.

In discussions, the foreign delegates shamed their English counterparts with an easy command of several languages, sometimes all at once.

'Perhaps they're speaking in tongues?' he said to Marie, in the bar.

They both realised, simultaneously, that they were staring at each other's tongues, lips, mouths. Later, they got out of an expensive taxi in Nottingham's Lace Market, busy even on a Thursday night, and wandered arm in arm, tingling, from one set-piece pub to another. They ended up in a swish bar in a decommissioned church, with high gothic windows, cut in half these days by a mezzanine lounge. Music from a live jazz trio filled the space where plainsong once ruled. Looking up at the high arched ceiling, he tried not to think of swelling organs.

They only just made breakfast next day, choosing not to sit together to avoid lewd suspicions that were in fact well-founded. The conference droned on in many accents, but Batten heard only the soft tones of Merlot Marie.

Unlike many conference romances, theirs stumbled along for two years, whenever geography, shift-work, thieves and bosses allowed. Which was not often enough. In the final months, their relationship was a matching pair of questions:

'When are you transferring to Leeds?'

'When are *you* transferring to Kingston-upon-Hull?'

Maybe if she hadn't also been a cop….Or if *she* had, but he *hadn't*? Or maybe what was missing was the final ounce of mutual commitment needed to tip the scales one way or the other.

They laughed easily together and had trust though. So he did something sensible for once, where women were concerned: he suggested a straightforward friendship instead of snatched sex.

'Otherwise,' he said, 'we'll end up buying a campervan with a pull-down double-bed, and leave it parked in a lay-by near the M62.'

She confessed she'd been thinking the same, then slapped him meatily on the arm.

'*My* version would have been a tasteful pied-a-terre, with central heating, soft music and a bath. You....*bloke!*'

Two years on, they were still close friends, but almost entirely by phone, text, email. The modern way, he thought. Please god it never becomes the norm.

Phones, texts and emails were proving useless to Sergeant Ball. Face-to-face ditto.

'Any sign?'

DC Magnus shook her head and kept quiet. Safer that way. Ball had sussed George Halfpenny's aversion to heavy digging and had instead tasked Nina Magnus with finding Stephanie Broke-Mondelle. Magnus did her best, but the result was the same. She tracked down the Scramblers, one after the other, but none of them could find her either.

'Sarge?' she said, taking a deep breath. 'I think we've got a problem.'

As he turned off the M1 into the suburban sprawl of Leeds, Batten remembered the landscape as it looked when he was a child. Much of the old terraced city had gone, demolished to make way for - what? Depots made of giant meccano; smug car showrooms, cloning themselves for what felt like miles; office blocks like stacked-up houses of glass. Sporadic municipal flowerbeds attempted to soften the sharp-edged terrain, and a few small trees had been planted in hope. He realised how lucky he was to have shipped up in the greenness of Somerset, where trees were taken for granted.

Even so, the 'Sold' sign in front of his Leeds house gave him a lump in his throat. 'Moving house', Zig. He made a start on the packing, to fend off nostalgia. The sooner his belongings were in store, the sooner he'd be....? He didn't know what he'd be. Not yet. As he taped down the lids of box after box, took down curtains and rolled up rugs, the house he'd painstakingly renovated became an echo.

Before packing his music collection he selected a few CDs for the journey south. Big Bill Broonzy, Loudon Wainwright the Third, Mississippi John Hurt. They've all got three names, Zig. What's that about? As a distraction, he played three-name-roulette, randomly pulling one CD at a time from the rack. Ladysmith Black Mambazo. Ching! Reverend Gary Davis. Ching! Crosby, Stills and Nash. Ching! This is getting creepy. Fats Waller. Ah. Elvis Costello. Joni Mitchell. You're on a losing streak. Wolfgang Amadeus Mozart. Ching!

The doorbell stopped the game. Merlot Marie.

'I was going to bring a crime-scene suit, keep the dust off. But your house was always clean, Zig. Whistle-clean, you. Always.'

She gave him the smile he would always miss.

'Still sniffing the lavatory brush, then,' she said, flicking his moustache. A flash of memory - a hotel bed, her fingernail slowly, tenderly teasing backwards and forwards through the hair on his upper lip. 'That's truly sensual,' he'd said. She'd smiled. 'Is it? I was just checking for mites.'

A fond kiss; but on his cheek. And I'm past tense now, am I? Put your Marie memories in one of these boxes, Zig, close the lid and tape it down. But keep it safe.

She threw herself into bubble-wrapping his paintings and prints. He would have to sell some, give some away. Would he ever live in a house as big as this again?

'If you hear gunshots,' she shouted, 'I've got bored and I'm popping the bubble-wrap!'

He'd bought an expensive bottle of Merlot for old time's sake, and poured her a glass. She guessed what it was, from the colour, even before she tasted it.

'Must have got some in my eye,' she said, turning away.

He sat at his big old desk, emptying the drawers. He'd gifted it to Ged, who would make sure it was used well. Most of the documents went into a green bin-liner for re-cycling, a few into the shredder first. Why *do* we keep all this stuff? He even found an old CV, from years ago, when he was trying for Sergeant.

'Don't leave any gaps in your CV chronology, Zig - the Chief Constable might think you were in prison!' His old mentor, DCI Phil

Judd, had laughed at the irony. He was dead now, cancer, at 58.

Batten scanned the single sheet of A4. There *was* a gap, of course - white space between birth and GCSEs, of little interest to employers but a significant gap for Zig Batten. The gap was also his litmus. A fling, a tryst, a liaison with the opposite sex, it only became a 'relationship' when he felt confident enough to tell the woman concerned about his early years - his birth, his parentage, his real name. He was thirty seven, and only three women had ever heard the tale. The third one was wiping away Merlot tears in the adjacent room.

Sergeant Ball gulped down his fears, dragged in the whole team and switched them to overdrive. When he offered free cider to whoever found Stephanie Broke-Mondelle, they got the message.

At last, Magnus waggled the phone in Ball's direction. It was pitch-black outside but nobody was going home.

'Best if you speak to her yourself, Sarge.'

'Speak to who? You've not winkled her out? You bloody star-'

'Not Stephanie Broke-Mondelle, Sarge. Sorry. It's the woman who cleans her house. She was there, earlier.'

'Doing *what*?'

'Um, cleaning, Sarge. But....alone.'

'Bugger. Put her through.'

Two short answers from Stephanie's cleaner and Ball's bad feeling became cold sweat. Instantly he sent out alerts - including one to himself: be on the lookout for an enraged Inspector Batten, soon to return from a whistle-stop tour of the polar wastes of West Yorkshire.

Batten's thoughts had drifted way beyond West Yorkshire, to the North Sea. His 'first dad', Yevgeny, was a Polish-Russian trawler captain who gave him and his brother their Polish and Russian first names - and a surname nobody could spell, let alone pronounce. He was drowned at sea when Zbigniev was barely eighteen months and his brother Dimitri was still in his mother's womb. According to Aunt Daze, a mixture of sadness and relief rose up as Yevgeny's trawler went down. Batten's parents had met on holiday in Whitby, but Yevgeny's bright charm soon faded. He was remembered only for his tongue-twister surname and the two sons he left behind.

Balakadaldiniov was the name on the marriage certificate, but even this was an anglicised guess. The Registry Office Clerk refused to accept names written in the Cyrillic alphabet, and Yevgeny's grasp of English was less secure than his ability to grasp English women. His tall, good looks were offset by long absences at sea, a liking for alcohol, and a distaste for the notion of housekeeping money.

Yevgeny's widow, June, was soon remarried, to Ronald Batten, a postman. But not for long. June and her new husband were killed in a pile-up on the MI near Leeds, when thick fog blanked the vision, and the judgement, of a local 'worthy', well-oiled in more ways than one. He was never brought to book.

June and Ronald had gone to buy Christmas presents for the kids, and for each other, but never made it. Zig and baby Dimi were being looked after by June's sister, Aunt Daze, a situation which continued permanently when she became their legal guardian. Zig learnt to talk quite early but could not say 'Daisy', only 'Daze', and the name stuck. And stayed forever.

Zbigniev and Dimitri, by contrast, were names that didn't survive the ritual of school classrooms, playgrounds, streets. Zig and Dimi were permanently re-born there.

Zig had a hazy memory of his real mother; little memory of a man who might have been Ronald, and no memory at all of Yevgeny. It had been worse for Dimi. His mother was a shadow and his real father had neither seen nor held him before being sucked down into the North Sea. Was this why Dimi became a troubled and troublesome youth, despite the ungrudging guidance of Aunt Daze, who raised them as if they were her own, with a balance of probity, grit, imagination and love?

Zig, tall and stronger than he appeared, looked out for his diminutive brother, protected him, tried to steer him past trouble. But Dimi came from another place entirely. During Zig's A levels there were frequent visits from the uniformed branch, all focused on Dimi. Shoplifting, when he wanted for nothing that was good for him. Vandalism, when his household gave him security and cleanness. Fighting, when Aunt Daze bestowed only love and warmth. Was Dimi the reason why, after finishing his English degree, Zig decided to join the police?

And how long had he been on the Yorkshire force before he crossed swords with Olly Rutter? Not long. What a world of change, Zig. *Now*, when you drive to Leeds from Somerset, you're briefly leaving Olly Rutter behind.

Marie was talking to him.

'You've drifted off again, Zig, haven't you? Gone to *Zig*land. I'm jabbering away, ten to the dozen, and you're a tailor's dummy.'

'Sorry, Marie. I do, don't I? Drift off to Zigland?'

She moved closer. And then closer still, thumb and finger on the top button of his shirt.

'I just wanted to say….have you got any more bubble wrap? I've run out!'

He whacked her with his duster. She pretended to fence with her scissors. Time was, they'd have a mock fight and end up in bed.

'No,' she said, stopping the game. 'I'm not being fair, Zig. I *did* say. Friendship. Just friendship now.'

He went to collect their takeaway meal, after putting his old CV in the shredder.

# Twenty Two

Neither Ball, the Scramblers, nor - when his car screeched into the 'reserved for Chief Inspector Jellicoe' space at Parminster - the decidedly grouchy Inspector Batten knew what to make of it.

'*Someone* must have seen her - or *heard* the nattery cow!'

''Fraid not, zor. Thin air. Disappeared.'

'So what is she? Abducted witness? Or a killer-on-the-run?'

And has she changed her name, Zig? *Stephanie Broke-Mondelle*? It's hardly Jane Jones!

'She paid the cleaner three months in advance, zor - never done that before - more convenient, she said. Never told the cleaner she was leaving. No mention of a holiday, no bookings in her name, nothing.'

Alarm bells, loud, in Batten's head. Or was it the metallic ring of Gribble's raised voice?

'She's presumably got a car?'

'Still in her garage, zor. Car keys and a spare in a pot on the kitchen table. We're checking the local taxis, car hire firms, coach companies - not a sausage yet.'

'Nearest railway station?'

'Cruck'n.'

'*Cruck'n?* Where the bloody hell's *Cruck'n?*'

'Sorry, zor. Crewkerne. Not far from her place.'

'CCTV?'

'Hickie's been, zor, checked. Nothing.'

'Smashed a camera, did he? Derailed a bloody *train?*'

Hick was competent enough, but even Detective Inspectors need a scapegoat. He rubbed his moustache. Perhaps it worked, or perhaps the obvious struck him.

'What form of transport do the Scramblers use, Sergeant?'

'They don't, zor. They scramble. You know, walk.'

'So what if she did the same? Is her walking gear still at her house?'

Ball cursed himself. Tiredness, must be. He hadn't looked, hadn't asked the cleaner. He'd send George.

135

'If she started walking yesterday, she could have gone bloody miles by now, in any direction she liked.' She hadn't nipped out for a quick scramble round the houses, Batten was certain of that. Not after bunging the cleaner three months' wages.

'Only reason I can see for her walking away, zor....'

'Yes. Guilt. Or fear.' Batten shrugged. *Could* she have poisoned Lawrence Vann? Or be running from whoever had? 'She still needs to sleep. Local hotels, B&Bs -'

'Already done, zor.' Ball swallowed the 'nothing'.

'Then check her friends in the area - if she's *got* any - and check if they've got a spare bed. And ask the cleaner if the posh cow owns a tent. And see if it's *missing!*'

And you, Zig, go and tell the Assistant Chief Constable (Crime) that protecting one key witness will cost him a fortune, and searching for the other will cost him a darn sight more. Because Stephanie's done a runner. And we haven't the foggiest idea *why*.


Olly just grabbed the door handle and yanked it shut. Nothing changes. He'd pulled it out of its socket once and the garage had to fit a replacement. But when Lady Wake was along for the ride, Baz had to open the Jaguar's rear door like a flunkey, step deferentially back while she glided in, and gently close it after her. She never said 'thank you, Baz', just twitched whatever fingers weren't holding her Gucci handbag. If the twitch was supposed to be an acknowledgement, well, me no speak aristocracy.

Exeter Races this time, just for the afternoon. At least he'd get an hour to wander round in peace, to think, to plan. Or try to.

A practised dip of his hand nudged the big Jag onto the A303. He could smell Olly's pungent cologne, seeping from the rear seat like a sweet fog; could feel the breath from Olly's big lungs; could imagine Olly's dark eyes staring at his chauffeur-skull as he drove. Can guilt seep out from the back of your neck? If it could, he was a dead man. Sooner or later even Olly would clock that his dreary, model-making, weight-lifting chauffer-dogsbody wasn't quite as dim as he looked.

Lawrence's quick thinking had saved Baz's bacon that day. And Baz had a life-changing bank-roll stashed away as a result. But Lawrence's life had changed too. Into death. When Manny McRory dragged himself up from the stable floor where a contrived punch from Lawrence Vann had knocked him, Baz wished he'd been there to slam the little shit down again, and beat his head into the concrete till it cracked and spilled like a soft-boiled egg.

It all went wrong, from the moment Baz grabbed the memory stick from the safe, out of his own….what? Greed? Despair? Desperation? Should have left it where it was. Lawrence would have found some other way; clever, resourceful Lawrence.

'A spot of bad luck, Baz. That's all. But, under the circumstances, we should fast-forward to the second - indeed, the third - part of the plan.'

Lawrence had adjusted his tweed tie, smiled his reassuring, persuasive smile, and briskly got on with it. The second part: download Olly's cash. The third part: download Olly. Cologned breath on his neck reminded Baz that part three never happened.

Not even Lawrence could have planned for the unpredictable behaviour of Manny's mobile phone. In the fight, as Manny fell to the ground, it popped gravitationally out of his coat, slid mockingly along his collar, travelled across the increasing slope of his shoulder and slalomed down his waterproof sleeve directly into his unaware hand. When he came round and staggered upright again, the phone was already surrounded by his dazed fingers which more or less automatically pushed the speed dial for Olly. Most days, the signal at Wake Hall was weak and intermittent. That day, the connection was instantaneous and Manny's incoherent scouse babble aroused Olly's suspicions right away. He was in a fast taxi almost before Baz had handed the purloined memory stick to Lawrence – a stick now impossible to return. Manny himself staggered as far as the office, but was so fuzzy he failed to fit his keys into either of the locks. He sat on the ground instead, his head against the door. He was still there half an hour later when Olly emerged from a taxi that smelt of burnt tyres….

'Oi, Michael Schumacker!'

Baz was doing ninety. Too fast even for Olly, on these roads.

'You trying to get there for *yesterday*'s race?'

'Sorry, Olly.' And what's aristocrat for 'sorry'? 'My apologies, Lady Wake.'

In the rear view mirror, he could have sworn her fingers did that little dismissive twitch. He certainly saw Olly clamp his claws together. Nothing changes.


'*I'll* tell you where she's gone, George - she's eloped! With Fat Jellicoe!'

Hick found his suggestion so hilarious he was in tears.

'Just think - Jellicoe, with a posh bird like that! She'd ask for a dray whate wane, and he'd plonk a pint o' lager and a whisky chaser in front of her! 'Gerrit down yower neck, moy luvver!''

'Very funny. Mr *Loft*.'

George Halfpenny could have done without a Jellicoe-like slap on the back from Hick. After the best part of a day failing to find Stephanie Broke-Mondelle's name on any accommodation register, car-hire agreement, credit card receipt, flight manifest, blah-de-blah, her bank had finally informed him that she withdrew five grand in cash a week ago. When he told Batten, he got an earful from him too!

Batten knew that, in theory, they could use the bank note numbers to pinpoint the locations where she spent them, assuming she did. He also knew that Stealthily Gone-to-Hell - George's nickname for her - had disappeared with deliberation. Following a trail of small notes *in practice,* well....

'Take a break, George,' Batten said to the prematurely-relieved Halfpenny. 'Then keep looking.'

He caught Hick's smirk in the corner of his eye. Unusually wide peripheral vision, that was what the optician said, last time he had an eye-test.

"Hickie?'

'Er, yes, sir?'

'Give him a hand.'

# Twenty Three

Sergeant Ball's desk was made of wood. That was Batten's first feat of detection of the grumpy new day - made possible by the total absence of paper on the smooth oak surface.

'I was reminiscing with Mrs Ball about Bonfire Night, zor, and I became inspired. Burnt the lot.'

In exasperation, Ball had actually stuffed any document of significance in a filing cabinet with his name on. The discards had been added to the funeral pyre of rubbish growing dangerously large in the corner of the room. Batten had insisted it be moved today, wanting neither a fire nor an untidy organisational culture to flare up amongst his over-stretched troops.

Until Ball mentioned it, he hadn't even realised Bonfire Night was long gone, as if he cared. He'd heard fireworks - still dealing with them, Zig! - when he first arrived in Somerset: screeches and bangs in the sky, an occasional fizz of colour, the barking of disturbed dogs, but had no Trick-or-Treat visits or Penny-for-the Guy. Not because he lived down a dark country lane, but because he'd hardly been home.

More recently, his few free nights-in had been spent with a small glass of Speyside and a large pile of paper of his own. Neither revealed the whereabouts of Stephanie Broke-Mondelle but his notes triggered other faint intuitions.

'You know what intuition is, Zig?' Ged had once asked him.

No Ged, but you're going to tell me anyway.

'It's thinking, Zig, that's all it is. It's the thinking you do when you think you're not thinking.'

'Ged, you're a clever lad and you get a gold star.'

'Prefer a fresh pint, Zig, if it's all the same to you.'

One small intuition led him back to Lawrence Vann's cottage. He'd sloppily assumed that because Mr Someone had already searched it, there was nothing left to find. Search it again, Zig, you unprofessional plonker. If you can't find Stephanie Posh-Posh, then find something else, something *useful*, at Wake Hall.

He had insisted on driving this time, the route from Parminster now engraved in his skull. And he enjoyed his Ford Focus - despite the ribbing he took for not driving something flashier. What, something like a Jag? Like *Olly's*? Sergeant Ball wasn't enjoying it one bit, slumped in the passenger seat, face more thunderous with every mile.

'Is my driving *that* bad, Ballie?'

'Zor?'

'Forget it.'

There were two versions of Sergeant Ball. The carefree workhorse mutated into a silent sulk-machine whenever 'Wake Hall' was mentioned. What's going on, Zig? How can two short words suddenly become kryptonite? After steering the Focus into the Wake Hall Visitors' car park, he put the question. Ball glumly shrugged.

'Christ's sake, Ballie. It's like interviewing a crooked lawyer with his crooked lawyer present. You can't go down a hole in the ground because someone says 'Wake Hall.' Spit it *out!*'

A rumble welled up within Sergeant Ball, grew deeper in pitch, and emerged as words carved slowly into stone.

'They had a farm here,' he said, flicking a vague hand at the horizon as if that was explanation enough.

'It's three guesses now, is it? Who? Who had a farm?'

More boulder-words rumbled downhill. '*They* did. Mum and dad.'

'Ah, you were farming stock, were you?'

'I was a kiddie. Too young. You don't see things. The struggle, both of them eking out a living. Just a giant open-air playground to me, animals to chase, birds nests, all that. The farm died before they did. But losing it...well. They lingered on for a a few years, bless both their souls.'

'I'm sorry,' was the best Batten could do. Awkwardly, he punctured the awkward pause. 'Explains why you're not a farmer, though.'

Ball's angry shoulders twitched in dismissal. 'What would I have farmed? A few acres of *nothing*?' He seemed to be woken up by his own raised voice, and opened and closed his clenched fists in apology. 'The bank owned more of it than they did. I was doing my police training when they died. Him first. Mum clung on for a month or two.'

Batten couldn't remember if he'd said 'I'm sorry.' He said it again.

'I had to have time off, from the training college. Second time – that was mum – one of the cadets, sly bastard, said 'skiving off again, Crystal?' They called me Crystal, you see.'

They still do, Ballie. 'Upshot was, I decked him, harder than I'd intended. Huh, 'intended'. It was red mist, that's all.'

That's all? Ball's fist was a bag of spanners.

'I could have been in trouble, but he was going to fail anyway, so they said. I think the tutors were glad to see the back of him. One of them, he took me aside, said 'I've been wanting to thump that pillock for weeks.' Bought me a drink at the graduation piss-up, said 'this is for you know what.'

Batten never understood why people told him things. Ged's boozy jibe rang in his ears. 'It's because of your Stalin-like appearance, Zig. Folk 'fess up to you sharpish, hoping you'll go easy on them. They don't want to end up in Siberia, in a Gulag.'

'What happened to the farm?' he asked.

'The farm?' Ball laughed, a ginger tomcat coughing up a fur-ball made of anger and stone. 'You're sitting on it, 'the farm'. Over there, give or take.' He flicked a thwarted farmer's hand at the horizon.

'What? They sold it? To *Wake Hall*?'

'Sold it? Wake Hall *bought* it. For next to nothing. Hardly the same thing. Zor.'

Batten gazed at the distant, empty fields of Sergeant Ball's childhood. It all looked like grazing land now, with barely a hedgerow. Whether for sheep, cattle or horse he hadn't a clue, and not a single animal grazed in the big fields today. The detective in him wanted to ask why. But Ball had clomped out of the car and was trudging towards Wake Hall in such slow silence that Batten wondered if it *was* Crystal Ball he saw, or someone else.

Staring across at the dirty-white limestone blockhouse, with its roads and tracks snaking off to distant fields and farmsteads, Batten mused that he now had one more thing in common with Sergeant Ball. They had both lost their birthright, if you could call it that. Had things gone differently, would Ball have been a farmer? He had the physique for it. And you, Zig? Cap'n Batt'n, swamped by giant waves on your North Sea trawler? You'd get seasick in a rowing boat on Roundhay Park Lake in Leeds.

He climbed out of the car, the warped reflection of Wake Hall distorted in the windscreen. Plenty of birthright here, Zig, for someone. And what of Lawrence Vann, what of *his* birthright? Who did he plan to leave it to?

A line from Brecht swam around in his head, imperfectly remembered. He had begun to worry about his memory - he could readily recall the beginning and the end of a great many episodes, events, quotations. But rarely the middle. The Caucasian Chalk Circle, was that the play he was thinking of?

'What there is shall go to those who are good for it....'

He glanced again at the empty, subsumed fields where Ball's farm had died. The middle of the quotation eluded him; he had no idea why. But he knew the ending.

'....The tractors to good drivers, that they are driven well,
And the valley to the waterers, that it bring forth fruit.'

He slammed and locked the car door. It beeped at him, in mockery.

Trusting that his Sergeant's professionalism still ran through him like letters in a stick of rock, he left him to it, and hunted out Rhona Fiske instead. His purposes were entirely to do with the investigation but there were worse tasks. He found her in the Hall's farmhouse kitchen, inducting a temporary cook. Batten made no mention of having recently questioned the permanent one. Debbie Farley would soon be sent home to recuperate, so they'd said, but he chose not to tell the crisp Ms Fiske, whose attitude to Debbie was a touch ambivalent. And he wanted to keep her sweet.

'You take a break now, Sandra, while you can.'

A relieved-looking Sandra nipped outside, cigarettes in hand. Cooks allowed to smoke? If you worked at Wake Hall, Zig, *you'd* smoke.

'Are the police trained to arrive just as kettles boil, Inspector?' she asked, with a more open smile this time. 'You're welcome to join me - for *yesterday's* coffee-break. It's been that kind of week.'

For both of us. They sat at the big kitchen table. As the cafetiere brewed, he put his questions.

'At *night*? *Lawrence*? Goodness me, surely you know enough about him by now? The thought of Lawrence tramping around, outdoors, at night, after *wildlife*? Apologies, Inspector, but it's laughable.'

Batten thought it was too. It was why he'd asked.

'Horses apart, it was a very different sort of wild life he pursued, believe me, once work was done. *Indoor* safaris were more his taste - yes, I am being suggestive, Inspector, because it's *true*. We can't *see* Lawrence's place from our cottages, but on summer nights, with windows open, certain *noises* were involuntarily overheard.'

Rhona Fiske suddenly pushed down the cafetiere's plunger, surprising him. But the coffee smelt better than her Earl Grey tea.

'And Lawrence wouldn't be out riding at night, would he?'

She looked at him wryly. Ham-fisted way of putting it, Zig, under the circumstances.

'Horses, I mean.'

Batten imagined Lawrence as a cultured cowboy doing circus tricks with wild horses, day and night. According to Allie Chant, Lawrence had taught the young Lady Wake to ride, and still gave her lessons. Has she found another teacher yet, Zig?

'Lawrence wouldn't dream of endangering a horse by riding in the dark, Inspector. No-one here would. Too many badger holes at Wake Hall. We hear clip-clopping at night sometimes, over there' - she pointed over her shoulder at the kitchen window - 'but that's the horse-sales people.'

'Wake Hall Horse?'

'Wake Hall Horse! Such a *silly* name. *We* call them *The Regiment*.' Rhona Fiske laughed, like a silver spoon weaving through coffee and cream. Batten was pleased he wasn't the only one to find Wake Hall Horse an odd name for a business venture.

'They're a law unto themselves, the Regiment. Evenings, weekends, bank holidays. If there's a horse to sell, it'll be driven off in a box quicker than you can say 'fetlock'. And 365 days - and nights - a year. They should remove the 'Wake Hall Horse' sign and replace it with 'We Never Close.'

A further thought struck Batten.

'How did Lawrence get on with the Wa - with The Regiment people?'

Rhona Fiske hesitated, before shrugging her shoulders.

'Like the rest of us, I suppose, Inspector. *We* were here first. They're the new boys and girls. Yet, almost overnight, they converted a ruined stable block into a vast horse factory. Right in our backyard.'

'There's a bit of rivalry, then?'

'Difficult to be rivals when there's barely any contact.'

Rhona Fiske paused and took stock. A careful woman, Zig?

'You probably remember, Inspector, that I'm the official keeper of the keys here?'

He did, it was useful information.

'The chatelaine?' he said.

Rhona Fiske gave him a look he'd seen many times before. A policeman? A *plod*? Correctly pronouncing a foreign word of more than one syllable? Shock her, Zig - say 'marmalade', too.

'Well, Inspector, *as* the chatelaine I have keys for every lockable door in Wake Hall - except her Ladyship's private rooms, of course. But I don't have any key for any door at Wake Hall Horse. Not a single one.'

'So no contact with them at all? That must be strange, given how close they are?'

'Well, not *friendly* contact. One or two comments have been made, I gather.'

'Made by…?'

'Now, now, Inspector. For gossip, you want the stable-girls, not me.'

He raised an apologetic hand. 'Not even Lawrence, then? He didn't mix with the new boys - and girls?'

She saw exactly where he was going, gave a little smile and a shake of the head.

'It's almost all boys - men, in fact. Extremely large ones for the most part. But no, he didn't. Without descending into gossip, it's safe to say that non-Regiment staff, Lawrence amongst them, are not made welcome over there.'

She pointed over her shoulder, then turned to look through the rear window at what little of Wake Hall Horse was visible - the side of a horse-box; part of a high stone wall; the edge of a large, closed gate. He realised he was admiring the soft curve of her neck.

'So, Lawrence didn't go on country rambles with his Regimental colleagues across the way?'

'Definitely not, though he liked his walks, did Lawrence.'

'Did *you* ever…?'

'Walk with him?'

Batten nodded. What else do you think I meant?

'No. I would have liked to - I'm a keen walker when time allows - but after my brief encounter with Lawrence's digits….In any case he normally walked with Debbie.'

Rhona Fiske beckoned through the glass at a newly-nicotined Sandra.

'I have to deal with Debbie's tantrums on a weekly basis as it is. So the thought of walking with Lawrence *and* Debbie….Hardly.'

She put the empty cups noisily in the sink, her coffee-break and their conversation now over. He was more disappointed than he should have been.

Responding to his radio, PC Jess Foreman loped into the kitchen-diner of Lawrence Vann's cottage and confirmed what Sergeant Ball had been told to ask him.

'Oh yes, that's what it is - we use one a bit like it ourselves, now and then. At night, out on rural patrol. For spotting poachers - or whoever else lurks around in the dark for no good purpose.'

Batten'll be pleased, Ball thought. He wasn't sure why.

'Common or garden now though, these, despite the price. Was a time the silly beggars'd hide in the undergrowth, not knowing we could see their heat signature. They've wised up o'course, but even a cold-blooded villain gives off heat. Can't stop doing *that,* can he?'

Jess chuckled, surprised when a glum Sergeant Ball failed to join in.

'Despite the price, Jess? How much we talking about?'

'Oh now, my mem'ry. Used to borrer one from the Fire Brigade, 'fore re-organisation. They use 'em to spot folk caught up in fires, see through the smoke. Couple o' grand maybe, for top of the range?'

Ball was correct. When Batten's lanky stride took him from the Wake Hall kitchen into Lawrence Vann's cottage he was pleased Jess Foreman had confirmed his hunch. One of last night's niggly intuitions had some substance after all. When he and Lee searched Lawrence's place, Batten had picked up what he thought was a snub-nosed telescope - it looked like the kind of monocular that birdwatchers use. It wouldn't focus so he swapped it for a pair of binoculars hanging from the same hook. These were strong enough to spot Olly's fancy Jaguar, and his un-fancy chauffer-bodyguard, sloping off by the floodlit side entrance of Wake Hall.

'So, it *is* a thermal-imager. Two *grand*?'

Why would Lawrence Vann spend two grand on a device for picking up the heat signature of wildlife in the dark? At night, the only wildlife of interest to him was shapely birds and trouser snakes - if Rhona Fiske was to be believed. No thermal imager needed in his bedroom, with its hot red feature wall. And the device was almost brand-new.

'Ballie, pull Hick and Halfpenny out of the Estate office, and get them to go through Lawrence's receipts – they're in a box by the desk, next door. See if they can find a receipt for this. Oh, and for the ordinary binoculars too.'

While Ball did as he was told, Batten retraced his steps through the over-tidy cottage. The tip of his gangly frame threatened the ceiling in every room - except the kitchen-diner. The roof was much higher there, with several feet of space above his head. It was a room he could happily live in himself; capacious and comfortable, with a shaker-style kitchen at one end, and a comfy-looking sofa, large pine table and expensive leather dining chairs at the other. Not to speak of a long shelf of fine whiskies. This room was brighter too, because of a long, narrow window which ran the full length of the back wall, just below the ceiling. Batten was staring up at this when Hick and Halfpenny arrived and were put to work.

'Ballie?'

'Zor?'

There was a tone of 'what next?' in his voice. He deserves the eyebrows for that, Zig. He's here to work, and when not reacting to Wake-Hall-kryptonite, he's good at it.

'Ballie. Kindly fetch me a step-ladder, would you, stout fellow? I mean, if it's not too much of an inconvenience, my good man?'

A small red smile creaked its way across Ball's cheeks. He brought the ladder, barely three steps and a noggin. Batten climbed onto the top rung but couldn't see out of the fanlight even with his neck stretched. He climbed down again, hunch still nagging.

'When we searched before, didn't Lawrence have *two* ladders?'

'Hasn't everybody?' asked Ball. But he was shedding the Wake Hall glums. 'I'll look, zor.'

This took longer than expected, because the long ladder was tricky to steer through narrow doorways. But once in place Batten immediately saw it would reach the fanlight. As he put a size-nine on the bottom rung another thought struck him.

'Ballie, tell George and Hickie to look for receipts for these stepladders too - then steady this bloody thing, stop me breaking my neck. And pass me that thermal imager.'

Atop the ladder, with a faint feeling of vertigo, Batten peered through the high, narrow fanlight, the only window in the cottage's rear wall. The shrill voice of Mr Willey, the estate agent who rented him his own cottage, came to mind. *'This delightful rural home has the benefit of additional restricted views to the rear'*. Because it did. There was no long vista, no tree-clad hills. All that Batten could at first see, forty feet from where he stood, was a high stone wall and beyond it, at right angles, the sloping roofs of line after line of stable-blocks. Further along, the high gates came into view, and then an over-sized and new-looking sign said 'Wake Hall Horse.' Well now, Zig.

He squinted through the thermal imager, not expecting it to work in daylight. To his great surprise, he was able to make out vague, shimmering, multi-faceted heat images of one four-legged creature after another. Dozens of them. And how much better would the imager work at night?

'This is like having X-ray vision, Ballie!' he said, an excited schoolboy. 'I'm coming down. Don't let this beast collapse, or I'll land on *you*.'

Once safely on the ground he had to practically push his reluctant Sergeant up the ladder, to confirm what he'd seen. From his wobbly perch, Ball took his turn to play doubting-cop.

'Don't see any direct evidence he was up this particular ladder, with this particular thermal imager, looking at *that*, zor. Do you?' He jerked his thumb at Wake Hall Horse. His scepticism was rewarded only by a prolonged stay up top, to confirm the second thing Batten had noted. The window frame was painted in bright white gloss, presumably to reflect as much light as possible into the room. A distinctive, smile-shaped indentation was visible on the lower edge of the frame, and the paint's hard skin had been disturbed there. Ball gave in when he saw a corresponding white stain on the lower lip of the thermal imager.

'He must have rested it there, on the frame, Ballie, and scuffed a bit of paint off.'

'Forensics'll tell us, soon enough.' Ball had learnt not to fuel his Inspector's triumphal mode. He climbed down, with barely-disguised relief, as Batten recounted what he poetically termed the logic of Lawrence's ladders.

'Paint and ladders, Ballie. Only pot of paint in the place is a half-full can of sexy red - same colour that's on the feature wall behind Mr Vann's bed. But the tall ladder's far too big for that room, it'd collide with the beams for a start. So why buy it? No sign of him painting anything in the kitchen-diner, and that's the only room the ladder fits in! He wanted to look out of that high window, I'm certain, and the only thing visible is Wake Hall Horse!'

Ball stayed in doubting-cop mode, imagining Derek Herring as defending counsel, painting for the jury a very different picture of Lawrence Vann - seedy philanderer and now peeping tom, lustily spying on innocent nocturnal nookie over at Wake Hall Horse, the dirty dog. But Ball's encounter with a slippery Manny McCrory came back to him. In the brownness of McRory's draughty shed forty feet the other side of this window, he'd felt a familiar tickle of suspicion. Maybe Lawrence had felt it too. Or more likely heard it, at night, and bought the wherewithal to *see*.

'We'd better press on, zor. Find what Lawrence Vann was looking at.'

Batten needed no prompting.

'Hick! Halfpenny! Where's those receipts? Get a move on! It's four scraps of paper!'

Strutting into the sitting room, Batten saw Halfpenny and Hick squatting in sullen silence, amid hundreds of invoices, bills and receipts. Batten had forgotten: Lawrence had amassed an entire yearsworth for his tax return. He pitched into the pile himself. It took another ten minutes to unearth three of the receipts. The one for the binoculars was in the desk drawer, in a file marked 'Guarantees'. Batten waved them all under the nose of his doubting Sergeant.

'Notice anything significant about the dates, Ballie?' Batten asked.

Ball gave in. He had to admire Batten's persistence. In mentoring mode, he picked up the receipt for the thermal imager, the binoculars and the two stepladders and passed them to Hick and Halfpenny.

'Come on, boys, before you go blind, tell me why the nice Inspector's so fizzed up by a few scraps of paper.'

The two DCs applied the remains of their sight. Hick beat Halfpenny to the answer.

'Got it, Sarge. Small stepladder was bought a year back. Binoculars - expensive - are even older than that. The pricier stepladder has got to be the taller one, yeh? Well, he bought that….two months ago - on the exact same date he bought that thermal thing.'

'So?' said a drained Halfpenny. 'He goes shopping, buys binocs and a ladder. S'not bomb-making, is it?' And in response to Hick's arch smile, he asked 'what?'

Hick's twitching face was gradually converting his computations into words. Ball saved him the trouble.

'If you've already got a newish set of steps, why buy a taller set, unless you want to reach somewhere higher?' Ball pointed to the kitchen-diner. 'No sign of Lawrence painting the ceiling next door. The only other bit you'd need a tall ladder to reach is the high window.'

'He could have been draught-proofing it? Something like that?' said Halfpenny, clutching at straws of pride.

'It doesn't open. It's a sealed unit, double-glazed,' countered Ball.

'Come on, George,' Batten cajoled, 'he buys the long ladder on the very same day he credit-cards an expensive thermal-imager. Why? He's not interested in spotting wildlife in the dark. And if he wants to go bird-watching - the tweet-tweet kind - he's already got a pair of top-grade binocs.'

'Lawrence Vann didn't need a thermal imager,' added Ball, 'except….'

Halfpenny gave a white-flag nod.

'What can you see from that window, sir?' he asked.

Batten told them.

'Well,' said Hick, 'you'll be wanting us to do a bit of quiet surveillance, sir, up a ladder, from that window there? At night? With that thermal - '

' - imager,' added Halfpenny.

Batten and Ball exchanged glances. How, when, permission, all would need to be worked out. Arguing 'reasonable cause' wouldn't be a pushover. They nodded, regardless.

'In that case,' said Hick, 'I expect we'll be on overtime, sir?'

# Twenty Four

Focusing too much on Lawrence Vann's cottage, Batten absent-mindedly overfilled the woodstove in his own. Surprised by balmy December weather, he was cooling off outside in the hamstone porch, enjoying the long view across the valley to Ham Hill, when the phone rang. It was irksome enough to re-enter the temporary sauna of his sitting room, but doubly irksome that the caller was Mr Willey from the rental agency. When it came to Estate Agents, Batten agreed with Woody Allen. You could become ill just by sitting next to one. Mr Willey's sham voice was squealing down the hot phone.

'Yes, very sad for the dear old fellow, but what a good innings, eh, don't you think? Ninety six?'

Batten politely agreed. Willey was talking about Mr Torrington, the cottage's owner, who had 'sadly died, quite unexpectedly'. Well, at ninety six. Batten assumed the extortionate monthly rent helped pay for Mr Torrington's nursing home.

'Only one remaining relative, alas. A cousin, male. Lives in a rather obscure place in Canada, the back of beyond - his words not mine - all moose and snow-shoes, I imagine?'

I imagine you could get to the point, lad. When Willey did, Batten wished he hadn't.

'Upshot is, the cousin wants to sell. Sell the cottage, that is, not the moose, hah-hah! And right away too. Wants to buy more moose perhaps, hah-hah.'

A Yorkshire silence.

'Sooo, apologies profound, Mr Batten, but this will mean inventories, viewings, surveys and such and such. Unavoidable disturbance to the even tenor of your domestic ways, alas, alas. But we *do* have a similar cottage for rent, *super* little place, barely a mile or two or three from where you are now. And *exceedingly* convenient for the A303, quite a bonus, eh?'

Yes, thought Batten, I can hear the traffic noise already, blotting out the birdsong.

'Sooo, I'm positive we can arrive at a *most* reasonable rental package, in view of any mild inconvenience….Hello?'

Batten was thinking of the 'mild inconvenience' that moving would involve. He looked out of the window at his long, green valley. He looked at the CD racks he had carefully fitted to the old stone walls, the shelves of book-bargains bought cheaply in the early morning chill at the markets and car-boots he had begun to discover. Several first editions - a pristine Jack London amongst them - sat proudly on the nearest shelf. He looked at his woodstove, absurdly hot now, but promising cosy winter evenings. He had revived it with black stove paint, found an old log basket in the loft and filled it with a flame-ready pile of logs. Applewood, by the smell.

Through the kitchen window his back garden was still bare soil, but it was *his* garden, because hard digging on his few days off had unearthed it, rescuing from deep layers of brambles and weeds the shapes of old vegetable patches and flower beds. He'd even found a Roman coin and a few shards of pottery that looked like the Samian ware he'd seen on archaeology programmes on TV.

He liked the feel of history around him. Saying goodbye to a loved house in Leeds, built with gritstone quarried from ancient hillsides, had not been easy. He wasn't about to flit from a 200 year-old hamstone haven too. Not without a fight.

Mr Willey was still squeaking down the phone, but Batten did important business face-to-face. Through gritted teeth, he made an appointment. Mr Willey could sweat for a day or two.


Nothing! Would Doc Danvers have called it nothing *plus*? No, Zig, he wouldn't. There was no bloody *plus* about it!

He'd carefully - gleefully - planned the midnight surveillance on Wake Hall Horse, from the fanlight in Lawrence Vann's cottage, but the results were a frustrating, counter-productive *nothing*! And Batten, having gambled on a little private intervention, would be in Gribble's bad books as a result - if Gribble ever found out. You forgetfully forgot to mention it, Zig, didn't you? 'Sorry, sir, pressure of work, sir.' No official permission. No *unofficial* permission either.

Showing off, weren't you? Should have been less bullish - especially when Halfpenny plucked up courage to ask the obvious question: 'what exactly are we looking for, sir?' Batten's only guidance was 'try and see what Lawrence might have seen.'

What might that be, Zig? What secret could Lawrence Vann spot from his fanlight window? The favoured hunch was drugs, because when Olly first arrived up north, bad heroin quickly hit the streets. Maybe heroin once more then, perhaps concealed in the wadded lining of a saddle - or very many saddles, given the production line of horses trucked in and out of Wake Hall Horse, day and night. What a convenient distribution system that would be. Or in the horse-boxes themselves, within the copious padding and protective linings used to safeguard the horses during transportation?

He advised Hick and Halfpenny to track the heat signatures of two-legged bodies doing more than just walking up and down; to track intensive and protracted human activity - men stripping out the guts of a saddle, or the sound-proofing in a box, and unpacking or re-packing the cavities with *something*, something more profitable. More deadly.

After two nights, Hick and Halfpenny were half-blind, after long stints on the ladder in their darkened room, peering through the thermal imager at the spectral heat signatures of horses that had been there in daylight anyway, at the occasional two-legged attendant on night patrol, and at nothing else whatsoever.

Batten had secreted the two DCs into Lawrence's cottage under cover of 'a forensic re-examination of Mr Vann's environments.' When the technical staff went home, the DCs stayed quietly inside, protected by the 'Police Line - Do Not Cross' seal, and locked in with their food supplies and their thermos flasks.

'Don't switch on the lights, don't flush the loos till you have to,' Batten told them, 'and keep your grubby gobs off his vintage whisky.'

And all without the knowledge of ACC Gribble. Or Rhona Fiske. Or, especially, the owner of Wake Hall. Batten would break a dozen rules to avoid giving Olly a heads-up.

'Worth risking another night, Ballie, do you think?'

Ball did a silent Falstaff impersonation. 'Discretion is the better part of valour'. He'd read it, on the Famous Quotations app on his mobile phone.

'A re-think might be in order, zor? No?'

Batten was *trying* to re-think. But the expected breakthroughs hadn't broken through; the 'witnesses' were fuzzy or flown; the forensics results were either compromised or yet to arrive; and other unsolved crimes were accumulating. He'd been promised a 'full and final' toxicology report on the poisoned soup first thing this morning. It was now one-o-clock and the report was AWOL.

'OK. Pull Hickie and George out of Wake Hall and put them back on the tractor thefts. See if Jess Foreman's snouts can add anything.'

Ball didn't remind Batten how dismissive he'd been about thieves nicking tractors, until he'd clocked the kind of money involved.

'And keep young Lee working on Stephanie Born-in-Hell. His eyes are in better shape than George's. You, me and Magnus'll sort out Debbie Farley and the rest. That Solo Souls bod, what's-his-name, is he back yet?'

'Vito Valdano, zor. Back last night, him and his sidekick both.'

'Oksana….?'

'Unpronounceable, zor. Oksana Thing.'

'Get a pecking order together then. If anyone wants me, I've gone thermo-nuclear with the toxics.'

Lady Wake ran a manicured fingernail through the dark hair on Olly Rutter's lower abdomen. She drew the shape of a three in the hair, and then traced a nine. Olly was good at numbers, but even he had no sense that it was '39' she'd written. And she wasn't trying to remind him about her imminent birthday.

'Darling?'

'Ungh?'

'You remember that spare fifty acres, good grass, over the rise behind Wake Hall Horse?'

'Yengh.'

'We-ell, I was thinking….'

Don't. Leave that to me.

'….those rather wonderful brood mares we shipped off. Remember?'

Course I remember. We cleared twenty grand, *after* tax. And a hundred grand on the other stuff. But the other stuff was *his* business.

'Yengh.'

'Such lovely mares, Olly. What if we'd kept them, here, with a few more? On the fifty acres? Some of those pretty Andalucians we saw in Spain perhaps?'

'Kept them? For what?'

'For breeding, of course, darling. Top quality, that's why they're in demand.'

Olly knew where this was going. Marianne was easy to read. Besotted he might be, but on *his* terms. He'd get her some more Spanish mares though, because importing them would suit his plans.

'We got a good price for those mares *because* they're in demand.'

'I know, darling. But instead of just buying, we could be *breeding*. Mm?'

He was right.

'Breeding. Imagine little foals dancing through the grass. Expanding into stud would diversify the business, Olly. Help to *maintain* it.'

Lady Wake didn't want to be the last of the Wakes. Each day, centuries of ancestors on the Hall walls wagged their chins and fingers at her as she glided beneath their gilt-framed portraits. She wished her soft, ineffectual *father* had wagged his finger at her occasionally. How much milk of human kindness did he think his daughter could swallow before she gagged? Marianne had always been the family rebel. But to be the *last* rebel? And Olly was strong, exciting. She made allowances for him, yes, every now and then....but to have a child - at thirty nine it was likely to be just the one - a child as strong and bold as Olly, well.

'So, what do you think, darling?'

I think pigs might fly.

'What's wrong with the way things are?'

To Batten's surprise, the Chief Toxic picked up the phone. 'Finishing touches' to the report had delayed it just a tad, he said. A tad *more*, Batten wanted to yell, as he flopped into Jellicoe's chair. Sensing the need to placate, Big Chief Toxic offered to email it there and then, and talk Batten through 'the more arcane elements of toxicological science....'

'A plant? He was poisoned by a *plant*? Is that what you're saying?'

'Plants plural,' corrected Chief Toxic. 'All the same plant, but the concentration was extremely powerful. A product of several plants, yes?'

Batten had never heard of aconitine.

'No, not nicotine, Inspector, though that is actually a poison too. *Aconitine* - from the Aconite plant. If I tell you that the Aconitum genus has over two hundred and fifty species, you may appreciate the toxicological difficulties a little better.'

No. I won't.

'But we *are* confident now that Aconitum Napellus is the villain, to be necessarily precise.'

'Necessarily because…?'

'Ah well, the many forms of aconite are all poisonous, but Aconitum Napellus is among the worst.'

Or the best, if you're a poisoner.

'It contains several alkaloids - aconitine, napelline, mesaconitine - '

'Yes, yes, but where does it come from, this plant - no, who would have *access* to it?'

'Ah, Inspector, you, me, and Everyman. And I *am* acutely aware that is not the answer you seek. Tell me, in your spare moments - '

*Spare?*

' - are you green-fingered at all?'

What is it with these people? I ask for a tox report and get Gardener's Bloody Question Time!

'I mean, are you possessed of a garden, Inspector?'

Well, in a way, he was. Recently, to clear his mind, he'd thrown his case notes onto the coffee table and finished clearing the thickets of weed surrounding his cottage. As he was raking the last of them into a pile, the farmer who owned the methane-heavy fields across the lane trundled by in his tractor and trailer. Kenny Layzell could well be the friendliest person in Somerset. He worked twelve hour days - nights too sometimes. But never Saturday night, when he did his best to do a week's talking and drink The Five Bells dry.

'Arternoon, Zig. Bin busy, an't you?' The downside of Kenny's openness was statements of the obvious.

'I'll be busier still, Kenny, getting this stuff dumped.'

The daunting piles of weeds, thorn and brambles would fill a skip, with some left over. Half an hour and two whiskies later, it was trundling down the lane in Kenny's trailer, on its way to the huge, steaming compost heap that was the farm's sideline. Batten did have a garden, visible now. Nothing was growing there, but he would fix that. In his *spare* time.

'Because, Inspector, if you do have a garden, Aconitum napellus - Aconite to the layman - may well be waving around in it. Quite tall, quite a pretty leaf and a sort of hooded flower. Mid-blue, this version. You may know the plant as Monkshood?'

He didn't. A poisonous plant, though? In a *garden*?

'Oh, a large number of garden plants are in fact poisonous, though this particular one is deadlier than most. There's a similar form, Aconitum lycoctonum, that farmers used to call Wolfsbane. Perhaps they still do. In the distant past, I'm told, they poisoned foxes with it.'

But Lawrence Vann wasn't a fox. Was he?

'Mother Nature is not entirely random, however, Inspector. She has endowed the aconites with an extremely unpleasant taste. As such, accidental poisoning - of the fatal kind - would be the rarest of events.'

And the soup would taste foul, Zig. Nobody would drink it. But Debbie Farley said hers was laced with brandy.

'Would brandy disguise the taste - enough to persuade someone to have a good glug?'

'On its own, I would doubt that. The soup in question, however, contained strong curry spices and a fair amount of sugar. And parsnips themselves, of course, have a natural sweetness. Collectively, they may very well have disguised the taste. But there is an additional point, Inspector….'

Batten hated it when boffins prefaced what they're paid to tell you with phrases like that. 'Incidentally', that was another one.

'As it happens, it's not terribly easy to *dissolve* aconite. The plants - and the roots, of course, which are in fact more poisonous than the leaves - were probably dried and crushed to a fine powder, but even so. In *alcohol,* however….You can see where I'm going with this, I imagine?'

He could. To collect several plants, grind them to powder and dissolve them in alcohol was a careful act of obvious deliberation. Our old friend 'malice aforethought.' The poisoner would then have….a serum? A distillation? A deadly additive, at any rate. Dump a large dose in a couple of innocent flasks of soup, screw the lids on, give 'em a shake, wipe off the prints and….

'Whoever put the poison in the flasks, could they have done it as a warning?'

Chief Toxic paused. Batten waited for him to say 'I'm not a policeman...'

'I'm not a policeman, but I very much doubt it, Inspector. If a warning was intended, why would the perpetrator use enough poison to easily put down a horse?'

# Twenty five

On the quiet, Sergeant Ball drew Hick and Halfpenny into an empty interview room. Bad news, boys, about the overtime. Complications, bureaucratic glitches, budget problems - take your pick. In the interests of the team, though, shouldn't we just put this one down to experience? I'll make sure your names are top of the list next time, if you get my drift?

They got Ball's drift alright. Colonel Batten had cocked up the battleplan and the troops were paying for it - or not being paid for it, to be more precise. Two sleepless nights up a ladder; half-blind; no overtime. They respected Ball, so they would do as he suggested and 'take one for the team.' As for the Northern git, they preferred him to Fat Jellicoe, but - just now - that was as far as it went.

Ball sped from his unscheduled bit of arm-twisting with Hickie and George to the headquarters of Solo Souls, to rendezvous with Batten and Magnus. He needn't have rushed. They too were delayed.

Batten had agreed to meet at Magnus's car, tucked away in a parking space behind the market, just off Parminster High Street. Even if he hadn't known which was hers, the deep, fresh scratch across both passenger doors was obvious enough.

It had happened to him, too, in Leeds. A yob finds out you're a cop, watches you climb into an ordinary-looking car, and the following day the windscreen's smashed or a long scar's been keyed into the bodywork. He'd expected more civilised behaviour down here.

Magnus was across the street, reluctantly engaging with Parminster's resident bag-lady, an excitable rag-doll of indefinite age but definite odour. He could not hear what she was gabbling at Magnus nor understand the frantic mime as her smelly arm whipped from left to right across her body, as if skimming an invisible stone across a non-existent sea. Then both hands came up to her neck and the fingers waved up, down and over, in semaphore.

'You saw someone scratch my car? Is that what you're saying?' Magnus was using short sentences and breathing through her mouth. 'A large man? What did he look like?'

The description came with a full supporting cast of gestures, grubby hands miming a three-quarter length coat, malodorous fingers flicking up and down to show a thick collar.

Magnus glanced across at Batten. This was not the time for official complaints. She had no desire to be labelled a whinger. She would take her own private revenge on the only large male in Parminster who wore a three-quarter length coat with fur round the collar.

In the car, she gave a non-committal shrug when Batten offered his sympathy.

'Happened to me in Leeds, a time or two. Makes you want to spit.'

'It does, sir, yes.'

It did. It made her want to spit.

Ball had tracked down Vito Valdano by the skin of his teeth. Having left the country the day Lawrence Vann was killed - a coincidence, Zig? - Mr Valdano had flown back briefly and was due to fly out again, to Albania this time - or was it Romania? - where he sponsored orphanage-based charity projects, allegedly. The team should be gearing up at Parminster, now they knew precisely what had poisoned Lawrence Vann, but as Batten put it, 'we'd better question Valdano first, before he de-materialises.'

They rendezvoused in the flower-fringed car park to the rear of Solo Souls. If they were expecting a mysterious, soulful building, they were disappointed. The exterior of Valdano's place of business was municipal to a fault and looked like a chartered accountants. Magnus went to question Valdano's assistant, Oksana Unpronounceable. Batten and Ball drew the short straw.

Vito Valdano met his two visitors in the Meditation Room of Solo Souls. Here, municipal was definitely not in evidence. It was like no other room Batten had been in, its walls a deep puce. If the room had windows, they were so well hidden by layer on layer of indigo muslin swags and dark sea-green drapery that barely a chink of light could enter. Presumably to compensate, candles in their dozens flickered in mirrored globes and in little lanterns and on tables and shelves and even on the floor, giving a disturbingly sea-sick light to the proceedings.

Batten and Ball shared knowing nods. Yes, we could probably do

Valdano for Health and Safety. The only seating was a semi-circle of Tibetan prayer stools - 'designed, Inspector, to straighten the spine, and of course as an aid to spiritual reflection.'

Vito Valdano had the advantage of previous practice when it came to sitting on his. Batten and Ball were two mismatched finials, wobbling precariously on a pair of upright sawn-off curtain-poles.

As for Valdano himself, he was as tall as Batten, and far better-fed. Rhona Fiske had mentioned his preference for macrobiotic cuisine, but this man was no scarecrow. A large, loose suit struggled to cover his frame, a suit in which no colour dominated but in which every colour imaginable was attempting to. Above his trimmed beard, Valdano wore an expensive-looking pair of gold-framed tinted spectacles. They'll be to stop him going blind, Zig, when he looks in a mirror.

'No, no, Inspector', Valdano was saying, 'Solo Souls is definitely *not* a 'dating agency' as you so inaccurately - and might I say tastelessly - put it. We provide for spiritually-inclined persons who happen to live alone - some by choice, some by misfortune, some by….well, simply because they *do*. Our gatherings are aimed at the minds and, naturally, the *souls* of participants.'

'These minds and souls don't roll up to your gatherings inside bodies, then, sir?'

'Inspector. Bodies are secondary, where Souls Souls is concerned.'

'But bodies need feeding, nevertheless? Which is what brought you to Wake Hall on November 1st, I understand?'

'Ah, yes, the day poor Mr Vann….'

Lost his soul. Batten had enough respect to keep this thought to himself.

'You knew Lawrence Vann, then, sir?'

'Wake Hall's Conference Centre is a major focus for our programmes and symposia, Inspector. I liaise with the Wake Hall staff, Mr Vann amongst them.'

'And Debbie Farley?'

'Ah, a most promising 'chef macrobiotique'. Oksana and I were facilitating at the Hall that morning. Before our programme began we visited the kitchen - to discuss menus for a future event.'

Some drippy course about getting in touch with your inner gazelle.

160

Isn't that what Rhona Fiske had called it?

'Alas, Ms Farley was about to depart….on the fateful country walk - I have read about it in the newspaper, Inspector. I do hope her health is improving?'

Ball gave up trying to work out what a symposia was, and chipped in.

'Mr Valdano, when you were speaking to Debbie Farley and Rhona Fiske, did you spot anything unusual in the vicinity? Or any*body*?'

Vito shook his beard. 'Alas, Sergeant, nothing. And nobody.'

Batten switched to the past, another very informative country.

'Why did Solo Souls fetch up at Wake Hall, sir, if you don't mind me asking?' What with Glastonbury and its wizards being only a bit further up the road.

'Well, I do not think of Solo Souls as 'fetching up' anywhere, Inspector. Lady Wake was the reason - a most excellent reason. We requested, she graciously assented. A most welcoming, liberal-minded patron, whose perspective on spiritual matters was - and still is - one of immense encouragement.'

Batten's view of Lady Wake tended more towards the physical.

'I wonder, sir, was there any encouragement from Olly Rutter?'

Did the slightest tremor creep across Valdano's face, or was it candlelight reflecting off his suit?

'Of course I have *met* Mr Rutter, through his….association with Lady Wake, but...' Valdano waved a handful of unspoken words and a full-stop, making the nearest candle flicker and almost die.

'So no *involvement* at all with Olly Rutter, sir?'

'As I have already said, Inspector, her *lady*ship is our patron.'

'And Derek Herring, sir? No patronage from *him*, through *his* association with Mr Rutter perhaps?'

'Mr Herring? I have *met* Derek, of course. Other than that….'

Valdano waved more unspoken words at the candle. This time it went out. His large body seemed to shift inside its technicolor cloak. For a moment, Batten envied him the tinted spectacles. If Vito had more to say, however, he wasn't saying it.

'Gentlemen, I have much to do. If there is nothing else…?'

Vito Valdano arose with surprising grace from his Tibetan prayer stool. Batten and Ball took considerably longer to extricate themselves

161

from theirs and to creak back to the car.

'Don't know about you, zor,' Ball said, 'but my arse feels like it's still in Tibet.'

DC Magnus had enjoyed a better deal. She and her interviewee shared an unspoken affinity - both women were British, born in England, but were still seen as foreign by some. Oksana Thing had been charming, Magnus said, offered a chair with arms and a seat, and made tea - 'I was expecting cauliflower and daffodil, you know, but it was just tea. Nice tea.' Sensing Ball's envy, she moved on. 'Anyway, she was very helpful, very open. Valdano's got quite a business here, sir. Not the odd evening class once a blue moon. She showed me a brochure. Residential courses galore - with posh food and a lot of well-heeled punters - short daily programmes, special conferences, the works.'

'Inner gazelles,' Batten said.

'*Sir*?'

'Never mind. Not some kind of front, is it?'

'Well, I don't *think* so, sir. It's a proper business - not a hundred uses for a dried chrysanthemum. Self-sufficiency, interpersonal relationships, art, literature, music. Loads, really.'

'You going to enrol, Nina?'

Magnus knew when to smile.

'Too pricey, Sarge.'

Batten wondered how much Valdano coughed up to Lady Wake for all this pricey, genuine activity, if that's what it was. He picked up threads.

'And this woman, Oksana Whatsername, she see anything untoward that morning?'

'Nothing, sir. *But*, she did see Mr Vann.'

Batten and Ball woke up. So far, only Lonny Dalway *might* have seen Lawrence that morning, and Batten was still unsure if he'd simply mistranslated Lonny's twang.

'Is she certain?'

'I couldn't see a reason for her to lie, sir. She knows Lawrence well enough - they liaise a fair bit. She says he was in his walking boots and waterproof, carrying a big hat. She waved to him.'

'And he waved back?'

'She said he did, yes.'

A final goodbye, as it turned out. Perhaps the last social gesture of his sixty year old life.

Magnus had effectively scotched one of the private hunches Batten shared with Ball, that Lawrence was somewhere else at eight that morning. It had been a poor hunch, a sign of how little evidence they had. But the toxicology report was real, at least. Maybe it would revitalise his tired team. Maybe it'll revitalise *you,* Zig. Because he was due to 'report back' to Gribble again, too soon.

He spent the evening trying to think through the investigation in logical steps, first with Dory Previn on the stereo, then Springsteen, then Mozart. None of them helped. He tried it in silence, with the same result.

Next morning, he couldn't even drive off in logical steps - the thatcher's van was still parked across the country lane amid piles of dead thatch, and next door's roof was still made up of ladders, tarpaulin, and what looked like a heap of twigs. He chicaned past the truck as best he could, making sure the Focus didn't end up scratched like Nina Magnus's, or in a ditch. He headed for Wake Hall.

Now he knew the source of the poison in Lawrence Vann's flask, it was more than logical to double-check what Jake Tuttle, Wake Hall's gardener, had been growing in his expansive domain. Batten found him in the brick-walled vegetable garden, surprisingly warm for so late in the year, and a tribute to green-fingered skills. Jake was bent over, pulling leeks - fresh-smelling, bright-white, near-perfect leeks. There must have been twenty long rows of them, amongst the salad greens and brassicas, the parsnips, spinach-beet and final flush of late-season raspberries. Batten scanned the large plot, surprised that such produce could be successfully grown in what to him was winter. He realised he was envious. His own garden was still bare soil.

Jake was standing now, hands on hips, a 'you again' look on his face. He'd already been put through the mincer by Sergeant Turnip. Ball, was that his name? And now climbing-French-beanpole-Batten was back. Batten? Ball….? They weren't winding him up, were they? Winding him up about cricket, the best sport in the world?

'Aconite? Yeh, I grow aconite. So what? Cuh, I suppose you want to see.'

Batten trailed after Jake whose quick, strong steps led them from the walled garden towards a tree-lined path running between two long lawns. The path joined the driveway to the main house, a dirty-white mass of limestone, sixty yards away. Jake pointed down.

'There,' he said.

Batten could see only grass, beneath bare trees. If this toe-rag's taking the piss….His look must have given him away because Jake deigned to explain.

'It'll come up soon, don't fret. It's winter-flowering. Yellow, looks a bit like buttercup.'

Yellow? Chief Toxic said it was *blue*.

'An' it's poisonous, which means the pesky rabbits won't touch it. Nor the deer.'

Poisonous? Well, well.

'I only plant it 'cos it looks good with snowdrops. Little low clumps of yellow, with the white.' He pointed at the bare trees. 'Grows here in winter, before these come into leaf an' kill the sun.'

Batten couldn't help thinking that more than sun had been killed, not far from here. But, buttercup-yellow? Is this toe-rag being evasive?

'You say it's like buttercup? So you could *mistake* it for buttercup?'

'*You* could. I'm a gardener. Even so, a banana's not the same as a *lemon*, is it?' He said 'lemon' as if Batten *was* one.

The invisible yellow aconite was beginning to get on Batten's wick. He consulted his notes. Jake Tuttle was getting on his wick even more.

'Let's cut to the chase, eh?' He pointed at the empty grass. 'You admit planting Aconitum napellus?'

'What do you mean, *admit*? I grow aconite, so what? *Winter* aconite, as it happens. And since you're collecting plant names, I happen to grow Eranthis hyemalis, not Aconitum napellus. *You're* talking about a different aconite altogether, Monkshood. Plenty of that growing in Somerset. An' it's got blue flowers, your version, not yellow. Flowers in September. About so high.' He held the flat of his hand above his knee.

'*Winter* aconite?'

'Yeh. *Winter* aconite. Watch my lips: Eranthis hyemalis. I don't grow Aconitum napellus, or any other kind of aconite.' Jake turned away. 'If you want me, I'm pulling leeks.'

# Twenty six

Vanilla wafted from the custard-filled Danish pastries, and a rich smell of fresh coffee filled the meeting room. Hick had been to his favourite café again, for another takeaway order. He smiled appreciatively when Magnus thanked him, but not when she called him a domestic goddess. He didn't smile at all when Batten opened the window, and the sweet aromas drifted away.

The toxicology report lay on the table like a dead lettuce. In the photocopied images that Ball distributed, Aconitum napellus seemed a harmless cottage garden plant, till Batten reminded them what it did to Lawrence Vann's face, still staring accusingly down from the centre of the murder board. The fact that Aconite grew in the wild and in local gardens didn't make their task any easier.

Jake's story had been thoroughly double-checked. They would keep at it, but so far he seemed to be just a gardener. That he was in the frame at all reflected the fact that - theoretically - he could have put poison in two innocent thermos flasks. As could a lot of other people. And without the decency to leave a fingerprint behind.

'Before we put these folk through the wringer again,' Batten said, with a hint of threat, 'there will be a short experiment.'

Some of the team returned instantly to their schooldays in the chemistry lab, with accompanying nudges and giggles. Jess Foreman and the older ones waited quietly. Batten picked up two of the takeaway coffee cups and replaced their plastic lids. He put both cups on the window sill, while Ball moved the furniture around.

'This is the farmhouse kitchen at Wake Hall,' Batten said, waving his arms at the rearranged meeting room. 'OK?'

Nods, shrugs. Schoolboy detectives now. He pointed at the window sill. 'The two flasks of soup - where Debbie Farley put them, around seven in the morning on the day in question.'

'Corroborated by Rhona Fiske,' added Ball.

'Now,' said Batten brightly, placing a sachet of sugar in front of each of them, 'the sachets represent phials of aconite, dissolved in brandy. We couldn't run to real brandy.'

Giggles.

'Or real poison.'

Silence.

'Task,' Batten said. Remember 'pin the tail on the donkey'? This is 'put the poison in the soup'. Without leaving prints. And nobody sees you.'

'And you haven't got long,' added Ball, folding his big arms and moving to the back of the room to watch.

They threw themselves into the experiment, had several tries, compared notes and tried again.

While they were comparing theirs, Batten looked back at his - the 'case summary' pages from his last meeting with Gribble. Hardly worth typing them up. Lawrence Vann was an only child with no living relatives, not even the clichéd 'distant cousin in Australia.' He had never married, and if any illegitimate children lurked in the Somerset undergrowth they were invisible. His mobile phone and laptop were missing, presumably stolen from his Wake Hall cottage by persons unknown. He didn't leave a suicide note. He didn't leave a will.

Batten turned the page. Experienced manager....financially astute....good with computers....no external business partnerships, no known overseas connections. His holidays were little more than a fortnight in Cyprus every year....a countryman....a skilled rider. And a bit of a stud, too.

'If you draw a line down the middle of your notebook, zor, and write 'Wake Hall' on the left and 'totty' on the right, you've pretty much got Lawrence Vann in a nutshell.'

Of the most recent 'totty', Karen Sellers was dead - from what seemed an accidental fall from a racehorse. Ann Kennedy was very much alive, with possible cause to do Lawrence harm, but Magnus had checked her story. When Lawrence was ingesting poisoned soup, Ann Kennedy was hanging fancy swags round the entrance to a large marquee, in advance of a posh wedding in Lyme Regis.

If, as Magnus thought, Lawrence was a complex philanderer in search of Ms Right, neither Ms Right, Ms Wrong or Ms Maybe had emerged from the undergrowth. After Debbie Farley, Lawrence had given up on Wake Hall women, and if he was exploring fresh flesh in the world beyond then he'd managed to do it invisibly. His personal phone and laptop might tell a story - if they ever turned up.

Batten couldn't fault his team though. They'd even poked distant relatives and fringe friends of possible vengeful women with a sharp stick, without result. Alibis unshakeable; motives undiscoverable. When PC Lee had felt confident enough to speak, Batten didn't disagree with him.

'If it's a scorned female seeking revenge, sir, then Hickie's just won Best Dressed Man of the Year.'

Wake Hall, the left hand column, seemed to be where the reasons were.

The exercise was becoming noisier; he should have said 'unheard' as well as unseen. But it was good team-building, despite the chaos and the increasing amount of white sparkly sugar on the floor.

'I think we get the point, sir.' Magnus had umph, he'd give her that. 'It's not easy to do - quickly, I mean.'

So they had discovered. Entering undetected; removing two lids; carefully adding two lots of poison; replacing both lids; shaking the containers; putting them back on the window sill; departing unseen.

'Harder to do with gloves on, too, so maybe allow more time for wiping prints off the flasks, sir? You know, stainless steel.'

'It's at least two people, gotta be. You'd need a lookout, even that early in the morning.'

Hick glanced round for his Sergeant's approval, but Ball was nowhere to be seen. Magnus waited in vain for encouragement from Batten. Instead, he thrust two long fingers into his mouth and whistled. In response, Sergeant Ball's unmistakeable ginger head appeared in the yard outside. He gave a snooty smile as he reached into the room through the open window and removed the two 'flasks' from the sill. Instantly he replaced them with an identical set. With a marker-pen, he'd drawn skulls and the word 'Poison' on the second pair. Batten felt his Sergeant should have been more respectful, but the schoolkids found it funny, all the same.

'We know Debbie Farley made a big batch of soup the evening before Lawrence died, and pretty well anyone on the list could have nabbed some, doctored it and poured it into two identical flasks before doing the switch.'

'Don't forget', Ball added, 'she always flings the kitchen windows wide open, every morning, around seven.'

The two empty coffee-cups with their felt-tipped skulls stared knowingly into the room.

'And we shouldn't dismiss those *not* on the list,' said Batten, without conviction. They were still searching for the tractor thief with a penchant for poisoning guard-dogs. How - damn it, Zig, *why* - would a dog-poisoner sneak unseen into Wake Hall and dose a thermos with aconite?

He re-focused.

'You've seen the flasks. Common as muck - you can buy them anywhere, scuff 'em up a bit. And Hickie's right, there'd need to be a lookout so it's at least two people.'

Before Hick could luxuriate in praise from Batten, George Halfpenny chipped in. 'I still don't see how it tells us who was targeted, sir. Vann? Farley? Both?'

It didn't. They'd worked intensively not just on Lawrence Vann. Debbie Farley had been through the mincer too, with similar results. Difficult childhood, but did well enough at school. FE college, a catering qualification, the usual training in diverse kitchens. Been in her current post for four years and no sign of her yearning for pastures new, particularly as Lady Wake loved her cuisine and said so. No dodgy friends or associates. A few blokes of one kind or another, nothing untoward about any of them. Well, apart from Lawrence.

The finger of suspicion stubbornly pointed at Wake Hall Horse. Find crooks, and you find crime. And, if you're lucky, the other way round. Which crooks, though? That Lawrence Vann was murdered because from a high window one dark night he saw *somebody* doing *something* was pretty much all they had. The poison shut him up before he painted pictures for the CID.

'Fair point, George. Best guess is that Lawrence was the target, and the perpetrators weren't about to play poisoned flask roulette with him. Hence both flasks being lethal.'

He couldn't bring himself to use a phrase like 'collateral damage' to describe Debbie Farley. He let them figure it out for themselves. Hick spoke up, emboldened by his moment of praise.

'What about more night-time surveillance, sir, from Mr Vann's window?'

Batten wasn't sure if Hick was just after the overtime. George Halfpenny looked aghast, but Ball had already talked Batten out of it. The evidential grounds for official approval were wafer thin in any case, and if they had a second unofficial try and Wake Hall's owner found out....They would have to come at things differently.

'Let's focus first on your lookout theory, Hickie. If switching the flasks is a two person job, which partners in crime might be contenders?'

Roddy Cope and Neil Tapworthy, the farriers, had already been questioned by George Halfpenny, so Batten had low expectations when he and Hick went to question them again, in the yard in front of Wake Hall Horse. He would have preferred to bring Halfpenny, but he was busy inserting tractor theft stats into spreadsheets for Batten's next meeting with Gribble. In his spare time, George was doing a degree in Business and Finance. He'll either leave the force early, Zig, or stay in and take over from the ACC.

Hick and the two farriers could have been dressed by the same blind fashionista, their colour-clashing ensembles of corduroy trousers and twill shirts perhaps coming from the same charity shop - though Roddy and Neil also sported long leather aprons and reinforced boots. Hick's brown Oxfam jacket didn't look too much out of place, so Batten encouraged him to lead.

'We're just double-checking, gents, won't keep you long from your.....'

Hick twitched his notebook and pen vaguely in the direction of the line of horses tethered to iron rings bolted into the stone wall, and then at the electric furnace glowing in the farriers' van. Batten had moved away from the red heat it gave off; maybe Hick would do the same once he was cooked. Hick still preferred gestures to words, but he was improving.

'I think you told my colleague you started here at....7.30 on November first? That right?'

Two bored nods.

'So did you *arrive* at 7.30? Or maybe a bit before?'

Roddy looked sheepishly at Neil, or the other way round. Batten realised he'd forgotten which was which.

'I was here by twenny past, I suppose,' said Roddy, the older man. 'Neil, though, he sort of likes a bit o' chat-up time, before work, don' you?'

Hick turned to the giant who was Neil. Batten wondered how he could possibly have confused them. Roddy was six foot, but a pygmy next to his young partner.

'And chatting up who exactly, sir?'

Neil shrugged his shoulders, two wardrobes disturbed by an earthquake. Batten wouldn't relish trying to cuff him. But he was handsome. And so were some of the stable girls.

'Just talkin'. Chaattin' up, well, thaat's diff'rent.'

Batten had never heard a voice so slow, so deep.

'Need a bit more'n ten minutes for chaattin' up.' Neil risked a shy smile.

'You were just talking, sir, that's fine. And who would you have been talking *to*?'

Neil shrugged his wardrobes at Hick. Roddy was impatiently tapping what looked like a large pair of pincers against his apron, keen to get back to work. They were only paid by the job, however long it took. Roddy butted in.

'Talkin' or chattin', whichever, it was Allie. You know, from over there.' Roddy waved his pincers in the general direction of the Estate stables, much smaller than Wake Hall Horse, and protected by post and rail fencing rather than a vast stone wall. Neil's head followed the pincers, his face a mixture of pride and embarrassment.

'S'right,' he said slowly. 'Allie. Allie Chaant.'

'At twenty past seven in the morning, sir? Where did this 'chattin' up' take place?'

Neil moved into chivalrous mode.

'Umm. Rather naat say.'

Batten would have hurried things along, but Roddy was of the same mind.

'Come on, Neil. Just show' em. We got work t'do, boy.'

The big farrier nodded, and slowly turned his enormous wardrobes

170

towards the staff cottages. They all followed, but even Batten's long legs struggled to keep up with Neil's giant strides past the long stone wall, then over damp grass that was very well-trodden indeed. He pointed to an unofficial track, just visible through a gap in the tall hedge between Wake Hall Horse and the corner of Allie Chant's little house. Hick got the picture swiftly enough.

'So, are we to assume this was your actual route to work that day, sir? And that you happened to arrive on foot, on this occasion?'

Again Roddy answered for the sensitive giant.

'Well, it's no crime, is it? He stays over sometimes, on the quiet. I started without him, that day. Eight-o-clock before he gets his trousers on.'

'I fell baack to sleep,' admitted Neil. 'Allie'd rushed off. Sh'as breakfast with her lot, 'bout haalf seven. Hope she won' get into no trouble.'

Hick and Batten raised mutual eyebrows: Allie and Neil were each other's alibi - if the truth was being told. If lies, then as a pair they were perfectly placed that day. Checking. More checking.

When Neil lumbered over to fetch a piebald horse that was next in line for chiropody, Batten tackled the older farrier. Both were still suspects, whatever the story.

'You and the big friendly giant seem to bump along together,' he noted.

'Well, we go back a-ways, me and Neil.'

'Back a-ways to where exactly?'

'Oh, well, racetracks, racing stables. S' where we first partnered up.'

Racetracks, Zig? Where Olly Rutter and Manny McCrory partnered up too?

'You'd have come across Olly Rutter, then, sir, at one racetrack or another?'

'Bump into all sorts, at the track. It's places like this now.'

Batten quietly noted Roddy's evasion.

'And you don't mind Neil getting his nookie on the firm's time?'

'It's now and then, Inspector, that's all. I like to work quick anyways, and Neil, he does the heavy stuff that would slow me down. And he keeps McRory off my back.'

An eyebrow travelled north.

'Well, Manny gets a bit....lippy, if there's a backlog. Or if you ask him a question he has no answer for.'

Batten remembered Ball's description of Manny: 'half a shovel of horse-shit and a shovel and half of scorn.'

'I said to him the other day, 'you seen my spare pliers anywhere, Manny, they've gone missing?' 'What do you think I am,' he says, 'a bloody lost property office?' And he can be a bully, when Bulky Hobshaw's there to back him up. Neil just slowly walks over and casts his shadow. Shuts the pair of 'em up. Ev'ry time.'

The thought of anyone shutting up Manny McRory and Bulky Hobshaw revived Batten's spirits, till he remembered the other pairs of suspects still to be questioned. Jake Tuttle and Rhona Fiske needed another look. In theory, either of them - or both together? - could have added strong poison to innocent soup.

And was Baz Ballard really a loner? Did he and a silent accomplice reach in through the window and switch the flasks? If Baz shared horse-box driving duties with Manny, what else did he share? And what of Vito Valdano and Oksana Unpronounceable, who were in the kitchen that morning? Out of the country right now, Zig, thank god. He didn't relish another squat on a Tibetan prayer stool.


Gribble could read a spreadsheet better than most. He grunted as his finger ran down the tabulated pages. George Halfpenny had more than lived up to his reputation, curse him. Gribble flung the report onto his desk where it came to rest against a framed diploma.

'Twenty four percent increase. In less than a *year*?'

*I've only just arrived! It's not my doing!*

'Got to be stopped, Inspector. I doubt even you will disagree?'

*Even* me? Gribble grabbed the report and throttled it.

'This is deliberate targeting, Inspector. Motor homes and high-end tractors.' He flung the spreadsheet down again, gouging it with his finger. '*Someone* is making a killing!'

Batten couldn't disagree. Someone *was* making a killing - and killing guard dogs too. Don't bother telling Gribble that, unlike dogs, your boys and girls only have two legs each. He'll just tell them to run faster.

But Gribble didn't. The Assistant Chief Constable knew they were putting in the hours - and that 'the Jellicoe problem' was not of Batten's making. If only Batten could be a bit more....deferential?

'I can't put any more feet on the streets, Inspector, so you'll have to do some juggling if you want to clear up these thefts.'

*If* I want to?

'But returning to the Lawrence Vann case. In view of the travel patterns of some of our suspects, I've had International Liaison open channels to the Greek police in Corfu. As you're the Investigating Officer, expect a phone-call from....'

He scanned his desk, failing to find the post-it note Mrs Pinch had put there barely an hour ago.

'Damn.'

He hit a button on his intercom, and moments later the crisp form of Mrs Pinch placed a typed-up version on the ACC's desk. Was she the efficient one, not Gribble? On her way out she gave Batten an almost imperceptible smile. He wasn't sure he could cope with a charm offensive from *both* of them.

'Grigoris,' said Gribble, reading from the typed notes. He's a Lieutenant - their equivalent of Inspector. Lieutenant Grigoris, of the Greek International Police Cooperation Division. He's in Corfu right now, but has your contact details. Keep this strictly 'need to know', mind. If Grigoris is chasing European criminals, there'll be confidentialities.'

So behave, eh, Zig?

'Very useful, sir. Thank you.'

And not before bloody time. He'd banged on about Olly Rutter's Mediterranean trips, and the need to suss the *real* reason for Derek Herring's jaunts to Corfu. Vito Valdano and Oksana Thing flitted around in that part of the world too....

'And I'll try to increase your civilian support, at least until....' He couldn't quite bring himself to say 'until you've solved this murder'. It was a strange case - he'd said as much to the media. If only it would disappear. But not like Chief Inspector Jellicoe.

'Much appreciated, sir. The paperwork does build up, as you'll know from your greater experience.'

Goodness, was that deference from Batten?

'And four or five civilian officers should have quite an impact, sir.'
No. It wasn't.

As Batten flung his Gribble-throttled spreadsheet onto his Parminster desk, Ball pulled a glossy brochure from the fresh bonfire of his own. He waved it at Batten, before squeezing, just, into his cubby hole.

'M'not saying this is a breakthrough, zor, but…?'

When someone's murdered, nobody tells the postman. Lawrence Vann's mail arrived regardless, and was forwarded to Ball for checking. It was dull stuff. Cattle-feed additives, machinery repair agreements, livestock control - how much bumph does a dead body need?

'I see it, Ballie - he *wanted* this one.'

Lawrence Vann received unsolicited brochures from every firm, consultant or chancer under the sun. But the accompanying letter Ball had spotted - 'thank you for your interest in' and 'we enclose our *Living Overseas* information pack, as requested' - caught Batten's eye too. As did the financial implications. He whistled when he opened the Cyprus real estate brochure - their 'Prestige Collection'.

'The *cheapest* villa's pushing half a million euros. What's that in pounds?'

Ball pummelled a calculator.

'Four hundred grand, zor, plus a lot.' He whistled too, with envy.

'Has George finished the bank search yet?'

Ball showed him. Lawrence Vann had a hundred grand in ISAs, bonds and cash, and an expensive pension plan offering £30,000 a year at age sixty five. Nice, but hardly a fortune.

'He could've just been dreaming, zor? You know, 'when I win the Lottery'?'

Neither believed it. If Lawrence wanted something, he got his hands on it.

'Was he planning to quit, do you think? The villa-with-pool in Cyprus? Ride his big white horse on a Mediterranean beach?' And alone, Zig - or in female company?

'Well, he *was* sixty, zor. Couldn't work forever.'

He couldn't. But with a pension plan kicking in at sixty *five*, there's still five years' cash to find. And as for the four hundred grand…?

'Put Halfpenny back on this, Ballie.' And sod the farm thefts. 'We've got to track Lawrence's money.'

'I'll break the news to George, zor. He'll be thrilled.'

# Twenty Seven

'You *have* locked the bloody door this time?'

Manny wanted to remind Olly that he'd locked the bloody door *last* time, but he knew what he'd get if he tried. Smarmy Derek Herring had already flashed a warning smirk. Olly got worse, no matter how much of his shit you shovelled. Today he was antsy in case Lady Half-Awake should 'drop by', find him up to his tricks again. What makes you think he ever *stopped*, you stupid cow?

'It's double-locked, Olly, yeh. No-one's getting in, I double-che-'

'Bring the bloody thing to life then, Mish,' Olly told his tame IT 'consultant'.

Mishimaro Tuji disliked his nickname, but he too knew what he'd get if he said so. At least Olly had stopped calling him 'Mush'. He booted up the shiny laptop, liberated from the desk in Lawrence Vann's cottage. Lawrence's i-phone was nowhere to be found, and Olly's missing memory stick had still not floated to the surface despite a covert search that would have impressed an archaeologist. Tuji prayed Lawrence's laptop held *some* kind of trace - they'd gutted everything else. Doubt was creeping in though. Lawrence was quietly going up in Tuji's estimations, Olly loudly coming down.

While resenting the racist cliché of Oriental inscrutability, Tuji nevertheless hid behind a blank face. He disliked being locked within this creepy Wake Hall office, with those freakish paintings of over-muscled horses staring down at him. The experience was disturbing; whispers and coded glances; snappy commands; snide comments; Olly's ridiculous throne of a chair looking like an oversized commode. Who was more intimidating, Rutter or Herring? Some days, McCrory was nastier than the pair of them. Tuji had never quite worked out the role of the room's other occupant....

'You trying for overtime, Mish, or what?'

'Almost there, Mr Rutter.'

'Almost there? You've had the bloody thing for *ever*!'

Tuji could have pointed out that all the freelance days - and nights -

Olly paid him for, had been spent hacking into every digital device Lawrence had access to. A man could go blind. How long did Olly think it took to crack Lawrence's passwords? Tuji blamed the technology.

'It's a surprisingly inferior machine, Mr Rutter. A somewhat indolent laptop.'

Olly had never got used to Tuji, to the clash between his Japanese features and his Oxford English.

'Made in Taiwan, was it?'

Made in ignorant England, like you, he would have liked to reply, had Olly been a seven stone weakling, and not paid so very well for his silence.

'Dual-processor, 250 gigabyte hard drive, but strangely low on RAM....ah, here we are.'

The five men gathered round the screen, grudgingly admiring the speed and accuracy of Tuji's fingers as they caressed the silver keys. Page after page of sub-screen code appeared and disappeared, flashes of data from the laptop's viscera blinked to the surface before being as quickly rejected. Tuji was an expert where a computer's intestines were concerned.

'I bet it's down to that oriental thing, where they slice open their insides,' Olly had told Derek Herring. 'He's good at guts, is Mish.'

Good or not, Tuji's evisceration failed to find what was never there, because all that was there was nothing. He gulped as he told Olly the news: if Lawrence Vann had downloaded a memory stick - of any kind - it wasn't on this machine.

Neither Tuji nor the four men looking over his shoulder would ever track down the laptop that *had*, because it was a disfigured, molten lump at the bottom of the Wake Hall furnace. Lawrence himself had put it there, shortly after using it to transfer an eye-watering sum of laundered money from Olly's stockpile to a well-hidden pair of secret accounts. He'd planned to melt down his beloved i-phone at the same time, for safety's sake, but couldn't bear to part with it.

'What do mean, there's *nothing*? Nothing's bloody USELESS to me! There's got to be *something!*'

'We may have to make plans accordingly, Olly,' coaxed Derek Herring, unaware of the real reason for Olly's wrath and trying his best to focus it onto adversaries rather than assistants. 'Our Mr Vann is an extremely clever thief, it would seem.'

Yeh, so clever that the old shagger's dead, Olly thought. Thrusting his over-cologned chin at Tuji's face, he hissed, 'Find. me. *something!*'

A perspiring Tuji searched the laptop's craw, scrolling through one likely document after another, looking for documents concealed within documents, for scraps and fragments hidden away for later re-compilation, for *something*. But Mishimaro Tuji failed. The hard disc had barely been used. He began to suspect Lawrence didn't *care* what they found. The most recent documents were domestic or trivial. A blank income tax form gave him hope - but blank it remained. No rogue data. Nothing.

At last, he found *something*, though its relevance defeated him. He turned the screen towards Olly. Was this Lawrence's first mistake?

'This is the last thing Mr Vann downloaded, from a digital camera -'

'A *camera*? The old shagger *photographed* my data? Bloody downloaded it onto -'

'We liberated his camera, Mr Rutter, and while it was definitely the source of the image here on the screen, that camera - I assure you - has never come into contact with a single pixel of your private information.'

'*What*? So all you've found is holiday snaps? IS THAT *IT*?'

Not quite. Tuji hit 'full screen'. As the picture expanded, so did the silence. Whenever Olly raised his voice you shut your mouth and hid in a trench. But silence was also a fitting reaction to the full-colour image that stared up from the laptop. Herring and McCrory gazed at its nudity with such facefuls of fascination that Olly clambered down from the heights of his tantrum to peer at it himself. A coyly smirking couple giggled out from the photograph, their naked lower halves scarcely covered by an unfolded Ordnance Survey map of the Somerset Levels. Their upper halves, by contrast, were wholly *un*covered, as naked as the day they were born. The male was Lawrence Vann; his female companion was -

'Good *god!*' said the fifth man, hand rising to his lips in embarrassment. 'That *can't* be -' he took an apprehensive step towards the screen.

'Don't tell me you *know* this titted totty?' asked Olly. 'Bit old for *you*, Vito - with the added downer that she's *female!*'

Vito Valdano ignored the homophobic jibe - he'd had far worse from

178

Olly - and stared harder. Instantly, fear swamped him. The naked woman in the photograph - there was now no doubt - was exactly who he thought it was.

'I'm afraid I do know her, Olly. Er, know *of* her, I should say. Her name is Stephanie Broke-Mondelle, and she….she has attended one or two of my programmes. Here, at Wake Hall.' Vito Valdano waved a rainbowed arm at space beyond the braying, horse-hung walls. 'Stephanie. Yes. That's, um, how I know her.'

He edged instinctively towards the door. When Olly discovered the far more significant reason why Vito knew Stephanie Broke-Mondelle… Colour bled from his cheeks. If he stayed in the office much longer, it might very well bleed from his suit.

As Vito went white, Olly turned red, his stone fist slamming so hard into the solid oak desktop that it visibly bowed.

'If that old shagger's bunged my memory stick to miss titty here,' he yelled, 'she'll need to have it surgically removed from her *arsehole!*'

He flung his hefty body at the office door, only to find it was double-locked. Olly glared back into the room, at the four perspiring men who had physically shrunk. A furious finger jabbed at each one in turn, then at the naked image on the screen, as he hissed a final command: 'Don't just flop there like cow-crap! *FIND THE BITCH!*'


What *is* up there, he asked himself? Ham Hill permeated his morning view each time he opened the curtains: its long bulk; the remains of its iron-age defences which had failed to repel a Roman onslaught two thousand years ago; its dignified stone needle, a memorial to those who fell in more recent wars, aiming now at the sky from the hill's highest point.

Hell's teeth, Zig, if the Romans have been up Ham Hill then why haven't you? Because, Zig, in sympathy for the dead, murder has a habit of delaying things. And I've gone off hills. He frowned at a mound of unwashed washing on the kitchen floor. Stick a twig in the top and you've got a scale model of bloody *Burrow* Hill itself!

Beyond the kitchen window, patches of weed-cleared ground in his 'garden' cried out for attention. Barely used fishing gear slumped forlornly against the wall of the lean-to. As for the contents of the fridge, he'd eaten the last of them for breakfast in the form of a thin omelette filled with a barely edible mixture of leftover goo. Perhaps a walk on Ham Hill would prepare him for the hated supermarket trolley-dash. Or postpone it. He pulled on his hiking boots.

And was pleased he did, not because of the terrain or the weather - dry and clear - but because of the grandness of the hilltop view. A passing dog-walker told her companion 'that's Stoke-sub-Hamdon, down there. That's Martock, and over that way's South Petherton, the one with the octagonalalian church-tower.' For non-locals, a metal plaque, mounted on a sturdy waist-high rock at the hill's peak, identified the names of places far and near, the ranges of distant hills, and beyond them the faint purple crown of what the plaque said was Exmoor.

He stared at the far distance and breathed in. It was good air and a little of life's normality returned to his lungs and heart.

'Oh, Inspector,' she said. 'I would have thought you'd seen enough of Burrow Hill by now?'

He stared back at her, in double confusion. They were both out of their professional zones, with no other point of contact to draw on. But here she was, nevertheless, offering a rogue conversation. Awkward, Zig. She's a witness, at the very least. Ideally, he would have liked to walk away.

Also, she must be deranged. *Burrow* Hill? Even incomers like him knew the difference between blobby Burrow Hill and *Ham* Hill, the vast ramparted fort on which his feet and hers currently shuffled.

'*Burrow* Hill?' he said. Surely you mea -'

'No, no, there,' she said, an unringed finger flicking out to point at the plaque. She delicately traced her finger along a thin track engraved in the metal. 'Burrow Hill, 5 miles' it said, next to a line pointing vaguely west. He ran his own finger down the arrow then up and out into space, squinting uselessly along it into the distance.

'I can't find it,' he said. Thank Christ.

'Over there. See?' She took his finger softly in her hand, surprising him, and guided it across the horizon. Yes, a near-distance mound capped by a single, distinctive tree came into view, lower down the valley than he'd imagined.

'Ah,' he said. 'Yes, I see it.' His finger was still trapped between hers. Gawkily, he withdrew, ending the awkward physical contact between policeman and witness. In the clumsy silence, normality dripped away.

'Are you on surveillance duties, Inspector? Checking out the scene of the….oh dear.'

They both looked westward, masking their discomfort.

'Well, you're certainly incognito,' she said, pointing to his boots and waterproof, older and considerably less expensive than her pale purple matching set, he noted.

'Believe it or not, I'm just walking.' He almost said 'and breathing' but in this unsought context it would have sounded absurd.

'Well, that's two of us. Today's the first chance I've had to walk anywhere since….'

Batten nodded silently. Speech could sometimes be a kind of cement, stiffening walls of recall when you'd prefer them to crumble away. As if sensing this she made to go, whether to leave him to his thoughts or to invite him to follow, he was unsure. Unsure, Zig? Aren't you supposed to be a detective?

In the end they both spoke at once.

'Ms Fiske -'

'I was just -'

'Please, you first,' he said.

'I was only going to say I'm popping into *The Prince of Wales* for a late lunch. And I've walked off enough calories to warrant a glass of wine, I think. And it's Rhona, by the way.'

Rhona? Rhona, my arse. Not with those eyes. You're Mona. Mona Lisa. But my name's Zig, and I've no alternative.

'Er, Zig.' He shrugged, as if a slightly foreign name needed an apology. Well, it often did, he'd found.

'Ah, is that Polish?'

He was uncomfortable being interrogated; he preferred to be on the other side of the table. 'On the day in question, Ms Fiske, was your presence on Ham Hill purely coincidental?' Or what?

'Kind of Polish,' he said. 'Kind of complicated.'

It was her turn to nod.

'Did you say *The Prince of Wales*?' he asked.

'I did. Just over there.' Her finger pointed beyond bare trees and stone.

'I had no idea there *was* a pub on Ham Hill.'

'It's excellent. Very friendly to walkers. And dogs. You can even buy dog biscuits at the bar.'

'Never acquired a taste, myself.'

Rhona Fiske smiled politely, and sauntered a toe-dangling pace or two towards the pub. Batten paused, undecided, till the thin omelette he'd had for breakfast became his excuse. A good lunch, that's all. Lunch. Without interrogation.

Ball envied Batten his weekend off, not that he hadn't earned it. Even then, the Saturday interview schedule had been pretty much steered by the Inspector.

'If I recall, Baz Ballard doesn't like uniforms - he has to wear one all day. He looks like an over-muscled butcher at the best of times, but when he puts on that chauffer suit, cuh.'

They had agreed: take PC Lee along, and have him stand there in his dark blue, with his silver buttons, and a notebook in his hand - and maybe his radio crackling, in that unsettling way? In the confines of a Wake Hall garage, it seemed to work, not least when Baz was asked about his horse-box driving duties with Manny McRory.

'I just do what Mr Rutter says. Manny sometimes needs a driver. And I'm a driver. Rocket science.'

Baz grinned at his own joke, while polishing the same chrome strip on the flashy Jag three times in a row. He'll be through to bare metal soon, Ball noted, before pretending to forget Baz's cloudy alibi for the day Lawrence Vann was killed.

'If Mr Rutter was off in Spain, and didn't invite *you*, well, you'd have been here, at Wake Hall, yes?'

Baz paused for a moment. They already knew where he'd been on the day Lawrence died, but these two could whistle in stereo for the full story.

'Drove to Cardiff, early doors.'

He could do early, when it wasn't work. And the only non-work time he seemed to get was when Olly was abroad. He couldn't remember the last time he'd had a fortnight's holiday, not that he had anywhere to go.

'Early, zor?'

'You know, 'bout seven. Miss the traffic.'

'Alone, were you, zor?'

'Just me.'

Ball knew the Jag's number plate had been logged as it went through the Severn Bridge toll. Baz knew it too.

'Cardiff, zor. Now, any particular reason why Cardiff?'

'Yep.'

You dumb clot, Ballie. Ask open questions. You're supposed to be showing young Lee how it's done.

'So, why exactly Cardiff, zor, on that particular day? For what purpose?'

As soon as Baz hesitated, he saw Ball cock an eyebrow, the way cops do. Even the young cop with the crackly radio noticed. Whatever he said, they'd have a smirk. He spat it out.

'I make model planes. Scale-models. Accurate.'

Ball was staring at this butcher-chauffer's squashed banana fingers, couldn't stop himself. Incredulity would have been written all over his face, if he'd been able to spell it.

'I can show you, if you like…?' Baz waved chrome cleaner in the direction of his Wake Hall rooms.

'All in good time, zor. But now, model planes? And Cardiff? How exactly do they fit together?'

'Big specialist supplier, in Cardiff. I'm running low on supplies. If you want receipts…?'

They did.

'And back by what time, zor?'

No point in lying, with cameras on the bridge.

'Six? Half-past? 'Bout that.'

'That seems a long time to just buy your….model plane supplies, sir, wouldn't you say?'

'Well. Good breakfast when I got there. My supplies. Late lunch in a pub. Nice walk round, cuppa tea, I like Cardiff. It's my day out. When the cat's away.' He shouldn't have said that, about the cat.

Ball and Lee trailed after the weight-lifting driver-cum-car-valet to his Wake Hall rooms where Ball was intrigued - and Lee gobsmacked - by a ceiling hung with impressively-fashioned models, perhaps twenty or more, some of them over three feet long. All of them were…..beautiful, painstakingly hand-painted, the product of considerable skill and delicacy. Ball recognised Sir Francis Chichester's *Gypsy Moth* amongst them, because at school he'd had a fight with a bully who said *Gypsy Moth* wasn't a plane, it was a boat, and nothing else. He didn't share this with Baz, whose receipts supported his alibi. They would check again.

Baz had a quiet smile as they left. Everything he'd told them was true, so they could check till the cows came home. But he hadn't told them everything. That he'd made an additional stop, at the Cardiff bank which held his safe-deposit box. That for only the second time, he'd used his little silver key to open it. That he'd enjoyed running his hands over the packs of ready cash. *His* cash now. Just a dry run, a practice go, so he'd be ready once Lawrence had trussed up Olly for the police.

The smile faded. He trudged back to the garage, polished the over-polished chrome on Olly Rutter's Jag.


Rhona Fiske was right about *The Prince of Wales* being dog-friendly, its walls hung with sketches and prints of one breed after another, and its flagstone floor draped with sleeping dogs. She was right about the food too. He was savouring an onion chutney even better than Aunt Daze's home-made version, and it went perfectly with the generous slices of honey-roast ham.

She picked like a bird at her salad, he noticed, then proceeded to tell him the story of her life, even though he hadn't asked, and hadn't intended to. Ged's remembered voice told Batten that 'folk 'fess up to you, Zig. You've got one of those faces. Ever thought about becoming an agony aunt?'

'And it's not so very long ago I was an Events Organiser, and doing rather well. Interesting work, nice flat, holidays. Men. Then, oh-lucky-lucky, mum developed Alzheimer's. There's only me and her. Well, only me now.'

She sipped at her glass of Sauvignon. He'd almost ordered a large glass of Merlot, but….

'I was being nursemaid, *and* trying to work full-time. 'Organising

184

events' - how ironical. I struggled on, but I was being called away more and more, by the neighbours mostly. At least she had kind neighbours. And more than once by your illustrious colleagues.'

'*My* colleagues?'

'By the police. Oh, for all sorts of things. Forgetting where she lived, for one. She'd go shopping, toddle home to the wrong house, try to put her key in the lock. It wouldn't open, naturally, so she'd bang on the door, shout 'Rhona! *Rhona!* Let me in!' She was a spirited woman, mum.'

He could imagine.

'There'd be a confrontation, of course. Hence the police.'

Batten had been there, as a young beat cop. Social workers with sirens, that's all we are, his oppo had said.

'In the end I sold my flat and went to live at mum's. Dad paid off the mortgage years ago, apparently. Trusting daughter - and gullible idiot. Hardly been there a week when a bailiff turned up with a final warning. She'd binned all the previous warnings - binned most of the mail, in fact. Not just the bills, but the offers of help and support. And she *never* answered the phone or the doorbell. The equity from my flat-sale paid off her arrears so we didn't end up on the street. What money remained kept us honest for a year. I couldn't go out to work, you see - or anywhere else. Holidays, men, everything stopped.'

He wondered if it had started again.

'Coincidence, of course, but she died just as the money ran out. It felt like spite. Oh dear, I'm gabbling.'

'No, no,' he said automatically. But she was.

'I didn't mourn as much as I should have done. Grief. Anger. They're bedfellows, aren't they?'

He nodded, meaning it this time. He knew a good deal about grief and anger.

'So, Inspector: a grieving, angry, broke, unemployed Events Organiser. Quite a catch.'

She'd called him 'Inspector', and he felt relieved. It was awkward, a first names conversation, when they were never likely to be on first name terms, were they?

'At the interview - for Wake Hall - I talked about my under-pressure achievements of the previous two years. It was a very long list.'

Batten suddenly remembered he had to do the supermarket. He tried not to look at his watch.

'Well, they were impressed with my dedication so, unfortunately, they gave me the job.'

'Unfortunately? I don't see ho -'

'And I didn't. At first. The misfortune was arriving at Wake Hall just as the economic recession plonked its muddy boots on the carpet. Head Housekeeper used to mean what it says on the tin. Now, it's an open-ended role - with a finite salary, mind - and a mountain of unpaid overtime.'

He thought of all the unpaid overtime he had worked. How many hours by now? And who gets the money?

'But at least your house is part of the deal?'

Batten remembered Rhona Fiske's neat hamstone cottage, arranged as she wanted it, he imagined, in comforting colours with rugs and prized possessions. It had an old inglenook fireplace, like his.

'Well, yes, it is a perk. And given the salaries at Wake Hall, it ought to be! It's not a huge place, even as cottages go, but when I saw it, I thought 'I can start my life again from here.' I don't know if I should call it 'home' because I don't own it, and frankly, I'm not sure where home is supposed to be anymore.'

He thought about quoting Robert Frost to her, but she didn't seem a poetry person. He quoted to himself instead: "home is where, when you go there, they have to take you in.' It always made him think of Aunt Daze.

'Well, it *is* a pleasant cottage,' he said, thinking that his would be too, if he ever found time to work on it. And Lawrence Vann's cottage was the nicest of the three, much good it did him. Lawrence's kitchen, with its high fanlight window overlooking Wake Hall Horse, flashed into his thoughts. A policeman's life, Zig. Can't leave your cop-brain in the locker, can you? Can't just have lunch in a pub with a....

'You're very good at your job, Inspector. Somehow you've persuaded me to stray beyond my professional restraint and here I am gabbling Wake Hall gossip like a stablegirl.'

'It's me who's strayed. Should steer my mind *away* from the job more often.'

She smoothed her napkin on the tabletop, folding it with precision into a perfect oblong. Even though it was paper, disposable. Habits get inside us all, Zig.

'When you were asking me before, Inspector, about Lawrence....'

Rather than 'fessing up', unasked, she seemed now to need his permission to continue. He gave one of his shrugs, the softer one.

'Perhaps I didn't paint a complete picture. When things were becoming a little....when the recession grew worse I mean, he did us all a favour, all the Wake Hall staff. No chance of a pay rise, but he spoke to Lady Wake on our behalf - he can be very persuasive when it suits - suited him. We get a mid-week half-day off now, all Lawrence's doing. We still put in plenty of hours, but I'm happier working five and a half days instead of six, believe me.'

Batten flipped further into cop mode.

'So Lawrence would have worked weekends?' Hick and Halfpenny's curtailed surveillance had only taken place midweek. Weekends might suit Olly better....

'Weekends? We *all* work weekends, Inspector. The Hall would grind to a standstill if we didn't. It's when many of our Residentials take place. We're supposed to work one weekend in two, but events don't run to such a steady rhythm.'

Rhona Fiske looked ruefully out of the window. Daylight was deserting the early winter sky.

'Do you know,' she said, 'this is my first weekend off in a month?'

So why are you sitting here with me, talking about a murdered colleague?

'I don't suppose I'll recoup my lost days,' she said. 'They just go, don't they?'

He sneaked a glance at his watch when she looked away. This day's nearly gone - and the supermarket still to do. He re-adjusted the tickly wicker chair, scraping its legs loudly on the flagstones. Rhona Fiske ignored the sound, still searching for something invisible through the tree-framed window. With a familiar touch of ambivalence, he stayed in his seat.

# Twenty Eight

Batten's weekend of washing and supermarket shopping seemed a thousand years ago, but at least he'd spent part of it in female company.

Now, the company was once more male, and ginger. He reached for the thermos flask, wondering if he'd ever look at one in the same way again. At least this one held coffee, not parsnip soup and poison. He topped up Sergeant Ball's mug before pouring one for himself. It was strong and very hot, exactly what was needed to keep sleep at arms length and compensate for the damp chill of the Somerset Levels. At three-o-clock in the morning.

'What do you think, Ballie? Someone sold us a pup?'

Ball sipped hot caffeine before yawning, lion-like.

'It's still early, zor. For thieves, I mean.'

Early? They'd been there since before midnight. A few ghostly sheep had baa'd past the muddied Ford Focus, and that was all. Ball pointed at the sky and mumbled 'tawny owl', but Batten only saw a brief shadow against the blackness. He'd never been to Muchelney before, wondered what it looked like in daylight.

'You know this village?'

'Oh yes, zor. A long history. Last year, mind, it was neck-high in flood water.'

Batten knew; he'd seen the pictures. They were parked in the dip of a small track way, hidden by a hedge, with just enough of a gap to see the Dutch barn and its shiny John Deere tractor. He'd never liked stakeouts - particularly ones that the still-absent Chief Inspector Jellicoe ought to be supervising - nor 'acting on information received'. Cold, wasted hours, and no warm bed. But they needed to catch the man who poisoned guard dogs, maybe people too. *Any* kind of arrest would please Gribble.

'Murder is rare, Inspector. Theft is common. If we can't catch a killer, let's catch thieves. Yes?'

Or catch a cold. But Jess Foreman had said his information was reliable, and since that was how Batten viewed Jess Foreman, here they were. Waiting.

He peered through the gap in the hedge, but couldn't spot the rest of the team, some hidden in sheds, the rest parked and ready in unmarked cars.

'How've you managed to keep Hickie still for this long?'

'Put him in with Magnus, zor. I think he's a bit in awe.'

'It better not be love.' You hypocritical sod, Zig.

'Ooh, no, no, zor. She'd eat him for breakfast and spit the bones. He's never worked with a, you know, a black female officer before. Behaving himself, is Hickie.'

Ball might have added 'unlike George', but his muted phone vibrated in his hand. The approaching vehicle, deep-blue, black maybe, glided like a ghost down the dark lane. Its engine made barely a whisper. Batten gazed in bemusement, then slapped himself on the forehead.

'That's why we haven't caught them, Ballie,' he hissed. 'Bloody electric car!'

In hold-your-breath mode, they watched two balaclava-clad figures noiselessly emerge. The taller one made short shrift of the locked cab; the shorter one hooked a tow line onto the brand-new tractor. Experienced, the pair of them.

'They'll not pull that thing far on battery power, zor, if they pull it at all.'

'They only need to nudge it down the lane, Ballie, out of sight and sound. Bet you a gallon of cider they've got a diesel truck waiting, clever sods.'

Slowly, the tractor crept forward. Batten watched the ghostly ballet, a silent electric car moving in an eerily straight line, pursued - but never caught - by a giant silent tractor, creeping along against a backdrop of dark trees and sky.

Then, at a signal from Ball the stage lights flashed on, the roads were blocked and the silence erased by loud '*Police!*' warnings. Batten saw the two balaclavas fling themselves at the darkness, saw the big frame of Jess Foreman envelop the tall balaclava in a huge bear-hug and dump it, in one brute yet flowing movement, onto the hard ground. The smaller figure ran like a hare into undergrowth, with police in pursuit. Ball was out of the car in a blink but had made barely thirty yards before he saw, then heard, the second thief painfully returning, arms wrenched backwards almost to breaking point, firmly gripped - to Ball's amazement - by the small clamps of no less than PC Lee.

'Well done, Jon,' Ball said. Lee looked pleased with himself.

Batten was smiling too. At last, something positive to tell the Assistant Chief Constable (Crime). And screw *you*, Fat Jellicoe.

To Batten's surprise, Somerset woke to snow. Not the dirty snow of slushy urban roads but a pure, deep, undulating whiteness. It excited the voice that crackled from Batten's radio. Snow news was *new* news. After gleefully reading out a list of road closures, school closures, airport closures, the voice began to wonder 'are we in for a white Christmas? Give us your view, folks! Contact me on....' The news voice had conveniently forgotten what the weather voice had said barely two minutes before, that the snow would soon give way to 'unseasonably balmy weather for December.' Might get to go fishing, Zig, with a bit of luck.

He switched the radio off and put the coffee on. Beyond the window the snow was a veil, hiding the ground he'd failed to cover, the evidence still unearthed. It's varnishing the scene of crime with a brilliance *you* haven't shown, Zig. Papering over your cracks.

He'd tried to *open* a crack or two where Manny McRory was concerned, shamelessly taking Magnus when he questioned him again, hoping the racism scrawled all over McRory would shake his control. Batten sipped his coffee - a bit too strong, even for him - and stared at the white snow. The ploy hadn't worked - Manny just leaned against the wall of his shed-cum-office and sniffed theatrically, as if Nina Magnus was an invisible bad smell.

'I felt like thumping him on your behalf,' Batten had admitted.

Magnus had a thick skin; didn't have much choice. To her, McRory seemed neither worse nor better than George Halfpenny. She could forgive George his choice of after-shave, but not the way he side-stepped his own intelligence for a mindless hatred of a skin colour different from his own. McRory and George were similar in another way, too. They were both sneaks. McRory had a snide answer, an excuse for everything. George spat insults in her face only when no-one was there to hear.

'Mind if I open a window, George?' His cologne had seemed even stronger that day.

'Not if you jump out of it, climb back on the boat.'

'You'd like that, would you? If I sailed away?'

'One less.'

'One less what, George?'

He just glared at her, eyes fixed in a look she'd seen many times before: inexplicable hate. His eyes are almost black, she said to herself. Perhaps it's my reflection.

Because of the snow, the perpetual blockage of the thatcher's van was missing today, and Batten drove off in a more relaxed state than was justified. Gribble had been overjoyed at the arrest of two tractor thieves during the well-planned stakeout near Muchelney. Something positive to tell the media, who would relish reporting that the pair were in fact husband and wife. Would they be able to resist a 'partners-in-crime' story? No mention would be made of the silent, electric car, though - why give crook-world fresh ideas?

Alas, there'd be no mention of guard-dog-killing poison either, because not a tiny trace of poison had turned up, despite ultra-careful searches of all premises used by the partners-in-crime and a series of sharp interrogations that *just* stayed within the code of practice.

Worse, crook-world carried on. Another motor home disappeared from Hinton St George, a few miles down the road, the following night. Two steps forward, three steps back.

Where Manny McRory was concerned, he and Magnus hadn't gone *one* step forward. Manny had been....canny.

'Weekends? 'Ey, Bulky, they wanna know if we work weekends!'

Bulky Hobshaw did as his name suggested - stood there, denying space to others. 'Weekends,' he spat, a short sentence kind of bloke.

'*Course* we work weekends, In*spec*tor! Don't you? Try shipping horses to a Surrey stockbroker on a Tuesday morning, yeh? Or a banker in Aberdeen on a Thursday afternoon. Where they gonna be, Bulky?'

'Not in,' Bulky said.

'That's right! They're at work!'

He pronounced it 'wairk'. Batten ordinarily loved the sound of scouse, but not from a mouth like Manny's.

'*They* might be nine to five, but we're not. Three-o-clock in the morning sometimes, us. That right, Bulky?'

Bulky shrugged. Resting his voice.

'So, you conveniently deliver their horses at weekends by turning up at three-o-clock in the morning?' He was trying to wind them up.

Manny shook his head pityingly, and used his adult-explaining-to-child voice.

'Sometimes, Inspector, we *leave* here early in the morning - or is it late at night, take your pick?'

'Night,' said Bulky, giving Magnus a gawp. 'In the *dark.*'

'We have to cover the distance, yeh?' Manny pointed vaguely at either Surrey or Aberdeen. 'Got to rest the nags, *and* arrive at a convenient time of day for the punter, yeh? Even you can see that?'

'We value *our* punters,' said Bulky, his big chest puffing out in proportion to the longer sentence.

Batten had wanted to knuckle the pair of them, on his own account now. Just as well it was winter; he could legitimately keep his clenched fist in his pocket.

In spite of snow and bad Manny-memories, he drove into the Visitors' car park at Wake Hall. Once in the welcome warmth of Debbie Farley's little cottage, he explained that her 'discreet police protection' was to be removed. She'd never understood why it had been necessary in the first place, and still had no idea, sorry, where Lawrence's laptop and i-phone were. Secrets? She didn't know he *had* any. Her sigh made the jasmine-scented candle flicker in its glass globe.

'I'll tell you what I am, Inspector. I'm a cook. A good cook, and that's all. I'm no wiser now why someone should want to poison me, than I was when....'

She shuffled menu sheets on the dining table that served as a desk, its liberty-print tablecloth covered in recipe books.

'So there's nothing you've remembered? Nothing's come to mind?'

'Oh, I wake up in the middle of the night with things coming to mind, horrible things, but not the things *you* mean.'

He could imagine. He'd been knocked unconscious by a drunk once, on the Saturday night punch-up patrol. He was out for a minute or two, and shoved into an ambulance. As the sirens whooped and the tyre noise, speed, laddering lights and swaying stretcher all merged into one white wall, he assumed he was dead. The memory was still there. And he was only punched. If someone had deliberately tried to poison him....

'But you will ring me, if anything....you know?'

She had his card, had Magnus's number too, and the usual support links. ACC Gribble thought the safest place for Debbie Farley was Wake Hall, and he had a point. Lady Wake valued her skilful cook, and if that wasn't protection enough, Debbie was surrounded by people all day, in busy kitchens and conference suites. At night she could lock her cottage door in the knowledge that she was two bricks away from colleagues either side. Batten hoped his wasn't too jaundiced a thought: if she's attacked at Wake Hall, it won't take long to narrow down the candidates.

'If you leave the Hall, though, you must let us know. You do understand that?'

She didn't really, but agreed. As Batten got up, she handed him a large biscuit tin.

'I don't want you to think I'm not grateful for all the, you know. These are freshly-baked, this morning. I was going to do chocolate brownies, but then it snowed.'

She smiled at his puzzled expression, her face illuminated now in the candle-light.

'Oh, you see, they're Welsh cakes, in the tin. They're supposed to taste better with a pinch of snow. Old wives tale, I expect, but I believe in such things.'

Better than parsnip soup with a pinch of poison. But he wasn't going to remind Debbie Farley of that. Happily, for the first time in a while, her complexion was less pale than the snow that had banked up against the herbs stubbornly growing in terracotta pots by the cottage door. He thanked her for the cakes.

In the car, he tried one. Share them please, she'd said, but with a single bite he was tempted to keep the whole lot for himself.


'What's your favourite machine, then, Dave?'

Tom Bowditch fluffed a hand through his thinning hair. He didn't care about premature baldness today. Life was good. He wouldn't make idle conversation with Dipstick Dave if it wasn't. But he'd done the sums after they'd nicked the motor-home, near Hinton St George, and he was close now to his £200,000 target, the target he hadn't mentioned to Dave. No chance of getting closer in the next few days, with the ground covered in snow. He warmed his feet on the electric heater. The old barn was a perfect base if they were active, but cold as a witch's tit when you had to pass the time talking to Dave the dork.

'I mean, all these machines, what's the best?'

Dipstick Dave didn't do idle chat either. But Tom was young; he made allowances.

'Kettle,' he said. 'Kettle best machine.' He switched it on, to prove it.

Tom shook his head. Liking Dave would be like liking piles. Two more jobs and that would be the end of it. Any jobs at all, except quad bikes - he'd told Dave no more of those. Not enough profit, given the risk.

And risk there was. Tom showed Dave the evening paper, 'Partners In Crime', splashed across the front page. 'Husband and wife tractor thieves arrested in police raid,' it said.

'Thieves *do* get caught, Dave. See?'

'No job for woman, Tom. Talk too much. I bet she wake farmer. *We* not get caught.'

No, we won't, thought Tom, because I don't take risks. And because nobody hears us. He finished oiling the rear wheel of his mountain bike, flicked it, saw the spokes spin and merge, soundlessly. The snow wouldn't last, the weatherman said, and then they'd be out once more, at night, bike silently rolling down tracks and lanes towards whichever machine had been targeted. If there *was* a dog, he'd retreat and send in Dave with his poison.

Then Tom would be in the cab in a trice before attaching the tow-rope. Chains and cables made too much noise. He'd give Dave his due; the diesel truck was a credit to his mechanic's skill - extra sound-proofing and a whisper-sweet engine. And you could barely hear the winch. Silently stealing a tractor was a breeze if all your bare metal was rubber-tipped, and you were liberal with the grease-gun. Grease, him and Dipstick Dave.

And Dave had made another of his phone calls, hadn't he? The cops had disappeared from Wake Hall, vamoosed.

'Now, Tom, we go, yes?'

No, Dave, we don't. We'll hit Wake Hall *after* Christmas. Tom got his way - after a row that almost ended in fisticuffs. Tom would reach his target soon, and slide silently away, on grease. Then no more pretending to *like* Dave 'Dipstick' Vossialevydipsic.


Derek Herring returned from Corfu with a spring in his step, not because his villa was finished, but because the new double shipments were about to begin.

He suspected, correctly, that police both Greek and British were monitoring his comings and goings, because barely an hour after his return, the northern Inspector's chunky red Sergeant asked to speak with him. He trotted out to the car park to be interviewed. Olly's policy was never to invite a cop *sans warrant* into your place of work or your home. Inquisitive little piggy-policeman eyes would always find something. Or leave something behind that wasn't there before. Derek knew. He occasionally paid policemen to do things like that.

'Sergeant Ball. How nice.'

'Zor. Thank you for nipping out to see me.' Ball was wondering what Derek would have done had it been snowing.

It's a question of style, Derek thought. Ball is....straightforward. Batten would have said 'dragged your fat arse as far as the car park, I see, Del.' Derek Herring wasn't sure which he preferred. But as he frequently said to Olly, one should engage with whoever is on the ground.

'Not at all, Sergeant. And how can I help you?'

Ball did his very best - and Derek admitted privately that Ball's very best was really quite good - but Derek Herring was not to be tripped up. He knew exactly what he'd told the police last time they'd questioned him, and he treated Sergeant Ball to a detailed repeat performance. Ball persevered out of stubborn professionalism - and because they were running out of leads.

'Sergeant. May I be direct for a moment? It seems to me that all your questions are in fact reducible to one: why did I poison Lawrence Vann? No?'

Ball gave a grudging sideways nod.

'And since I did not poison Mr Vann - indeed I can think of no reason why I or anyone else would wish to - your question is doomed to be ever unproductive. Do you not think?'

Ball didn't not think, no. In fact, his thoughts were more on tonight's skittles match at the alley in his village pub, The Jug and Bottle - they had a crunch game in the Crewkerne and District league. When a heavy wooden missile left his mitt and smashed into a clutch of ninepins, he'd be thinking of Derek Herring. Every question he asked - night transport, Olly Rutter, Corfu, Lawrence Vann - Del had a bloody answer for.

'I stick to the facts, zor, and the fact is that Mr Vann was murdered. It's also a fact that you were present at Wake Hall on the day it happened. Unless my facts are wrong?'

'I do have rooms here, Sergeant, but I am not the earliest of risers. I was barely beginning breakfast when - as I understand it - Mr Vann and Ms Farley left for their country ramble.'

Yes, and you made damn sure plenty of people saw you at your cornflakes - or *said* they did. Ball changed tack.

'You've had dealings with Debbie Farley, have you, zor?'

'Dealings, Sergeant? I have eaten her cuisine. Does that qualify as a 'dealing'?'

How the hell should I know? Ball thought. I'm just flying a kite.

'You've not spoken to her, then, since she left hospital?'

'Spoken to her? 'I trust you are well, Ms Farley.' 'Excellent coq au vin.'

'But not discussed Lawrence Vann with her, for example?'

'Words of condolence, naturally, Sergeant. But she and I move in different circles, as you surely must be aware. I can think of no reason why I *would* discuss Mr Vann, or anyone else, with her.'

Unless…? Against his better judgement, Derek wondered about the fresh police interest in Debbie Farley. The covert search of her cottage had turned up neither i-phone nor memory stick, but if she had them, they could be concealed elsewhere. He'd persuaded Olly to steer clear while police protection was in place. But what of his other advice, that one should deal with whoever is on the ground? Her protection had been removed. Was she worth a closer look?

'I've been more than patient, Sergeant. If I may return to my work?'

Work? Do crooked lawyers actually *work*? Ball gave another grudging dip of his head. I'll see you again, Derek, he said to himself, as the silk suit headed into Wake Hall. Not in a car-park, though.

# Twenty Nine

The Estate Agency reminded Batten of the Parminster CID Centre - drab walls and over-flowing waste bins. He perched on a squeaky plastic chair, surrounded by rack on rack of 'bijou' dwellings and 'investment' opportunities. The glum surroundings helped him revert to type. Stubborn. Direct. Crap detector in the 'on' position.

'What's he want for it?' he asked the slightly nervous Mr Willey, who blinked back at him.

'For the cottage. What's the sale price?'

'Oh, oh I see. Well, I'm not altogether sure if the price has been *fully* established yet - '

'OK. What's the partially established price then?'

'Oh, hah-hah, yes. Well, I may have to check with the vendor, for accuracy. I mean, price details, oh dear, in a potentially rising market, well...' Mr Willey threw up his hands while rapidly re-calculating a much higher sale price than the one he'd fully established with the Canadian cousin two days ago.

'Just give me a ball-park figure then', asked Batten.'

'Er.....'

'I *am* talking about a cash sale. Easy and quick,' said Batten archly.

'Ah well, a cash sale, yes. And of course it is a *highly* sought-after property, hamstone walls, well-appointed, spick and span -'

'It's spick and span *now*,' said Batten. 'It wasn't when I moved in, though your blurb said it *was*.'

Mr Willey looked sheepish, but managed to twist his lips into an insincere smile. Batten inwardly screamed . 'Stop *pretending*! You make yourself smaller, more ridiculous!' He went for the kill.

'Mind you, with four months of my rental agreement still to go, I don't suppose any of us are in much of a hurry, are we?'

Mr Willey weighed up his options, almost audibly. A cash sale, in a slow winter, in a recession. And at the inflated commission he'd told the Canadian cousin was 'our international rate.'

'Well, ah, you see, properties of this type, with parking, a garden, views of such magnitude -'

Batten's crap-detector buzzed. When folk use words like 'magnitude', they're just trying to bump up the price.

'£210,000,' he said. It was a fair offer.

'Oh, I doubt the vendor would accept a penny less than £249,950, which of course *is* advantageously below the higher property tax threshold' retorted Mr Willey.

'Pity,' said Batten. '£210,000 was my absolute ceiling.'

It was also the sum total of the equity on his big old house in Leeds. He pushed back the plastic chair and reached for his coat.

Less than thirty minutes later, he had bought outright his Ashtree cottage, subject to the usual checks and surveys, signing a house purchase agreement for £210,000, cash.

Less than thirty seconds after Batten left, Lesley Willey reached into his desk, took out a lighter and a small cigar and ducked through the agency's back door. He always treated himself to a small cigar when he made a sale. Lately, he'd hardly smoked.

When the phone rang that evening in the warm hamstone cottage, it was the owner-to-be who answered. Ged's voice hallooed down the line.

'You're lucky, Zig. I wish *I* was chasing a killer. Metal thieves, me! This lot, they'd nick a tin leg while the owner's wearing it!'

'Have a night off, Ged. You're not on duty now.'

'Wish I *was*. Early Christmas shopping, late at night - makes no sense, does it? Well, Mandy's doing the shopping. I'm lugging the bags and the gutted wallet.'

Batten pointed out that the background noises didn't sound at all like a shop.

'Bloody detective. Have a night off yourself. I've just nipped into Weatherspoon's - nearest place of safety, before you give me grief on that as well - and I've treated myself to a defiant pre-Christmas snifter. Mandy's trying on bras, says she doesn't need help from my clammy hands, thank you very much.'

'How is Mandy?'

'She's on a roll - wouldn't you be? Conspicuous consumer spending, mid-week, in a recessive economic environment? In other words, pissing my money at the wind.'

Batten could have pointed out that Mandy's career in town planning gave her at least as tidy an income as Ged, but Ged just needed to sound off.

'Anyway, what do you care how Mandy is, you deserter?'

Batten and Mandy had never got on. In the early days they'd had to compete for Ged's time. Latterly, their social relations had stabilised into small-talk. She was good for Ged, though - a strong woman complementing a driven man. And she's more than *you've* got, Zig.

'I was being polite, Ged. You remember 'polite', don't you?'

'Hah bloody hah. *Polite* is when your old northern mucker - disorientated, skint, and suffering from post-shopping stress disorder - *still* remembers to ring you up and ask what you want for Christmas - that's *polite!*'

Batten lay back on the sofa and looked at the honey-coloured walls, beamed ceiling and old latch doors of the warm cottage that from today was to be his permanent home. The hamstone inglenook was a perfect frame for the cast-iron solidity of his slightly gothic wood stove. Here and there, faint dots of wood-ash confirmed a balance of form and function.

'Very thoughtful of you, Ged. But, you know what? I think Santa's already been.'

The quiet bits of Handel's 'Messiah' always made him drowsy, and he was nodding off in the warmth of the woodstove when the phone bleated again. Ged, trying to have the final word as ever.

'*Who?*' he asked, more rudely than he'd intended.

'Lieutenant Grigoris,' said the voice again. 'I call from Greece, from Corfu.'

He remembered, apologised, turned off the CD. They shared hellos and roles and reasons, before moving to Olly Rutter. Batten was surprised that the Greek police had no record of him. His passport had never been scanned at Corfu airport nor had he arrived by boat - not legally, at least.

By contrast, Derek Herring was well known to the Greek police - they even had a nickname for him.

'Pappas, my colleague - he is from Kefallinia - he call Mr Herring 'Mithratis'.' He pronounced it 'myth-ratties.' 'Mithratis is Greek word, of course. A little fish, like whitebait. But more fatter.'

A fat whitebait? Batten couldn't imagine a more apt term for Derek Herring. He began to enjoy his conversation with Grigoris, and more so when he learnt that Herring had hit the radar because of his connections with 'dangerous men, bad Albanians - give good Albanians a bad name, yes?'

'But why, Lieutenant? These Albanians - and Herring - what are they up to?'

'This we are not sure, not quite yet. These men are new. The Balkans drug route, may be? Suspicions, yes. Proof, not.'

The equation dragged the dead face of Lawrence Vann into Batten's head. He ended the call, switched on the stereo, hoping 'The Messiah' would remove it.


Spending Christmas in the sun seemed an excellent idea to Lady Wake. She was convinced it was *her* excellent idea, but Olly knew different. He'd been dropping the odd word into conversations for days, and she'd duly fed them back to him. After pouring two large glasses of single malt, she poured herself onto a chaise. Olly stayed where he was, sitting on the old cast-iron radiator in the draughty drawing room. Just as well the weather's warming up again - not much heat coming out of *this*.

'How hot is southern Spain in December, darling, would you say?'

'Mm, dodgy. Storms, if your luck's out. For sun, you want the Canaries, Gambia, places like that.'

Certainly not southern Spain. The whole point of being away for Christmas was to have a lead-lined alibi. Del Herring would be in Corfu. Neither of them wanted to be in southern Spain when the Andalucian mares were loaded into their giant horse-box. With the other stuff.

'What about Lanzarote?' he asked. 'Nice villa, heated pool. Could be bliss. Bit of riding - one kind or another?'

Her eyes smirked back at him from above her crystal tumbler. Lady Wake made more allowances for Olly than felt comfortable, but she still tingled whenever he made rude suggestions. Because he always carried them out so very well. Christmas in Lanzarote - what an excellent idea.


The spirit of Christmas was struggling to dispel Sergeant Ball's grumps.

Despite the bizarre rise in temperature, his head cold lingered on, as did his shift. He'd been called out to Oddcombe where a reported tractor-theft turned out to be feuding farmers playing silly sods over a piece of mechanical junk. He'd barely parked the car back at Parminster before he was called out again, to Burrow Hill this time.

Unseasonably warm weather or not, what possible excuse did they have for cavorting half-naked amongst the leafless trees, on a red tartan blanket, barely twenty yards from a public right-of-way? Even then, had they kept their grunts and giggles down a bit, the passing dog-walker - puritanical, fierce - would have failed to spot them, and would have failed to call the police. Ball's misfortune was that when Jess Foreman responded to the call, he recognised the pair of them. And rang the Sergeant.

'Time was, they'd get a clip round the ear and be sent on their way. But, with 'em being a bit old for a clip, and being who they *are*, and being where they *were*, I thor' I'd better call *you*. In case of any connections.'

But connections were there none, so Ball was lumbered with two embarrassed wrinklies. At least PC Foreman had made sure that Harry Teign and Eth Buller were now fully clothed again. They look marooned, Ball thought, without the rest of the geriatric Scramblers milling around them in their walking gear and funny hats. Harry and Eth sat abjectly on a fallen tree at the edge of the apple orchard that fringed the approach to Burrow Hill.

Ball had seen everything now. *These* two? Canoodling? In the open air? They've got to be sixty-five if they're a day!

'And the pair of you were....doing what you were doing, *here*? Of all places! A man was murdered, for god's sake, just *there*!' He pointed up and across at the single tree and the round mound framed against the sky. 'I mean, where's your respect for the *dead*?'

Eth Buller's face refused to emerge from behind her tiny hands, so Harry Teign had to do the talking.

'You see, Sar'nt, here's where we first walked out together, Eth and me. I can tell you *when* exactly - it war today, five year ago. That right, Eth?'

A nod from behind two small hands.

'We's each lost our spouses, see, ten year or more now. Only so much y'can do on your own, en' there?'

Sergeant Ball was unsympathetic. 'You *weren't* on your own,' he said, nodding at the still faceless Eth. 'There's the *two* of you. Partners in crime.'

'Crime? You don' call this *crime!*'

'The law does - crime is that which breaks the law.'

Unless of course they're just getting forgetful? In which case maybe he could hand them over to Social Services.... From behind Eth Buller's hands, a small voice peeped.

'I suppose we *were* 'returning to the scene of our crime'. It's just as Harry said, today's kind of a....a anniversary, see?'

Ball didn't see. He had a long list of other things to see. Harry cut in.

'Ohh, you do see. He do, Eth. Just here's where we, you know....an' *when* too, when we first.....oh zor, *you* know! A canoodle, two adults, in the fresh air. A anniversary, that's all it war!'

Ball watched as Eth's face slowly emerged from behind her shamed fingers. It was full of consternation, but innocence too. He regretted calling her a criminal.

'Zor, please,' she said. 'We 'ent got two pennies to rub together, so no posh anniversary's goin' appen, es it? We just thought we could spend time here, in our special place. In our anoraks.'

Should he remind them they weren't *in* their anoraks - or in much else - when the police arrived? He didn't have the heart. Caution them? Or thank them for removing his apprehensions about life and love in the third age? Tenderly, Eth gave Harry a little tap on his arm.

''S'all your fault, Harry Teign. 'Cottage pie!' S'when he says 'Cottage pie', Sergeant. That starts it.'

*Cottage pie?*

'See, Sar'nt, oi war saying to Eth that on a anniversary, you wan' somethin' more'n cottage pie, if you get my drift? So, bein' as it's so warm, we comes here, for the memories. An' we got a bit carried away. Bit more spice than we intended.'

It was pointless telling them he'd once had cottage pie laced with chilli sauce, which made for a tasty dish. Instead, he told them to stick to indoor games in future.

'And by the way, 'indoors' does *not* include pubs, cider farms,

National trust properties or any other indoor spaces where you might feel inclined to hold an anniversary. Is that *understood*?'

They nodded meekly. Eth nudged Harry again.

'One good turn, Harry. Go on. Better tell him. Please.'

Harry screwed his face into a knot.

'She says we're not to tell.'

Eth nudged harder.

'It's too big a burden, Harry. She know that.'

'She?' asked Ball.

'*Stephanie*,' said Eth more firmly. 'She ring us. What, three day ago?'

Harry nodded reluctantly.

'She won' exactly say where she is,' he added. 'Safe, though. Cryin' down the phone, Stephanie war.'

Ball wondered why he bothered. *How was your day, darling?* Oh, uneventful: geriatric sex rituals in the open-air; a new way of looking at cottage pie - almost forgot, two over-spiced wrinklies found a missing suspect *we've* spent a small fortune failing to!

He kick-started himself. Harry Teign and Eth Buller were taken off to give statements, and receive a firm warning: when Stephanie Broke-Mondelle rings again, insist she contact the police. And persuade her to return. Soon. To answer some very particular questions.

# PART THREE

*Buds*

# Thirty

It's just country walks. That's what he told himself. A stroll in the Somerset air with an attractive woman. And a witness - or *something* - in a murder case.

So, which half of your body is currently making the decisions, Zig? The top half, where your brain is rumoured to live? Or the other bit?

This was their third walk together since what he hoped was an accidental meeting on Ham Hill. Their first had been a ramble round The Seavingtons through fields that in summer, Rhona said, were a white and blue beauty parade of linseed flowers. In the brownness of winter, they'd found broken pieces of fossil, quite large pieces, like ammonites, just lying on the surface where the plough had thrown them. He'd taken a piece home; it was sitting on the pine blanket-box that doubled as a coffee table, next to the carp fishing magazine he still hadn't read. The fossil stared up at him whenever he sat on the sofa. I am much older than you, it said, and though only a piece of stone, am I not wiser and more careful than you?

Nevertheless, after a coy 'we must do this again', he had agreed to a second walk, a different route across Ham Hill, because she liked the pub food there. Perhaps they'd hear the exultation of larks, maybe even spot them, high in the bright sky, though they both knew it was too late in the year.

'You can probably see most of your beat,' she said, waving her hand at the horizon.

As if I want to. He kept shamefully quiet, though, in case of bedroom developments. From high on the quarried ramparts of Ham Hill, even through strong binoculars, he failed to locate his cottage beyond the tapestry of trees on the far side of the A303.

'Let me try,' she asked, taking the glasses. 'Over there, is it?'

He gently moved her pointing finger a little to the north.

'Which village?'

'Just outside Ashtree,' he said. After a pause.

'Oh, I know Ashtree. We ran a conference in the hotel there once, when Wake Hall was overbooked.' She raised the binoculars, scanning the very private territory he'd nevertheless pointed her towards.

'You can't see it from here. It's in a dip, I think.' She handed back the binoculars. They smelled of her perfume now. 'What's your cottage like?'

Such moments, Zig. You didn't buy the place so you could live there as a hermit. Did you?

Today, she took his arm and led him down a stretch of the River Parrett Trail, near Martock. He kept telling himself that getting to know South Somerset was all part of the job. You big liar. And he must have drifted off to Zigland again.

'You don't have to talk to me, you know,' she said. 'You could go and join that walking group, the….'

'Scramblers.' `

'Yes. Except it's for the over-sixties.'

'You're not a member then?'

'Oh, you noticed.'

'You'd have whacked me with your rucksack if I hadn't.'

'I'd have driven you straight to the opticians if you hadn't. And left you there.'

He smiled at her banter. Or was it edge? He watched the river swirl and eddy past a clump of reeds.

'I hope I never need glasses. They remind me of my mother. Three pairs, she had, but every other sentence was 'what's this say, Rhona? I can't find my specs."

It was too soon to share mother-memories with Rhona Fiske. That would only happen when he was definitely in a 'relationship'. Did he want to be, or only *need* to be? He swished at the reeds with a stick.

Later, from the car, the round mound of Burrow Hill popped up yet again, in the near distance through bare trees. Hoppity little blister, they should rename it Frog Bump or something. She followed his gaze.

'I expect you're sick of seeing it.'

A wordless bluster.

'Pity. It's such a wonderful view,' Rhona hinted.

He didn't feel like trooping up Burrow Hill to re-visit a crime scene.

Follow your desires, Zig? Or follow hers? And why aren't they the same? They parked more or less where Sergeant Ball had parked Batten's Focus on the day Lawrence Vann was killed.

'Race you!' she said, and ran at the slope like an athlete. Shamelessly, he admired a different view as her fine body swept past. He gave her a few metres start, then outpaced her easily, while wondering how the ageing Scramblers had ever managed to sprint up this slope towards the siren-screams of Stephanie Broke-Mondelle.

'A gentleman would have let me win,' she laughed. He smiled back at her.

'Then you wouldn't really have won, would you?'

Getting beyond winning and losing, was that what made for a healthy 'relationship?' He rarely got that far. She?

Her ringless finger was pointing out landmarks and explaining the horizon. Even a man used to the big scenery of the Yorkshire Dales and moors and coast was filled by the vista.

Does everyone see a view like this in the same way, he wondered? Staring at the church spires and orchards and distant hills, he allowed Olly Rutter and Lady Wake and Derek Herring and Manny McRory into his head. Lawrence Vann was already there. Had any of these four dislikeable suspects ever stood in this spot, on the crown of Burrow Hill? And if they had, what did they see? He could imagine Lady Wake sizing up the horses grazing happily in the distant fields - and sizing up the fields themselves. Derek would be looking at the mud on his hand-made shoes, Manny at his watch. But he could not imagine Olly Rutter looking at all, could not imagine him bringing a single grain of appreciation to this magnificent view. Perhaps Doc Danvers is right, Zig. Perhaps you do have poetic tendencies.

'It's hard not to like Somerset,' he said, 'with all this to stare at.'

He pushed away the sharp memory of a dead, distorted face staring at *him*.

'For me, it's the orchards,' she said. 'Proper apples, for proper English cider. Not the stuff made from foreign apple mush fizzed up in a machine.'

'I had to arrest a few folk who were fizzed up on that stuff, way back when,' said Batten.

'I thought they'd all be on Yorkshire bitter, way back when?' She deepened her voice into a cod Northern accent when she said 'Yorkshire bitter', and he tried to find it amusing. Failed.

'If it's cheap and strong, they'll sup it, whatever it is', he said. 'Then it's 'look, I'm Superman.'

'And fight for the hand of Lois Lane?'

'Just fight. They'd punch Lois Lane if they'd drunk enough.'

'Similar jobs, you and me,' she said.

'Where'd you get *that* from?'

'Oh, dealing with the dregs, perhaps. In my case, the domestic dregs - scraping together the underpaid scraps of staff and the kitchen crumbs and pretending Wake Hall is somehow stately - and for whom? You, well, the criminal dregs, I suppose?'

Dregs and crumbs. Yes. Not the fine wine cellar, the haute cuisine. He'd only once considered leaving the police force, when - briefly - it seemed his only purpose was keeping the dregs off the streets so over-privileged folk could lead expensive lives without discord or disturbance. He stayed because Aunt Daze reminded him - with fire in her eyes - that she wanted safe streets too.

Aunt Daze was replaced in his head by the well-connected Lady Wake and her manicured lawns and the wasteful, half-empty wastelands of Wake Hall. The thought began to taint the view, his frown only fading when Rhona tapped him playfully on the nose.

'You've gone all quiet. Means you're hungry. I'll drive us to Perry's for lunch.'

'Perry who?' asked Batten, thinking for an absurd, jealous moment that he was a male friend of Rhona's.

'It's another cider-farm, with a nice café. You can try some of their vintage ciders - there's barrels of them.'

Batten had a last look at the apple orchards that made up a good chunk of the view from Burrow Hill. But the moment had passed, and a contrasting image filled him. He was a young policeman, looking down from the high bluff above the River Aire as it squeezed its brown way through the brick and concrete confusion of the Leeds he remembered: tight chimneys of back-to-back houses in streets with darkly ironical names like 'Pleasant View'; four-lane roads raised on concrete columns above more roads below, each road swirling between clumps of high-rise flats like little offshoots of the brown river; scrubs and scraps of waste ground waiting for still more buildings to grow there; factories and warehouses now prettified and sold off as loft-living; and the big Victorian cemeteries where far too many blackened memorials to dead children told of 19th century urban plagues - scarlet fever, tuberculosis, rubella, diphtheria, and the rest. Thousands of little apples that never came to anything at all. Little buds that fell, too early, from the tree.

He was no longer hungry. But they went for lunch anyway.

Baz Ballard had the sort of face that looked like nothing went on behind it. Just as well. In Olly's thought-trap of an office, visible thinking was dangerous. That twerp of a Sergeant had unnerved him, with his questions about Manny McRory and the horse box.

'For Chrissake, Baz, all you gorra do is *drive!*' Typical Manny. 'Done it before, yeh? A time or two?'

Three times, in fact, where a horse-box was concerned - the first time for no better reason than Bulky being over the limit because of a skinful the night before. Bulky had acquired a brute of a black eye by the time Baz drove back into Wake Hall Horse.

And, yes, all Baz *did* do was drive - because on all three occasions Manny had dropped him off at a local pub before the horses were unloaded.

'If you get kicked in the head by a frisky horse, Baz, and Olly's left without a chauffeur, he'll have my guts.'

Nasty thought. But he didn't believe Manny's concern, and not just because Manny was only concerned about Manny. There were plenty of other drivers, when Bulky wasn't around, so why Baz?

'Because Olly owns you,' he said to himself. Olly didn't do trust; he did ownership.

There'd been something *off* about those journeys. A jack-in-the-box at the best of times, Manny was knife edge on all three trips. Baz had mentioned this to Lawrence, over a glass of twelve-year old Islay malt. Why hadn't he just used his mouth on the whisky, and kept his worries to himself?

Too late now. Behind his blank face, the problem was clear: he was an accomplice to *something*, he wasn't sure what, three times over. He glanced over at Olly. Normal people stared into space; Olly glared at it. Baz could wrap his boss in red tinsel and add a gift tag saying 'Arrest me', and still the cops wouldn't believe Baz wasn't in the know.

As he buffed the leather peak of his chauffer's hat, he resigned himself to the possibility of jail time. Not ideal, but at least he'd have the funds to grease a palm or two. He squeezed himself into the hat.

Olly Rutter was glaring at his own concerns. Once the double shipments started, any worries about his dented finances would begin to go away - but when would the *police* go away? They weren't protecting that dumb chef anymore, but hardly a day went by without plonker Batten or one of his flatfoots turning up to poke a nose into what used to be his trough of easy money.

'I would suggest softly, softly on the shipments, for the time being, Olly? No?'

'*Del*, kindly concentrate on the legal stuff and your Corfu connections, would you? And I'll decide the rest. *Yes?*'

That's what he'd said. What he meant was 'Softly, softly, my arse! I've got losses to make up!' But he couldn't say that to Del, because he hadn't told Del about the losses. Anyway, Olly wanted action; he was a doer.

He'd happily *do* whoever had thieved his memory stick, and do Lawrence's posh totty too, if he could get his hands on her....

'You know, Del, I get sick to the teeth of you saying 'one must engage with whoever is on the ground,' but sometimes you're right.'

Debbie Farley *was* still on the ground. If Lawrence Vann told anyone what he was up to, it'd be a woman, and Debbie Farley went on all those nice chatty walks with him, didn't she? Well, Marianne might have to find a new cook.

Bloody Christmas had almost arrived too, uninvited. He was supposed to be taking Marianne to Lanzarote, hardly had time to give it a thought. But *after* Christmas, it was New Year resolutions. And Debbie Farley would be one of his.

'Baz! *Baz!*'

'Boss?'

Baz's newly-buffed chauffer's hat went spinning across the room.

'Wake up, you dozy sod. Fetch me a disposable phone. *Now.*

That evening, the smell of apple-wood wafted from the glowing woodstove in Batten's stone-walled sitting room. It reminded Rhona Fiske she was a reformed smoker.

'Oh I'll never smoke again, but it pops into my head sometimes, that cigarette moment.'

Batten had never smoked, never understood those who did.

'Do you remember that Bette Davis movie, the old black and white one? Where she lights the two cigarettes in her mouth and gives one to her man? Or *a* man anyway. Imagine if it had been two Nicorette patches!' Rhona did a Bette Davis impression. 'Dahling, wear this one for me!'

He wasn't sure what a Nicorette patch was supposed to do. It made him think of nicotine - a poison, Chief Toxic had said. He'd misheard: it wasn't nicotine, but aconitine. A more deadly poison altogether. And he didn't much like Bette Davis. Rhona was gabbling.

'How often do you watch an old movie, and there's the two of them in bed, 'afterwards', with the sheets pulled up discreetly over the lady's mazumas and they've both got a touch of spray-on sweat on their foreheads, and he's got a smudge of lipstick on his cheek, you know. And they're panting, after their romantic exertions?' She giggled. 'And then the man reaches over to the bedside table' - her hand grazed Batten's chest as she reached for an imaginary pack of cigarettes - 'grabs a ciggie, lights one up and smiles like the cat who's had the cream!'

Yes, yes, I get the picture. I'm a detective, for god's sake. It's not hints from you I need, it's permission from *me*.

'Well, I don't suppose they can show that *now*, with these anti-smoking laws? No post-coital cigarette. Healthier, of course.'

'I think if that law covers bedrooms, I'm seriously out of date.'

'But you see what I mean, don't you? Cigarettes - they were a sort of language. And if we don't speak Cigarette anymore, what do we speak instead?'

What's wrong with plain old talk, he asked himself, while failing to notice he'd hardly said a word? Turning to look at Rhona Fiske, attractive in the firelight, he cast his mind back - how long since he'd last had sex? His lust-meter was hovering at eighty five percent, but he was dog-tired, and unsure. If she can pretend to be Bette Davis, who else can she pretend to be?

# Thirty One

Hopes were quickly dashed when a Fat Jellicoe sighting turned out to be just another large drunk. ACC Gribble had mixed feelings either way. He was getting it in the neck from the Chief Constable as it was. But when the super-sized embodiment of his mistakes *did* turn up....

Batten had turned up too, for his weekly report. Another set of mixed feelings - though it was a surprisingly low-energy version of the Northern nugget, Batten-lite, that sat down in front of Gribble's station-platform of a desk. Gribble had seen the look many times before, in others, and in his own mirror. This man's exhausted. Weeks of pushing hard at a locked door, it did that. But how to stop? Gribble's role wasn't to make his detectives happy, but it was important that he kept them alert.

'When did you last take a break, Inspector? From police work, I mean?'

Batten was too fuzzy to do anything but shrug. His Saturday night bedroom romp with a Wake Hall witness had tired rather than refreshed him, but he certainly wasn't going to mention that to Gribble.

'And your next rest day, when is it?'

'Friday.' He should have said 'sir', he knew.

'And what will you do on Friday? Relax? Touch of fresh air?' Through the office window, climate change had sent 'one of the warmest Decembers since records began', despite the bizarre brief interlude of snow.

'Sorry, sir, don't see the relevance.'

'Well, I'm wondering, I suppose, if you're getting a bit too close to the case?'

*Christ, Zig.* Don't tell me this desk-jockey knows about Saturday night's organ recital with Rhona Fiske? *How?*

'Too....*close*, sir?'

'You know, wood for the trees. Time to get a bit of perspective? I don't like the phrase myself, but 'clear your head?'

Phew. Not *'keep your trousers on'*. Or 'clear your *desk.*'

'Yes, sir. Clear my head. Good advice, sir.'

The pleasant thought of 'stepping back' lasted only as far as Parminster. He barely got a toe on the now visible office carpet before Ball thrust a sheet of A4 paper at his face.

'If that's a holiday chit, Ballie, roll it up and stick it somewhere personal and tubular. The Assistant Chief Cock-and-Bull has instructed me *to clear my head.*'

Peering at the report, he saw the word 'Toxicology' and jumped to a wrong conclusion. It was not additional info about the soup swallowed by Lawrence Vann, nor about the lethal poison found in his system.

'All the same, zor, it's progress. Isn't it?'

Yes and no. The thieves removing tractors and mobile homes from Somerset's roads - and not because of green politics - were still adding pound signs to the 'value of goods stolen' column in George Halfpenny's spreadsheet. Batten had redoubled the search for sightings or evidence, and while they had failed to apprehend the thieves, they *had* taken into custody a dog, a poisoned guard dog - dead, but fresh. And *this* one wasn't going in the bloody incinerator.

'I don't care if you've never tox-screened a *dog* before! It'll extend your CV, *won't it?*'

'Inspector -'

'And *don't* tell me you'll have to send it off and it'll be six weeks coming back. We're not talking about fancy paperwork for an inquest. One side of A4 will do. It's a *dog.* It's been *poisoned.* How hard can it be to tell me by *what?*'

The toxics had grudgingly agreed to take samples and test them, and - 'if initial screening is productive' - send 'informed indication of the toxins involved.'

Which is why Ball was so excited.

'Forget the fancy language, zor - you can see as well as me what's killing them. Zor?'

Batten *could* see, but didn't like what he saw. Adulterated heroin - 'in extreme concentration' - did more than frighteningly kill a guard dog doing what a guard dog should. Bad heroin also said Olly Rutter. It was his early, nasty trade mark. When Olly arrived on Batten's old patch in Leeds, ten years ago and counting, bad heroin quickly flooded the streets. *Time to step back a yard or so?* He was stepping back further than that.

He took the tox report into his cubby-hole and spun round and round in Fat Jellicoe's chair. Tractor thieves - poison - Wake Hall - Olly Rutter - murder. He spun faster. Could centrifugal force somehow push the circumstantials into place? And connect them in a chain of evidence?

Hell's bell's, Zig, there's not even a chain of *logic*? *Clear your head, man!*

Somerset snow was a faint memory, and the water warmer than it should have been. He set up his rods opposite a little island by a bed of reeds in Ashtree Lake. It was a balmy Spring friday. In December.

'I dunno what to tell you, Zig. The carp 'ave been up, they've been down. Up again today. Never nudged an angler to surface-fish in December before, but *I'm* goin' 'ave a try, and you could do worse.'

Vic the water-bailiff waddled back to his shack, with its corner-curled photographs of large carp pinned to its walls. A much younger Vic smiled out from one of them, a monster mirror-carp held proudly in his sagging arms. The caption read 'Ashtree Lake Record Carp: 37 pounds.' Batten didn't think he'd get anywhere near, but he'd try.

There was stillness, at least. And surprises. What looked improbably like a banded demoiselle perched itself on the end of his carp rod and waved its delicate see-through wings at the watery world. The very latest he'd seen such creatures was the back end of October, but it was December now so maybe the book of nature was being rewritten. Suddenly the brighter, flashing blue of a kingfisher whisked across the lake, dipped its sharp gash of a beak in the calm waters and disappeared as fast as it had arrived. And then all was peace and stillness again.

He gazed at the world of colour: the blues and silvers of the sky, and the iron-grey water with its shimmery reflections; the greens, shade after shade of green, in the trees beyond, in the grass of the bank beneath his feet; the yellow-greens of the bamboos; the almost black green of the rushes, then straight ahead, fringing the island, the rich mid-green of the beds of reeds, or were they bamboo too?

Whatever they were, an invisible giant suddenly walked straight through them, powerfully sweeping first a single stem aside, and then another, and then whole clumps of them, to left and to right, only the stems moving at first, then ripples on the water too as if invisible floating

216

feet were stamping and stepping there. And then the stems snapping back upright again but with no sign of the man himself. It was the carp, of course, large carp, swimming just beneath the surface and pushing aside the vegetation, like a large invisible man walking through green bamboo.

Although hoping to clear his head, the thought of an invisible man stayed with him. That was what they were searching for. Who was he, this unseen man who had poisoned two people? And how does he remain invisible? Does he slide beneath the surface, like carp in a deep lake, disturbing the water for a faint moment before disappearing? Flutter away on see-through wings? Or flash briefly-blue across one's vision like a kingfisher, then just as quickly disappear into the dark trees?

And just how do you catch an invisible man? *Easy,* Zig. Use invisible bait! There's no shortage, it's all around you. If it wasn't invisible you'd be able to see it. You pratt.

His carp bait, by contrast, was highly visible. It was a large piece of bread crust, which would hopefully convince a surface-feeding carp to suck this tasty morsel down into its rubber-tyre of a mouth, hook and all. Vic was right. In this unseasonably warm weather the carp were beginning to glide and weave just beneath the surface. He flicked the bait into the margins, where the branches of an overhanging tree teased the calm water.

His breath held and his body tingling, he'd already watched languid carp stir beneath the tree, and had flicked several offerings of bread crust there, to encourage them. As he watched, faint shapes disturbed the surface, then large, suspicious noses and mouths nudged and nibbled at the floating bread. A few pieces disappeared with an audible 'schluk'. Others, his bait amongst them, were ignored. But only temporarily. A nose broke the water next to his hook, a large mouth sucked at the edges of the bread, tantalisingly turned away, then immediately turned back and slurped the bait down below the surface. Hooked! Batten's strong carp-rod bowed and danced as the carp tore powerfully across the lake, line stripping from his reel so fast it would have sliced into his finger had he been stupid enough to get it in the way.

He could still remember the first fish he ever caught, a tiny silver thing but a huge experience, a tingling connection between man and dark nature, the tremble of life vibrating backwards from fish to line to rod to

217

angler's arm, hand, brain, heart. The pounding pull now flowing from his rod into his stiffening shoulder told him that this carp was big, muscular, and powerful, and he knew he had at best a fifty-fifty chance of landing it as it ploughed this way and that across the lake, diving at the reed beds by the island, searching for weeds and underwater obstructions in which to snag the thin strand which precariously connected it to Batten. His reel whizzed and whined as more line was dragged from it by the carp's unpredictable surges.

Time drifted, being meaningless anyway in this reverie of combat, and he had no idea how long it took to turn the fish and regain some of the stripped line, and then a little more and a little more again. He eased his landing net quietly into the water in anticipation of netting what he now knew was the biggest fish he'd ever hooked in his life. Big, and clever. When the carp saw the net, it suddenly changed direction, diving at the roots of the sunken tree and so nearly smashing into them. But Batten held his nerve and, his arm now tired and aching, turned the carp's head back towards open water and gradually again towards the waiting net. Very carefully, with massive pleasure and relief, he eased the carp into the net's triangular jaw and lifted his spent adversary from the water.

'Big lump o' fish, Zig, by the look of it!' shouted Vic, from his shack. 'You wanna weigh it?'

He did, and with Vic's help and on Vic's scales the mirror carp weighed in at 28 pounds. It was the biggest fish Batten had ever landed. And it was beautiful.

'Suppose you wanna photo too, Zig? An' d'ya want me to stuff it an' pop it in a glass case for you?'

'Just a photo, Vic, thanks. Unless you've got strong liquor and two glasses in that shed of yours?'

A still trembling Batten faced the camera, lifted the big carp, its giant mirrored scales glistening with gold, and smiled a smile that, like the experience itself, would be frozen in time. He gently returned the fish unharmed to the lake. As he watched its tail disappear into the depths of the sunlit water he realised he had a lump in his throat. Ged would have said 'bloody hell, Zig, it's a *fish*. You didn't want to *marry* it, did you?' But Ged, for all his good-friend qualities, was not an angler. And he would never understand.

That evening, while downloading photos of the giant fish onto his laptop, he recalled what he'd been pondering just before he hooked it: catching the invisible man, with invisible bait. Sure, Zig, *easy*.

With a barely-touched nightcap of Speyside at hand, he flicked through the daily paper, a predictable alphabet soup of insinuations and fantasy. Sometimes he wondered if even the football results were true. Miss Sylvia Morrison, one story said, was luring neighbourhood dogs into her home with tit-bits, drugging them and selling them on. 'Who's to say how many dogs?' a neighbour was quoted as saying, 'and they can go for hundreds of pounds, you know.' Miss Morrison told a reporter all she did was help re-home stray animals. Sometimes she fed an undernourished local dog, yes, and then patted it and sent it home. Her neighbours didn't like her, she added, because she shamed them into taking better care of their pets. One resident, who did not wish to be named, said '*Her*, she's drugging them by the dozen. One went missing only yesterday. What's she done with it, eh?'

Batten sighed. The deeply gullible would swallow the story whole, and those only half-disposed to accept its insinuations would simply take longer to multiply each half-truth by two. All the story did for him was re-fill his cleared head with poisoned guard dogs, bad heroin, and Olly Rutter.

Then he laughed at his own blind stupidity. Zig, you're an idiot! Invisible baits are staring you in the face! Half-truths. Insinuation. Rumour. Might such baits entice and snare an invisible man? If something is hiding below the shiny surface of Wake Hall, then why not drop a hook in the water? He raised his glass, began to work out how. The golden whisky tasted sweeter than before.

# Thirty Two

'Ballie, what's it say on this empty key bob? I can't make it out.' A key-fob found in the pants pocket of the dead Lawrence Vann plopped onto Ball's desk.

'Wake Hall…something.' Ball got a magnifying glass from his drawer, did a Sherlock Holmes. 'Dunno.'

'Could it be Wake Hall Horse?'

'*Could* be. Don't think it is though.'

'But it could be?'

Anther peer from Sherlock. 'Could be Wake Hall *House*? Wake Hall *Hunt*? Here, Jon, your eyeballs are younger than mine.'

Lee stepped over, instinctively keeping the Sergeant between himself and Batten, and inspected the fob.

'Er, Wake Hall *House*? Could even be Wake Hall *Hearse*.'

They were reminded that Lawrence Vann's funeral had still not taken place, despite Lady Wake's agitations.

'It's *Horse*, I'm sure it says Horse. Wake Hall *Horse*.'

Lee withdrew to the safety of his desk.

'You're the Inspector, zor,' soothed Ball. 'It says 'cider penny a pint', if you like.'

Ball grinned as Batten disappeared towards the car park. You're up to something, zor. He wasn't going to ask Batten what the CPS might think was written on the key fob. It wouldn't be Wake Hall Horse though.


'Inspector. It is still Inspector, I assume? Not yet demoted to Constable?'

Batten gave her a water-off-a-duck's-back look.

'Mm. Clearly not *yet*. Well, how immensely satisfying to see you again,' she said, swishing herself onto an antique chesterfield the size of Batten's car.

She had moved on from sherry this time and was plugging away at a pale-gold liquid that filled two-thirds of the largest cut-glass whisky tumbler he'd ever seen. It was expertly swirled by a fan of manicured fingers. Didn't get those done at the local nail-bar, Zig. Her shot-silk kimono had given way to what he guessed was a fashion version of riding gear: jodhpurs, leather boots, silk shirt and hacking jacket - all so exquisitely cut and so palpably expensive that only a madwoman or a complete spendthrift would allow them anywhere near a horse. Well, Lady Wake, if the cap fits. Batten guessed she'd left the riding crop in the bedroom.

'I'll try not to keep you from the stables for too long, Lady Wake,' he said in his best two-can-play-at-that-game voice. 'Just a couple of questions, if I may?'

As at their last meeting, the tanned hand waved vaguely. It seemed her speaking voice was largely reserved for sarcasm, or for other people.

'It would have been helpful, Lady Wake, last time I popped in to the Hall, if you'd pointed out Mr Vann's extensive experience in the world of finance.'

'You didn't ask, Inspector. As I recall. Mm?'

'But you were aware of it?'

'Aware? Of course I was aware. Its relevance? *That* I am mystified by. Oh dear, I assume you will now have to tell me.'

'It's extremely relevant if Mr Vann's financial skills cross-fertilised with the....parallel skills of your Mr Rutter? Particularly in Olly's capacity as, what, 'business manager' of your horse-sales empire?'

Lady Wake's manicure eased her vat of liquid towards her lips, which drew in a considerable draught of the stuff. He could hear Aunt Daze. 'By 'eck, she's got a thirst on, that lass. She could sup rain from t'top of a tramp's hat.'

'Allow me to correct you, Inspector. We do deal in high quality horses, yes. But Wake Hall Horse - the registered business name - is an *enterprise*, not an empire. An enterprise, incidentally, which provides paid work for a significant number of staff in an area of high rural unemployment.'

Batten nodded in mock-sympathy. Wake Hall Horse? *The Regiment* sounded better.

'And Lawrence Vann?' he asked. 'Was he involved with this enterprise, perchance?'

''Perchance', Inspector? '*Perchance*'? How very Edwardian.'

'Shakespearian, I would have thought, Lady Wake.'

She waved his correction away with the tiniest twitch of her mouth. 'Lawrence was Estate Manager. I think you already know that.'

'I do. But Wake Hall Horse is part of the estate he was manager *of*, presumably?'

Or maybe it takes place on another planet. Or in a dream. Or only on paper. They were looking at this possibility too.

'I imagine, Inspector, that Lawrence would initially have advised in some minor fashion. As the enterprise grew, Mr Rutter - and I, of course - brought in additional staff. We could hardly expect Lawrence to do *everything*, could we? The sad but illustrative fact is that Wake Hall Horse continues to function very smoothly without Lawrence, whereas the rest of the estate which Lawrence so expertly organised has urgent need of a replacement manager. Indeed, I am about to interview three potential candidates for the post, so *do* excuse me.'

Ah, that explains the posh horsey get-up, Zig. Impress the candidates with expensive fancy-dress. She ought to pop a couple of mints though, before she breathes on them.

'Just one final thing, Lady Wake. It's a question of keys.'

'Keys, Inspector? I have *staff* to deal with keys. I *pay* a chatelaine. Why would I jangle keys myself?'

Yes, you pay Rhona Fiske. But she's not allowed keys to the office of Wake Hall Horse. Which is always locked. Even when it's occupied....

'It may or may not be significant, Lady Wake, but I was wondering why Lawrence Vann, who you say had nothing at all to do with Wake Hall Horse, had in his possession a key fob - but no keys, alas - with what appears to be 'Wake Hall Horse' written on it?'

She gave a look now of *ultra*-boredom. Batten paused, dolloped a touch of decorum onto his voice.

'When I say 'in his possession', of course I mean it was found on his body.'

Lady Wake flinched.

'So I was wondering what might have happened to the keys? And why?'

Her tanned hand placed the drained cut-glass tumbler on an inlaid side-table - a shade tentatively, Batten thought. In lieu of a wave of her manicure, this time she merely raised her eyebrows at him, and waved her whole lithe frame out of the chesterfield.

'I neither know nor care,' she hissed, and eased herself through the central door without a further word. He heard the dead-bolt click on the other side.

Batten didn't mind. She would tell Olly. Perhaps he was at this very moment concealed behind one of the trio of old-oak doors which grew smaller as Batten once again walked away from them, past the grim portraits and fading tapestries and into fresher air. He hadn't caught a fish yet. But where fishing was concerned, he knew how to be patient.

Olly Rutter frowned at the reception hall's trompe l'oeil door. He was a doubly worried man. Last night, Marianne had given him a painful weal on his naked buttock, swishing her riding crop with surprising tension. This Lawrence Vann business was playing havoc with her mojo. He would have to keep a careful eye. Against his better judgement, he'd grown to like her more than was good for him - or perhaps to like what she *did*.

His real worry, though, was those keys, and what they represented. Plonker Batten had only confirmed what he already thought: it *was* Lawrence in my bloody office, doing his damage. And the damage is still out there, waiting! Which of the old shagger's bed-warmers did he slip my data to, before he croaked? I should have been more hands-on....

Olly rarely doubted himself. But all this *rural* stuff! He'd never got used to the smell of Somerset, a cow's arse of a place as far as he was concerned. And now, stolen keys; missing data; gutted bank accounts; an edgy bed-mate. Once Christmas is over, though....hands-on it will definitely be.

He couldn't concentrate. Rubbing the weal on his buttock with a claw like a tarantula, he turned painfully towards the bathroom, to smear something cool on his hot backside.

'It's being held in the Chapel, at ten....Yes, of course ten in the *morning*! What did you expect, a torchlight procession?'

Rhona Fiske was a bit brusque, he thought. Overworked, as usual. Or having post-coital regrets. Or something. His invited presence at Lawrence Vann's Memorial Service was more to do with decorum than detection anyway. Not to notify the police might have seemed suspicious. To someone.

In the absence of living relatives, it had fallen to Lady Wake to arrange Lawrence's burial. It was difficult to do so without a body, which the police were not yet willing to release. Instead, she decided that if a service did not take place soon, the 'fringe connection' - suppliers, part-timers, and those linked to Lawrence only by 21st Century networking - would forget he had ever existed. A Memorial Service would provide some kind of closure - and persuade staff to get their minds back on their jobs.

Batten had no idea there was a Chapel at Wake Hall and wondered if they'd searched it. They had. The 'Chapel' had long ago rendered itself to Caesar and was now The Silver Room, in the Conference area. He half-expected to find thirty pieces of the stuff lying on the carpet.

But it was not a wasted morning - unfortunately. Once parked, he took an illegal short cut across the freshly barbered lawn to the rear of the Conference suite. He'd been to Wake Hall so often now, he was almost a native. Ducking past the Banqueting Room - a posh caff with bits of chintz nailed on - he glanced in through the modern stained-glass windows, past green glass grapes and red glass apples into the room itself.

Jake Tuttle the gardener was backed against the far wall, arms raised in defence, face grim. The focus of Jake's defence was a sharp, threatening finger attached to the linen-clad arm of the shapely body of no less than Rhona Fiske. Batten watched as her hand stabbed at Jake's face, before jabbing him in the chest three or four sharp, admonitory times. Whatever she's mouthing at him, Zig, it isn't Christmas greetings. Was this a falling out between partners in crime? He would have to enquire.

At the Service itself, Batten had been given a seat at the back of what could only be described as a muddled room. Ancient carved fireplaces at each end pleasantly framed an antique altar-plinth, used in these secular days as a dais, but their harmony was jarred by a powerpoint projector and large white screen bolted unceremoniously into the ornate panelling and old oak beams of wall and ceiling. Modern, bright blue conference chairs had been placed in a broad semi-circle around the dais which was garnished, today, with an embroidered black ribbon tied off in a bow. As he watched, an enlarged, reincarnated Lawrence Vann smiled out of the screen. Batten tried not to connect the wavy-haired, maturely handsome face with the expressionless mug-shot pinned up on the murder board back at Parminster. Or with the grotesque, sunken death-mask he'd encountered on Burrow Hill.

Lady Wake was on the front row, wearing a black silk dress below her white silk face. Whether hers was genuine sadness or a dressed up mourning, he was simply unsure. Olly arrived at the last minute, sullen, openly bored.

The male contingent did little more than mumble 'Amen' when the time came, though one or two seemed more troubled. Batten focused on a tall character towards the back, a familiar face but….He added stubble to the chin and a muddy-grey hat and it became Lonny Dalway, the milkman, clean-shaven and trussed into an old suit that Batten guessed only emerged from the wardrobe for occasions like this. He caught Lonny's eye. A sad nod, beyond any pretence. Batten wondered how many of the payers-of-respect would summon such genuine sadness for Lawrence Vann.

Not Manny McRory or Derek Herring. They were nowhere to be seen. Wake Hall Horse was noticeably under-represented. Next to a bored-looking Olly, the habitually blank face of 'chauffeur' Baz twitched a little. He'll be thinking of spark plugs, or weight-lifting, Batten thought, his gaze moving from Baz to the many women there. How many of them had pillowed their heads beneath the scarlet feature wall in Lawrence's bedroom? If Ann Kennedy, who had almost borne his child, had been invited, she had chosen to stay away.

Lady Wake gave a speech of welcome and condolence. Fitting words, supported by more powerpoint photographs, about the life and achievements of 'Wake Hall's wonderful Estate Manager', but necessarily edited. Felt words, though? Maybe, Zig.

After the predictable readings, guests were invited to make impromptu comments about 'the Lawrence you knew'. Lonny Dalway's lips twitched in a silent statement of thanks as Rhona Fiske rose to say a dignified goodbye 'on behalf of all the Wake Hall staff.' Jake Tuttle looked on inscrutably. Roddy Cope, the farrier, nodded to the beat of an invisible hammer. His giant sidekick Neil did the same, more slowly.

Debbie Farley, as waxen-faced as when Batten first saw her on a stretcher at the foot of Burrow Hill, cried unashamedly even as Allie Chant, the Head Lad, gave her what might have been a reluctantly supportive hug.

Batten looked around to check the reaction of Olly Rutter, but the space next to Baz was empty. Olly Rutter had already said goodbye to Lawrence Vann.

Afterwards, Batten mingled with the few folk that might be forthcoming. June the cleaner was hardly a reliable witness, but she was fluent.

'We-ell, they had their moments, Rhona and Mr Vann, god bless him.'

'Moments?'

'You *know*, arguments. *Words*. When they thought nobody's listening. Not that I *was*, mind. Who's in charge of this, who's in charge of that. And, glory-glory, they didn't half go at it sometimes, you know.'

Batten didn't know.

'Ohhh, they could have been an old married couple having a tizzy over the price of fish. And that finger of hers, a wonder it hasn't dropped off by now. Wagging it in Mr Vann's face. And *him*. Nice enough he may have been, but Mr Important sometimes, you know. Standing there with one hand on his hip like a teapot, the other hand patting the air as if it was a baby's head. Like a referee. In football. On the telly. You *know*.'

'Er, no, I don't.'

'Ohhh, Inspector, you *do*. Calming things down. With his hand. Steady on girls, put down the handbags. You *know*.'

'And it worked, did it?'

'Mm. So-so. She went red in the face a time or two. And once she nearly clocked him, with that big bunch of keys of hers. Didn't though, not as I saw. They bumbled along, pair of 'em.'

'Bumbled along?'

'You *know*, bumbled. 'S'what we all do, isn't it?'

It was the following day before Batten caught up with Jake Tuttle, whose rare 'office' moments took place in a confusing variety of ramshackle sheds. Today it was a cobwebbed tool store smelling of linseed oil.

'*Animosity?* What, towards Rhona? Where'd you get that from?'

Jake was treated to a Batten shrug.

'Me and she….we get on OK. Mostly. 'S'only when she acts like she's my boss that I stick up for myself. She's no more my boss than you are. Lawrence is my boss. An' he lets me get on with it. An' I *do*. Getting on with it's how I work best.'

'But there must be t-'

'Look, I got a suggestion for you. Stop bugging *me*, and go ask *Rhona*. Oh, an' while you're there, ask her what she thinks about these interviews, for Lawrence's replacement. Ask her if *she's* had her interview yet? I know she applied. Dead man's shoes don't bother *her*. She'd love a job like that - chance to be *really* bossy. But you get on an' ask her yourself. An' I'll just get *on*.'

Cups and plates played a tune next door. He wondered who'd made the cake she was slicing. In Rhona's cottage he felt a loyalty to Rhona's cake, but cake made by Debbie tasted better by a distance.

'Nearly there,' Rhona sang, from her little kitchen. Batten's thoughts moved from food to Jake's jibe about a dead man's shoes not bothering Rhona Fiske.

'Hey, if you get Lawrence's job, they'll have to give you his big cottage, won't they?'

His question was clumsily-disguised. Kitchen noise screeched to a halt. She strode into the sitting room and eyeballed him.

'I mean, if it were me, I'd assume the bigger cottage came with the bigger job,' said Batten, with a hint, now, of bluster.

She said nothing, just stared. Why are you here? Cop, or lover? asked her left eye. Make up your mind! said the right.

'Assuming I knew anything about it, of course.'

Full-on Batten-bluster now.

'Whether you did - *know* anything - or indeed knew absolutely nothing at all, you would doubtless be given both job *and* cottage, because you, *Inspector*, are of the *male* persuasion.'

Rhona Fiske folded her arms - and her face - into a knot.

'Er -'

'And being of the male persuasion, you would instantly benefit from

Lady Wake's exclusion of all *female* applicants - regardless of irrelevant trifles such as *ability* - in her quest for a Lawrence Vann, version *two*! Right down, I imagine, to the *COCK and the BALLS!*'

The energy from her raised voice swept her from the room and she was through the front door like an angry ghost before he could invent an apology. *SLAM*!

He felt like a burglar, left alone in her home. The desk drawer was unlocked. He could see diaries and hand-written notes on a side table, through the half-open bedroom door. Cop or lover, Zig? Before he could decide, the door burst open and Rhona's furious face reappeared.

'And do feel completely free to search through my belongings, with your grubby, suspicious *policeman*'s fingers!' she snapped.

Her voice was a snarl, then the door slammed for a second time. Lifting himself awkwardly from his easy chair, he dusted off his embarrassment. Since her 'invitation' wouldn't stand up in court, he slunk away. There's no evidential value in an unauthorised search. Every cop knows that.

'Look, Inspector, I'm busy. Plants don't stop growing 'cos the police turn up. You might be 'just doing your job', but I'm trying to do mine.'

'A quick word, Jake, won't take a -'

'What, are you my dad now? You sound like him - 'only take a minute, Jake, there's a good boy.' I told you, I'm busy!'

And *I'm* busy - and embarrassed and pissed off and my theories are all to cock. So don't push it. Lad!

'If you wish, we could do this down at -'

'What? Down at the station? Do the fuzz *really* say crap like that?'

Jake's hand reached across the tool-store for a large sack of potting compost and swung it into a waiting wheelbarrow as if it was weightless. Stronger than he looks, thought Batten. He changed tack. Bad habits running ahead of your common sense, eh, Zig? Just ask, shut up and listen, and you'll both be on your way.

'One simple question, Jake. Rhona Fiske: why'd she threaten you, just before the Memorial Service?'

Jake looked pityingly at him.

'What? Is that *it*? Tuh. So you snoop as well. D'you really want to know?'

Batten zipped back a tempting sarcasm.

'For what it's worth, she was giving me a bollocking. An' I *deserved* it. On that occasion only.'

He began to remove tools from the rack and pile them noisily, one after the other, onto the wheelbarrow beside the bag of compost, as rumpled now as Jake's face.

'I didn't mean anything bad. But once in a while, I suppose, Jake's a pratt. Rhona, see, she was in the Banqueting Room, her and Debbie. They were at the buffet table, checking everything was there, for the guests. Or are they a congregation?'

Batten wasn't sure.

'Debbie was reading items from a list while Rhona checked them off. You know, potato salad....yes....sausage rolls....yes. I remember thinking, well, this is the most cooperative these two have been for a while - put me in a cocky mood, I suppose. Anyway, Debbie pauses so I - I wish I never had now - I says 'Soup?' Just came out. If I'd thought, you know....'

Batten didn't know.

'So Debbie starts wailing - you'd think she'd be bone dry by now - oh well, she plain *fled*. An' Rhona, she gave me one eye an' then the other, eyes like nails, you know?'

Batten did know, yes.

'Anyway she give me a shove, an' not a soft one, I thought she was going to clock me. Where Lawrence is concerned, she says, button your lip an' keep it buttoned. When did *she* start liking Lawrence? And then that bloody finger of hers, digging me in the chest. I tell you, if she'd been a man I might have clocked *her*. If I don't button it, she says, one word in Her Ladyship's shell-like and, flip-flop, I'm pushing my belongings down the road in a wheelbarrow just like this one.'

With a puzzled squint, Jake noted the pile of tools in the overloaded barrow, sighed noisily and began to remove and re-hang all but a shiny, sharp spade.

Why don't you borrow it, Zig, the spade? Dig yourself out of Rhona's bad books - if you get a chance. Or just dig yourself a hole, and crawl in.

Once in a while, you know, Zig's a pratt.

# Thirty Three

He was growing used to the staccato Greek voices in the background whenever Grigoris rang, and to the charmingly-accented English spoken with confidence by Lieutenant Grigoris himself. For the sake of confidentiality, Batten took Greek calls only at home.

'*King Zog*? Wasn't he king of Albania? Years back?'

'Is so, Inspector, is so.'

'But he's dead, surely?'

'Dead? Of course dead! But *this* King Zog, he is much alive - and much bad. It is not his real name, but a knock-name.'

'A nickname?'

'Ah yes. His real name we will discover, soon. *Our* King Zog he has big boat, it sail from Albania to Corfu, Corfu to Albania, sail back and forth many times. When it come to Corfu, your Mr Herring he is no stranger to this boat, so we are told.'

'Told by...?'

Grigoris paused - a rare thing. Brisk verbal energy was his default position. For a moment, Batten heard only distant Greek voices in the background.

'Told by a dead man, Inspector. A dead man *now*. Three days ago this man was a living man, *our* man. We paid him, it is true, for information, and we hoped for more. But....'

'I assume we're not talking about an accident?'

'Accident?' Grigoris gave a grim laugh. 'Drowned by accident, may be - but both his hands they are missing in this accident. The man Zog, we think it is his....signature? Is correct word?'

Batten too fell silent. If Herring is involved with someone as ruthless as 'King Zog' - whoever he is - then Olly Rutter's snout is rooting in the same trough.

'It is correct? Signature?'

'Sorry, yes, correct. His *hands* though?'

'His tongue? His ears? What does it matter? It is life that is lost. I pray he is dead before they cut off his hands, but I do not know this. His widow, she does not know this also. So you can see? Your Mr Herring, he is become more important to the Greek police now?'

Batten could see. It was why the job mattered. Someone has to pay - if not, all is anarchy. Herring and Rutter would pay. He didn't care how.

'Looks like promotion already for you, zor,' said Sergeant Ball as Batten's body squeezed into the now over-full CID office, weaved through a chicane of staggered workstations, and edged past the sharp corners of a vicious block of gunmetal filing cabinets. It was just as well his mind was still in Corfu - there wasn't room for it.

'Some cider-induced babble just escaped from your Somerset choppers, Ballie. Run it by me again, eh?'

'Said it looks like promotion, zor. For *you*. Congratulations!'

'And where'd you hear this drivel? Tribal drums in the skittle alley?'

'I deduced it, zor, like Sherlock Holmes. It's an inescapable conclusion.'

He's in a perky mood today, Zig. You might have to whisper 'Wake Hall' in his ear.

'And on what, precisely, has Sherlock inescapably based this conclusion?' Batten stepped into his cubby hole, confronting a mess of messages, reports and policy documents that hell's postman had sprayed across his desk.

'On your second message down, zor, the one from the Chief Constable her very self.'

Despite his mind being on an Albanian thug called 'King Zog', he pretended to flick through a risk assessment policy statement for staff below the rank of Superintendent, while giving the message a glance. It merely said he was to turn up at Yeovil, tomorrow, where the Chief Constable would see him at 9am. So, Zig, perhaps Lady Wake *did* take the bait - and spat it back at *you*. At least he wouldn't have to trog up to HQ at Portishead. Either way, he was unkeen to go.

'Pound to a penny it'll be 'stop upsetting Lady Wake'. And read your own messages in future. Shylock.'

'I did, zor. *Mine* says I'm to drive you there. So you arrive on time, I expect. Or to get *my* promotion?'

'Get a kicking, more likely. After she's kicked *me*.'

'Only Inspector grade and above are entitled to Mrs Kirkwood's stilettos in their 'nads, zor. I'll get a quick jab from a lowly minion, mark my words.'

The following morning, at precisely ten seconds before nine, a silent aide waved Batten towards the Chief Constable's door. Ball had already been siphoned off, as predicted, by 'a lowly minion'. Batten was expecting a Mrs Pinch, prim and trim with her hair in a bun, but the Chief Constable's aide was male, bald, bottle-shaped and so meticulously neutral he could have been Swiss. Or perhaps American, given that his ID badge said he was Hank Gage. Batten silently renamed him Blank Page, before turning past him to face the Chief herself.

Angela Kirkwood's local office was a pastel-green garden, a flowery gauntlet of plants, power and pollen. Plants grew on the floor, on filing cabinets and window-sills; plants lividly floral or deeply green; maidenhair ferns, parlour palms, busy-lizzies, orchids galore. Jesus, Zig, she doesn't carpet people in here, she tests them for allergies.

The Chief Constable's immaculate uniform and the top of her deep-auburn head sprouted from the green jungle. He guessed the report she leafed through almost certainly had his name in it. To his great surprise, the Chief asked him to sit down. More accurately, she *told* him to, so he did. Briskly. He'd never been in the same room as a Chief Constable before - let alone face to face - and he didn't like it.

'You're leading the local team on the Burrow Hill murder, Inspector?'

'Ma'am'.

'And you suspect there may be a connection between the murder and Wake Hall?'

'Yes, ma'am.'

'Which is also the reason you've seen fit to robustly interview Lady Wake herself, I presume?'

Here we go, the posh pals protection racket. It's a bollocking, sure as eggs is eggs. So, Zig? Crawl into a foetal position and grovel? Or go down fighting like a man?

'Pardon me, ma'am,', he said, 'but that's three questions you've asked. May I have my three now?'

'No, Inspector, you decidedly may not.'

'May I ask *why*, ma'am?'

Angela Kirkwood had, amongst her numerous skills, a formidable command of silence which she bestowed on Batten for a full five seconds, during which a long day seemed to pass. But the Chief was a fair woman. And sharp.

'Inspector, you've already wasted *two* questions, so granting you a third should hardly trouble me. Ask away.'

You pratt, Zig. Make the third a good one.

'I was just wondering, ma'am,' he said, 'if I should look forward to a personal interview with you during every case I investigate?'

Chief Constable Angela Kirkwood was more than sharp and good at silence, she was also a good judge of character. Which explained why she had never entirely warmed to the character of Marianne Wake, who used the advantage of her social position without always embracing the responsibility that went with it. But what of the character of Inspector Batten? As she watched, he nipped a wilted flower-head from an orchid and bulls-eyed it into the wicker wastebin. He had balls, she'd give him that. She was less sure if he had judgement.

'I think, Inspector, you would happily kick down an unlocked door to catch a criminal?'

'Catching crooks is what the police are about, ma'am, isn't it?'

In response she smiled - on the inside. Oh, to have the luxury of saying the very same thing to the press or in committee, where she must maintain the necessary public relations line - prevent crime, ensure public safety, support the criminal justice system. And be efficient. Well, Batten was certainly efficient - because he cut corners, not least in his 'conversations' with Marianne Wake. Nevertheless, she found herself smiling at the thought of this lanky northerner slicing through the Wake Hall claptrap - having kicked down those old oak doors she'd stepped through once or twice.

Then the Chief realised she was smiling on the outside too because the lanky northerner was wryly smiling straight back at her. Nothing wrong with upward pressure from your staff, she thought, if they clothe it in a bit of charm. And anyway, she was enjoying herself.

'Have you come across Contingency Theory, Inspector, on one of your training courses?'

'No, ma'am.'

'It's sometimes known as the 'it depends' theory. And that's the answer to your impertinent question - *it depends*. If you get results, good. If you break too many sensitivities in getting them, not good at all.'

'Ma'am, when you say 'break *too many* sensitivities', does that mean I'm allowed to break *some*?'

'That's your fifth question, Constable,' she said. Batten was reminded of Lady Wake, who'd played the same trick of demotion on him. Without the smile. Or the power to make it happen.

'It is, ma'am. My apologies.'

'Inspector, we both know that good policing involves taking risks. How could it not? But we also know that taking risks requires careful professional judgement. Yes?'

'Er, yes, ma'am.' He blinked away the image of a post-coital Rhona Fiske.

'Therefore, whenever you display careful professional judgement, I shall not be on your case. I'd much rather congratulate my officers than ....*police* them.'

'Ma'am, I've - '

'So if Marianne Wake is involved in criminality you will collect the evidence very professionally and pass it to the Criminal Prosecution Service who will very professionally decide what to do with it. Is that clear?'

'Ma'am, I've always -'

'I shall risk some plain speaking with you, Mr Batten. I've read the report of your transfer interview - and of course your personnel record.' She tapped the file that lay on her desk. 'The evidence suggests you are a palpably good detective.'

He blushed slightly, but the Chief Constable summarily closed the flimsy file.

'The question is,' she added, 'are you able to be a *better* one?' The Chief stared across her desk, and this time the smile had gone. 'There's a tad too much insolence in you, Inspector, and it may well stifle your development - if we let it. Treading on toes may occasionally have value - *when* it stems from a professional desire for results. But am I certain that yours does?'

For a second time, she bestowed on Batten her formidable command of silence. An ice-age of tortured time ticked by.

'The jury's out,' was all she said before reaching across her meticulous desk to nip a tiny, dead leaf from an otherwise exquisite pink orchid, flicking it into the wastebin without taking her powerful eyes off Batten. She would have enjoyed saying 'You missed that one, Inspector.' Instead, her final words were, 'Now bugger off, and if you want to keep your job, get better at doing it!'

When Batten emerged, more chastened than he was prepared to admit, from the Chief Constable's indoor allotment, Sergeant Ball was nowhere to be seen. Instead, Hank Gage/Blank Page, the bottle-shaped aide with his mute button on, floated silently towards Batten and handed him a scrupulously-written memo, the initials HG scrupulously entered in the box marked 'from'. A uniformed officer of similarly Swiss neutrality, car keys jingling soundlessly in his hand, appeared from nowhere and waved an arm towards the door.

As Batten sat beside his silent driver in the scrupulously-driven police car, he re-read the memo. Its few words referred only to a 'rendezvous point' with Sergeant Ball, and an 'incident' taking place there. In doodle mode, Batten took out his pen and altered the HG to BP. It could hardly be called an act of 'too much insolence' but it passed the time, and briefly took his mind off the fact that, like it or not, he was being driven at speed to urgently re-join Sergeant Ball. On bloody Burrow Hill again.

It was not Ball but the unmistakeably shambolic figure of DC Hick that greeted him. Some people should be permanently excused clothes, he thought. Or ties, at least. If today's tie had been chosen to match Hick's manure-brown Oxfam jacket and his pale beige face then a colour-blind geek had chosen it. The acid blue spots continued to vibrate even when Hick's febrile body briefly came to rest, and the tie itself circled the side of his neck like a noose. Perhaps he's a 'bring back hanging' cop, Zig, dressing to advertise.

'Hickie, you're whiter than a nun's arse, lad. Seen a ghost?'

'Seen a *ghost*? Worse! Worse than ghosts or ghouls or….or….stuff!'

'Just spit it out, lad. What *have* you seen?'

Hick pointed jaggedly up at the round blob of Burrow Hill, shaking his head in a random mime of twitches and jerks. Stop him, Zig, or you'll be picking his dislodged head out of the sheep-shit.

'I haven't got time for charades, Hickie. Just *tell* me. *Please!*'

'It's her, sir. Again! *Her!* Just you go up. She's standing by that sodding tree. And not talking for once. What she's *doing*, I couldn't tell you. She's in a dream. Sergeant Ball can't fathom it neither. He said to send you straight up, see if *you* can make sense of her.'

Batten followed DC Hick's arm as it pointed skywards, and sighed at the thought of clomping up Burrow Hill in the murky-mud. Sod's law, you put a shine on your good shoes to look your best for the Chief Constable - dressing up for a dressing down - and half an hour later they're sponging up Somerset sheep-poop. If it was possible to thump a hill, Zig, I'd happily knuckle this squitty little excuse for one!

Nearing the top, through the clearing mist, he saw the same ghost that DC Hick had seen. Hickie was right; she was back. The statuesque figure of Stephanie Broke-Mondelle was unmistakeable at this distance. He imagined Gribble's posh-yokel voice - 'Good! You won't need to waste any more of my disappearing budget *failing* to find her!' Batten re-focused on the obvious questions: where had the nattery cow been, and what the hell was she doing *here,* on Burrow Hill?

Stephanie was standing completely still at the base of the single tree, gazing at the cluster of bouquets and messages that friends and strangers alike had deferentially laid there, in memory of Lawrence Vann. Batten looked across at Ball, perched like a frozen Buddha on the viewing platform. At least the mud's ruined *your* good shoes too, Batten noted. His questioning eyebrows drew only a puzzled shrug from Ball, hunched up against the deepening cold, hands out of sight in sullen pockets. The rain had ceased, but the warm December glow had given way to a wind with spikes on. *Do* something, Zig, before we all freeze to death.

As if sensing his thoughts, Stephanie reached into her bag and produced her own little memorial bouquet of the reddest roses Batten had ever seen. She gently kissed the flowers and laid them with great tenderness at the foot of the tree, but a little away from the rest of the tributes, as if she wanted to make a shrine entirely of her own. Stepping back, she stood quietly for a moment as tears, not rain, ran down her face.

Then she moved resignedly towards Sergeant Ball. When he nodded in Batten's direction she obediently changed course.

'I'm ready to talk to you now, Inspector,' was all she said before making her way down the damp, southern slope of Burrow Hill.

With some relief, from the wind at least, Batten ushered Stephanie Broke-Mondelle into the small office of the Burrow Hill cider farm. For the second time, he found himself thanking the green eyes of Erin Kemp, the manageress, for the temporary loan of her workspace. It was Mrs Kemp who had phoned Parminster after seeing the missing Stephanie Broke-Mondelle click open the gate at the base of the hill. Batten thanked her for that, too. *What is it about women, Zig, that makes you remember their eyes, even when there are so many other goodies to look at?* In the case of Erin Kemp it was because she had 'warmth' written on both of them.

Stephanie's eyeballs were a different story. She had 'sadness' written on one and 'confusion' on the other. She declined Ball's offer of a warming cup of tea with a brief, sad shake of her head, thwarting his plan to piggyback on refreshments for a witness - if that's what Stephanie was - with a 'two sugars please, got any cake?' But at least they were indoors now.

Despite their three chairs being barely a foot apart in the cramped office, Batten was unsure if Stephanie was warm or cold, or indeed if she knew or cared if she was one or the other. Though 'ready to talk to you now, Inspector', all she had voiced so far was regret at placing Harry and Eth in a difficult position. She chose not to mention Lawrence's i-phone and the silver key.

'So you *had* left the county, then?'

'I do apologise, Inspector, but yes. I'm a walker, you see. Nobody notices yet another rambler with a rucksack, do they?'

No. They bloody well don't.

'I set off at first light, walked ten miles cross-country and hopped on a bus to Exeter. Two little stopping trains from there, then a mile or two more on foot. It's almost funny, where I ended up. Even amongst the….sadness. And given what my fellow walkers will have said about me.'

Batten raised an eyebrow.

237

'That I talk too much, Inspector. Surely they will have told you that?'

Inspector and Sergeant flashed polite Tweedledum-Tweedledee smiles.

'I transgressed, I know, leaving the way I did. I'm not one to hear voices, but on this occasion voices whispered 'Stephanie, time and distance, dear, distance and time.' And not merely because I discovered a horribly dead body on a favourite hill, Inspector.'

Stephanie paused. She would not tell lies to the police - but neither would she disclose the fear that made her flee.

'In my absence you will doubtless have investigated my background. Mummy and daddy were hardly squeamish types. How could they be, in their profession? Military surgeons, both of them. Everything calm and precise. If you had seen them slice a Sunday roast.... No, a body is a body, Inspector. Usually.'

He wanted to tell her he'd never come across a body that hadn't been a struggle to look at.

'Not up there, however.' She flicked a tentative finger towards Burrow Hill. 'As soon as I saw *that* body, I immediately knew who it was. I was too enthusiastic, you see, and I accidentally dislodged his hat....' She closed her eyes to quell the images. 'When I looked down at his poor face, with such pain carved into it, and seeing my Lawrence, my poor Lawrence....it was simply too much for me to bear.'

Tears came, despite her efforts. She let them flow. Batten and Ball shared looks of amazement. *Lawrence*? Lawrence and *Stephanie*? Bloody *hell*.

Drying her lips and eyes with a white silk handkerchief the colour of her face, she took a deep breath.

'Do you know Mr Valdano, from Solo Souls, Inspector? Either of you?'

Both men nodded, concealing their further surprise at the mention of Vito Valdano.

'Well if you've met Vito, you'll know all about 'Discretion', I expect?'

Batten pretended he did. 'Nevertheless,' he said, 'please tell us in your own words, while Sergeant Ball takes notes?'

Stephanie obliged.

'I keep being told that sixty is the new forty, Inspector. And when I turned sixty last year, I decided I'd very much like to be forty again. I knew about Solo Souls of course, having attended one of Mr Valdano's meditation courses, at Wake Hall. I'm afraid it did nothing for me. I told myself it was because I'm too restless, but when I did manage to reflect, I realised that in fact I'm....well, I'm too physical. That's why I began the South Somerset Senior Citizens Rambling Group, you see.'

'The Scramblers?' asked Sergeant Ball.

'Oh dear, how we rush to abbreviate. But yes, if you must, the Scramblers. It absorbed a good deal of my physical energy, all that wonderful walking, as I intended it should.'

Her eyes wandered to the office window, and to the framed view of Burrow Hill beyond the glass.

'I suppose, too, that I harboured thoughts of meeting....*the man*, from amongst my motley walkers. Not 'the man of my dreams.' I'm not a fool. An outdoor man who felt as I did, that sixty can be forty again. I must have bemoaned my disappointment to Vito during a coffee-break. It wasn't coffee, alas, but dandelion tea or something equally undrinkable.'

As if to remove the taste, she sipped water from the plastic bottle she fumbled from her bag.

'And Mr Valdano?' prompted Batten.

'Oh, Vito was rather sympathetic. Quite a helpful chap, despite his strange apparel. He told me he could offer....now what did he call them? Private services? Unadvertised private services? Well, I misunderstood, and rather rudely told him I wasn't searching for a massage parlour! Terrible, terrible Stephanie. But he forgave me, and offered me 'Discretion'.'

Ball's puzzled face mirrored Batten's.

'I'd heard of web-dating, of course, but, oh dear, *computers* - they're science fiction to me. And it sounds as if spiders are involved, no? The thought of being ensnared, like a fly in a spider's web. But when Vito explained that 'Discretion' was a venture that didn't involve computers at all.... He said it was a sort of private portfolio of....needy people. Needy, but of, well, a certain standing, yes? And Vito *connected* them, made personal introductions - entirely discreet ones, hence the name. One hand-picked member to another, you see? And it didn't cost the earth.'

Batten's cocked an eyebrow.

'I'm so sorry, it's detail you require. A thousand pounds, that was the fee, for each introduction. Vito said we could have as many as we wished....'

I'll bet he did, Zig, and what a nice little unadvertised private income that would add up to. He imagined the amply-fed man-of-the-spirit, perched on his prayer stool, planning a well-paid pander service for folk 'of a certain standing'. They would be questioning Valdano again, assuming he'd flown back from wherever he'd flown *to*.

'I had just the one introduction', Stephanie said, her eyes focused once more on the hill beyond the office window. 'It was all I required. It was Lawrence. I knew, almost the same day, that Lawrence was the one.'

Ball looked up from his notebook. Batten was thinking the same thing. Didn't Stephanie *know* of Lawrence's reputation? Dumb she's not, but deaf and blind? She caught their look.

'Oh, I was under no illusions about Lawrence's past. He told me all about his women, his 'adventures'. But he was searching - as was I. When he spoke of the future, *our* future, deep in my heart I knew he was telling the truth. Lawrence was tidying up, you see. Thirty years at Wake Hall was too long, he said. It was time to make ready.'

'Make ready? For what?'

'Oh. To leave, Inspector. For Cyprus. He intended buying a villa there.'

Not with the contents of his official bank account, Zig. Ball's fingers remembered rattling a calculator, translating half a million euros into pounds.

Stephanie fussed a handkerchief across her eyes and nose, wiping away the significant omissions in her story: Lawrence's i-phone and his little silver key. She would never understand i-phones, but had quickly realised the key would open a safe-deposit box - *where*, she knew not - and that the box contained Lawrence's financial future.

'I was deeply moved when he asked me to go with him. I prefer Italy myself, but I would have followed him without hesitation to the moon.'

Her handkerchief failed to soak up real tears now. Lawrence was gone. As was the key. Before returning to her fate, she had dropped the little silver memento - unused - down the first convenient storm-drain she came to. The i-phone went into a tidal part of the River Exe. She would keep this knowledge to herself, forever. *Her* Lawrence would be remembered for unworldly reasons, and nothing else.

'Of course, she had warned him off by then.'

'I'm sorry? Who had warned him off?'

'Oh, I assumed you knew. Lady Wake. She was the reason he joined 'Discretion', you see. I suppose in a way I should thank her. He told me exactly what she said: '*Lawrence, I intend Wake Hall to be Somerset's rural employer of choice, particularly where female staff are concerned.*' Stephanie hardly needed to ape the accent; she sounded almost as posh as Lady Wake. '*And a certain person's reputation, doubtlessly distorted, may be unconducive to this aim.*'

Batten was wondering how Lady Wake's liaison with an over-sexed crook like Olly Rutter qualified her as a moral crusader. He recalled, too, the rather different picture of Lawrence that Lady Wake had painted for *him*. Will a truth serum ever be available to the police? Stephanie finished the dregs of water in her plastic bottle.

'After thirty years of loyal service, Lawrence was hurt, in his quiet way. In any case, he had pre-emptively changed. Intelligent, of course, and tender. And never slapdash with me. A *giving* man. Perhaps I *am* a fool, because I'd grown to love him, deeply. And an even bigger fool now, aren't I? Because he's gone.'

This time, she simply allowed the tears to drip from her cheeks onto white hands that lay like sad saucers in her lap.

'Shall we take a break?' Batten asked. He wanted to swap thoughts with Ball. The two men promptly accepted Erin Kemp's offer of tea. Stephanie slowly composed herself.

'Do you believe her?' asked Batten.

'I'm leaning that way, zor. You?'

Batten wasn't sure. He tested some possibilities.

'If Lawrence Vann swaps Debbie Farley for Stephanie....is Debbie angry enough to poison him?'

'Maybe, zor. Hardly a *surprise*, though, Lawrence playing musical beds. And they still did their walking. Can't quite see it.'

Batten couldn't see it either. And if Debbie did bump him off, why then poison *herself*? Far better to poison *Stephanie*, her replacement under the duvet.

'OK, if not Debbie, then what about Stephanie herself? So far, Ballie, we've only got her word that it was all sweetness and light with Lawrence. She might be making up the script as she goes along.'

Batten was recalling the moment when Stephanie placed her red roses not on the informal shrine on Burrow Hill, but separately nearby. Was she simply saying farewell personally to the murdered Lawrence? Or to the Lawrence she had personally murdered?

'Give her an Oscar if she is, zor.'

'Glug some tea, Ballie. It'll keep your mind open.'

'Oh, it's wide open, zor. You could park a bus.'

'Park this one, then: for all her talk of the future, what if Stephanie was really the *past*, as far as Lawrence was concerned?'

'One of his rejects, zor? And she bumped him off for a bit of vengeance? Mmph.'

Batten didn't like it either. Wake Hall still topped the list.

'Be interesting if there was another woman *after* Stephanie, though, wouldn't it? Or *during*?'

Ball drained his tea.

'Who, though, zor?'

'Let's ask her.'


They did. Vehement denial - anger - more tears - and another delay. As a line of enquiry it was as useful - and as useless - as the rest of their theories. But the delay gave Batten time to wonder what to *do* with Stephanie Broke-Mondelle. Detain her? On what actual evidence? They could hardly lock her up for 'wasting police time.' He'd enjoy asking the ACC. And enjoy asking him if in fact they should be arranging expensive police *protection* for her, as they had done for Debbie? That would make the cogs turn behind Gribble's eyebrows, or is it an abacus he keeps up there?


Stephanie was talking again.

'As I said, Inspector, it was rather ironic, where I ended up.'

See, Zig, if you have a bit of patience....

'You'll hardly be surprised to learn they asked me to leave in the end - with great politeness, of course.'

'I'm sorry, *who* did?'

'Oh, the monks. In many ways I was sad to go. With their help and support I grew calmer, you see. The day-to-day tasks, the structure, it rather settled me down until I found my voice again. They're not a completely silent order but I became just a little bit too verbally expansive for them, I fear.'

*Monks*? A *monastery*? She was hiding in a *monastery*? He looked at Ball.

'Don't try blaming *me*,' Ball's face said. 'Would *you* have thought of looking in a monastery - for Stephanie Broke-Mondelle?'

Batten shrugged. He didn't even know monasteries still existed. Ball shrugged back. Sometimes it's all you can do. And then get on with it.

Gribble's a bigger risk-taker than *me*, Batten thought. Once he'd weighed up the evidence and the probabilities, the ACC's response to Ms Broke-Mondelle was a mixture of lateral thinking and bold action. And a touch of poker-playing too.

'Definitely charge her with wasting police resources. Because she *has*,' was Gribble's first pronouncement, even before Stephanie had signed her rambling statement. 'She's cost us a small fortune.' His second pronouncement was more left-field. 'This monastery? Would they have her back?'

Batten didn't know, and was tersely told to go and find out....

'The monks are not over-keen, sir, but they *are* charitable. Of course, she'd need to turn down the natter switch.'

'She capable of that?'

'Maybe, sir. But....'

'Spit it out, Batten.'

'Well, sir, now she's back, to send her off again, so close to Christmas? It seems a bit....'

Gribble's face was vocal. Inspector Curmudgeon-of-the-North is capable of *sentiment*? 'Well, she'll not be spending Christmas with Lawrence Vann, will she? Not going soft, Batten?'

*Are* you, Zig?

He couldn't dispute Gribble's view: there were no grounds, no legal basis whatsoever to detain Stephanie for Lawrence's murder. But if she wasn't the killer, the danger from whoever *was* could be all too real. Stephanie maintained that Lawrence had told her nothing of significance, but....

'Very few people know she's back,' argued Gribble. 'And nobody at all ever managed to discover where she'd been. Not even the *police*.' Batten was treated to a hard stare. 'So, if she *returned* to her monastery, quietly, quickly - with transport and liaison kept strictly confidential? And if the monks agreed to contact us at the first sign of concern? *We'll* know where she is, but nobody else will.' He didn't add 'and it'll be cheaper.'

Batten would at least have the pleasant task of persuading Erin Kemp to forget who she had seen on Burrow Hill, but he did whinge to Ball about the risks in Gribble's plan. Rather than take his Inspector's side, Ball upped the stakes. There's something in the cider down here, Zig.

'Well, they owe me a whopping favour, zor, the pair of them. Don't see why this can't be it, do you? I mean, they already know where she was.'

Batten surrendered - but took revenge, insisting that Ball go along as police presence. Better him than the sworn-to-secrecy Hick.

Her face hidden, Stephanie Broke-Mondelle returned to her safe-house-cum-monastery on the Somerset-Devon border, not in a police car, but in the back of an old Land Rover driven by Harry Teign and Eth Buller. On the return leg, they didn't need Sergeant Ball's keep-your-mouth-shut warning, but they got it anyway.

# Thirty Four

This time, Batten phoned Grigoris, cutting through the long-distance Greek gabble by plugging away in English, repeating the Lieutenant's name again and again till he came on the line. He was enjoying his conversations with the rich Greek voice at the other end of the phone, and his socks were up on the sofa to prove it.

Stephanie's revelations about Discretion, and the unexpected link to Lawrence Vann had freshened Batten's interest in Vito Valdano. Could Grigoris add anything of value?

'For your Mr Valdano, Corfu is an airport only. A jumping point.'

'A jumping-off point?'

'Ah yes. He go to Albania, to Romania, from there. He come back to Corfu only for the plane to England. We will now look, of course, more close, but Mr Valdano he has no interest to the Greek police, not yet.'

Blast.

'It's orphanages, right? Where Valdano goes, in Albania?'

'In Romania also. But, Inspector, what we see is not bad things. Our contacts, they say he do good.'

Charity projects. Precisely what Somerset police enquiries had unearthed. Batten told himself to be less prejudicial. There's no law against a man wearing a technicolour suit. Nor against the tingling of plod feet.

Grigoris was jabbering in English, again shaming Batten's non-existent Greek.

'And I am soon wishing you a Happy Christmas, Inspector. The English, they like very much to celebrate Christmas, I think?'

Maybe not the Polish-Russian-Yorkshire English, though, Zig?

'And a happy Christmas to you too, Lieutenant. But not for criminals, eh?'

'Ah yes! A bad Christmas for bad men. I hope is so, Inspector. I hope is so.'

Manny McRory was not a Christmas person. He didn't need an excuse to neck a few double scotches, and that's all Christmas was to him. This year, though, he had *herself* to consider. Barely a shopping day left, and he hadn't bought her a thing. I don't *do* Christmas! And I don't do live-in girlfriends either. Until now.

He switched on the pressure hose and zapped the side of horse-box 1 with foam and water. It seemed like half the mud and horse-crap in Somerset was stuck to it. He felt the power of the machine in his hands and grinned in satisfaction as dirty brown crud splattered into the gutters of Wake Hall Horse, and dark blue bodywork reappeared.

He couldn't decide whether to be pleased or worried about Carrie. Pleased, for sure. Best sex he'd ever had. Not a looker, but what a pair of bedroom eyes. She even had a job, that research place, even had her own money. She was useful, was Carrie, but she worried him. Hankering after this, hankering after that. And now she wanted 'to have Christmas together'. Christmas night, he was supposed to be on the road; another 'special' collection for Olly.

He pointed the pressure washer at the box's bonnet and grill, its caked-on road dirt spattered red from collisions with god knows what, black specks of dead flies and tar stubbornly sticking to it. Usually, he was a king on a throne in the high cab of the powerful truck but he was having mixed feelings as he stared at it now. Manny-bloody-Santa, stuck in a giant horse box on the M27. Carrie alone in the echoing house on Christmas night, her bedroom eyes staring at repeats of Only Fools and Horses.

He'd have to have a word with Olly; groaned at the thought.

Not for the first time, Batten celebrated Christmas early. Being new and single, he'd pulled rank and put himself down for the Christmas Day shift. Rhona was spending Christmas in Edinburgh, and Batten was still unsure if he was miffed or relieved at not being invited. Under the circumstances, it seemed unfair for Sergeant Ball to be sitting in a near-empty Parminster office instead of spending Christmas Day at home en famille.

So, days before the nation tucked into its turkey and stuffing, Batten was digesting his, flopped down on the old sofa in Aunt Daze's little sitting room in Leeds. The yellow paper hat he'd been wearing had fallen off, and lay on the brown patterned carpet like a blob of marzipan on a Christmas cake. He and Aunt Daze had pulled three crackers, and not one of them went 'bang'. Her hat, a mauve crown, was still in place, seemingly glued to the hairspray that buttressed her special Christmas hairdo. Batten chuckled: her curly locks had hardly moved when he'd leaned down to give her a seasonal kiss. The third cracker they'd pulled was for Dimi, his younger brother. Perhaps he would turn up later. Don't say 'like a bad penny', Zig, whatever you do.

'You've surely got room for a glass o' this, Zig?' She waggled a bottle of vintage port, a Christmas gift from Mrs Yeadon, next door. Just like last year and every previous year, as far back as he could remember. If Mrs Yeadon had a first name he still didn't know it. He lazily held up a thumb and forefinger, barely an inch apart, before correcting his rudeness.

'Sorry. Too full to speak. Just a small one thanks, Daze.'

He'd stopped calling her 'mum' the day after she'd told him about his real parents. At a very early age, other kids are happy to remind you what funny foreign names you've got, you and your brother. Kids at school, kids in the street. And it isn't long before you pester your 'mum' to tell you why. Dimi still called Aunt Daze 'mum' when he was drunk or drugged - which Zig suspected was the reason he hadn't turned up. He'll be shoving something illegal down his neck. Or up his nose. And when he finally arrives he'll emit a false buzz of happiness, till it wears off and an angry younger brother crawls out of the debris.

They clinked glasses, said 'Merry Christmas'. It was fine port, rich and not too sweet. Aunt Daze had poured three glasses.

'E'll come,' she said.

Dimi turned up at six-o-clock. They'd finished eating at three. He tucked into warmed-up turkey and soggy sprouts, talkative and affable between mouthfuls, full of wholly artificial chemical Christmas cheer.

'D'you get taller, Zig? Or 'm I shrinking?'

'Eat your sprouts, Dimi. Supposed to make you grow.'

Because he never really had. Five foot seven in his shoes, give or take. Aunt Daze believed it was the sudden lack of nurture in those crucial early months of life, when the confusion of death and loss, the legal chaos left behind for the living, had fallen out of a Christmas sky. No crib for a bed alright. He didn't lack love though. She gazed across at him, watching his lips and mouth chew the white meat, watching the small movements of his knife and fork, watching his hands, his nails, the joints of his fingers, his skin, the tiny hairs growing next to his knucklebones. Batten wouldn't be surprised if she could see into his arteries and veins. He could only guess what was inside them right now, but it would be a professional guess. Zig the cop. Dimi the drugged delinquent. Aunt Daze refusing to value one adopted son above the other.

Because his bulk was so intimidating, Olly had a knack of making his minions feel grateful for even the tiniest concession to their needs. Which was why Manny was relieved and uncharacteristically smiling as he drove home to tell Carrie the good news. Olly had agreed: the M27 'special' collection could wait till Boxing Day. What Manny didn't know was that, on Derek Herring's advice, Olly had already decided to postpone.

'Christmas night may not be the optimum time, Olly. Rather conspicuous, a lone horse-box on empty roads, when everyone's indoors enjoying Christmas cheer? Perhaps we could wait twenty-four hours or so? Every horse in England will be heading out on Boxing Day, to one event or another?'

Olly was well aware. Marianne had nagged him to take her to the meet at Crewkerne - 'it's a Boxing Day tradition, darling, the Seavington Hunt. You'd enjoy it.'

No he wouldn't. Him and the local snoots would never see eye to eye, he had no illusions about that. And he sweepingly assumed they'd all be there with their shiny black boots and their red finery and their yappy hounds, ganging up on a clockwork fox, or whatever they used these days. As if he cared. He could ride well enough, for a big man, but would much rather watch horses *being* ridden, by *little* men in coloured silks, at Wincanton or Cheltenham or Exeter races - horses that could make you money. One way or another.

I'll be a darn sight warmer in Lanzarote. And safer, he said to himself.

Horse *boxes* could make you money too. While Manny headed home, and Olly flew to warmer seas and alibis, two nameless and dark-featured men

248

- one tall and thin, one short but solidly-built - were sweating in the Spanish sun. With the ease that comes from experience, they loaded three fine Andalucian mares into a legally licensed horse box. If from a distance, in silhouette, the men looked like Don Quixote and Sancho Panza, that was as far as the similarity went. Before sunrise, they had carefully refitted a false panel over the sound-proofed compartment concealed behind the driver's cab. Two young olive-skinned girls, sisters, were already strapped tightly into its narrow dark space.

'Vacuum-packed for export,' Don Quixote had jibed in vernacular Spanish to Sancho Panza. The two girls had deep brown eyes like little pools of beauty, closed now, in drug-induced sleep. Even when awake they had not understood the men's language. Not a word of their native Albanian had been spoken in days, on sea or land. Greek, yes; some Italian; Spanish today; English, soon. It might be better for the two girls if they never woke up.

Ball was grateful beyond words for his Inspector's generosity.

'It's a no-brainer, Ballie. Kids need their Santa-dad at Christmas. Long sleigh ride from the cop-shop to your chimney-stack.'

For the briefest moment, Batten saw a tiny shadow flit across his Sergeant's ginger brow. And you never even mentioned 'Wake Hall', Zig.

'It's just the wife and me, zor, matter of fact. But Di - her name's Di, not sure if I've said - she'll be, yes, she'll be more than grateful. If you're sure?'

Batten was sure. For him Christmas was an itch; a place of dark memories. Without his northern obligations he'd run a mile the other way.

'You'll owe me one, though. A day's fishing. Long weekend up north. I'll give you a nudge.'

Later, it was Ball doing the nudging.

'I know, zor, but she insists, does Di. And when Mrs Ball insists....'

Batten was flattered to be invited, but on Christmas night? In Yorkshire, Christmas night was always for family, for kinfolk. It wasn't till Boxing Day that *friends* got a look-in.

'Bring someone if you like, zor. If that's what's holding you back?'

*Bring* someone? Who, Kenny Layzell from the farm up the road? The senior citizen midget barmaid in The Five Bells? I've only just arrived. I don't *know* anyone! He imagined what Ball would say if Rhona Fiske hadn't been in Scotland and he'd offered to bring *her*.

'No, it's not that, Ballie. I wouldn't want to be in the way. You know.'

Ball was under instructions not to know. He'd phoned his wife, told her the nice Inspector was covering Christmas Day, and she'd insisted that Batten be rewarded; she had her reasons. An invite to their village 'panto' wasn't much of a reward, but the copious food and drink before and after might qualify.

'It's a tradition, zor, on Christmas night in our village. The pub's not open, but the landlord gifts us the big back room with the stage. You won't be short of company, zor. Everybody turns up. We knock together a sort-of daft panto - could be a part in it for you, if you play your cards right. Zor?'

Batten was cringing at the thought of doing am-drams in front of a pack of baying kids of all ages. But Ball had his number.

'Course, once the youngsters are off to bed the piss-up begins. Goes on forever, zor, right through to early doors.'

Say yes, Zig. Beats eating and drinking alone. And you'll earn brownie points for getting Mrs Ball off your Sergeant's back.

As he drove down dark roads from Ashtree to the village of Stockton Marsh where the Balls lived, Batten wondered what kind of an evening he was in for. It had been a very slow Christmas Day at Parminster, but at least he'd cleared most of the still-absent Jellicoe's paperwork from his in-tray into someone else's. The few staff on duty had made the best of it, with warmed-up turkey and cold mince pies, but it was the warmed-up turkey some days ago, on Dimi's plate in Leeds, that still lingered. He wished his prediction had been wrong. Once the turkey was eaten and his substance abuse wore off, Dimi reverted first to Mr Sulk, then drifted through various forms of Mr Regret to Mr Angry, until a final Mr Slam yanked the door shut behind him as he left.

''A still think of 'im as young,' murmured Aunt Daze.

He's thirty five, Zig. A thirty five year old teenage delinquent with a tidy income but no identifiable job. Aunt Daze poured herself another port. Batten clicked the catch on what Daze called her whisky cupboard. Peace on earth to all men. And maybe Dimi too.

Hidden compartment and human cargo undetected, the horse box with the Spanish number plates trundled along empty roads towards the coast and its ferry ports. Don Quixote was a ferry port veteran now: hand over your documents for checking; drive up the ramp of the huge car ferry; chug into a bay; switch off. His export papers for the three brood mares, his veterinary certificates and horse passports, they were all in order. The two olive-skinned girls would probably be a touch smelly by then, but this would be of no concern to Don Quixote. Who would detect a touch of sweat and human manure against the stench of horse urine? Once the horses were seen to, he would double-lock the doors behind him and climb the big ship's familiar iron stairway to the bar. Sancho would have got the drinks in.

Batten wasn't too sure about dropping his car keys in the shoe-box sprouting from Sergeant Ball's bag-of-spanners hand. Funny night for a wife-swapping party.

'Car keys, zor, or you don't get a drink. House rule,' smiled Ball. 'Don't worry. Someone sober will drive you and your car back home.'

When he saw the impromptu bar, stacked to the rafters with alcoholic delights, he happily flipped his keys into the box alongside several others. Instantly, Sergeant Ball poured him a pint of local cider.

'Try it, at least, zor. Don't think you'll be disappointed.'

He wasn't. It was strong and dry. Deep and crisp and even better than beer. He sat down at the adjacent table, savoured his drink and looked round the big room, a Christmas tree at one end and a small stage dressed with tinsel and fairy lights at the other. He scouted the place for company, preferably under forty, female, intelligent, shapely and single. What do you think this is, Zig, Christmas?

In fact it was Mrs Ball who sat down next to him, wearing a pair of plastic reindeer antlers, and with a battery-powered Christmas tree brooch pinned to her well-cut pale-blue jacket. The brooch flashed green and gold a few times, till she apologetically switched it off.

'Trying to force myself into the mood, for the panto,' she said quietly. She sipped her half-pint and unclipped her antlers. Her upturned jug of a husband smiled encouragingly at her, while adding more car-keys to the shoe-box and playing barman. It was his turn, this year, she explained.

Di Ball went on to explain a great deal more, including why a shadow had clouded her husband's face when Batten called him a Santa-dad.

'She was just a month old, Gemma, when we lost her. Premature babies, you know.... Well, you probably don't. It felt cruel, anyway. I mean, we're not exactly small are we, me and Chris? But poor Gemma, she was barely bigger than your pint-glass when she died.'

Batten needed a drink, there and then, but couldn't raise even a finger to his cider. He glanced across at Ball. Even after Di's story, it seemed wrong that they were childless. His Sergeant looked exactly like a dad should look, like he'd always been one. Mind you, until a minute ago he was Ballie, not Chris. Hardly surprising they called him Crystal, behind his back. Di took a few sips from her glass, but Batten still dare not touch his own.

'After it happened, I thought I'd shrivel up to nothing if I didn't stop the tears. But when the doctor said there'd be no more babies, well, I cried till I was sand.'

She drained the last inch of her cider; Batten snatched the chance to drain six inches of his own, replacing the glass on the table with very great care indeed.

'When, er, when did she....when did Gemma....?'

'Oh, easy to remember - not that we'd ever want to forget.' She smiled. To his relief, there was tenderness but no tears in her eyes. 'It was Christmas Day. Seventeen minutes past three. In the afternoon.'

He'd meant 'how long ago?'

'Twelve years,' said the now-gravelled voice of Chris Ball, as he quietly placed two full glasses on the table. 'Twelve years ago.' He touched his wife's hair with a giant, gentle hand before returning to his duties at the bar.

'It's why Chris has stayed, of course. In Somerset.'

Batten did puzzled eyebrows.

'With a child buried here. We couldn't leave her, could we?'

He thought of his mother's grave, three motorways and a ring-road to the north. And then Di Ball surprised him, leaning over and planting a warm thank-you kiss on his cheek.

'You'll understand now,' she said, 'why Chris being at home today meant such a great deal to us. To me.'

Batten smiled and stroked his moustache. It was wet, from the cider. All he could manage was a 'don't-mention-it' hand, meaning it. Di and Chris. He wanted to ask them how they emerged from such pain with their humanity intact. He wanted to drag Dimi here, now, to listen to their answer, Di and Chris.

'Please,' he said. 'Call me Zig.'

Whether it was the cider or the general air of Christmas cheer, Batten didn't know, but he did begin to feel less like a stranger. Just as well, because it turned out he *had* been given a part in the 'pantomime'.

'We couldn't really cast you as the villain, zor, er, Zig. Wouldn't be very welcoming, would it? And the local kids insist I'm the baddie. Once a year, get their own back on Mr Plod.'

'So.....?'

'Oh, nothing difficult. You come on at the beginning and just stand there. It's a non-speaking part. You're a tree.'

'A *tree*? I've got to pretend to be a *tree?*' That's for luvvies, Zig, isn't it?

'Piece o' cake, zor. Just stand there with your arms out, and hold these.' From a black bin-liner, Ball produced two large branches made from some kind of lurid green plastic. They were the right size and shape for a fan-dance, but there was no way Batten was doing one of *those*.

'And when Royce the Voice says -'

'When *who*?'

Ball pointed across the room to a tall, large-nosed man, peering over his glasses at a crumpled page of notes.

'Royce Beckett, he's The Narrator. Has to be, he's the only one who has a script, for what it's worth. We call him Royce the Voice. When he says something like 'the wind shook the trees', well, you give your branches a wave. Wave anything you like, if you like. They'll love it.'

Momentarily, Batten was back at primary school, in the Nativity play, frozen with stage-fright. He was wearing a vaguely Biblical headdress fashioned from an old striped tea-cloth, and a tickly beard made out of

253

cotton wool and sellotape. He had just fluffed his big line. Third Shepherd only had one line, and it wasn't 'Miss, I need the toilet.' He propped the plastic branches on his chair; went to the loo.

Carrie was having a leisurely soak in her scented bath. At the last minute, Manny had dashed out to buy her some expensive rose-petal things that melted in the water. Bath bombs. *Bombs*, in a *bath*? What next, a grenade with the turkey? With or without, she'd told Manny the bird would be on the table at six, and he'd better be back in time to carve it, or else. He'd nipped over to Wake Hall to double-check the horse-box for tomorrow. Olly was obsessed with double-checking.

The engine was running sweetly, the lights and tyres were fine, and he paid extra attention to the ventilation ducts that fed the hidden compartment behind the driver's cab. The last thing they wanted was a couple of stiffs on their hands, after all the effort and expense. They'd make the switch behind closed doors, while transferring the horses, then Bulky would drive the next leg, over towards Bristol. It would be dark by then. Three silver-grey Spanish mares, Andalucians this time, and good ones too. A nice bonus. He switched everything off, locked up, and hopped into his Range Rover. Then he hopped out again; double-checked the horse-box doors.

From his grassy hill - a wooden box - at the edge of the little stage, Batten had a fair view of the panto and what seemed to him its rag-bag of bizarre and random characters. As a nod of welcome, the opening narration began 'the morning sun warmed the lonely apple tree with its rays.' A cardboard sun on a piece of string descended from the ceiling and hit him sharply on the head. He flapped his plastic branches in what he hoped was a sun-warmed manner.

''S'not an *apple* tree!' a young voice shouted. ''S'a *fir*. 'S'*evergreen*.'

The lurid green plastic could have been anything, but to avoid a bad start, Royce adapted. 'The morning sun warmed the lonely *fir* tree with its rays,' he said, shooting a glare at smarty-pants in the audience, and Batten once again wobbled his ridiculous pair of branches, this time to evergreen applause.

A seemingly plotless series of village in-jokes and rude double-entendres followed. Bill the Barman, played loudly by Sergeant Ball, was arrested for selling watered-down cider, and brought before The Lady Magistrate.

'On yower knees!' ordered The Magistrate.

'Have mercy!' screamed Bill/Ball.

'Soylence!' said The Magistrate, played with red rouge and panache in a frizzy gold wig by Malcolm Burley from the National Farmers' Union. 'And in future address me as 'Moy Lady', if you'll be so koynd!'

'Have mercy, Moy Lady!' screamed Bill/Ball. 'It's the shortage of apples! What else could oy do?'

'How shall he be punished?' cried The Magistrate, a question which drew a long list of ingenious and painful ideas from children young and not so young in the well-oiled audience. Even Bill the Barman winced at 'sit him on a sharpened carrot!'

In the interests of harmony, Royce the Voice said 'suddenly, a gentle breeze caressed the trees'. He'd learned his lesson, and kept things arboreally vague. Batten gently shook his plastic branches, to enthusiastic applause from Joe Porrit who Batten later learned was a tree-surgeon. When Royce said 'the wind ceased, and silence descended,' Batten stopped shaking as another placard on a piece of string was lowered too quickly from the ceiling by Jean Phelps, the librarian, hitting him sharply on the head.

'Whoops!', said Jean.

'Shhhhhh!' said the placard, in large letters.

'Typecast again!' stage-whispered Jean.

As the in-jokes passed him by and the powerful cider clouded his mind, Batten's attention drifted. The frizzy gold wig of 'Moy Lady' bounced across his vision as Malcolm Burley enjoyed his in-drag moment in the spotlight, circling the kneeling, cringing figure of Bill the Barman, whose elasticated false-hair-forelock grew longer and longer each time he gave it a tug. The cackling from the now-wild audience became louder still, came in tipsy waves, in echoes, and through the sharp glare of the stage-lights Batten could only just make out the blurred, swaying faces of children and parents and the white smears of teeth.

And then the faces and teeth were grinning sneeringly down at him from old ancestral portraits hung from high walls, and the walls were in

Wake Hall and he was on his knees before the imperious figure of Lady Wake who had hard gold hair, her cheeks and eyes like hard red balls of anger. 'You've a tad too much insolence in you, Inspector,' she hissed, before viciously cutting her giant leather riding-crop across his dazzled eyes. Through tears, he glimpsed a kimono-clad arm and sharp-nailed fingers gripping a golden goblet of hot blood, his blood, raising it towards her vampire lips and drinking greedily, draining its thick red contents down. His hands shook as they gripped at two absurd green plastic branches and he almost fell from his grassy hill, from his wooden box. He was a tree indeed, a single tree, a killing tree, on a low bump of a hill in a place he hardly knew and every Scrambler and Gribble and child and woman and man was laughing, cackling, screaming, screaming at him, but one silent face amongst all of them screamed a poisoned, dead-eyed, wide-eyed gargoyle scream at his hopelessness, his inability, at his failure, at the Third Shepherd's one fluffed line.

'The wind ceased, and the noyt was still,' said the rich West Country burr of Royce the Voice. In his peripheral vision, Royce saw that though the wind had ceased, the tree had not.

'The wind ceased to shake the branches of the OBVIOUSLY DEAF TREE!' he yelled, amidst hoots of cider-laughter from the audience. Joe Porrit, the tree-surgeon, offered to hop onstage and 'do a bit of loppin' if yer loyke!' - an offer forestalled by the smiling hands of Malcolm Burley from the NFU who, ducking his frizzy gold wig towards Batten, grabbed the tree by its forearms, and gently eased both plastic branches down. Evergreen or not, they fell deciduously to the floor, slipping from Batten's sweaty and cider-loose hands. 'Falling leaves!' quipped Malcolm to a dazed and slightly drunk Inspector from the CID. The audience loved it.

As the half-empty ferry rumbled past the harbour bar, Don Quixote slowly sipped the one and only beer he'd drink before disembarking at Portsmouth. Back in Spain, he'd be into his second or third by now, but not with the British police waging seasonal war on drink-driving. Don Quixote winced at what Rotten Fish - his collective name for Rutter and Herring - would do if he jeopardised a special shipment. King Zog was nasty enough. But Rotten Fish? Worse.

Batten could barely suppress his joy when the Very Fair Fairy made her entrance. She only came on near the end - Ball had said so - and the end couldn't come soon enough. His gut-wrenching embarrassment was a touch vain: he was a tree; a slightly tipsy tree; a very badly-acted tree. Only in his personal nightmare was the audience watching *him* instead of the real show.

The bulky roundness of old Mae Potter from the Grower's Association almost demolished Royce as she swept onto the stage carrying an oversized wand and wearing an enormous leopard-print faux-fur coat.

'What's that *fur*?' chorused the Chorus.

'To keep me warm, stupid!' replied Mae.

'No, what *fur*?' the Chorus sang back.

'I just told you what fur!'

'No, *what* fur?'

The exchange went on - to Batten, it went on and on and on - until Mae yelled 'because I'm the Very Fur Furry, that's what fur!' To hoots and applause, the Very Fair Fairy then trounced the Mad Bad Fairy in a wand-fencing contest, before pardoning one-and-all, including the still-kneeling Bill the Barman - 'and my rugby knee's killing me!'

Batten waved his plastic branches one last time as the 'cast' took their bow. He needed a drink, but was just sober enough to know it was food he needed first, to dilute the impact of the formidable local brew.

Manny still thought of long-distance phone-calls as exotic, so was not put out when the call ended after barely sixty seconds. Derek Herring had phoned from his private villa in Corfu to wish him Merry Christmas, or so it seemed, and to wax lyrical about 'a couple of very pleasing presents' he'd received. He hoped Manny was 'doing something nice for Boxing Day' - a coded confirmation that the two olive-skinned girls should be collected as planned. 'You have a good one too', Manny said, before returning to watch 'The Snowman' with an already-sniffling Carrie.

'No sense skimping on good nosh tonight of all nights, is there? It's only once a year!'

Batten had his mouth satisfyingly full so was unable to give the obvious reply to Sergeant Ball. Skimp? They certainly hadn't. He finished his steak pie. He was saving a bit of room for the dozen different puddings lined up on a long table behind him. Winter or not, one of them was an enormous summer pudding that seemed about to burst. He'd planned to help it, once the savoury stuff was gone.

Mrs Ball had introduced him to the other chompers at his table, but the only name he could recall was Norm Hogg, not because he sounded like a smoker's cough, but because he was half way through the game pie that Batten had privately earmarked for himself.

'Garrrrhhhh!' said Norm's pained voice. 'Some silly sod's put a bloody tooth in my pie! Supposed to be silver threp'nny bits in pies at Christmas! Oh-*oh*.' His tongue shifted meat and pastry from the roof of his mouth, and found a cavity that felt deeper than a mineshaft. 'Bugger. It's *my* tooth! Good Christmas for my dennist, this 'un....'

He finger-fumbled along the inside of his jaw and produced a dirty-brown pellet, which he glared at gruffly before wrapping in a dirty-brown hankie.

'Saving that for the tuth fairy, eh, Norm?'

'Tuth-fairy, my arse - ooh, sorry Mrs B. 'N what the bloody 'ell's *that*?'

Norm's finger poked at the pie. Sticking out of the yet-to-be-chewed part was a sharp-looking piece of....something. He flicked at the pointed little object, and drew it out with a puzzled finger and thumb. With his other hand he smoothed gravy, bits of pastry and small chunks of indefinable meat from the surface of the tooth-destroyer. Not satisfied, he dunked the object in the nearest glass - after first ensuring it wasn't his own - swished it through clean cider and held it aloft for all to see.

'Look at that'n. '*That's* what's done my tuth! And what's it doin' in a *pie*? Eh? You two're supposed to be coppers, en you? You're my witness, pair o' you! Whoever put that in my pie, I'll sue 'em!'

To humour him, a po-faced Sergeant Ball produced a see-through evidence bag. He squeezed it open, held it beneath Norm's giant hand and caught the tooth-destroying object smartly as it fell. They all stared at it, amused - apart from Norm. It was a smallish triangle of what looked like white perspex. Two sides were smooth and bevelled, the third side jagged and sharp where presumably it had been snapped off a larger object. The jagged edge had traces of something black on it.

'Wha's it, then? It 'as to be *something*'?'

258

'Norm, I haven't the faintest idea,' Ball said, cocking a questioning eyebrow at Batten, who stared and shrugged.

'Looks like the corner broken off, what, a plastic sign?'

Batten held the object up to the light, but before he could take a closer look it was flicked out of his grasp by the tipsy hand of Pete Beecham who was just passing, on his unnecessary journey to the bar. He peered at the object.

'I'll tell you what that is, gents - and you, Mrs B, apologies - I fit about ten of 'em a week.'

'You a dennist now, Pete? Thought you fixed cars for a livin'?'

'I do, Norm. 'S why I recognise it. It's the grade of plastic, see. That'll be a bit of black lettering, just there. And you couldn't miss that slightly rounded corner, could you?'

They could. The whole table raised collective eyebrows at Pete.

'Tuh. It's off a number plate, en it? Broken end off a number plate. Off a car. Or some kind of vay-hickle, as we say in the trade. And since you ask, it's a pint of best.'

'Put it on my tab,' said Ball to Pete's departing back.

A puzzled Norm could only splutter, 'I've lost my tuth to a *number plate?*'

You can't even be off-duty on Christmas night, can you Zig? A piece of number plate? In a game pie? He made the link, relieved that Norm got to the pie before he did. Go on, Zig, get your Sergeant's attention. Batten glanced over, nodded at the evidence bag, at the pie. Ball caught up, nodded back, did his duty.

'Norm, who'd you get these pies from?' he asked, reluctantly.

# Thirty Five

While no stranger to a thick head, Batten had never experienced a Somerset cider hangover before. As soon as he woke, he decided never to experience another. Vague memories of being driven home in the early hours were coming back to him, as was the sensation of sharp nails being driven into his skull, from the inside. He struggled downstairs, made strong coffee.

When he managed to raise his head to the clock he saw it was the middle of the afternoon. Squinting through the window, his eyeballs briefly encountered sunlight before he snapped the curtains shut to kill the glare. Someone had driven his Focus here at some point. It was parked outside. And his car keys must have miraculously migrated from Sergeant Ball's shoe-box because they now lay on the doormat, beneath the letterbox. Best place for them, since he already felt like a car-wreck.

As the coffee went slowly down, embarrassing memories of a strange Christmas night came too quickly back up. Just as well Sergeant Ball isn't one for office gossip. Is he?

If anything, Manny preferred doing the short 'special' collections by himself. The Boxing Day run, thankfully, had been an easy one-man job despite the engine overheating on the way back. He didn't like those Spaniards though, the tall one with the thick eyebrows and that squat, fierce-looking splodge who just stared at you all the time and never said a word. Reminded him of Batten and his blob of a sidekick - unpleasant thought.

Less could go wrong when it was a one-man job. On the long journeys Bulky sang from the same hymn sheet but he was a bit conspicuous. Baz wasn't a whole lot smaller. And he'd never been quite sure of Baz, whatever Olly said.

Was Manny becoming touchy about his size? Probably all Carrie's fault - you let a woman into your life and it all goes arse over tip. Mind you, they'd had a cracking Christmas Day. When he got back from checking the horse-box, she was still in the bath, surrounded by scented bubbles and bits of flower petal. He'd poked his head round the door, seen that bedroom look of hers. She'd slowly crooked her finger at him.

'Join me,' she'd whispered. He was out of his kit in a flash, been smelling of roses ever since.

But that felt like weeks ago now, because Olly got back from Lanzarote in a foul mood and worked everybody hard - even Del looked like he wished he was still in Corfu. Doubling the size of the special shipments meant twice as many brats to shift. And it's not as if Olly needs the cash.

'They're hardly going to notice the space got tighter. *Are they?*'

No, Olly.

'Just make sure the ventilation's working, and they don't wake up before you hand them over. *Right?*'

Yes, Olly.

And as if things weren't busy enough, Del quietly popped an untraceable phone into Manny's pocket. Which meant a different kind of 'special' was on the cards. But Manny enjoyed that kind of challenge - and the tidy bonus for completing it. He checked the phone's battery. It would ring, soon.

Once back in harness at Parminster, Batten forgot about cider hangovers - till Ball brought up the matter of Norm Hogg's tooth-destroying pie.

'Right, I remember now. Road-kill, yes?'

The logic was simple enough: if you find a bit of number-plate in a game pie, chances are you're eating meat from a road-kill. Batten remembered Norm Hogg's other information, too.

'Oy bought 'em off Mick. 'E do a tasty game pie, Mick.'

They'd both been surprised when Mick's surname finally popped out, because they recognised it. Mick Baines had been interviewed twice already. He was one of the Scramblers, the walking group who'd found Lawrence Vann's poisoned body at the top of Burrow Hill. He had a memorable girth and wore a loud canary-yellow cap.

'I had to put a bit of pressure on him, zor,' said Ball, 'before he coughed. He has a sideline, selling pies at farmer's markets, car boots. Him and Norm go way back. Norm bought a few pies, cheap, as his contribution to the panto food.'

Batten was feeling queasy again.

'He swears it was just this batch of pies, zor. Cheeky beggar blamed the Christmas rush. Ran out of meat, so he helped himself to the free stuff.'

'Where'd he get it?'

'There's always fresh road-kill over Wake Hall way, he says - usual formula, animals and late night traffic. 'Accidental meat', he says it's called. He tootled over in his van after dark, just the once, so he claims, couple of days before Christmas. Picked up the best stuff, right off the road.'

The best stuff? Badger? *Fox*?

'Swore he only put rabbit and pheasant in the pies. But if any are left we could have them tested, zor?'

Batten weighed up any fanciful connections between Mick Baines, the Scramblers, dodgy pies, and a pair of poisonings. Here, the coincidences seemed just that. Then he weighed up the lab-test fees, the hassle, the delays, Gribble's reaction.

'Just book him with what we already have, Ballie. Not sure I want to delve into that particular food chain. We know where he is if anything crops up. And he'll not do it again. Will he?'

Ball's ginger smile was laced with a touch of the devil. No, Mick Baines would definitely not do it again.

If the police hadn't been so insistent, she would have just got in her little Nissan and quietly driven herself to her mum's for Christmas, and then just as quietly driven herself back. She'd never enjoyed Christmas anyway, not since the old man had....But he was gone now - she couldn't care less where. What bugged her was the embarrassment of mum's battered old rust-bucket of a car rolling up to collect her, in full view of half the staff, with a broken exhaust blowing out smoke and hullabaloo. Faces had appeared at windows. There'd be smirks at her expense, she was sure of that.

And now here she was, back again, a glorified waitress tonight, serving dinner at the long table where Lady Wake and Olly Rutter sat in the same silence that had travelled back with them from a less than joyful Christmas in Lanzarote. While not the most observant person in the world, even Debbie spotted that Lady Wake's chair was a touch further away from Olly Rutter's. Or the other way around? She'd had such a bad time of it lately, she couldn't be sure of anything. But there it was, in her stride as she served, a pace or two further between ma'am's chair and the yeti's. Mr Yeti. The Abnormal Snowman. Which is what she called him in private.

'Thank you, Debbie,' said Lady Wake, a little coldly. 'We can manage dessert ourselves. Do take yourself off now.'

Sod them both, Debbie thought. I'm done my special tipsy trifle, and it needs serving properly - in delicate stemmed dishes, with a final sprinkling of toasted almonds and sugared mint leaves. She could just see the big yeti's banana fists slopping two rough portions into thick glass bowls and plonking them down on the polished oak table. If I didn't need the job, she thought. And the cottage. And a Lady who likes my food. And a safe place to be.

When Debbie had gone, and Olly had slopped tipsy trifle into two wrong bowls, Marianne Wake listened to the silence for a while. She was, she knew, experiencing the downside of her liaison with an 'erstwhile' gangster. Exactly how 'erstwhile' *was* Olly? There had been far too many police visits of late. He had spent much of their break in Lanzarote deflecting every question, every concern – when he wasn't whispering into his mobile phone. She was discomfited. 'Bedroom Olly' was how she thought of him now, because it was the only place she still trusted him to carry out his promises. Though he'd never actually promised to *breed*. At this present moment, her reaction to that was somewhere between disappointment and release.

In his distant dining chair, Olly thought his own thoughts. Going to pack my trunk and toddle off into the sunset, am I, because a *woman* has a dose of the sulks? I'll brush Somerset off my collar when *I* choose, not you, *Lady*.

In the cold silence, he chomped on the whiskied goo of Debbie's trifle. Pretty good nosh again, he thought, even if it's cooked by a ghost. She looks a wreck, that one - ever since Lawrence had his little accident. Something on her mind? Something the old shagger gave her? Told her? He tried to imagine Lawrence Vann doing pillow talk. Huh, shag and snore, more like.

Olly scooped up trifle, blind to his habit of projecting his own relationship assumptions onto others. Time she got her warning, the cook. Time to act.

Toying with a silver spoon that had been in the family for over two hundred years, Lady Wake glanced across at Olly with mixed emotions of disquiet, confusion, and stubborn lust. She recalled what that odious Inspector had said. 'If Olly's reformed, I'm Chief Constable of Somerset.' She didn't know. She just didn't know anymore. Olly swallowed the last of his trifle. Does he have to scrape the sides of my cut-glass bowl like he's gutting a deer?

But it wasn't the bowl that Olly was gutting, in his head. It was Debbie Farley. Once he made a decision, things moved with rapidity. Olly clanged his silver spoon into the glass dish, making Lady Wake wince. He stood up so quickly and with such a mean look in his eyes that she pulled her Irish linen napkin up towards her throat in a futile gesture of protection. But Olly flicked back his heavy oak chair and strode wordlessly past her, moving much more quickly than a large man should do, wrenching his mobile phone from his pocket as he slammed through the dining room door.

Had Lady Wake been less anxious and more observant, she would have noticed that it was not a gold-plated smartphone that was clamped in Mr Yeti's fist, but a cheap, disposable, totally untraceable model.

Batten had mixed feelings about questioning Vito Valdano again, but it had to be done - not just because of Stephanie Broken-Record's revelations about 'Discretion' but because Valdano was actually in the country.

'Don't worry, Ballie, we'll interview him in his *office* this time.'

Vito Valdano was no stranger to slings and arrows, and despite the cold rumble of fear in his stomach, he did his best to play pat-a-cake with the police. His opening salvo, once Ball and Batten were ushered into his 'study' - 'we do not have 'offices' here, Inspector' - was to ask them if they would like to sit down. As the ceiling was hung with a motley mix of moon-crystals on strings, tiny starlight LEDs, sky-coloured dream-catchers and white wooden wind chimes in the shape of little planets, the lanky Batten had to choose between conducting the interview with his head in a starry constellation or plonking himself down on the only available seat. While the dreaded Tibetan prayer stools were not in evidence, he still had difficulty looking and feeling authoritative while crunched into a small white-leather bean-bag. Even when the crunchy cushion came to rest, he still felt like a golf ball on a tee.

At least it was worse for the chunkier Ball, whose attempt to take notes while straddling a hill of beans threatened to pitch him onto a dangerous carpet of prickly sea grass dotted with random and presumably soulful little islands of crystal and pebble-stone, from which the smoke of a dozen joss sticks drifted up like thin grey snakes on the ladder to the stars. They stink of cat-piss, Batten thought, but refused to give Valdano the satisfaction of seeing him wrinkle his nose.

'I hope you are not uncomfortable, gentlemen?' asked their host, without a hint of a smile. 'We find soft seating very conducive to meditation and reflective endeavour, so I trust such benefits will filter through to you.'

Batten noted that Valdano himself was sitting behind an enormous and opulent sandalwood desk in a deeply upholstered white leather chair the size and shape of the Thai royal throne. One-nil to you then, Vito.

'Tell me, Mr Valdano, how long have you been boss of Solo Souls?'

'Inspector, we do not use such terms. There are no 'bosses' here. No Superintendents, no Senior Managers. Spiritual interaction is not responsive to control and command. How could we presume to 'manage' the human soul? Purely for the purposes of clarity and communication, I am known as the -'

'Soul proprietor, zor?' suggested Ball, from his bean-bag.

'Certainly *not*,' said Valdano in a tut-tutting, disappointed voice.

'King, perhaps?' suggested Batten, jabbing a long explanatory finger at the Thai throne.

'Inspector. Your tone, as that of your Sergeant, is not merely frivolous, it is offensive. And inaccurate.'

'Please correct me then, sir,' said Batten. 'What *are* you called?'

Valdano reached across the landscape of his desk and drew from a little soapstone dish a business card of the most delicate eggshell blue, overlaid with mazy smoke-yellow strands. Batten guessed it was a trendy graphic designer's idea of what a soul looks like. He'd already assumed that Valdano's title would be the dreaded 'Facilitator' so was hard pressed to remain professional when he read 'Solo Souls: connective tissue for adventurous spirits', and beneath it, 'Vito Valdano: Energiser.'

With his teeth clenched behind tight lips, Batten handed the card with mock solemnity to Ball who read it and immediately tightened *his* lips too. Batten pretended to clear his throat.

'So, perhaps you could answer my question, sir, which was how long have you been the....Energiser' - Batten cleared his throat again - 'of Solo Souls.'

'I fail to see any relevance in your question, but the answer, for what it is worth, is five years.'

'And before that?'

'Before that? Before that we were all younger, I imagine. Can you be a little more precise, Inspector?'

'I can, sir. I'm asking what you did *before* Solo Souls?'

'Many things, Inspector. I was searching for the way - as we all do, no? - and I found my vision: a facility focused on single, sensitive people. Without my belief in the spirituality of the single woman and man, there would not *be* a Solo Souls.'

Make things easier if there *wasn't*, eh, Zig? But as a single person himself he felt a background loyalty. He buried both thoughts.

'Mm. So, as Energiser, you presumably take....sole responsibility for all practices and policies of Solo Souls, without exception?'

Vito ignored the jibe and gave a noncommittal flick of the head. His large throne was beginning to feel just a little smaller beneath him.

'And in that same sole capacity, you would have been responsible for liaising with Lawrence Vann? Sir?'

'Inspector. All this has been asked, and answered. Previously.'

'I do realise that, sir, but Sergeant Ball and I were wondering if by any chance you've recalled any information about Mr Vann that may have for some reason slipped your mind? Previously.'

Vito Valdano paused. He saw the trap, but all he could do was shake his ample head. The police were the least of his concerns. If *Olly* discovered that his match-making sideline had paired Stephanie with, of all people, Lawrence Vann, late of this parish....

'So, no special links with Mr Vann? No unadvertised private services you might have put his way?'

Another shake of the head. And a cold-hot-cold-hot prickling of his skin.

'Stephanie Broke-Mondelle, then? Any special links with her, at all?'

Valdano dared to hope he was on slightly firmer ground here, not least because Stephanie had conveniently disappeared.

'Stephanie? Yes, of course, she has attended my meditation programme. I do believe she valued the experience, Inspector.'

'And was she offered any unadvertised private services, at all? Any *discreet,* unadvertised, private services?'

The ground turned back into quicksand. Vito Valdano practised his yoga breathing but it failed him. Nets tightened around his throat. How could the police and Olly be ploughing the same furrow? He knew Derek Herring was not above bribing the occasional policeman but surely he had not greased the palms and pockets of these two?

'Perhaps, Inspector, your description explains itself. 'Discretion' - to which I imagine you are referring - is deliberately named. We do not advertise. Nor divulge. Nor make public any matters that are meant to be private.'

'So if I were to ask you, sir, if you 'privately' introduced Lawrence Vann and Stephanie Broke-Mondelle, you would categorically deny it?'

Sweat was worming its way down the back of Valdano's neck and saturating his shirt. He tried to dam the flow with a badly-disguised roll of his shoulders.

'Given the recent tragic circumstances, and the moral imperative to assist the police in their necessary work, I would most reluctantly have to say yes, Inspector. But may I trust that discretion will also be practised by the CID?'

'And Lawrence Vann, sir. How did you come to have him on your books?'

'Books, Inspector? *Books*? Solo Souls is not an Accountancy firm. We deal in the *spirit.*'

'Oh, it's all free is it, sir?'

'Everything has a cost, Inspector. Lady Wake is a generous patron, but Wake Hall as a venue does not come free. Food is not free. Staff need to live. Goodness, Inspector, have you no grasp of economics?'

Yes, I have. And of tax avoidance. And dodgy book-keeping. So don't push your luck, Vito.

'Well, I'll rephrase, sir. Under what circumstances did you *assist* Lawrence Vann? Where he was concerned, what was the nature of your....intervention?'

'As I told your officers previously, Inspector, Mr Vann and I liaised purely within the broad context of Wake Hall. And I do not intervene. I *connect*.'

Vito knew he was more or less telling the truth, if with misleading vagueness. Lawrence and Stephanie had been more than happy to be *connected*, but this was a side issue now. Olly Rutter's fixated search for stolen data was Vito's true concern. If Olly found Stephanie, how long would it take him to unearth Vito's foolish role in 'connecting' her to the man who had stolen it? He dabbed at cold sweat from his brow with a rainbow-coloured handkerchief.

Both detectives were puzzled at the beard-shaking impact of a couple of vaguely awkward questions on this slippery man. He was beginning to melt. With something approaching disappointment, Batten nodded to Ball who consulted his notebook before continuing.

'Well, zor, first of all you appear to have been deliberately withholding information from the police about your highly significant connection to Lawrence Vann and Stephanie Broke-Mondelle, and you've also wilfully concealed 'Discretion'. We assume it is a registered business, zor?'

Vito merely shrugged. Raps on the knuckles he could take. Did these two have any idea of the stinking quagmire they had barely dipped their toes in?

'And it seems strange that just after your private relationship service comes into effect, Mr Vann is murdered, his walking partner poisoned, and the person you've 'connected' him to, Ms Broke-Mondelle, conveniently discovers his body before disappearing into thin air. You will forgive us, zor, if we fail to accept all these events as purely coincidental?'

Yet to me they are, Vito wanted to say. As far as I am concerned, they are. Whatever the consequences, he would bear them. He dare not explain to the police the far more significant trap he'd fallen into, because to name Olly Rutter and Derek Herring would bring the sky down on his head. It would be suicide.

Yes, he would reluctantly accompany them to the police station and make a statement. Did he have any choice? A more desperate concern was what would happen when they let him out.

# Thirty Six

Radiator hoses. Bloody horse-box goes through them like piss through a sieve. As if I haven't got twenty other things to do! But at least he'd tracked down what was making the bloody engine overheat.

Manny had his head under the bonnet and engine oil smeared on his hands and face when Batten and Ball strolled uninvited through the gates of Wake Hall Horse. The gates he'd forgotten to lock. His first instinct was to check if Olly's hands were within slapping distance, but Baz had driven Lord and Lady Muck to some posh business 'do' in the Jag, a good hour ago. He hoped the engine oil was hiding how red his face felt. Bad enough letting the cops walk straight into Wake Hall Horse. If they had a warrant for *this* particular horse-box, he was a goner. Thank Christ the office was double-locked, at least.

McRory wasn't to know that even had the gates been locked, Batten would have kicked them in - or got Ball to do it. Batten was boiling. All the graft they'd put in on Vito Valdano revealed not a single link to the murder of Lawrence Vann. Small crooks, small crimes, no leads, dead ends. Whenever they came close to a breakthrough, it darted out of range. Was Olly Rutter *psychic*, all of a sudden? Batten had decided it was time for another fishing trip, fresh invisible bait on a sharper hook.

He'd never seen the vast interior of Wake Hall Horse in close-up. He and Ball stared at the interlocking lines of stables, dozens of them, the yards and track-ways, the big barns and storerooms, all encircled by a high wall that must have used up an entire quarry of stone. Batten was reminded of the dense network of apple orchards at Burrow Hill. They were multi-coloured though. Wake Hall Horse was a random mix of dirty-browns.

'Gents, gents, I'm up to my neck. Whatever you want it'll have to wait. It'll *have* to.'

Ball gave McRory a 'don't push it' stare.

'Look, if I don't fix this box, I'm for the high jump. Losing us money. Been off the road for weeks. *Week*s. Engine's knackered, needs a new one. Wouldn't like to tell Mr Rutter for me, would you, eh? He'll go *spare*.'

Ball left the speaking to Batten.

'We're not interested in *you*,' he lied. 'We're looking for Bulky Hobshaw.' As well as being on a wind-up-Manny mission. 'Is he around?'

Why did they want Bulky? *He* hasn't cocked up, has he? Typical, no Del, no Olly. Just Manny, manning the walls on his own again.

'You want to know if Bulky's around? *Bulky*? Cuh. Do you think you wouldn't notice him if he was? You a pair of comedians now?'

We are. And you'll get a punch-line if you don't watch your lip.

'When will he be back?'

'Back?'

'Yes, back.'

'When will he be *back*?'

Batten had recently been in a panto. Never again. He put a commanding arm round Manny's grubby shoulder and drew him to the far side of the horse-box, away from Ball's ears. Suspecting the worst, Ball turned his back. I neither heard nor saw a thing, Your Honour.

'In my capacity as Investigating Officer in a murder case, I've asked you a simple question. If I don't get a straightforward and accurate reply in the next ten seconds, I'm going to ram your lippy gob so hard into this engine-block your teeth will shatter. And for an encore I'll slam the bonnet down on your cocky little head!'

'You ca -'

'And if you utter words *remotely* resembling the sentence 'you can't talk to me like that', I'll do it even harder the *second* time. Are we CLEAR?'

Batten removed his arm from Manny's shoulder, and brushed away dirt. Manny was speechless, until he remembered something about ten seconds.

'He's delivering. Back tomorrow. Leicester, I think.'

'Don't think. Check.'

Manny failed to prevent Batten following him into his sentry-box office, where a pile of grubby diaries poked out of a wall rack. He grabbed a diary with 'Box 7' scrawled on the cover.

'There,' he said, pointing at 'LEICESTER' and 'BULKY' blocked in against today's date. 'Satisfied?'

Batten gave it a dismissive glance and without preamble dragged a diary headed 'Box 1' from the rack. Manny visibly tensed as Batten flicked through the stained pages. Ball was right: 'BAZ' was scribbled here and there.

'What's this?' he asked the cowed Manny, his long finger jabbing at the word 'IMP' scrawled on some of the pages. 'This refer to *you*?'

Manny wanted to roll back time, to a point where he'd remembered to double-lock the gates. He bit back a sarky reply before choosing the most straightforward.

'That's Imp. You know, Import.'

'When you bring horses from overseas?'

'Yeh. Like I told your Sergeant, we're *international*. No Mickey Mouse stuff here.'

He pointed into the distance, easing the two cops away from the horse-box whose illegal imports were far more profitable than a few Spanish nags. 'Imported three top-notch mares the other day, if you want to see. In the fields, over there. Andalucians. Her Ladyship's favourite.'

The two detectives trudged towards the rear gates to pretend to look. While Manny was juggling keys and fiddling with locks, Batten riffled through more of Box 1's diary pages. Those for the weeks before and around Christmas were missing. Flicking back, he noted an 'Imp' crossed out, around the time Hick and Halfpenny were doing their night-time surveillance. He carefully committed future import dates to memory, before gazing through the now-open rear gates towards field upon field of beasts. He'd never seen so many horses in one place before, not even at The Grand National - eighty, ninety of them, maybe more. The strong equine smells no longer bothered him.

Even a townie could spot the Andalucians, grazing a little way off in a separate field: magnificent silver-greys with lush manes and long tails. How could something so beautiful be called a beast? They were fine-faced creatures, magazine-cover material.

With disdain, he thrust the open diary into the less attractive hands of Manny McRory.

'A lot of missing pages here. Bit careless, that?'

Manny pointed accusingly at an invisible pack of horse-box drivers.

'Law unto themselves, this lot. Barely read 'n write, some of them. Wrong entries, wrong pages, I can't keep up. Gets on your *wick*.'

He closed the diary, pulled it tightly to his chest with a pair of brown claws.

'We'll come back. When Bulky's here.'

'Er, can I tell him what it's about?'

Batten wiped his sticky hands on the wooden gatepost.

'No.'

He was glad Ball was driving, because he didn't want to pollute his own steering wheel with the residue from Manny's diary. His hands would need soap and water and a scrubbing brush.

'Successful trip for a change, zor.'

'Yep. McRory almost peed his jodhpurs.'

'So when *are* the next imports due?'

Ball had thrown off the Wake Hall blues, and was back to his old sharp self.

'You spotted that?'

'I did, zor. But I don't know if Manny did.'

Probably. Or he'd work it out later. For Batten, it mattered little. Dates could change, but could Olly Rutter?

'It was handy, you taking Manny off for a gentle talking-to, zor.' Ball smiled a ginger smile. 'Gave me a chance to have a butchers at his favourite horse-box.'

'What, the broken one?'

'Oh yes, zor. The broken one with the warm engine. And fresh oil on the floor, below the sump. And something much more interesting than even that.'

Batten didn't mind indulging his Sergeant in these games of protraction. Rural policing meant doing a lot of miles, and the games passed the time. He leaned back in the passenger seat.' I don't suppose you're talking about Manny's after-shave, eh, Ballie?'

'I'm not, zor. I'm talking about Manny's number plate. On the front of his horse-box.'

'It wasn't RUT73R, was it?'

'No, zor. And nor was it entire.'

*Nor was it entire?* Where does he get these yokel phrases from?

'I'll have to check, mind.'

'Oh, I'm sure you will, Ballie.'

'Don't suppose you had a chance to look, zor?'

'Boredom alert, Sergeant. Spit it out.'

'Right, zor. Well, it would be nice if they match - the missing corner of Manny's broken number-plate, and a certain piece of plastic found in a Mick Baines road-kill pie on Christmas night....'

Batten jerked up in his seat and looked admiringly at the upturned jug expertly steering his car at speed down a narrow Somerset back-road towards Parminster. Because, if they do match....Batten was trying to remember the statement that Mick Baines had given.

'Because if they do match, Manny's lying through his teeth, yes? Horse-box 1 is fully serviceable - and the bloody thing *must* have been on the road around Christmas time!'

'S'right, zor. Even though it's been *off* the road for weeks.'

'W*eeeks!*'

Batten's imitation of McRory's high-pitched scouse was pretty good, for a Yorkshireman with a fear of amateur dramatics.


'Want tea, Tom?'

Dipstick Dave selected a caddy from his well-stocked shelf. He waggled the label in front of Tom's face. Tom wanted something warm, for sure. The barn was icy. But Orange Pekoe tea? If he wanted orange, he'd *eat* an orange.

'I'll stick to this, Dave.'

Dave frowned as Tom spooned two helpings of cheap instant coffee into a mug with 'Happy Birthday' printed on it. Tom should use *that* mug on birthdays, not any old time. And stop putting three sugars in his coffee. Might as well just drink sugar. Or milk. Yes, he should drink milk, from little baby's bottle! He was angry with Tom, didn't know why.

Two nights before, they had finally hit Wake Hall.

'Piece of pizz, Tom.'

Tom hadn't disagreed - the security was a joke. If they'd put their minds to it, they could have broken their six-minute record. But for Tom the tingle had gone.

He swallowed his thick, sweet coffee, and watched Dave's now-familiar tea ritual. Was Dave really from Eastern Europe? Give him a teapot and he turned into a bloody Geisha girl. He was sick to the back teeth of caddies of tea. He was sick of this chilly barn, sick of sleeping in daylight and going to work in the dark. But mostly he was sick of Dave.

Sometime today, though, a nearly new Massey Ferguson tractor from Wake Hall, complete with false plates and papers, would be heading off to a container-ship bound for points east. His share of the profit would ring the £200,000 bell, the private target he'd set himself. When the money came through, he wouldn't be sick of Dave any more. He'd be gone, and Dipstick Dave could shove his tea - and shove himself - back in his caddy.

'I'm going for some air, Dave.'

'Air? You think no air in here?'

'It's just an expression, Dave.' *For Christ's sake!*

'Hey, Tom! You not wash dirty coffee cup!'

But Tom had slammed the door on him.


Gribble's theory that Wake Hall was the safest place for Debbie Farley had a weak point. Wake Hall's green fields and fine vistas may have been appealing to the eye, but Debbie's body and soul needed more. She was stir-crazy. Christmas at her mum's bungalow had been claustrophobic to a fault, and now after shifts in hot kitchens and dining halls, she needed long hikes, different country, good air. Debbie needed to walk, walk, walk.

'I could go with her, sir,' Magnus offered, when the problem was raised at the daily briefing. Magnus was ex-Army, an experienced yomper in her own right, so Batten agreed. But it was not to him that George Halfpenny, afterwards, snidely hissed 'aww, nice girlie hike with your colour-blind lesbian chum, eh?'

'The trouble with you, George,' she replied, 'is you give real men a bad name.'

For Parminster locals, there were two towns: Parminster, and Parminster Top. Street parking in the high street was a nightmare, now that a new one-way system had 'improved' the place. But up the hill in Parminster Top there was parking a-plenty, and Debbie Farley left her Nissan Micra there in a little cul-de-sac before joining DC Nina Magnus on a welcome country hike through the valley of the River Ile.

A morning walk would have been preferable, had half-days and shift patterns coincided. Making the best of it, they planned to walk till the sun disappeared then grab an early evening meal somewhere. And walk they did, through woodland, by the winding river and under open skies, swapping tales and ignoring the clank and clutter of working lives left temporarily behind.

This closeness to nature moved Debbie to recommend an 'exciting organic-food place I know.' Magnus had set her stomach on a home-made burger and, to hell with it, chips and mayonnaise too. But this was Debbie's day, so she reluctantly postponed her pure beef for 'something healthy', in a new bistro called 'Meat-Free Meet'. When her aduki-bean curry arrived it was less of a disappointment than expected, or perhaps the glass of premium lager made it seem so. Debbie tucked happily into the roasted pine-nut pesto that sat like a beige-green beret above her tofu and aubergine flan.

Earlier, through powerful binoculars, a small, wiry figure had tracked Debbie Farley on her country walk with 'the butch black one' - which was how the man described Magnus to his well-spoken contact. They used cheap, disposable mobile phones. Not once did they refer to Olly Rutter and his determination to 'fix the old shagger's cast-off.' No names were mentioned.

'She's giving it mouth, the white bitch? Get me?'

The wiry man was correct only to a point; had he been closer he would have heard Debbie unburden her grief and loss to a sympathetic woman who just happened to work for the police.

'Your assessment?' asked smooth voice.

Lifting his binoculars, the wiry man watched animated lips pour out word after word, saw the butch cop listen in that calculating cop way. He recognised it, he'd had experience. In code, he reported what he saw.

'Oh dear,' posh voice replied. 'It seems to be time for a little persuasion.'

Before dusk fell, binoculars again picked out the two women as they stepped through the badly-painted mauve doors of an under-heated little restaurant half way down the hill from Parminster Top. Seconds later, the women appeared at a table in the window.

'Easy,' said the wiry man, as he slipped what looked like a long metal tube beneath his dark coat. He checked his pocket for a stubbier piece of metal, and locked the car, its false plates securely in place. In near darkness, he scuttled across waste ground to the path by Debbie Farley's Nissan, and strolled nonchalantly past. A thick clump of shrubs separated the parked car from the empty, unlit recreation ground beyond. The man ducked into the shrubs and slipped between two tall viburnums. From beneath his coat he drew the high-powered air-rifle.

In some ways he was being over-dramatic, since Parminster Top in midweek midwinter was a ghost town after sunset. It took him only two shots to smash the bulb in the street lamp next to the Nissan, leaving a wide pool of darkness all around it.

'Easy,' he said again, creeping forward to a vantage point behind a large laurel bush whose mid-green leaves looked black in the gloom. He was now one long stride in the darkness from Debbie's car.

'Well, it's....interesting,' said Magnus in answer to Debbie's enquiry about her bean curry. She gestured at Debbie's lower lip, from which a dab of pesto was dribbling.

'Oops, sorry,' Debbie giggled, wiping the green paste from her mouth. She was beginning to relax, to enjoy things again. Despite the scrubbed wooden table that was a little too big, and the uncomfortable chairs with hard rush seats that were a little too small - and despite the lack of red meat - Nina Magnus was enjoying things too. They'd had a lovely walk, and once Debbie had unburdened her sadness over Lawrence Vann, they had yakked like old friends. Better than spending time with George Halfpenny.

The wiry man's plan was simple. Taking chances with the fuzz would earn him a slapping, so if the butch cop saw the dumb chef to her car, he'd abort, and follow in *his*. Country lanes all the way. No shortage of ditches to run her into.

But if Debbie Farley came alone, he'd wait till she unlocked the Nissan then make it look like a mugging - a rough one. Stars were visible above him now, and that's all *she'd* be seeing. He'd check her pockets, the boot, glove compartment, take her bag, her rucksack, her keys - but not her mobile phone. She'd be needing that. In a little while, a disguised voice would remind her that one mugging can easily become two. And the second one…. Keep your trap shut though, keep out of the witness box - and you won't end up in a box of your own.

Nina Magnus would have happily ordered a second lager and continued chatting to Debbie Farley, had she not been driving - and if Mike wasn't coming round. She needed to get home, whizz a hoover round the carpet, hide some of the clutter. And put clean sheets on the bed, just in case. She'd bumped into Mike - literally - while shopping for a pair of walking boots. Almost knocked him over, in fact, big as he was. Mike was a walker too, she discovered, after she'd said yes to a coffee. She'd never heard of the Lycian Way. It was a walking trail in Turkey, he said, and he was planning to hike along part of it in the Spring. If he could find someone to go with….

In the shadows, the man pulled on a black ski mask. All his clothing was black, right down to the gloves that covered surprisingly strong hands, one of which gripped a stubby steel pipe. It wasn't heavy enough to do permanent damage, but it would knock the silly bitch senseless. And he wasn't exactly a novice, was he? A stout branch snapped from a nearby tree lay handily nearby. Once she was down, he'd scrape the branch across her neck at the point where he'd clubbed her, and drop the branch on the ground. He could already hear the cops trying to sound smart.

'Opportunist crime, wouldn't you say? Used what was to hand. Her blood on the branch, fragments of bark in the wound. Some yob, for drugs money, my bet.'

'Well, I think he's quite good-looking, your Inspector, and very sympathetic.'

'Oh, he is - but he won't be sympathetic if I don't see you safe, believe me.'

They had reached Magnus's Toyota now. She dropped her rucksack in the back, sneaking a quick look at her watch as she did so. They'd chatted on, and it was later than she thought. Debbie Farley pointed up the hill.

'You *have* seen me safe, Nina. My car's just up there - street lamps all the way. And I'll tell you something, first time in a while I've *felt* safe, thanks to you.'

Magnus was flattered. Yes, she'd done a good job on Debbie. Listening, settling her down, a bit of advice. She'd told her that what's hurting now won't hurt forever, and meant it. She'd got over Steve, her ex, hadn't she? Mind you, *her* ex was still alive, more's the pity. Mike seemed a far nicer man. She sneaked another look at her watch. Mike.

Debbie drew car keys from her pocket and started up the hill, holding up a hand, fingers raised, as Magnus made to follow.

'Nina, please. I told you, I'm safe now. Go on, get in your car, 'stead of bobbing up and down next to it like the pavement was on fire.'

They both had a giggle. Lord, thought Magnus, am I *that* transparent?

His fingers gripped the stubby metal pipe as movement in the distance became Debbie Farley, trotting helpfully towards him - alone. In truth, he would have enjoyed hurting the black cop - but he knew what Olly Rutter would do if he tried. Debbie walked confidently up the slope till she noticed the pitch-black area round her car. Not so jaunty now, eh, bitch? But she paused only to draw a tiny pocket torch from her handbag, and switch it on. The thin beam barely pricked the blackness. He focused on the rucksack she still wore. Can't climb into the driver's seat with *that* on your back, can you?

As if hearing his thoughts, she opened the car door, lifted both her arms to the back-straps and began to squirm out of them. In the process, her neck presented itself to him as if in sacrifice. Thanks, he might have said, had he been less vicious and more polite. Instead, he slammed the hard steel pipe into the base of her skull. The result was instant. Debbie Farley dropped like a rock, her backpack sliding almost comically down her arms as she fell to the ground. It landed beside her, no more awake than she was.

Magnus had only gone a few yards when the eyes in the rear-view mirror stopped being hers and became Batten's. 'He won't be very sympathetic if I don't see you safe.' She'd said that to Debbie, seconds ago, and here she was, driving *away* from her responsibilities, zipping the car through Parminster's one-way system like a lovesick schoolgirl, just in case Mike….She looked in the mirror once more - this time to turn right. And then to turn right again.

The wiry man took no chances. When he lashed a savage boot into the senseless Debbie's ribs, she didn't even grunt. Satisfied, he counted the spoils: her handbag, her keys, her backpack. They would all go into the hold-all he'd brought with him, once he'd searched the boot and the glove-compartment. If Lawrence Vann had been stupid enough to hand over any interesting items, the silly cow might just be carrying them with her. Keepsakes from a dead ex-lover, awww. He bent down for her keys.

With another glance at her watch, Magnus pulled the Toyota into the only free space she could find on the road to Parminster Top and hoofed it the rest of the way up the slope towards Debbie's car. Just two minutes, Nina, just to check, just to be on the safe side. Just to cover your back.

Reaching for Debbie's keys in the ring of darkness surrounding the Micra, the wiry man saw movement, saw a figure jogging up the steep slope as if towards him. The black cop, well, well. Honest, Olly, I didn't have a choice, she just came at me….Gripping the metal cosh in his eager hand, he crouched out of sight in the even darker shadow behind the boot. Two birds with one stone, hah-hah.

The Micra was still there, she recognised it, even in the darkness, seen it often enough at Wake Hall. But where's Debbie? And that street lamp's gone. And why's there a sack next to the car? *It's not a sack, it's*….Alert. Training kicking in. Kicking in *now*, yes, but what had she been thinking before - oh, just an off-duty/on-duty ramble in the country, no need for a torch, handcuffs, mace, a baton.

Had there been less dark, the metal cosh would have sparkled as it rose in the air. Nina Magnus did not see it as she approached the sack that was not a sack, nor did she see the heavy branch that the wiry man had laid handily on the ground. The cosh swung viciously down towards the back of her head, just as she collided with the unseen branch and stumbled over. She felt the whoosh as the metal bar fizzed past her head, missing her skull by a hair. Instinct made her roll away, her trailing foot hooking the branch and dragging it towards her. The cosh rose again as Magnus's hand felt roughness against her fingers which closed around the hefty piece of wood with its scars of torn bark and scalpel-sharp splinters at one end.

Wincing when the cosh struck her hard on the hip, she swung the wooden bough upwards at her attacker with very great force. She felt the collision, heard the crack and the rip as the heavy bough snapped into the wiry man's arm, its scarred edge slicing through the cloth of his sleeve and across his skin and deep into flesh.

He staggered back in shock, dropping the metal cosh which rolled away into darkness. Warm blood pumped from his slashed arm and ran down into the fingers of his glove - and then suddenly the pain came and the click of broken bone. His yell merged with a blast of shrieks from the gloom, as the floored Magnus used her only other weapon, a mountaineer's warning whistle, kept in her pocket for emergencies.

In hot anger, he lurched towards the source of the noise. He liked a challenge. But his sleeve was sticky with blood, his arm hot, and there was the handbag, the backpack, the keys to deal with, his airgun in the undergrowth, the car to search.

Shrill blasts from the whistle seemed to pummel his face. He jumped back, shocked, tripping over Debbie's fallen backpack and screaming as he landed on his damaged arm. Scrabbling to his feet, the wiry man in the black ski-mask and the blood-stained gloves, the man who liked a challenge, the man who was unarmed now - and hurt - in the shriek-filled pool of darkness of his own creation, turned and ran away, scuttling like a crab to the safety of his concealed car.

Magnus didn't think her hip was fractured, but by god it hurt. After phoning for help, the light from her mobile revealed a wet redness sticking to the rough bark of the broken branch. It wasn't Debbie's blood - she'd already checked her and done the necessary - and it wasn't her own. Whose blood was it then?

# Thirty seven

Vito Valdano was losing weight. He knew he needed to, but preferred a controlled, voluntary process based on consuming less food. Instead, he was leaking watery fat from every pore, uncontrollably. He tried to practice what he preached, but meditation calmed neither his pores nor his mind. A sweat-drenched, rueful, petrified Vito hissed 'think, man!' to himself.

If he had never met Derek Herring, and if Derek Herring had never introduced him to Olly Rutter….but he couldn't go back in time, couldn't undo harm or disconnect connections. Could he?

Vito Valdano was proud of Solo Souls. He believed in it, and his decision to use the profits to 'put something back' into the world was genuine. He was himself an orphan, as far as he knew, having been dropped on the doorstep of The Salvation Army at two days old, or was it three?

A Children's Home: what a misleading phrase. A proper 'home' barely figured in his childhood memories. Placing orphans from Eastern Europe into stable homes in the West was intended to be a compensation, a re-balancing of ills. Vito Valdano's legacy.

Derek Herring was on the same delayed plane, to Corfu. They'd recognised each other, Wake Hall being their common ground. The night ferry to Albania was long gone, and in the airport Derek overheard Vito enquiring about local hotels. Goodness, I won't hear of it. My spacious villa down the road. Please, let me emulate traditional Greek hospitality towards strangers. Not that you are. A stranger, I mean. Yes, isn't Lady Wake a wonderful woman….Me? Legal services, for the most part. Oh yes, Wake Hall Horse. My goodness, what a success that's been….

Back in Somerset, Derek had kindly offered to become involved, 'pro-bono, of course', in the legal niceties of the orphan re-homing project. He had even talked Olly Rutter into adding his support, he said. They had business links everywhere, and what worthwhile interventions they could make on Mr Valdano's behalf.

Why did he not see, when Derek next invited him to the Corfu villa, that his fellow dinner guests were well-heeled, clean-shaven gangsters? Had his vanity added even more tint to his already-tinted spectacles? He accepted help, signed 'accords' that Derek said were to ensure his new sponsors 'donated from their wallets and not merely from their hearts.'

His orphanages became swift roads to perdition. The orphan support networks he so carefully coordinated continued their benign work, attracting unsuspecting, needy children in numbers he would previously have been proud of. Not all these children arrived at their intended destination, however. A few here, a few there, were intercepted and efficiently transported westwards, for purposes he refused to acknowledge. He was told what would happen to him if he went to the police.

When he bravely objected, the big-faced Albanian who called himself King Zog *demonstrated* the consequences, using a 'spare' ten year old orphan girl - 'the broken one,' they'd called her, because of her misshapen hand. King Zog thrust a shoe box at Vito, made him open it. He could see - and smell - the severed, malformed hand even now. 'You like both your hands?' King Zog asked. 'You want to *keep* them?'

Vito's howls at his own naivety changed nothing. Yet he did not give up. He compensated, expanding the more-or-less legal sides of his business as best he could, while the illegal side expanded regardless. If he could create an unsullied nest-egg, he told himself, perhaps he could escape, start again, provide a legacy elsewhere. Once the police had finished with him, he'd throw himself into his work, afresh.

The truth seeped out like watery fat from involuntary pores, and his inner voice asked its bitter question: if there *is* an escape from Olly Rutter, is it the kind you need a nest-egg for?


Rhona Fiske wasn't returning his calls. What if he turned up outside her cottage in a police car with its lights flashing and the siren going nee-naa-nee-naa? By association, Nina Magnus popped into his mind. I bet she's taken some stick, a cop called Nee-naa. He had no idea she was taking far worse stick than that.

DC Magnus's *ears* had taken some stick from Batten, for not safely seeing Debbie Farley back to Wake Hall.

'*Have you got shares in the NHS or something?*' Batten roared down the phone, before Magnus was driven off to A and E for x-rays. Debbie Farley - still concussed - was back in the same hospital ward she'd left only a few weeks before. 'What kind of nervous wreck will she be when she *does* wake up?' he'd yelled.

'At least there's DNA evidence, zor. Could be a breakthrough.'

'Huh. If the toxics get their finger out.'

'Don't forget she's still young, zor, is Magnus,' Ball reminded him. 'Not the finished article yet.'

Ball's nudge made Batten ease back on the throttle. According to the Chief Constable, *he* wasn't the finished article either.

But was he finished as far as Rhona Fiske was concerned? He was still unsure how much it mattered. He'd enjoyed the walks, the meals, the brief fling, but…. Loose ends, though. He didn't like loose ends - which was why he'd tried to ring her three times already. To do what, Zig? Apologise? Ask for a re-match? If his self-awareness had seeped an inch closer to the surface he might have seen it was the *cop* in him that didn't like loose ends. In his private life, he had nothing but.

Nevertheless, here he was, the early bird, driving into Wake Hall instead of driving into Parminster, with the loose end of Rhona Fiske on his mind. He'd go to her cottage and find her, before she started work. He didn't fancy tracking her down in the Wake Hall kitchen, with the permanent cook now hospitalised for a second time.

Approaching the empty visitors' car park at the back of Wake Hall, it was not Rhona Fiske he saw but Manny McRory. He was struggling with a pair of holdalls, while searching his pocket for car keys. Manny straightened up when he recognised Batten's Focus, panic on his face and a thick white bandage on his right arm and hand. Batten was still in his seatbelt as Manny bolted past Roddy Cope and Neil Tapworthy, swerved round the farriers' van and sprinted away like a crazed whippet, despite the holdalls that clattered against his short legs as he ran. He headed for the grassy open ground that separated Wake Hall Horse from the staff car-park where a mud-spattered Range Rover waited.

Batten was dumbstruck. That's as clear an admission of Manny-guilt as a cop's likely to see, Zig. So *wake up*! Clambering out of his car he yelled 'Stop! Police! - but when his conscious mind kicked in and saw how far the scampering whippet had already travelled, he knew even lanky legs wouldn't catch him, particularly in these shiny slip-on town shoes. And you won't get your Focus over that swamp Manny's running through - you'll have to drive all the way round, Zig, and he'll be in the wind by then! Searching for something to throw, he grabbed at a heavy metal horseshoe from the farrier's van.

Roddy Cope's hand shot out and strong fingers firmly clamped onto Batten's arm. He cursed loudly, swung a fist, hard. Before it could connect with Roddy's chin it hit an invisible wall and disappeared into the steel vastness of Neil Tapworthy's giant claw. So these two *are* involved! Batten's fingers were trapped in a vice. Absurdly, he imagined two thieves either side of what felt like a crucifixion.

'I'll do the pair of you for assault, you bastards! I'll do you fo - '

Roddy Cope's much calmer voice cut in.

'They don' have to be red, to be red hot,' he explained, his free hand indicating the horseshoe. 'It's just out the furnace, that'un.'

Neil Tapworthy's massive spare hand selected an identical horseshoe and a deep, slow voice said 'This 'un's cold, if you waan' throw it.'

A chastened Batten turned towards the car park, expecting to see Manny driving off. But Manny was still slithering through the slime-trap of his own short-cut. He'd slipped on the skiddy surface, dropped his holdalls in the mud and his white bandaged hand was now a dirty brown. He got to his feet, reclaimed his luggage and legged it again. Without conviction, Batten heaved the horseshoe into the air - and watched it land with a disdainful plop barely thirty yards away. He cursed, frustration overcoming him. Not exactly Batten/Ball, Zig!

'I'm useless at bloody *cricket*!' he wailed.

'*You* might be, but I'm not!' Jake Tuttle had heard the commotion. 'An' I hate that whiny sod.'

Jake grabbed a cold horseshoe and with a practised whip of his cricketer's arm whizzed it powerfully at the fugitive. The horseshoe flew and whirled through the air, a spinning missile, homing in, closer and closer on Manny McRory's head - till he ducked at the last second and smugly watched it thump into the earth at his feet. Even at that distance Batten could have sworn he heard Manny's sarcastic scouse laugh as he sprinted the last few yards towards his car. He certainly heard the crunch of fractured bone as Manny's foot went into a badger-hole and stayed there, while the rest of his screaming body flew forward and slammed into the mud. A millisecond later, a pair of heavy holdalls slammed into *him*.

# Thirty eight

Carrie Sansom's warm Christmas bliss was cold porridge now. The police wouldn't allow her see Manny, who was under close arrest. What did they think he was going to do, hop away and hide? On a pair of sticks? It's a mistake, she convinced herself. All he did was buy and sell horses, and there's nothing criminal about *that*. One of the four-legged beasts had even kicked out at him, broke his poor wrist. And now a broken foot to go with it. Oh, *Manny*.

She'd given the police her home and work phone numbers, insisted they keep her informed. Thank heaven for Mr Herring, who said he would do his utmost to ensure Manny was bailed, yes, so she could look after him properly at 'home'. Derek chose not to burden her with his more informed opinion that, since Manny was apprehended in the act of escaping, and since forensic evidence would almost certainly tie him to the attack on Debbie Farley, the chances of bail were somewhat less than nil. Neither did he tell her that inside knowledge of the forensic evidence had triggered Manny's failed departure in the first place. If only the idiot had been quicker about getting off the premises….Derek was *not* going to tell Carrie that Olly's blue rage meant Manny was a darn sight safer on remand right now.

PC Jonathon 'Jon' Lee phoned Carrie Sansom at work and gave her the bad news: I regret to tell you that Mr McRory will be staying where he is for the foreseeable. He felt like saying it was *good* news, surely? Who in their right mind would want a weasel like Manny round the house? But he felt sorry for her because, down the phone, her sadness seemed genuine - to him at least.

Had he better ring Batten, though, and mention the other thing he'd discovered about Carrie? Lee's confidence was improving but, hell's teeth, Batten still called him Jonathon. Be nice if *he* improved as well.

'*Where* did you say she works, Jonathon?'

'SARL, sir. Somerset Agricultural Research Laboratory. It's out Yarcombe way.'

Batten wasn't going to admit he didn't know where Yarcombe was. He was still getting over the fact that Manny had a girlfriend. *Manny?* Puts you in the shade, Zig. You don't know if you've got one or not!

'She isn't some kind of boffin, is she?' Better not be a toxic.

'From what I can gather, she's a dispatcher, sir. Organises all the stuff that comes in and goes out.'

'*Stuff*, Jonathon?'

Stuff *you*! Call me *Jon*!

'Materials, sir. The stuff they research. Soils and Fertilisers. Seeds and -'

'Plants. Yes. I get it. Don't tell me she's allowed near the poisonous stuff?'

'Sends and receives, sir. It's her job to arrange secure transport. I thought you'd need to know.'

He was improving, was Jonathon. He made a note to tell him, sometime. But other things were more urgent.

'Any sign of Sergeant Ball?'

Derek Herring was wrong about Olly's blue rage. It was hot purple. And since Derek shared office-space with Olly he had little choice but to live with the escalation, keep his head down and do his best to keep the profits up. But even Bulky was keeping his distance from Olly now. The rest of Wake Hall Horse had formed an unofficial no-fly zone around him.

Olly's current target was McRory. Buggered up a simple task, *and* got himself nabbed into the bargain! Just as well he's inside. If I get my hands on him he'll be *underneath*!

Manny's only choice was to keep Olly's name out of it, admit to maverick behaviour, and serve whatever time the beak threw at him. Olly was certain the bitch cook would keep *her* mouth shut, but the pigs were now grilling Vito Valdano, a man who never used one word if two were available. Who *can* you trust to do a simple job?

His answer stared back at him from the bathroom mirror in his horsey office. Time for a new strategy. Time for hands-on. Olly had complete confidence in himself, once precautions were taken. The gold-plated memory stick, worn like a trophy round his neck for so long, was now locked away in a very private bank vault, along with any other gubbins he wouldn't want the cops to feast piggy little eyes upon. And he'd made

Tuji failsafe the technology. Batten could search the office right now and all he'd find would be hundreds of dull-as-ditchwater horse transactions - all genuine, all profitable - and *tax* paid on all of them.

He changed into an unremarkable outfit that would later be a pile of ash, tucked a ski-mask and a pair of gloves into his pocket, and reached for the metal object Manny had purloined some time ago from the back of the farrier's van. He looked out through the spy-hole in the office door. The distorted form of a distorted Baz was visible, sans chauffer-uniform, leaning on an old, dark green car so nondescript Olly wasn't even sure what make and model it was. He'd already given Baz a slap, to wake him up. Soon be nightfall. Then Do-It-Yourself.


By the time his cash for the stolen Massey Ferguson tractor turned up, Tom Bowditch had come close to strangling Dave Dipstick Vossialevydipsic. Don't forget to wash dirty cup, Tom. *Yeh, yeh.* Why you not put bolt-cutters back on rack, Tom? *Because I'm going to use them again!* You want tea, Tom? *No, Dave, I don't want tea. I detest your bloody tea!*

But the money *had* arrived, in twin packs of used notes as he'd insisted. Ten grand each. Tom grabbed his share and stuffed it in his pocket.

'It only money, Tom.'

You think? It's more than that. It's freedom. Freedom from *you*, Dave. He snatched his jacket and picked up the old Land Rover keys.

'We need plan for tomorrow, Tom. Two quad bike. Wooden shed. Easy-peasy-lemon-squeezie, yes?'

Easy-peasy-lemon-squeezie, *no!* I *told* you last time, Dave, no more quad bikes! No more of anything! He clutched his keys, one hand on the door knob. Should he just give Dave the whole nine yards, and have done with it? We *don't* 'need plan for tomorrow', Dave. Tomorrow I'm *gone. Dipstick!*


Sergeant Ball realised he'd never been in a vehicle driven by DC Hick, and thanked his lucky stars that Hick was not behind the wheel this time either, but strapped more or less safely into the passenger seat where he flicked haphazardly at his seat-belt strap and played games with the switch of the electric window. For a good mile, Ball tolerated the random fall and rise of the passenger window - and the consequent random blasts of rain and cold air - before even *his* saintly patience ran out.

'Hickie!'

'Sarge?'

'You training for the Arctic Police? Shut the bloody window!'

'Sorry, Sarge.'

Hick did his best, but left and right and north and south were all much of a muchness to him, so instead of closing the window, he pressed the switch that fully opened it. A boreal blast of air hit Ball full in the face before Hick managed to reverse the process. To his credit, Ball turned his eyes only briefly towards heaven before returning them to the road.

It hadn't been a good day. Di had come down with the flu she'd caught from *him*, so he had to walk the dog in the pitch dark, then get in for the early shift – which teamed him with Hickie. Is it an *act*, or can Hick *really* be as ramshackle as he seems? They were driving back to Parminster now, with news guaranteed to put the Northern Fork into another rage.

'Not in a million years, Sergeant. Make it two million. That's how sure I am.'

The Head of Security at the Somerset Agricultural Research Laboratory where Carrie Sansom worked was a curious mixture, his combat jacket and trousers topped off by a white lab coat with a pen sticking out of its top pocket. The pen reminded Ball of Derek Herring, and instinctively he throttled the plastic armrest of his swivel chair. On the other side of the desk, the Head of Security was still shaking his over-sized head at even a tentative link between Manny McRory, Carrie Sansom and the plant poison that had killed Lawrence Vann.

'And it's not only that she can't despatch anything remotely poisonous without two separate checks, each signed off by two independent staff, and then by *me*.' He paused for proud effect. The busy Ball hurried him along.

'I'm guessing there's a 'but also,' zor?'

'There is, Sergeant. A simple one. We don't *do* any research on flowers - not the garden variety. We deal with crops. Whatever the nation can *eat*. Without being poisoned.'

'But could someone have smuggled plants *in*, zor, and done a bit of, well, a bit of private *distillation*, on the side?'

The Head of Security made his eye-sockets considerably smaller, to show he wasn't amused. But then, neither was Ball, who knew a straw when he clutched one.

'*My* system works the same way for materials coming *in*, Sergeant. And we'd hardly be encouraging staff to knock up a bit of belladonna in their lunch hour, would we?'

DC Hick's only contribution to the interview was to nod at this final pronouncement. Because he agreed with it or because he happened to twitch at that point, Sergeant Ball realised he hadn't the faintest idea.


With no reason to notice the empty, dirty-green parked car, Vito Valdano waddled slowly past it and made his way into his apartment. He was under doctor's orders to walk more, which was not something he enjoyed, though it did him good. Vito was glad to be home. Calmer. He felt calmer now. A chilled glass of Chablis - a small one, doctor's orders again - and a Cello Concerto, Elgar's perhaps, before sliding into his waterbed.

He failed even to get as far as the fridge. The sudden, downward arc of a pair of hard metal farrier's pincers coincided with the side of his skull, and the body beneath the skull responded correctly, by dropping to the floor, senseless....

Why were the numbers on his bedside clock shimmering above him, in a heat haze? They had no reason; it was cold here. And dark. As they gradually came to rest, the numbers said 03.20. He must have been lying on the floor for....how long? And why was the side of his head so numb and sticky? And, agh, so painful? He slowly crawled towards the clock, felt for the bedside lamp and switched it on. The light made him feel nauseous; more so when his red-stained shirt came into focus. He saw bloodstains on the carpet too, where his head had rested. Something unseen, some*body*, had hit him, and he'd blacked out.

Tottering to his feet, a whale on a tightrope, he was heading towards the bathroom when an object on the coffee table drew his eye. It was a shoe-box, and had not been there earlier. He remembered the last such object he'd seen, in Albania, remembered its sickening contents, the severed misshapen hand of a ten-year old orphan girl, a King Zog warning. *Vito's* warning. The memory made him nauseous again.

Vito Valdano knew he was a figure of fun to some people, to the police certainly, but he was not without courage. Wiping his mouth on a multi-coloured handkerchief, its shades of red uncomfortably dominant, he grasped the shoe-box lid and flipped it aside. The box seemed empty, some kind of savage joke, but when he peered more closely he saw a small red and white object in one corner. It was a mere inch or so of....something. He tentatively prodded it, picked it up, brought it closer to his tinted spectacles - till the sticky pain in the side of his head drilled grisly realisation into him. His trembling fingers held the severed lobe of his own right ear. He threw it down in revulsion. And failed to make it to the toilet-bowl.


Rather than clear his head, a long spin in Jellicoe's generously-sized office chair made Batten dizzy. Despite well-intentioned early bird efforts, his relationship status with Rhona Fiske was as cloudy as before. With most of the dwindling staff of Wake Hall, she had come out to enjoy the sight and sound of police and paramedics slapping handcuffs and splints onto Manny McRory, before unceremoniously driving him away. Had she pointedly avoided Zig Batten, or was she merely being professional? He'd been too busy to know.

She wasn't the only loose end. Batten had tugged at the loose end of Manny McRory several times, but failed to unravel him. Manny was saying only what his crooked brief would allow - and his crooked brief was Derek Herring. Hope of proving a link between Manny, his girlfriend and the aconite that poisoned Lawrence Vann was fading, along with any chance of a murder or conspiracy charge. At this rate, they'd convict Manny of motiveless GBH on Debbie Farley and Nina Magnus, and criminal damage to a lamp-post.

So he could have done without a case of the glums from the stone-faced Sergeant Ball, who waved Batten towards an empty interview room smelling of sour coffee and disinfectant. Don't tell me it's the Wake Hall wobbles again, Zig? When a hovering DC Magnus joined them, Ball closed the door and the three detectives stood in a vaguely embarrassed silence for a while. Batten's eyebrows were dancing. His best guess was that Magnus had taken exception to the reprimand he'd given her for failing to protect Debbie Farley, and wanted redress. Tough. Compared to some Inspectors, he was a fluffy bunny.

'Sorry, zor, but I've got to pass this one over to you. I wish there was an alternative.'

Right again, Zig.

'It's about George Halfpenny, zor.'

Ah. It was the other thing. Batten was relieved. He knew Ball had quietly sorted out some minor racial tension between George and Nina. Has it recurred, got out of hand? Ball seemed tongue-tied. Seems it has.

'Best thing, Nina, is you just tell the Inspector what happened, in your own words. OK?'

He pulled out a chair and she sat down at the table opposite Batten and Ball.

'Thanks, Sarge.' There was another awkward silence. 'It's a bit of a long story, sir…?'

Batten opened his hands and pointed ten long fingers loosely in her direction.

'Well, I'm at this hen-night, last night, in Yeovil - it *is* relevant, sir.'

She'd caught Batten's involuntary raised eyebrows. Keep the bloody things under control, Zig, or you'll be here forever.

'Tell you the truth, I'm a bit over-the-limit after, so it's back to the multi-storey, change out of my heels. I keep a pair of flatties in the car. I'll get a taxi, I decide, leave the motor where it is.'

*Are* we doing racism, Zig? Or drink-driving now?

'I hear his car, first off, then I notice it creeping in. He's scanning, like he's on the lookout, but he doesn't see me. I'm parked in the shade of one of those big concrete pillars, and I'm sitting on the edge of the back seat, changing my shoes. Bending down, like you do, you know? The interior lights are always switched off in the car - '

'Because of surveillance, yes. *Who* didn't see you, Magnus?'

'Just tell it in your own way, Nina.' Ball had a pleasant way of asking his boss to shut up.

'Next, a big silver Mercedes drives in, slow. I'm thinking, here we go,

293

drug dealer, bit of late night business - and we're never off-duty, are we? Well, the Merc sidles up to the first car, which of course I've recognised. And even if I don't, the window comes down and he's there in the driver's seat. George Halfpenny. Even crouched, as I am by then, I can see straight in.'

She had Batten's full attention now.

'Well, the Merc's window comes down a crack, and George's hand passes across a piece of paper, just a single sheet. There's a pause, a few seconds maybe, then a gloved hand comes out of the Merc - I'm guessing, but it looks like a wad of cash, in a packet. George leans over and grabs it, sharpish, and both windows roll back up. The Merc drives off. I realise then, it's not drugs. Better if it was. I'm in shock. Shock.'

You'd have been in shock too, Zig, watching one of your own doing that.

'I got the licence number, sir.'

'And we ran it this morning,' added Ball.

Batten could only think of one silver Mercedes within their current sphere of interest.

'Derek Herring?'

Ball hesitated. 'It's a case of yes and no, zor.'

And it was going so well.

'Yes and no?'

'Tinted glass, sir. The passenger seat was empty, I'm pretty sure of that, because it was on the side nearest me, but from where I was crouching I couldn't identify the driver. Might even have been female. Sorry, sir.'

Sorry, she says. Would he ever understand women? A clear, caught-in-the-act ID of Derek Herring would have been icing on the cake, yes, but he still wanted to praise her, tell her he envied her guts. And she's saying sorry.

'Not easy, Nina, telling us.'

'No, sir.' Even a racist colleague is a colleague.

'What did George do?'

'Nothing, sir. Just sits in his car for ages, the window down a touch. Felt like ages anyway. I'm still crouching. I thought my hip would give out.'

He'd forgotten: McRory's cosh had badly bruised her hip and thigh. She'd shamelessly hitched up her skirt in the CID Centre and showed them.

'Then after a minute or two, the window rolls down all the way and a cigar butt lands on the car park floor.'

Ball produced an evidence bag containing the remains of the cigar. Every little helps.

'He just started the engine and drove off. Funny thing, I didn't even know he smoked.'

'Right, then, Ballie -'

'There's a bit more, zor. Go on, Nina. His defence lawyer's going to grill you about it anyway.'

DC Magnus seemed reluctant to speak, till Ball's ginger smile encouraged her.

'It's why I recognised George's car, sir. Straightaway, I mean. There's a big deep scratch right through the bodywork, across both doors.' She paused. 'It was me who put it there. Revenge. My car's got the same damage. Well, you've seen, haven't you, sir?'

Batten had. But never imagined George Halfpenny doing it.

'I'm owning up, sir, but I don't regret it. I had to do *something*, after the things he's been saying to me. I'm sorry, sir, but he's an arrogant racist twat!'

He'd never heard her swear before.

'And the snide remarks, when no-one's there. May not sound much, but you're not black, sir, are you?'

No. But I'm an alien townie in rural Somerset - a refugee with a Yorkshire accent. It gives me a tiny glimmer of understanding, at least. He also understood how a clever legal mind like Derek Herring's might undermine the evidence.

'Decent CCTV system in the multi-storey?'

Nina Magnus nodded. Ball smiled momentarily.

'Locked away next door, zor. You can't see the Merc driver, but the camera does a screen-test on George - and both number plates are clear as day. We're looking at his bank transactions too. George is a goner, zor.'

But what damage had George already done? Batten recalled the crossed out 'Imp' in McRory's diary, and the failed night-time surveillance from Lawrence Vann's window. What else did Herring know? At least they'd kept the lid on Stephanie Broke-Mondelle. Unless *Hick* too....?

He gave a long, pained sigh, which the others fully understood. They hadn't joined the force to catch criminals within.

# Thirty nine

Olly felt better - nothing like gutsy hands-on to warm the blood. And when the double shipments began to flow.… A pity the forensic evidence against McRory was too conclusive to sidestep. Hell's teeth, it would be a pain replacing Manny. If I could get my hands on whoever invented DNA….

Don Quixote and Sancho Panza also felt better. The big Albanian, the one who called himself King Zog, had tried it on with his sinister stare and gory stories of people losing hands and arms for failing to toe the line. In bad Spanish it all sounded as stupid as 'Zog.' And the tall Spaniard with the thick eyebrows wasn't an easy man to intimidate; he had stared coolly back, the stocky figure of Sancho Panza adding weight, if not height, to the effect. Zog was already limp and sweaty from the freak temperatures in Spain - this time last year it was cold and rainy - and a soggy sponge called Zog is going to make them quake in their espadrilles?

It's hard enough drugging *two* kids and loading them into the horse-box - and the horses too. But you want us to load *four* of them into the same space now, minus a hand or an arm? And then drive unnoticed to the ferry port? Well, who's the fool?

Agreements were reached, and the Spaniards' share was increased by a factor of two. King Zog would claw back a little from his agents in the Balkans, a little more from Mr Fish, his private name for Derek Herring. It was still top money.

'*What*? *Ge-orge*? You pulling my leg?'

'I'm not pulling your leg, Hickie, and I certainly wouldn't pull anything else of yours. It's true.'

It wasn't that Hick didn't believe Sergeant Ball. But it was….*hard* to believe. They weren't exactly mates, him and George, but their desks butted up and they were often teamed together. As the news sank in, and he trawled back over the weeks and months, amazement turned to plain bloody anger.

'So, Sarge, when me and George spent two nights doing surveillance from Lawrence Vann's funny window, looking through that thermal imager thing....?'

'He knew it was pointless, yes. He'd sold you out. Sold all of us.'

Hick recalled George's lack of enthusiasm, thinking it was just George being George.

'*I* spent most of those two nights up that ladder, Sarge! George kipped on the sofa half the time and ate chocolate the other half! It's a total waste, he kept saying. How do *you* know, I said? He just shrugged. Said he'd rather be at his laptop.'

Ball imagined George adding figures to an Excel spreadsheet. Totting up. Doing *money*.

'How much cash, Sarge, did he....you know....?'

'A grand a time, looks like. Four or five grand maybe.' Ball chose not to think how much George might have 'earned' had he not been caught. 'You alright, Hickie? Gone a bit pale.'

Five grand - that's what turned him pale. George sold us out for five grand? *Is that all we're worth*?

'Well I hope he gets ten years, Sarge. Twenty, the lying shit. And no parole!'

'Hickie?'

But Hick did not reply. He was staring at nothing, doing nothing, as Ball left. The Sergeant had never known him so still.

Batten's eyes were as flat and hard as stone. George Halfpenny drew on the final dregs of his bravado but failed to out-stare his ex-Inspector. Anyone entering the interview room, as Ball now did, would think it was a poker game. But Halfpenny's tells were giving him away, almost more than the evidence. Have George and Hickie done a swap, Ball wondered? George displayed the jerks and twitches that Hick had temporarily suppressed. Guilt, fear, and sweat. Ball had seen all three, plastered onto faces in faceless interview rooms like this one, with its twin tape machine and its metal table bolted to the floor. But never when the crook was a skilled and - till now - *trusted* DC.

Batten scraped two chairs towards the chipped table, and he and Ball ominously sat down. Halfpenny's instinct was to shuffle as far back into his seat as the seat would allow, but it wouldn't be far enough.

When Batten broke the news to Gribble, the ACC's head sank briefly into his hands, and not because Halfpenny's arrest would add badly to the Jellicoe problem. It was the cold, sick feeling of betrayal. Batten was reminded of his own private vengeance in Leeds, on PC Kerr, which Ged had called into question. A few small shavings from Batten's personal morality may have dropped into a hole in the ground, but *all* of PC Kerr's were at the bottom - George's too, now. Kerr was bad enough, stealing from the old and the vulnerable. But George had shafted his own.

Gribble, though, had earned his position. His dismay was brief.

'Use the bastard.'

'Sir?'

'No speakie Yorkshire anymore, Batten? Herring doesn't know we've nabbed his little snitch, does he?'

'No, sir. I'm certain he doesn't.'

'So. *Use* the bastard.' Uncharacteristically, Gribble jabbed a finger at the ceiling. 'Before our hands are tied.'

'What did you have in mind, sir?'

'Dangle a deal. We go easier on Halfpenny than he deserves, and in return he feeds Herring a well-chosen pack of lies. He'll lie with plenty of conviction, will Mr Halfpenny, I would imagine?'

Batten had hoped the ACC might suggest this. With the next 'Imp' from Manny McRory's horse-box diary fresh in his mind, he knew precisely which pack of lies to prepare.

This time, the silver Mercedes rolled into the National Trust car park at Montacute House, and came to a halt opposite Halfpenny's still-scratched car. Each rendezvous point had been different, and George was always instructed to park first - presumably so whoever was in the Merc could check for surveillance. They'd be hard pressed to find the three cameras that were trained on the meeting today. From his vantage point behind the tinted windows of an unmarked car, Batten couldn't spot them, and *he* knew where they were.

For one final time George handed over a summary of police action in the Lawrence Vann case, and the exact date and time of a planned police raid on Wake Hall Horse. The planned raid was true, but the date was fiction. The real raid would be much earlier, *before* stable doors were bolted, before the horse - and whatever else - was gone.

A thousand pounds in used notes poked from a crack in the Mercedes' tinted window towards Halfpenny, then both windows rolled up, and the Mercedes drove away. Barely a fragment of the driver's face was visible, and Batten knew a half-decent defence barrister would have a field day if Halfpenny – or anyone else - tried to swear it *was* Derek Herring. But have patience, Zig, the wheel's still turning.

A third car drew up and George Halfpenny - still gripping his thirty pieces of silver - climbed into the back seat. Sergeant Ball prised the bribe from George's hands and snapped the cuffs back on. Against his better judgement, Ball had made Hick drive, to ensure his furious fists didn't stray from the steering wheel.


To be a policeman, Zig, are you required to believe in the notion of a parallel universe? Here he was, second time in a week, fifty feet from Rhona Fiske's snug cottage, with its chance of amnesty and maybe even horizontal reconciliation. Alas, important police business was his reason for being there, and he hadn't the time to drum private apologetic knuckles on her door.

Batten's police business seemed anything but important, except to Lady Wake. She may have been on social terms with the Chief Constable, but ACC Gribble had never actually spoken to her before, so it was with some interest that he'd taken her call - once it found its way past Mrs Pinch. He'd assumed she would berate him about the expensive Massey-Ferguson tractor recently stolen from Wake Hall, and want to know 'if the police intend to do *anything* about it. Mm?'

But it was something else entirely. Although Lady Wake did not deign to say so to the ACC, she was reclaiming her birthright. She had decided to let Olly Rutter manage Wake Hall *Horse* for a little longer – pending the completion of certain legal niceties. But the Estate itself was *hers*, and she would run it how she chose. She had a request, she told Gribble. In which case, he would have liked to say, kindly present it *as* a request, not a haughty command.

'Have you any idea how much material has been removed from Lawrence Vann's office - and indeed his home?' she asked.

Yes, I have. It's common practice during a murder enquiry. We do what's called 'investigation.' Instead, he mumbled a sentence containing 'regret' and 'inconvenience.'

'Yet I wonder, *do* you in fact realise *how* inconvenient it is? *Mm?*' Temps had been attempting to run the half-gutted Estate office for some time now, and with difficulty, given the absence of key office documents and technology. 'And you *are* aware that a new Estate Manager will be in post in precisely seven days time?' Gribble was not aware. 'And that a fully-equipped, fully-documented office will be fully expected by then? Do I make myself *clear?*'

Very clear indeed, Lady Wake. I'll make sure Inspector Batten returns all that can be returned, to office and to cottage - though the cottage itself must regrettably remain sealed for a little longer, for forensic reasons. But a fully-functioning office, certainly, Lady Wake, forthwith, pronto, crawling on hands and knees, forelock at-the-ready in deferential fingers. Two of them. And how very useful that you should telephone....

In the spirit of cooperation, a police van drove into Wake Hall the following afternoon and, under Batten's supervision, a mixed bag of officers unloaded box after box of documents and equipment, returning most of them neatly to Lawrence Vann's office - and in the interests of efficiency, some to his cottage as well.

PC Jon Lee, the slightest member of the police contingent and in nondescript plain clothes today, helped to hump several boxes into what used to be Lawrence Vann's home, before somehow being left behind inside when the cottage was locked and its 'Police Line: Do Not Cross' seal was put back in place. Instead of documents, one of the boxes contained all the provisions Lee was likely to need for a day or two. He'd readily agreed to play clandestine gooseberry - even if it meant being quieter than a mouse - hoping the brownie points might help his ambitions to permanently join CID, an aspiration much dented when the tractor thief he'd robustly arrested turned out to be a less than robust female. This time, his only gripe was that he didn't fancy sleeping in front of a hot red wall in Lawrence Vann's dubious bed, with its multiple notches on the bed-post.

Batten had reassured him.

'You won't be sleeping much, Jonathon. You'll be up a long ladder most of the night, watching Wake Hall Horse from the fanlight window. With your radio in one hand and a thermal imager in the other.'

Vito Valdano drew curious glances when he stepped into the Parminster nick, to fulfil his bail conditions. His tinted glasses, beard and loud suit were set off today by the bright white bandage encircling his skull, retaining a large piece of gauze over his right ear.

'He looks like Van Gogh,' Hick whispered to Magnus.

'More like Pudsey Bear', she said, not bothering to lower her voice.

Vito firmly declined to comment on the injury when questioned by Sergeant Ball. He *very* firmly declined to answer any questions at all concerning Olly Rutter.

'You're not having trouble hearing me, are you, zor?' asked Ball, pointing at the gauze.

Valdano shook his head, before remembering that it hurt to do so. He'd had enough of the police, of criminals, of....*people*. He would maintain his silence, meet whatever judicial penalties came his way, and when they were behind him he would depart. And hope to begin again, elsewhere. Not in the Balkans, though. And certainly nowhere near Corfu....

....Where Derek Herring's plane had landed in surprisingly hot sunshine. King Zog had agreed to bring forward the next double shipment by seven days, but had trimmed a shade off the profits in return. They remained substantial. Derek saw no reason to inform Zog that the earlier delivery was to pre-empt a police raid on Wake Hall Horse. A boat stays afloat far better if it isn't rocked.

He'd been thinking a good deal about boats - yachts - recently. Trimmed or not, the extra profits would boost the capital in his offshore account. Soon, the yacht 'Victorious' would be moored in Corfu harbour, its new captain engaging in a little private-sector business of his own.

By contrast, Lieutenant Grigoris of the Greek International Police Cooperation Division was doing *public*-sector business - of the watching and waiting variety. He'd tracked Derek Herring's movements ever since his plane touched down, again, at Corfu Airport.

'He is back, the fat whitebait.'

'Our loss is your gain.'

A puzzled silence from the phone. Grigoris spoke his second language so well that Batten occasionally forgot he was Greek. He simplified.

'Is he behaving himself over there? You know, being a good boy?'

'Ah, good boy, yes. Being good boy - with bad men. The big yacht, from Albania, it come in harbour, pick up Mr Herring, then they sail away. But it will return, in the….fallness?'

'In the *full*ness? The fullness of time?'

'Ah yes. 'In the fallness of time.' And then we shall see….'

Night by night, in the bedroom, Lady Wake was slowly becoming Lady Fast-Asleep. Yet where business was concerned, she was swiftly reverting to Lady Wide-Awake.

'Olly. I no longer have *time* for gallivanting overseas to marry up mares and stallions. The stud will have to wait, I'm afraid.'

And which bloody stud are you referring to? *Mm*?

'You seem to have forgotten I have a large *Estate* to run. And in the permanent absence of Lawrence….'

He'd whiz down to the Camargue by himself then - and be nowhere near Spain or Wake Hall when the shipment rolled off the Portsmouth ferry. Even Bulky could handle a simple collect and transfer. Maybe the added bonus of three more Spanish mares would sweeten her Ladyship, get her mind back on the stud again. He hoped so; he was getting horny.

She was a puzzle, Marianne. At least the cops had buggered off - the ones she'd actually *invited in* - so he could safely get down to some proper business: a double shipment, in and away. And a whole week ahead of the police-raid he wasn't supposed to know about.

'Bulky!'

'Mr Rutter?'

'Special job for you.'

# Forty

PC Jonathon Lee was playing games with his name. He hated Jonathon. Loft Hick was right - it was a choirboy name. What about Jonny, like that bloke who used to play rugby for England? Good, yes, but according to Luce 'Jonny' *has connotations.* Jonno? Yergh, too posh. Or the French 'Jean', Je-awn? No - Hickie would deliberately call him *Jean* or Jeannie. How's Jean Lee today? Does Jeannie with the light brown hair require tea? Sod it, stick to plain Jon.

After nearly 36 hours, plain Jon was bored to his bootstraps. He'd finished reading his book, a Christmas present from Luce. It was a book of babies' names - and she wasn't even pregnant. The book was a waste of time anyway; she'd more or less told him it was going to be either William or Kate. It wouldn't be another Jonathon, that's for sure.

Even his beloved smartphone was a disappointment. Should have downloaded more games beforehand - the wifi at Wake Hall was rubbish. If he had to send another uneventful 'touching base' text to Crystal Ball, well, he'd scream, blow the whole surveillance. As for listening to his i-pod, the inside of his ears were raw. When Rufus Wainwright sang 'My Phone's On Vibrate For You' he switched off in exasperation. What I want is a good hot meal in a room with the curtains open and all the lights on, a cold beer, and a proper sleep in my own bed with Luce and, sod it, a baby too!

Nothing of significance had happened since he arrived, other than occasional security patrols. At first it had been a novelty, watching the shimmering heat signatures of horse after horse and of the occasional two-legged creature. Now it was plain boring. The first night, a big horse-box had chugged into the yard and he'd become animated with excitement. Was this Jon Lee's triumph, his entry into CID? With declining hope, he'd watched two men unload and stable a pair of four-legged heat signatures so small they could only have been Shetland ponies. Minutes later, the men had departed and he was left watching the lonely heat haze from the box's engine, which grew smaller and smaller as it cooled. To pass the time, he made a bet with himself over how long it would take for the heat signature to disappear. He lost. Now here he was, for a second night, up a ladder in a pitch-black room, looking out of Lawrence Vann's fanlight window, squinting through a thermal imager focused on Wake Hall Horse. He peeled open an energy bar, his third, and began to chew.

He was on his fourth energy bar when a dark blue horse-box rumbled into the yard. He checked his watch - almost one-o-clock. He bet himself that this box would be carrying Shetlands too. Lost again. Three large heat signatures shimmered back at him, before being eclipsed by a two-legged signature so colossal that it could only be the bloke they called Bulky. The huge shape rolled out of the driver's cab like a giant tangerine, before the reds and yellows of legs and arms drew a four legged shape from box to stable, and then another. When he's finished unloading horses, what will Bulky do with the illegal stuff?

He watched, tense, phone at the ready. Batten had said the protective padding of the box's interior could be a good place to hide drugs - or hide *something*. Hick had told everyone twenty times that 'horse' was slang for heroin, but Lee's bet was on blood diamonds - he'd seen a documentary on TV. He adjusted the imager because his eyes were sore and because it seemed to have developed a fault - at the worst possible time. As he panned across and back, a fuzzy image kept appearing from behind the slowly-cooling driver's cab. Not a moving image, but hot nonetheless. It's Bulky's takeaway curry, Jon! Almost big enough to feed him for a day!

But as he stared, the takeaway curry *did* move - or he thought it did. And then it didn't.... And then it did! He re-adjusted the lens - yes, definitely, a movement, and again. Not a Shetland pony, Jon. You've lost your bet - far too small, and not enough legs. Not enough....legs? The blurred colours shimmered again and the heat signature that he'd thought was all one....was becoming two, three....four? And surely the wrong shape? For *horses*.

Jon Lee tasted the green bile of realisation in his craw. He raised the thermal imager again, hoping he had made a mistake. But they were still there. Four small two-legged signatures. Oh, Luce. Oh, god, Luce, Luce. Revulsion fizzed his fingers into life and he grabbed at his radio, jabbed down on the speak button, did exactly as Batten had instructed him.

'*Go!*', he hissed. '*Now!*'

Blocking the exit roads and tracks, securing the scene, rigging up temporary lights, collecting evidence, managing the host of dressing-gowned employees who had flooded out to check on the commotion - Batten's team was trained well enough to deal with all this. They were trained at making arrests too, but none of them had ever arrested a colossus like Bulky Hobshaw.

'Perhaps he'll come quietly, zor, being a man of few words?'

Fat chance. Nine cops surrounded the giant, in the yard of Wake Hall Horse, like nine minions worshipping a huge idol. They gave warnings, said what could be said about 'not making things worse for yourself', but Bulky showed no sign of holding out his hands for the cuffs - even if they had a pair big enough. When he yanked a heavy iron crowbar from the driver's cab, there was a distinct feeling of 'after you'.

Batten reluctantly nodded to Jess Foreman. From the corner of his eye he saw the white-faced Lee wince as Foreman assumed the stance, gave the warning. But rather than move away, Bulky raised his iron crowbar and charged *at* the big beat copper. Lee's face twitched as Foreman's finger drew back. Batten heard the click from ten feet away. None of them liked the tazer.

Bulky Hobshaw liked it even less. Whether it was the tazer that stunned him, or the bone-crunching boom as his metric-tonne body slammed into the ground, Batten didn't care. For safety's sake, they put ankle-restraints on him as well. The sigh of relief they collectively exhaled was sickeningly premature, but not because of Bulky.

How can a key feel like wet jelly in your hand, yet still slide into a lock and open a door? He stepped into what was usually his hamstone haven, a good-sized cottage that, right now, felt no larger than an airing cupboard - without the air. Right now, he was a Lilliputian, tiny in the face of a repugnant night and day. He needed a burning hot shower to remove the crud of being a cop at times like these. And if this Lilliputian was simply washed down the plughole, so be it. Managing to ignore the half-empty bottle of Speyside, he flicked the switch of the kettle.

Neither hot tea nor a searing shower helped. Calculated savagery was not new to him; he had seen the human cost of criminal profiteering too often before. But not like this. He had no idea how to deal with what he'd

306

seen in the darkness at Wake Hall Horse. How was he supposed to erase acid imprints from an unreachable part of his skull? How could he clean his heart?

He'd sent PC Lee home early, but not because he needed sleep. Lee was in pieces. Or just smaller pieces than the rest of them? Batten lay on his bed, staring up at the ceiling's heavy beams, hoping their solidity might strengthen him. But he could not keep his eyes from closing, could not stop himself re-living the foulness of the night and day. In that strange land of shadow between eyeball and lid, hazy shapes swirled and re-formed themselves like the heat signatures that had shattered PC Lee....

'Tell me he's made a mistake, Ballie.'

Sergeant Ball double-checked the locks on the police van that was only just big enough to hold the shackled figure of Bulky Hobshaw. Like Manny McRory, Bulky knew that silence was demanded of him now, and provided nothing but. Ball turned back towards Batten whose long frame was uncharacteristically slumped against dark blue horse-box 1 with its broken number-plate.

'Lee, zor?'

Batten nodded.

''Fraid not. Isn't just you, zor. I'm screaming inside for it to be a mistake. All of us are. But it's not.'

When the agitated Lee described what he had seen through the sanitising lens of the thermal imager, Ball recalled his very first interview with Manny McRory. Something about him sleeping in the cab of the horse-box, on a pull-out bed? So where does it pull out *from*, he asked himself? From a void behind the driver's seat, that was his answer - exactly where Lee had spotted what he said were four small heat signatures. Too small, and the wrong shape, he said, to be horses.

The panel concealing the void was so cleverly designed and fitted that it took some time to even locate, and a good deal longer to loosen, while preserving whatever trace evidence might still remain. At a signal from the Head of the Scene of Crime unit, Batten and Ball climbed over fresh horse-muck and old straw towards the front of the box, and the panel was finally lifted away.

What hit them first was a rush of foul air, a gag-inducing stench of urine and faeces which made them temporarily step back. One of the SOCO's lost his dinner there and then, and Batten almost joined him. Ball's ginger features turned to chalk. What hit them next was the sight of the narrow concealed compartment, along the length of which ran a kind of slatted shelf and little else, except four large water-bottles screwed to the back panel, behind the driver's cab. From each bottle dangled a thin plastic hose the size of a drinking straw. The last time Batten had seen anything of the kind it had been attached to a budgerigar's cage.

But it was not pet birds being hydrated here. It was children. Four of them were squeezed diagonally into the space, tightly strapped to the slats, their thin clothes filthy, their skin discoloured with road-dirt and their own excretions. They were all girls. Three of them were small and barely awake, their expressions blank, half-drugged still. The fourth was larger, older - twelve or thirteen perhaps, Batten guessed, when his rational mind kicked in. This girl was awake, wide-eyed, fearful, her glance flicking left and right across these strange men in crumpled paper suits, whose hands were encased in the same latex gloves worn by the men whose needles had drugged her. She could not remember how long ago.

Batten allowed himself a moment of self-justification: like Jon Lee, Lawrence Vann must have seen all this, or something like it, through the same thermal imager, on the same ladder, from the same window. And paid with his life. Could it be that, right now, they had one or both of his killers locked up? He hoped not. The worst crimes demand that justice be done to the worst people. He wanted Derek Herring to pay. They'd look harder at Vito Valdano and his orphanages now. Lady Wake, too, if she was complicit. And Olly Rutter most of all.

Snatches of hummed Vivaldi interrupted these thoughts as Doc Danvers stepped into the horse-box. Immediately, the humming stopped and a long silence began. Even when his work was complete, Danvers seemed reluctant to speak.

'Never thought to see you tongue-tied, zor. If you don't mind me saying.'

Danvers waved the arm of his suit towards the ambulance that now contained three small, olive-skinned, blanket-wrapped figures.

'Just when one feels one has seen everything, Sergeant....'

Ball's face was reply enough. A baleful sigh from Batten snapped them out of it.

'My apologies, Inspector. Information is what you require - not that I can say much at this juncture.'

Makes a change, Zig.

'All four girls have been given a strong soporific, the exact nature of which is yet to be established.' He waved his arm again, this time at the horse-box. 'Toxicology screening will be required, of course, but those contraptions screwed to the wall in there....they very likely contain rather more than water and glucose.'

Batten inwardly snarled, at the callous criminality of 'people' who could drug four kids, ship them off to a living death, then *keep* them drugged by doctoring the very water they must drink to stay alive.

'The older girl....' Danvers had countermanded her removal to the ambulance, for forensic reasons. She still lay more or less where they had found her, un-strapped now and blanket-draped. '....my female colleague is on her way....the rape kit, I'm afraid.'

Looking up to the sky gave Batten no comfort. Danvers was making an odd little sound. Was that anger on his face? Pain? A single unprofessional tear escaped from his eye, and lay on his cheek, lost.

'My apologies, Inspector. I have a daughter, much the same age.'

Thank god I *don't*, thought Batten, striding away across the long yard to give the Doc - and himself - plenty of private space. He looked through the rear gates at the vague shapes of horses in the dark fields beyond. Behold a pale horse, Zig. An image of Di Ball drilled into his head, and he wondered how his Sergeant would answer when he got back home and she asked 'how was work, my dear?'

Turning to check on his Sergeant, he was surprised to see the figure of a perturbed Lady Wake arrive at the police tape, not dressing-gowned like the other Wake Hall residents, but fully-clothed and lipsticked. Did you think she'd turn up in a polyester housecoat and curlers, Zig? He did his duty and headed back, to put himself between her Ladyship and the potential explosion that was Sergeant Ball.

Before he had gone ten yards, he was astounded to see Nina Magnus raise the tape with one hand and beckon Lady Wake - quite firmly - with the other. Batten lengthened his stride, but Magnus was way ahead of him, her body language loud. She steered Lady Wake by the elbow towards the ambulance, talking animatedly. If she doesn't calm down, Zig, *she'll* end up before the Chief Constable. He could not hear what was being said amongst the hubbub of police and onlookers and the hum of the arc-lights, but Her Ladyship didn't get a word in as she was nudged, brusquely, from ambulance to horse-box.

Batten was jogging now, but could not prevent Magnus steering Lady Wake - oh, Zig, don't mince words, she's practically *pushing* her - into the box through horse dung and used straw to the hidden compartment which still stank of shame and excreta, and contained a thirteen year old victim of trafficking and abuse. By the time he arrived, Lady Wake's face had disappeared behind manicured hands, her shoulders trembling as sobs and a sort of keening issued from her, echoing round the despicable, tiny space.

When her fingers slid from eyes to mouth, mascara had scrawled Arabic-looking letters on her cheeks. He expected her to produce a silk handkerchief to wipe it all away, but her hands simply dropped to her sides. She stared in silence at the olive-skinned girl, somebody's daughter, in the dirty, slatted prison with its water-bottles and restraining straps. A death mask froze over Lady Wake's features, till a whip cracked inside her and anger burned the mask away. She recovered herself, and with whatever bearing she could muster, turned towards the tradesman's entrance of the Hall. Has she noticed there's horse dung on her designer footwear, Zig? Whether she had or not was immaterial. The Wakes do not scrape their shoes on the grass in full view of untitled folk. That's breeding for you.

'Is she pissed off with me, do you think, sir?' Magnus asked as they watched Lady Wake's back grow smaller.

'*She* isn't, Magnus. But I've every bloody right to be.'

'Have you, sir?'

It wasn't insolence. She'd asked him politely. It was a perfectly sensible question. Magnus gestured towards the Hall.

'I mean, who's here, sir, that's responsible - apart from *her*?'

What could Batten say? Only in dreams was Bulky Hobshaw the brains of the operation. Dozy Baz Ballard was nowhere to be seen; McRory was in a cell; Herring in Corfu; Olly Rutter predictably overseas. For now, Lady Wake would have to serve as scapegoat, justified or not.

To add to Batten's frustration, the police interpreter finally turned up - only to announce that she spoke Spanish, Italian and Greek.

'So? What's the problem?' asked Batten.

'The problem? These girls are *Albanian*. I recognise the language but I can't translate it - not with anywhere near the accuracy required by the courts.'

He felt like telling her to bloody well bugger off and stop wasting his time then, but professional control held long enough to ask her politely to find an Albanian translator who *would* satisfy the courts, and pronto. She looked squarely back at him, raising her eyebrows and tapping her watch. He hadn't noticed; it was three-o-clock in the morning.

Batten had to wait his turn in any case. Doc Danvers and his colleague were left in privacy to do what must be done, before the older girl, tears flowing now, was gently moved to another ambulance. The SOCO's then had the grim task of making a second sweep of the hidden compartment.

Ball was nowhere to be seen. Batten eventually spotted him in the shadow of a feed-store, sitting alone on an upturned bucket, a paper cup overflowing onto shaking hands. Batten had never seen him fail to drink hot tea before. Magnus had gone to track down an interpreter. The others were corralling and questioning Wake Hall staff, Estate and Horse alike. You're running out of troops, Zig. He beckoned to Jess Foreman and they made for the second ambulance. Work must be done, and screw the rules.

Trying to make themselves as small as possible, they sat opposite the older girl, smiling, nodding their reassurances. Jess Foreman slowly and gently wrapped another blanket round the girl's shoulders. He'd make a good Father Christmas, in kinder circumstances, Batten thought. In the absence of an interpreter, signs and gestures would have to do.

'Zig,' he said, pointing at himself. 'My name, is, Zig.'

The rich burr of Jess Foreman added his name, then Batten gestured an invitation to the girl. Her reply was too faint to hear. More gestures, then a stronger voice.

'Ve-ra.'

'Vera?'

She nodded, tapped her chest. Her name meant 'summer', he was to learn. Gesture by gesture, he moved towards asking her to identify mugshots, in mixed pages of innocents and suspects. She shook her head at page after page, as first one suspect then another was ignored. Another page, another, another - then a tightening of her lips, a trembling of her thin body - her finger jabbing at a photograph, poking it, slapping it hard, clawing at it with such vigour that Jess Foreman had to gently prevent her from hurting herself. They gave her more time, to be certain. She had pointed at the chubby, impassive face of Derek Herring.

Batten felt a brief vindication, till Vera pointed at *him*.

'*Me*? Zig?'

She shook her head, looked away in frustration, pointed at Foreman.

'Jess?'

Again she shook her head, waving her hands excitedly, jabbing at the photograph, beating her fists on the padded stretcher. Her head dropped, but lifted once more, a little shame-facedly, and she pointed at Jess and Batten together - 'she means 'men', is that it, zor?' - before her finger slowly edged down from Batten's face till it pointed at his groin. Batten and Foreman looked at each other in surprise. She was pointing now at Herring, then at Batten's groin, then at Herring again. You didn't need to be a detective. They took a break, telling themselves it was for the sake of the girl.

'I suppose he'll have used a condom, zor?' asked Foreman as he poured coffee into thin paper cups. Batten nodded in resignation. Herring was no fool. The coffee was scalding hot but Batten didn't care.

When they resumed, Vera stabbed her finger yet again at the photograph of Derek Herring, as if trying to erase it. Then she bared her teeth and snapped them together, tapping her chest with her finger before stabbing at Herring's face once more.

'Zor, is she saying she *bit* the bastard?'

'I think so, Jess.' And who could blame her?

He played her gestures back to her, but she shook her head with vehemence, beginning the mime all over again.

'You....*bit*....him?' mouthed Batten, trying to ape her movements.

She shook her head in frustration, waving her little hands, beginning to cry. Batten tucked her blanket more tightly around her but she pulled it away, pulled it from her shoulder and jabbed her finger now at the flesh behind her neck, and then at the face of Derek Herring, her agitation sending a stream of high-pitched Albanian into the air.

'He….bit….*you*?'

Would Herring be so reckless? Surely not? But Vera was snapping her teeth together, stabbing at the photo, nodding her head assertively - yes, yes, yes! Batten mouthed 'fetch the Doc' at Jess Foreman, and eased Vera's blanket very carefully around her again.

Avril, Lady Wake's bemused and bleary-eyed maid, finished bagging up Mr Rutter's clothing and belongings, tucking them away into cardboard boxes and a large suitcase. Lady Wake had privately removed the more pornographic of Olly's possessions and hidden them away. There are some things one doesn't allow the servants to see.

'What shall I do with them now, ma'am?'

Lady Wake, her mascara once again in place, was unsure how to answer. What were her expectations? That Olly would return from his stallion-hunt in the Camargue, scoop up his belongings and quietly drive away? Mm. Hardly. He had a large stake in Wake Hall Horse, for one thing. And he was….Olly. She made a decision. Olly could continue to buy and sell horses for the time being, if he chose. But he would not be sleeping in her bed, or living in her home, or even crossing the threshold. He would find another horse to saddle, soon enough, and gallop off to the land of mixed memories. In the meantime, perhaps a restraining order would be useful, or is it an injunction? She'd speak to her solicitor.

'Have it all put in the office, at Wake Hall Horse, Avril, mm?'

The office had a sofa-bed, a bathroom and a kitchenette. Palatial, under the circumstances.

'Sorry, ma'am, but the police have still got it cordoned off.'

'In that case, Avril, when they have gone.'

Avril hesitated.

'Is there a problem?'

'It's only that, we don't have any keys, ma'am. To the office.'

Marianne Wake remembered. Neither did she.

'Ah. In that case, leave it *outside* the office. For the time being.'

'But won't it get wet there, ma'am? Or damaged?'

Yes, it very well might. Rain was forecast, she seemed to recall.

Ordinarily, Doc Danvers would have told Inspector Batten ten times over that *of course, mais oui,* they had spotted, swabbed, measured and photographed the bite marks on the older girl's neck. But Danvers was not himself today. Who was? Batten gritted his teeth, till the thought of Derek Herring's teeth made him stop. He took a breath and carried on being leader, praying that Vera's unconfirmed story was the evidential truth. He'd already informed Gribble of 'possible developments', and they'd agreed that DNA testing was an absolute priority, in the hope that it hadn't degraded. Gribble didn't mention the cost.

With difficulty, Magnus had tracked down a female interpreter, and the pair of them gradually teased out the stories of the four young girls. He wasn't in a rush to hear them, but he knew he must.

'What'll happen now, sir?' For some reason, Hick had straightened his tie. He looks older, Batten thought.

'Sorry, Hickie, happen to what?'

'To them, sir,' he said, waving in the general direction of the girls.

Whatever it was, it couldn't be worse than the future that *had* been planned for them. He said a silent prayer, that a child's life could recover from a start like this, and stopped himself thinking of brother Dimi.

'Not sure, Hickie, not yet. Sergeant Ball's talking to the agencies. Then we'll see.'

'They'll get shipped back over my dead body, sir. Wanted you to know that.'

Batten nodded, gave Hick a pat on the arm. Get in the queue. He bit into a sandwich from the large tray sent over by Debbie Farley, a further thank-you to the police. Now we're closing in on Lawrence's killers, she'll hopefully sleep better in her bed tonight. Better than you will, Zig.

All the ham sandwiches were gone so he chewed on home-baked bread, mozzarella, sun-dried tomatoes, spicy rocket. And was that a hint of lemon zest? Did he have a right to be enjoying such food, barely fifty yards away from a stinking prison for innocents? He put the other half of the sandwich back in its wrapper, just as Sergeant Ball mimed a phone with one hand and beckoned with the other.

'It's the Assistant Chief Constable, zor. For you.'

Batten groaned. This would be the third time today. Because they did have daylight now, of sorts. Rain clouds hung over Wake Hall, and the tail-of-winter wind was a knife. He looked around him in the grey light. Dressing-gowned staff had reappeared in their work clothes and he could hear the thrum of tractors and farm machinery, the rattle of buckets, the whickers and whinnies of horse after horse. He found himself wondering what had happened to the three mares - three Trojan horses - who had innocently travelled in the dark blue box with its broken number plate.

Gribble's news was a surprise he might have predicted had he not been preoccupied with....all this.

'*Greece*, sir? Wh-?'

'Pour a pint of caffeine down your neck, Batten. Herring's in Corfu, and when he hears of our success he's hardly likely to stay there, is he?'

'No, sir.'

'And he's not going to swan back here, to give us the pleasure of arresting him. *Is* he?'

'He's not, sir, no.'

'Your pen pal, Grigoris, he still keeping an eye?'

'He is, sir.'

'Well then. We'll take up his long-standing invitation, and book you a flight. International Liaison are well-primed. You'll be ready on the ground in Corfu to bag Mr Despicable, if we get lucky with his DNA. If not, you'll damn well better find something else. Whatever the method, I want his foul carcass extradited. I want to see his face when he finds himself in an unaccustomed part of the courtroom.'

Batten's heart sank at the thought of flying *anywhere*. In his head, an Airbus spiralled into the ocean, his screaming white face framed in a window seat. He'd much rather be in bed with Merlot Marie, the true reason for the internationalism Gribble assumed he had.

But Gribble was right; very soon, jungle drums would alert Rutter and Herring to Bulky's arrest and what it meant. George Halfpenny was in a cell, which gave Batten a temporary edge. If the toxics got their fingers out, it wouldn't be a George, but a gleeful arresting officer who first

315

enlightened Herring to the evidential fact that his DNA and, failing that, his bite marks, had been recovered from the neck of a trafficked thirteen year old Albanian *child*. Would that be worth a three thousand mile round trip?

Batten suggested Ball travel with him, to share the experience. And the burden.

'I wouldn't be much use, zor. And you must have seen it on the telly, the freak weather out there.'

'Yes, it's sunny. Not like here,' said Batten, watching clouds imitate black anvils.

'That's just it, zor, the sun. 35 degrees of sun. Me, I'm GB, through and through.'

Batten had no idea what Ball was talking about.

'*GB*? Great Britain? You'll be coming *back*, for Christ's sake! What makes you think the Greeks would want to *keep* you?'

'No, no, zor. GB. It's what the lads call me - behind my back, of course. I thought you knew, zor'

He knew nothing of the sort. Ball's 'lads' called Ball 'Crystal' when he wasn't in earshot, and they sometimes called the pair of them the fork and spoon - or, more pointedly, 'the fork 'n spoon' - but apart from that he didn't think they'd dare call Sergeant Ball anything other than Sarge.

'GB - it's not 'Great Britain'?'

'No, zor. GB is....it's my colouring you see, zor....'

Batten was too tired, too drained. He gave Ball the eyebrows.

'Ohh, it's Ginger Biscuit, zor! Those lads have a cruel streak, when it suits them.'

Had circumstances been less grim, Batten would have had a long laugh at his Sergeant's expense. *Ginger Biscuit*? Today, he gave the briefest nod. Ball would probably return from a freakishly hot Greece looking like an orange marshmallow. He would have to go by himself. 'Abroad' to date had been a couple of dull holidays in Spain and three brief art and literature trips to Paris, Amsterdam and Rome as part of his degree. Greece was an unknown quantity, and this was hardly the best time to go, with the economy falling and the temperature rising. Assuming he had a choice.

Gribble didn't mention it was Chief Constable Angela Kirkwood who insisted Batten go to Corfu. Nor did he mention her initial suggestion, to send Fat Jellicoe - 'or is he already concealed over there, in a Greek *bar*?' Gribble's counter-suggestion, that the Force's International Liaison Officer was the best person for the job, cut no ice with the Chief. Batten was going.

'He's been on three International Cooperation training courses, according to his file, but I don't see any record of him *doing* any cooperation!'

The Chief Constable had also noted with unprofessional delight the freak weather that was sweeping across the Aegean, bringing high temperatures previously unheard of this early in the year.

'It'll do him good. Teach him diplomacy. Sweat off some of that northern insolence.'

And if he behaved himself out there, she thought - and didn't burn to a cinder - who knows?

# Forty one

Batten *had* slept, but awoke unrested beneath his beamed ceiling. Despite attempts to deflect them, disturbing images swam through his dreams, flowing slyly into past images from previous cases, submerged but never sanitised - the dangerous dregs, the consequence of policing. He laughed grimly at the irony of recall. As a detective, he relied on a fathom-deep memory-bank of villains' faces and methods; of their weak points and flaws; of resources and contacts and strategies to be used against them. But memory's strength is also memory's curse. Even as he arched and curled in his bed, it was a different bed, ten years ago in a smart detached house in north Leeds, that wrapped itself around him.

The child had just celebrated her fifth birthday. Her face was blue; her eyes wide open, eyeballs barely contained within their sockets. Dark red wheals were visible around her tiny neck. A young and green detective then, he'd arrived late at the scene, to confront his first body. The wheals were beginning to show - as thumb marks - either side of her throat. They stared at him, like eyes.

The thumbs that had made the dark bruises belonged to an expensively-clad investment banker who also happened to be an addict on a very bad heroin trip. He also happened to be the dead girl's father. Suspected source of the tainted heroin was Olly Rutter. Insufficient evidence, as usual, where Rutter was concerned.

He'd strangled the cat as well, the young banker - though at least the cat had managed to inflict some desperate scratches on the flesh of his crazed arms before it finally croaked. His child had simply succumbed in bewilderment. What was this painful birthday game that daddy wanted to play? Daddy's name was Sebastian, Batten remembered, against his will. And the five year old had been reading a Winnie the Pooh picture book. It still lay open on the bed, the death-bed. Foolishly, he'd picked it up, the clammy feel of his crime-scene gloves branding the moment into his memory, The fly leaf said 'Happy Birthday, Grace, from Daddy'. Then there were five kisses.

He pushed the image away, only for it to merge into the face of a childless Sergeant Ball. Had *he* been present ten years ago in that fashionable house in north Leeds, would his formidable hands have found their avenging way to the addict's throat, crushing it till the red marks of *his* thumbs were imprinted there? And how many plods would it have taken to crowbar his fingers away again? Sebastian: father and killer of five year old Grace. Sergeant Ball: painfully childless. Would anyone have been strong enough to stop him?

Ball's face became the face of Mrs Ball, at the village pantomime, on Christmas night. Sergeant Ball and his wife had buried their child, and could have no more. She was telling Batten about her lost daughter; and asking if he had children of his own. That night, other nights, now, the same thought swam to the surface: Batten was childless; and chose to be. Children were just too easy to lose. Or to turn into orphans. And how could you ever recover from that?

He'd barely noticed that his breakfast coffee mug now sat next to a tumbler of Speyside. They'd saved four kids from further despair, yes, but not from that already undergone. And how many more lost children were in transit, while he sat in his kitchen having whisky for breakfast?

Could he cope with finding out? Right now, he wasn't even sure he could cope with driving to Bristol airport. What would Gribble do if he refused to go? Corfu is more than a thousand miles, for god's sake. Wake Hall's barely ten, Zig, and you're having trouble with that. He wanted to stay in his warm cottage, cocooned, protected, secure.

Then the Chief Constable's question clipped him round the ear. 'You are a palpably good detective, Inspector. But are you able to be a *better* one?'

'No!' he wanted to yell. 'No, I'm not! Just leave me here to bumble along. Send someone else, not me!'

There *was* no-one else. Ball had refused. None of the others had the experience or the seniority. Make a decision, Zig. Greece, or here? Soiled and productive? Or clean and bloody useless? Which is it going to be?

He still had not made up his mind by the time he parked at Parminster, and for the briefest moment he thought of not getting out of the car. He knew what was waiting for him.

'Coffee, sir?'

'No thanks, Magnus.' His veins were already running with caffeine, even a tot of whisky, to his shame. No more coffee, no tea, none of Hick's bacon rolls and Danish pastries, no spinning round in Jellicoe's chair; no daydreams; no Zigland. No procrastination.

'It's on your desk, sir.'

He thanked Magnus, and closed the door of his cubby hole. The cleaners had been in; he could smell lavender polish. The white, typed sheets of A4 lay on the buffed oak surface. Four transcripts of four interviews with four Albanian children. The pages felt like rough sandpaper as he skimmed through them. Sometimes the act of translation de-personalised a witness statement, even softened it. Not these.

Magnus and the interpreter had done a difficult job with sensitivity, connecting dots, suggesting patterns. It came as a surprise, an unpleasant one, to learn that none of the girls were related. Bad enough being a lost child on a nightmare journey, but in the company of *strangers*? The younger girls had similar tales: an orphan; a runaway; a child abandoned by her family. All had been 'befriended' by older children, passed on to 'helpers' who fed them, gave them temporary shelter while they waited for a place at 'the orphanage'. But no genuine orphanage was involved; they were waiting for the journey to hell.

All three spoke of feeling strangely sick, of falling asleep. The differences in their accounts were small, a simple reflection of the fact that they had woken up, parched, at different times of the day or night. They talked of *before* the horses, and *with* the horses. One girl remembered road noise; one was sea-sick. What they could not remember were faces. The 'doctor' with the needle wore a mask; there was a very tall man with thick eyebrows who spoke a language they had not heard before; there was a man like a giant.

Vera, the older girl, had a different story. Danvers surmised that all four had been given the same drug dose but, Vera's body mass being greater, she was awake more than the younger girls. A mixed blessing.

*This man, the thin one, who did very bad things to you, did he come on the first boat?*

*No. The other man, big, with the big face, he cursed him. He said I was worth nothing now, and he would not pay for me. The thin one argued back. I did not see but there was shouting, then loud bangs. No, the thin one did not come on the first boat.*

*And the big man, did he?*

*Yes, he and a woman took me on the boat. She called this man Zog. She was his wife, maybe.*

*Would you recognise these two again, Vera?*

*The woman, I don't know. The man, Zog, with the big face, angry face. He did not like me, he said I am waste of money. Yes, him.*

He could barely read the rest. It was a painful process, filling in the gaps in her innocent misunderstandings. Because she was now 'used goods', she was passed round as a sex toy.

*The man, Zog, he called me bonus. What does it mean, bonus?*

Derek Herring had been given a bonus too. And left his DNA and teeth marks behind to prove it. Bile crept into Batten's throat as he realised the dispensable girl was 'lucky' to be alive.

A still-pale PC Lee was tapping diffidently on the cubby-hole's glass door. Batten was spinning and spinning in Jellicoe's chair, spinning round madly, a finger and thumb jabbing at his moustache, his eyes screwed closed. Was he trying to make himself sick, to purge himself?

'Is anything wrong, sir?'

When the required documentation arrived, Batten saw that his destination airport was Corfu Town, a few miles from Derek Herring's villa - but unlike the other English travellers who landed there, Batten would be heading not to the beach but to Police HQ.

'*Must* I go to Corfu? Sir.'

ACC Gribble could have said 'try asking the Chief Constable,' but this was bad psychology for the-man-from-the-north.

'Had a chance to look at a map of Greece, Inspector? Find Corfu?' he asked instead.

Answer came in the form of 'the Batten bluster', as Gribble had privately dubbed it, a cocktail of facial tightening, shoulder shrugs, and plosive sounds that could have a variety of meanings, none of them 'Sorry, no.'

Gribble patiently produced a map, inviting Batten to discover Corfu's whereabouts amongst the vast archipelago of Greek islands. When it was eventually located, Gribble asked 'anything special about it,

Corfu? In the scheme of things?'

Batten stared at the map. He wasn't good at maps. He lacked the internal geography needed to readily translate two dimensions into three. Corfu looked to him as if a giant foot had smeared a brown blob of dog dirt across a dark-blue pavement.

'Um...it's....it's....Ah. Yes. I see.'

Corfu, he realised, was as close as it was possible to get - while still remaining an island - to Albania.

'Albania, Batten. Bane-of-our-life Albania.' Gribble tapped his finger sharply on a brown streak on the map, as if disciplining it. His forefinger flicked at the thin blue channel separating Albania from Corfu. 'Imagine this channel. Cargo ships, passenger ships, fishing boats, island ferries, private yachts. Thousands of them. Then the other routes, to and from Corfu - Sicily, Africa, France, Spain. Imagine trying to identify a single shipment in all that traffic.... A tiny piece of seaweed in an entire sea? Impossible, without inside information.'

'Which Derek Herring might be persuaded to provide, sir?'

'And you'll do the persuading, won't you, Batten?'

Batten wondered why Herring should be any more forthcoming than the silent Bulky Hobshaw and Manny McRory. Pack your Superman suit, Zig.

'Whatever we achieve, Batten, it won't make News At Ten. We're not naïve about that. But there's something fishy *there*' - he stabbed at Corfu - 'and the smell has invaded *our* patch.' He waved his spare hand at most of Somerset. 'Doing nothing is *not* an option. Clear?'

Batten nodded, a resigned, back-to-work nod this time, and took his leave. Retracing his long steps down the manicured corridors he tried to forget that when Gribble referred to a 'shipment' it was a sad euphemism for the nauseating truth. Drugs were not being trafficked. Nor blood diamonds, nor uranium, nor guns. Children were.

In the car park, he slapped himself on the head when a tired penny dropped. *Ginger Biscuit?* Shamed by his own stupidity, he saw what he should have seen right away: the real reason why Sergeant Ball had declined to travel.

# PART FOUR

*Blossomings*

# Forty two

While Zig Batten was failing to sleep at 30,000 feet, Tom Bowditch was wide awake at sea level - the Somerset Levels to be precise - and humping the last of his belongings out of the orchard-hidden barn and into the back of his old green Land Rover.

How many times had he told Dipstick Dave that the tingle had gone, that stealing tractors was a chore-bore? Tom would never be a 'proper' criminal - too bothered by the risks. Dave didn't listen. Not only could he barely *speak* English, he couldn't *hear* it either. Or wouldn't.

But Tom had grown a shell. Dave's freaky language and his tea caddies and his stupid unpronounceable surname – he'd called time on the lot. Even now, Dave was scouting expensive machines that needed separating from their owners. He couldn't stop. 'Just pack your gear, Tom, and *go.*'

He was still packing when Dipstick Dave's big four-wheel drive swished almost silently into the orchard, half a day earlier than expected. A grim-faced Dave climbed out and stared at Tom. Unsmilingly, he pointed at the back of the Rover.

'Bolt-cutters, Tom. We will need. Tonight.'

*Jesus wept.*

'What d'you mean, *we?*'

Dave pointed towards Taunton.

'Brand new John Deere tractor. No guard dog. Easy-peasie-lemon-squee-'

'Dave! I'm gone. I won't be *here* tonight. *Any* night. Are you deaf, or just *STUPID?*'

Dave was focused on the bolt-cutters, nothing else. He jabbed a finger. 'Will need, Tom.' He tried to yank them out of the Land Rover. Tom, taller, stronger, pushed him back. *You, Dave, are getting on my tits!*

'For your information, *Dipstick*, the bolt-cutters are *my* property - *mine!*'

Dave refused to hear. When he was focused, that's *all* he was.

'Will *need. Tonight!*'

He heaved Tom aside, grabbed at the heavy-duty cutters, but Tom heaved back, harder, grabbed them first, his veins raging.

'*You want these, do you?*'

Dave clawed at the cutters with one hand, screwing the other into a fist and slamming it at Tom's head - too slowly. Tom might not be a 'proper' criminal, but neither was he a poisoned dog. His young, strong arm fizzed the heavy steel cutters high into the air and swung them fiercely down, months of fury hissing out of him like steam from a boiling kettle.

The beaming face of Lieutenant Grigoris of the Greek International Police Cooperation Division met Batten as he emerged, weeping with sweat, from his mad airport taxi. He had understood little of the taxi-driver's supercharged conversation, being more focused on the multiple bends they had boomeranged round. He thanked the stars it had been a short trip, strapped as he was to the hot back seat, wet lettuce in a dancing sauna.

Grigoris took Batten's bag from the driver and loud strains of Greek batted between them, underpinned with much arm-waving and the curious backward flick of the head that signified 'no'. No money changed hands.

'My cousin', explained Grigoris as the taxi lurched back to Corfu airport for more victims. 'Best driver in all of Greece, you very locky.'

Lucky to be alive, thought Batten as he wiped sweat from the back of his neck with a soggy handkerchief. Grigoris produced a small but welcome bottle of ice-cold water which Batten swallowed in seconds, holding the cold carcass against his neck and forehead and once again enjoying the bliss of feeling cool.

Inside Police HQ, the air-conditioning was an embrace. Grigoris led him to a large room full of mismatched desks, only two or three of which showed signs of occupation. Following Batten's eyes, Grigoris explained 'many police before, but now, empty desks. Is same in England, no?'

Batten didn't know how to explain 'economic recession' to this puzzling, moustachioed Greek detective whose casual dress was offset by a neat, thin tie sharply-knotted to the neck, despite the heat. He just smiled and gave his customised shrug.

'Of course, it is the world recession - but what can be done?' said Grigoris. 'Many debt in Greece. Euros, euros, euros. The number, is too long to write, yes? My cousin - the one in America - he telephone, he say 'Makis, you in hock forever till you die!' So, empty desks here, you can see. In Athens - worse.'

Batten mumbled about public sector cuts in England too, without mentioning the absent Chief Inspector Jellicoe. Perhaps Somerset Police could borrow some unemployed Greek cousins?

Shortly after Batten's plane landed, Olly Rutter's plane took off. A copy of his flight itinerary on Sergeant Ball's cleared-for-action desk confirmed the exact time when Rutter was expected back from his highly convenient visit to France - at which point Ball would pose the questions he and Batten had drafted. Ball looked forward to the confrontation. But he'd let Rutter discover for himself the import of the desk's other photocopied documents - a restraining order amongst them. Rutter could return to Wake Hall Horse if he chose, but he had no hope of getting through the overblown doors of the Hall itself. Lady Wake's lawyer - even better paid than Derek Herring, Ball imagined - had seen to that.

To Batten's unsurprised annoyance, the toxics had yet to complete the DNA analysis that might topple Rutter's toxic lawyer. Instead, the two inspectors sifted official paperwork. Batten tried to recall what he'd half-learned about 'Standardisation of Information Sharing Across European Borders' at his Merlot Marie conference.

'I hate these guys,' said Grigoris, gesturing at the twin piles of paper that now lay on the desk between them. Batten wasn't sure if he meant the bureaucrats who spewed out the paperwork or the traffickers who inspired it. At least he was cooler now, more settled, keen to take a stab at Derek Herring.

His readiness did not quite chime with the rhythms of Lieutenant Grigoris, who stood up, clipped his phone to his belt and turned to pick up his dark glasses. As he did, Batten noticed - foolishly, for the first time - the dull metal of the stubby automatic that sat in a little leather holster strapped to his waist. You're not in Somerset now, Zig.

Outside, Batten's skin ran with sweat under the acute heat of the sun and he was glad when their route took him into the shade of the giant, ancient fortress that dwarfed the town. Grigoris said there was a second fortress too, not so different from the first. A pair of giant totems, Zig, protecting Derek Herring from English invaders? He hoped not. They headed neither to the harbour nor the Port Authority, but to a nearby café-bar.

'You like Greek coffee, Inspector?'

Batten didn't say he'd prefer to skip coffee-breaks and get stuck into Derek Herring - nor admit this was his first time in Greece.

'Never tried it. And, please, call me Zig.'

'Sig? Like Sigarette?'

'No, Zzzig. It's….it's a long story.'

'Endaxi. OK. *Sig*. And I am named Makis.'

They shook friendly hands.

'But first, you try Greek coffee!'

When the tiny cups of coffee were placed on the blue and white tablecloth, Batten's immediate thought was 'well, this won't take long'. He had yet to adjust to the Greek pace of life, forgetting Gribble's reminder that, for the Greeks, GMT meant Greek Maybe Time. Neither could he adjust to the coffee, which was mouth-shakingly sweet. Grigoris watched his face in vain for signs of approval.

'I think the English, they like sweet things? Like much sugar, no?'

'Some do,' replied Batten politely. 'I keep off the sugar if I can.'

Grigoris' reaction was to flick no more than a finger at the waiter, who appeared instantly at the table. Perhaps *he*'s seen the gun too, Zig.

There was a brief explosion, not of gunfire but of loud Greek gabbling and Batten's cup was summarily replaced with an identical one.

'I ordered for you a sketo. No sugar. You ask for it, sketo, when you order Greek coffee next time, endaxi?'

*Next* time? Not bloody likely! Then he saw the tight lips of the Chief Constable mouthing the word 'diplomatic' at him.

He sniffed the black, tarry-looking, sugar-free liquid and to his surprise, liked its deep, rich smell. As it cooled, he sipped it, his approval bringing a broad white smile to Grigoris' face. He sipped again, more deeply. When he next raised his cup, Grigoris touched his arm, showing his own discarded cup, almost a third full of untouched coffee-grounds.

'My cousin' - he didn't specify which one - 'he talk English like the English talk. He joke with me.' And in an English accent never heard on English shores, Grigoris said 'Makis, you are a detective. Your job, deah boy, is to get to the bottom of things. But, I trust, never to the bottom of a Greek coffee!'

And Grigoris laughed such a moustachioed, blue-sky laugh that even the passing waiter joined in, despite holding aloft a tray piled high with freshly-squeezed orange juice, iced coffees, and little bottles of cold water weeping ecstatic tears of condensation down their shaking sides.

Before Batten could himself join in, Grigoris was on his laughing feet and striding back towards police HQ. If he's unusually brisk for a Greek, thought Batten, it's almost certainly the caffeine. He failed to decipher the Greek lettering above the doorway as he left. 'Kafenion', it said.

Two hours later, Batten would have settled for more Greek coffee. His head was swimming with details of suspected land and sea trafficking routes from the Balkans to almost everywhere. Neither were the grey waters of the English Channel a barrier to the transportation of children.

'You dig tunnel under sea, what you expect?' asked Grigoris. He pointed across the room to an empty desk. 'Pappas there - he in Kefallinia now - your Euro-tunnel, he call it tunnel of hell.'

Batten reminded Grigoris that, small mercy, horse-boxes weren't allowed in Euro-tunnel. Grigoris reminded *him* that Great Britain had twelve thousand miles of coastline. There were ferries to check, private yachts, fishing boats, freighters.

'At least the private planes seem more focused on drugs than children - that's something,' countered Batten.

'I have less faith, Sig. Have bad minds, these people. Think, 'many bags of drug piled in a plane, almost like a bed. Why not some children to sleep on them?''

Neither man smiled. Batten pleaded tiredness, went back to his hotel, hoping not to dream.

While Batten was turning in, Baz Ballard was turning blue - from a back-from-France Olly slapathon.

'Why didn't you *stop* the silly cow, you bloody dolt?'

Stop her? How exactly? Lady Wake had at least allowed Baz time to carefully box his prize collection of model planes and store them in a dry barn, 'for a limited period only.' She'd be needing his rooms, she said, without deigning to say why. Baz would cope. He'd been turfed out of places so often he was part-nomad, though never from a gaff as posh as this. A bed and breakfast joint, a mile down the road, would do. He didn't know for how long.

Olly glared at the carefully-worded legal document Lady Wake had unsmilingly thrust at him on his return, flinging it onto the giant desk in his Wake Hall office. She's pushing my buttons, the snooty bitch! And she'll have you in a cell, too, if you put a foot wrong. He wasn't giving her - or any woman - *that* satisfaction. Where was bloody Del Herring when you needed him?

'And didn't you have the sense to bring my *clothes* in out of the rain, you dozy pillock?'

Baz chose not to remind Olly that he'd never been allowed keys to the double-locked office. Not officially. He kept quiet, and tried to think like Lawrence Vann.

# Forty three

Waking early, Batten discovered that Corfu Town woke earlier still. He ate breakfast at the taverna near his small hotel, surrounded by multiple shades of blue - the sky, the sea, Greek flags on yachts anchored in the bay, window shutters and tablecloths, his painted blue chair - and by squirts of blue smoke from the motor-bikes, mopeds and pick-up trucks which disturbed his peace, then returned it by departing, then stole it again. It was a small price to pay for the freshness of the experience. He ate simple bread and thyme honey, refused the instant 'Nes' he was offered and asked for the unsweetened Greek coffee he had begun to enjoy.

Though already missing the sunrise vista from his Ashtree cottage, and the slow greening of the trees across the valley to Ham Hill, the view here was expansive, to say the least, and he wondered why he had travelled so little. Mountains, green islands, a crystal sea, tall Venetian buildings, their balconies drenched with geraniums, and the daily panorama of people - simple and exotic, taking their time, waving, greeting, talking. Fresh loaves of bread and plastic bags of peaches and melons bobbled their owners along the hose-piped pavements. He watched as feet flip-flopped from the nearby mini-market to a host of wooden house-doors, some grey with age and sea-salt, others carved and heavy with blackened iron fittings, and one, close to where he sat, adorned with panels of multi-coloured seashells set into the frame.

When Grigoris sat down at his table, Greek coffee in his long-fingered hand, Batten barely noticed his arrival. They raised their cups in greeting, and sat for a while. After Batten enthused about the invigorating sights and sounds of the street theatre in front of them, Grigoris tilted his head to one side.

'Ah yes, but there is the backside of the coin, no? There is the winter. Much rain sometimes, in the winter. The tourists, they go, and the people here they live on what they have leaved behind, till they come back in the next year. Not always they come back, not in the same number, and then the winter is hard.' He pointed at the silhouetted mountains of Albania, across the bay. 'Sig, I tell you, these bad men know this. And they tempt the weak ones, with bad money, blood money. You see?'

Batten saw.

Moving centre-stage in the street theatre, Grigoris became a trafficker, an evil grin out of Victorian Melodrama plastered across his animated face: 'Hey, Nikos, want to collect a package for me, from over there? I make payment to you, cash, used notes, make you rich, no problem.'

The nasty grin disappeared and sadness took its place.

'And then the package, it gets more big, then more big still, then is the size of a child, yes? And the tempted ones, they cannot go back, cannot be free. They must hide their cargo, sail the boat, keep silent. If not -' his finger made a slicing movement across his throat. 'So, the cargo, it makes its journey. Poor hidden wretches.'

He mispronounced it 'ratchets'. Batten didn't correct him.

'You have children, Sig?'

'No.' He almost added 'thank Christ' but was unsure how the Greeks viewed blasphemy? Churches were everywhere, he'd noticed.

'You are locky, Sig. I have three children. All fine girls. I think of the fathers of the girls you have found. Smuggled with animals. Animals, Sig! I think what I must do if is my girls taken this way. I cut my throat. Unless I can cut the throat of the man who took them.'

Or the woman perhaps, Batten mused, as the unwanted image of Lady Wake's slender throat lurched into his head.

'It would make you feel that, Sig, if you had children. Cutting a throat. You would feel it.'

Batten felt it anyway. He thought of the childless Sergeant Ball who, thank Christ, had stayed behind in England.

The interview room in the prison wing wasn't much to look at, but neither was the ratty face of Manny McRory. Ball and DC Magnus stared at it again, once more asking their questions - new ones, trick ones, fast ones. Nothing. Not a grain of even circumstantial evidence to link the canny sod to the murder of Lawrence Vann. And, sod's law, he was in custody when the Wake Hall raid took place. Magnus spent the interview staring at Manny's bandaged wrist, and making sure he knew it. *I had more impact on* you *than you on me, at least.* But a stubborn Manny stuck to his line.

'Maybe it's not *my* DNA. They make mistakes, you know, these white-coats. I seen a programme about it, on Sky.'

Ball changed tack. 'How well do you know Vito Valdano?' He'd long ago stopped gracing Manny with 'zor.'

'Well I've *seen* him. He glows in the *dark*, that one.'

Magnus chipped in.

'Bit too *colourful* for you, is he?'

Manny directed his reply squarely at Sergeant Ball.

'Valdano isn't horses. *I'm* horses. So our paths don't cross, get me?'

Ball had been getting Manny for far too long.

'So, being 'horses', how come you failed to notice anything strange about that horse-box of yours, the dark-blue one? The one you swore wasn't on the road round Christmas time, wasn't even roadworthy? You never realised it had a secret compartment, six inches behind your driver's seat?'

Manny's bespectacled lawyer - not quite a Derek Herring, but expensive all the same - gave a tiny negative wave of his hand. Try and prove it, Manny's smirk said.

'No groans of pain, no sounds of crying, no children's voices - all those times when you were merrily driving along? *Deaf*, were you? Or *immune*?'

Raising his voice made Ball feel better - and made the lawyer glare disapprovingly over his specs. Manny wasn't falling for it in any case. Did they really expect him to say, 'Ah that's where you're wrong - it's all sound-proofed!'

The ginger Sergeant could go whistle. Olly had a long arm, and prisons are dangerous places. Manny knew. He'd had experience.


Grigoris was a good host, a Greek host. They could only wait now, he said, for documents, for proof, for permissions.

'Ah, but I have surprise for you, Sig. Not far away, near the Spianada, we have cure for English home-sickness, yes?'

What, you've teleported my cottage to Corfu? With my CD collection and a bottle of Speyside? And a naked, unattached Merlot Marie?

'In Corfu Town, hard to believe but true, we have cricket pitch!'

Oh Christ.

'I bring you there, later. We sit, drink coffee, watch cricket. You feel like at home!'

He was shocked to learn that not every Englishman was cricket-mad, especially one with grim memories of a reluctant school playing field where he dropped more catches than a Russian trawler. And as for the snide references to Batten/Ball....What he wanted to do, he explained, was walk, and soon, early, before the crazy sun held sway. A puzzled Grigoris, who could not understand the English walking cure, pointed the route and took his leave.

Batten strolled away from the old harbour, away from the whine of motor-bikes and tourists, down side streets and through tiny squares, some with the same twisted, wizened trees. Olives, were they? He should buy a book on trees. What kind was the killing tree that sprang from Burrow Hill like an exclamation mark? Maybe it's the question-mark tree, Zig?

After a while he found himself at the sea once more, by a sand and pebble bay. It was still quiet as he sat down on a low wall, Albania barely a mile or two across the channel, but the connecting water almost at his feet.

Gazing at the blue surface, hearing the rhythmic shudder of the waves, he fell inwards, to the deeper waters of the soul. He wasn't the first to hear messages in the suck and slur of the sea. The crest of your joy, Zig. The slough of your despair. Joy. Sad. Joy. Sad, as each wave rose and broke and retreated. At University, he'd read Mathew Arnold:

'Socrates long ago
Heard it on the Aegean....
Begin, and cease, and then again begin....'

That's you, Zig. Begin; drift; fall away; start afresh. North. South. Merlot Marie. Rhona Fiske. Begin, and cease, and then again begin. And it's why you're still a cop, isn't it? Crime, law, crime, law, slowly catchee monkee. But you do catch 'em. Begin, arrest, and then again begin. Achieve something, somewhere. Carry *something* through to a finish of sorts.

Out in the blue cove, unusually, the wind fell away. Flat glass calm baffled the waves. He could barely hear the sea. He was in a photograph -

no, a soothing, blue paletted seascape, a picture of peace - the sad, sour taste of his work briefly forgotten. Still-life with daydream-detective.

Then a young girl ran by, raised an awkward arm and the canvas ripped and splashed as a stone hit the water. Had Batten been less understanding, been Derek Herring perhaps, he would have angrily grabbed the child by the offending arm, swung her up and out, and flung her after her stone onto the now-shattered surface of the broken sea.

# Forty four

Sergeant Ball's satisfaction at the jail-time awaiting McRory and Bulky Hobshaw soon disappeared when he assessed the remaining holes in the jigsaw. Fragments of proof, much silence, little else. Unless Batten brought it back from Greece alongside a handcuffed Derek Herring, there was no significant evidence against Vito Valdano. Nor Lady Wake. And as for Olly, he countered all Ball's questions with a sneerily repetitive song.

'I've been betrayed....I nip abroad for five minutes and they shaft me, the ungrateful sods....Who can you *trust*, these days?'

When asked about Valdano's missing ear, a homophobic Olly suggested they look for a jealous male lover. His advice was doubly academic. There were no palpable suspects, and should one be unearthed, Vito would not be pressing charges. He refused to say why. Ball doubted he'd ever slap cuffs on Olly Rutter.

He looked across the now-tidy office at the remains of the team. Magnus had just come back from her country jaunt to the monastery, to collect Stephanie Broke-Mondelle, and was leaning back in her chair, eyes closed, recovering from the temporary but explosive release of words that had swamped the journey. Ball imagined a group of contented monks soundlessly applauding Stephanie's exit. Would she still be articulate when more difficult questions were put to her?

The desk next to Hick's had been empty - loudly so - for too long, so Jon Lee had moved there. Ball dropped the brown diary for Horse Box 1 into Lee's in-tray.

'*You* try Baz Ballard, Jon. See if you can get beyond 'I'm just a driver', eh? The sod must know *something*.'


It was almost the size of Corfu, the grin on the handsome face of Makis Grigoris.

'So, let me get this straight. Derek Herring failed to fly out of Corfu *this morning*, because a Greek pickpocket - quite coincidentally - stole his passport?'

'It is so, Sig. Exactly so.'

'And it happened just before Herring boarded a plane to Costa Rica - which *coincidentally* has no extradition treaty with the UK?'

'No, no, he was *booked* to Costa Rica, yes. But he cannot fly direct from Corfu.'

That makes a difference?

'Sig, you are not of Greece. Here, such things we believe in.'

Grigoris's belief in such things was so deep the moustache framing his smile had practically disappeared round the back of his head.

'Was it this Greek belief that made the passport end up with *you*? Or is this pickpocket one of your 'cousins'?'

Lieutenant Makis Grigoris of the Greek International Police Cooperation Division merely shrugged and continued to smile. Batten envied the lush band of hair which framed his mouth. Thicker and darker than yours, Zig.

'Many months we have watched your Mr Herring, Sig, while we watch his friends from over there.' He dismissed Albania with a wave. 'They are clever, these men. Their ship, their *yacht*, it sail far to sea when they talk business. We can not listen, can not watch. I am patient, Sig. We Greeks have a saying, 'all things good to know are difficult to learn.' But many months? Long time not to learn of these men. Or perhaps you like it more if we let Mr Herring to catch his plane?'

Batten was getting the measure of Grigoris and his Greek ways. Energy. Determination. And a bit of judicious, non-judicial manipulation when needs must. It made Batten feel better about his own injudicious moments. But what did Makis have on this handy pickpocket, to persuade him to target Herring at a busy airport, near security staff? Batten could only smile at Grigoris's comment that 'we had much luck, yes?' Luck, indeed.

'He is known to us, this thief. He and his woman also. She is sometimes a flower-seller, she work where the big boats come in, where money is - 'Fresh flowers, my friends, for your honey-at-home? These posies, they make her hot for you, you understand?' She winks them, waves flowers in their faces, detracts them.'

'*Dis*tracts them?'

'Ah, yes. Distracts. She does this. *He*, he steals.'

'But this was the airport, Makis, not the harbour.'

Grigoris threw his arms upwards in a Greek shrug.

'It is the recession, Sig. One must....diversify? The word is correct?'

Just smile, Zig.

'At the airport, is different. Here, people make ready to fly - is always so - check tickets, check papers, have them in hand. And when your Mr Herring he do the same, they pretend big argument next him. She shout at her man, he to her. Much pushing and bumping, things drop to the floor, sorry, sorry, sir, she drive me crazy this woman - you have wife, sir, you know what they do to us, yes? - ah, you drop your papers, please, let me help you. See?'

How could he not see? Grigoris was a natural actor. He would have made a far more animated tree than Batten, in Sergeant Ball's Christmas panto.

'So Herring ends up with no passport?'

Grigoris gave a characteristic, mock-apologetic forward dip of his chin which seemed to trigger a momentary palms-up movement of his hands.

'No, no, he still have *a* passport. But he go to flight desk and they see it is not *his* passport. Poor man - he cannot fly! Then Mr Herring he scream blue murder - but the thief and his wife they are disappeared.'

'So whose passport was it?'

Again the wide smile.

'You know, Sig, I forget. But it will be investigated, of course. Some other time.'

For a moment, moustache smiled at moustache, then Grigoris clapped his hands together and pointed at two objects also smiling at Batten from his temporary desk. Grigoris picked up the first and casually waffled it like a fan before passing it across.

'Of course, Sig, if Mr Herring is arrested, his true passport may be needed. It is fortunate that our thief he is an honest man, yes?'

Batten flicked the passport open, to find Herring's chubby unsmiling face glaring back at him. He turned to the second object, Herring's wallet, which had also been 'retrieved'.

'Your thief doesn't know how to stop, Makis.'

'Ah yes, he is kleptomaniac, this thief, Sig.' Catching Batten's look of surprise, he added, 'Kleptomaniac, it is of course Greek word. Greeks have given your language many long words, I think. No?'

Relax, Zig, he's way ahead of you. The wallet contained half a dozen business cards. He recognised some of the Albanian names from the briefing Grigoris had given him the day he arrived. 'Import/Export' was a popular business activity in this neck of the woods.

'There is also this, Sig,' said Grigoris as he placed an additional object on the table. Batten had often watched it scratch notes and sign documents - most recently when Manny McRory was questioned 'with his lawyer present.' He rolled the gold-plated fountain pen towards him, to read the inscription: 'Victorious'. Well, Derek, maybe not this time.

'Our thief, Sig, he is much pleased with this fine gold pen. I think maybe it becomes lost?'

'Lost?'

'But then found again? Our thief, he finds it, yes? There must be a reward, for all his efforts, you agree?'

Grigoris watched Batten's eyebrows reach his hairline.

'Do not worry, Sig,' said Gigoris. 'It is traditional!'


ACC Gribble had picked up and put down the phone so many times in the last hour that his station-platform of a desk was starting to feel like a giant receiver. Momentarily he forgot who he was listening to, until strains of Yorkshire bit his ear.

'What do you expect, Batten? This isn't some American TV crime show! DNA analysis is a painstaking process. Bite-marks require an electron scanning microscope. We do *not* want errors....Yes, I *have* stressed its importance!' .....No, he hadn't visited the Lab himself....No, he hadn't 'put a bomb up the toxics'. Who do you think I am, Sylvester Stallone?

'Just remain vigilant, and be ready. Clear?'

There was an audible sigh.

'Clear, sir.'

Gribble put the phone down yet again. He was as worried as Batten that Derek Herring might still elude them, use a fake passport, sneak away in a small boat at night. Until concrete evidence arrived, the Greek police could only do so much. Hand hovering over the telephone, he took Batten's point. Against his better judgement, he lifted the receiver, dialled. Put a bomb up the toxics.

# Forty five

Nina Magnus had barely sat down at her Parminster desk when *her* phone rang. Has the bloody thing got *eyes*? Even then, she was surprised to hear the voice of Vito Valdano's assistant, Oksana Unpronounceable. She'd only met her twice, if an interview can be called a 'meeting', only remembered her because they shared common ground - the feeling of being somehow foreign, though they were both born here. Magnus was more surprised still to discover the call had nothing to do with Vito Valdano.

'Missing? Well, how long for?'

She wanted to put the phone down right away. Missing Persons, yuk. Nine times out of ten they weren't missing at all. But when they were....

'Right, he's your older brother? How old *is* he?'

A forty two year old brother who's a sort of mechanic and who hasn't been heard from in five days. No, she's never met any of his girlfriends. How to ask about *boy*friends without giving offence? Forty two though, he's hardly going to tell his younger sister *everything*!

'You just get Voicemail? Mm. Have you been round to his house?'

OK, his *flat*. Rented? Right. Well if he's never there, how do you know he's missing? As if I'm not busy enough already.

'So where else have you looked? What about his social life? Where does he work?'

Oh, freelance. On the road. Well that's helpful, not. It's the curse of modernity, thought Nina Magnus. Oksana hadn't actually *seen* her brother since Christmas. Texts and phones, a pretend relationship.

'What does he talk about, then, on the phone? Does he mention places, people?'

Oksana Unpronounceable was curiously hesitant. He mostly asked about *her* job, she said, about the interesting clients she met. She had some very well-heeled clients, seemed to spend half their lives on expensive residentials. She wondered why they bothered having homes or farms at all, if they were never there. Some of them even had little estates - oh, no, nothing as grand as Wake Hall.

Magnus couldn't understand this hunger for gossip; bro and sis, on the mobile, swapping snippets from a Somerset version of *OK Magazine*. Dave couldn't get enough of it, Oksana said.

'Right, so he's a Dave. His surname - can you spell it for me?'

Magnus wished she hadn't asked. She put down the phone and looked at the long jumble of seemingly random letters on her notepad. The family name began with a V - and an alphabet later it ended in -sic. Hell's teeth, no wonder they call her Oksana Thing. It *is* unpronounceable!

Grigoris was doing the talking, and he did it well. I'd like to see you do the same in fluent Greek, Zig. Mind you, with crime scene photos and Herring's DNA results spread across the table like placemats....They hadn't even mentioned dental records and bite mark comparisons, not yet.

'And so, I offer you again, to make a statement...?'

Herring stared first at the opulent Greek moustache and then at the lesser English version, before silently shaking his head at both. The interview room was hardly palatial, with its metal table and chair bolted to the floor, but it was bigger - and considerably cooler - than the grimy cell he'd been unceremoniously dumped in by a taciturn, unsmiling and very large uniformed Greek policeman. He was happy to dally, at least for now.

With deliberate nonchalance, Batten produced Herring's 'stolen' wallet and slowly removed its business cards, laying them on the table one by one, a dealer in a poker game.

'Lieutenant Grigoris has very hospitably offered to contact these people,' said Batten, casually flicking a finger at the cards. 'Purely on your behalf, of course. He takes the view that, when they discover your very serious difficulties, they may be moved to....intervene....in some way?'

Grigoris fanned his fingers demurely, a benefactor embarrassed by the discovery of his charitable act. Herring's stare intensified.

'He acknowledges that these people, your *friends*, will be surprised, *disturbed*, to learn of your rather repellent involvement with....?'

'The girl she is called 'Vera'.

'With *Vera*. Who is....?'

'Thirteen years.'

341

'Yes, thirteen years old - thank you, Grigoris.'

Again the fanned fingers. Batten examined the DNA results, as if refreshing his memory.

'But being men of the world, their friendship will no doubt outweigh any revulsion at your unfortunate behaviour? Lieutenant Grigoris suggests calling *this* man first, who he tells me is most influential in the import/export business. And who will be most upset to hear of your….predicament.'

He picked up the nearest card, and read the name.

'Gjin….Zogic? Am I pronouncing it correctly?'

Grigoris dipped his chin and turned his fanned fingers upwards.

'It is close. May be he is half-Albanian, half Serbian, so….'

'Gjin Zogic. Is he the one they call King Zog?'

'King Zzog, ah yes. But not King *Zzig* - we must not confuse this name with *your*s, Sig, no, no!'

The Greek moustache bobbed up and down as Grigoris chuckled merrily to himself. Herring's hard stare remained, but was there a tinge of fear in it now?

Ten minutes later he was staring at scrawls and scratches on his cell wall. A graphic gallery of obscene graffiti reminded him of his own foolish lapse of control. Batten and Grigoris were giving him 'thinking time', he knew, not that King Zog's capabilities - and his reach - needed thinking about. He was inescapably in trouble. And his skin was sticky, dirty, almost melting in the sweaty heat of the airless space. The ceiling fan, in its protective mesh cage, was completely still. He turned his back on the obscene scrawls and weighed up his options.

'How long should we give him?'

In the near-empty office, Grigoris was eating a large, runny peach. He dabbed at his moustache with a paper napkin before answering.

'A little more, I think. It is growing hot in there now. The fan' - he made a twirling gesture with his free hand - 'I am afraid it is broke.'

Batten smiled at the archness of his Greek colleague, who had flicked the ceiling fan's switch to the 'off' position before Herring even reached his cell.

'You know the fable of the wind and the sun, Sig? It is from Hyssop's fables, I think?'

'You mean 'Aesop's'?'

Grigoris looked puzzled. He thought he'd said that.

'But, no, I don't know it.'

'Ah, it is this: the wind and the sun they make a wager, yes? Which of the two can first make the man to take off his coat.'

'The man? Which man?'

'It does not matter! *Any* man! A man wearing a *coat!*'

'Sorry.' Diplomacy, Zig, remember?

'And so the wind blows at the coat, pulls at the sleeves, to drag the coat from the man's back - but the man he feels the coldness of the wind, he pulls his coat still more tight around him, yes? And the more the wind blow, the more he pulls tighter his coat.'

'Right.'

'Ah, but the sun, the sun, she has only to shine on the man, to make him hot. She shines more, so he is more hot still. And you can see, Sig, yes? The man, he sweat so much, he must take off his coat!'

Grigoris laughed his disarming, moustachioed laugh, which persuaded Batten to join in, till Grigoris abruptly stopped, his face tight, hard.

'So we let him sweat more, your Mr Herring. And then, I am certain, he take off his coat.'

How could it be so *hot*? There should be a law against freak weather. An informed inner voice listed real laws, ones that would very likely and very soon be used against *him*. For a rare moment, he heard his mother's voice in his skull: 'even clever-dicks like *you* get their comeuppance!' She'd hated it, that he turned out to be intelligent. Or was it envy? He'd stuffed her away in a sanatorium, till the liver damage polished her off. Would you like a nice marble headstone? they'd asked. Cremation, he'd spat back.

And cremation was what it felt like now, in this sweat-box of a cell. Derek Herring was wilting; his determination not to take his own advice had weakened; he'd begun to deal with whoever - and whatever - was on the ground. As a lawyer and a realist he knew that prison was unavoidable. It was merely a question of how much. And *where*.

Curse that little Albanian bitch! And curse King Zog, who swore he'd dumped her, replaced her with a fresh one. Dammit, they had a signed contract! But the two-faced crook had shipped her regardless, a child-bomb full of Derek's DNA! The Greek moustache had made it brutally clear: if he could prove the assault on the girl took place in Greece, then in Greece Derek would serve his time. He would not survive that. Away from the air-conditioned comfort of his Corfu villa, the prison heat would degrade him - if King Zog didn't degrade him first.

He looked down at his uneaten 'meal', a shapeless lump that might once have been moussaka, as appealing now as the plastic plate it had died on. Even the plate was melting. Time for realpolitik, Derek Herring decided. Cash in the bargaining chips called Olly? Or those called Zog?

There used to be a lot more of us, at these daily breakfast meetings, Rhona Fiske remembered, looking across the big farmhouse kitchen table at her fellow team leaders. Allie Chant tapped her nails against her coffee cup, trying not to want a cigarette. Jake Tuttle did what he usually did - chewed smoky bacon with his surly mouth wide open. At least it was Debbie's morning-off today. Rhona remembered another morning-off, weeks ago, that had removed Lawrence Vann - only for a 'new' Lawrence to sneak into the gap created. They had met the freshly-appointed Estate Manager, another stuffed shirt, who had politely said 'no' to daily breakfast meetings with the other team leaders.

She wondered why it was so eerily silent this morning, till she remembered the farriers had gone - no familiar noises and acrid smells. And the constant trundling of horse-boxes in and out of Wake Hall Horse had ground to a halt since Bulky Hobshaw's arrest. No-one believed the stable-girl gossip that Olly Rutter was in the doghouse - till his belongings turned up in a heap, dumped outside The Regiment office. Rhona herself had spotted the hairy mammoth, thumping past the stable blocks, alone, face like thunder.

She tasted the dregs of her coffee. Will this recession never *end*? Allie's fingernails tapped; Jake Tuttle's teeth clacked, in disharmony. And my *personal* recession? Whatever possibilities there had been at Wake Hall, she had failed to take advantage of them, failed to make them real, despite her efforts. All she had made was mistakes. It angered her.

The exploratory fling with a tall policeman had also fizzled out because - because what? A little too....unforthcoming, Mr Moustache? And did he realise he rhymed with a disparaging name for the police? She'd never actually *called* him Zig the Pig, but to think of him that way at all, well, it wasn't....conducive, was it?

Sliding her breakfast plate into the sink, she realised Debbie's morning off meant washing up to do. Sighing, she pulled on her well-used rubber gloves.

Batten had forgotten to eat, his focus entirely on gutting a Herring. Derek's intestines, though, were still in place, his mouth firmly shut.

'Mr Fat Whitebait can chew air, but Mr Makis Grigoris, he chew only *food*! We eat, Sig, *now*!'

From a taverna chair overlooking the bay, every wall and street-lamp was plastered with so many election posters that Corfu Town looked like a giant collage. Dozens of political parties seemed to be in contention. To Batten's foreign eye, yet to fathom the Greek alphabet, each poster was a jumble of acronyms and undecipherable slogans. He asked Grigoris what the various parties represented.

'Sig, you are not here for enough days,' pity and dismissal in his voice. 'The reasons are very long - much, much history. You choose please, Greek politics, or Greek food? And by the way, the cheese pies are *excellent* here.'

Batten tasted the joy of crisp pastry and warm feta. The fried courgettes, sweet and salty, were a delight. He'd ordered slow-cooked lamb because the misspelt menu said it was lamp-in-the-oven. It lit him up.

Was this to be his final meal in Greece? He loathed the fact that Derek Herring would decide. Grigoris had propped his mobile on the taverna table. It was silent.

With every mouthful, Batten's eyes returned to the phone, willing it to make a statement. Instead, a loudspeaker mounted on a dust-covered van sent staccato Greek politics clacking into the evening air.

'At least tell me what *this* lot are saying, Makis.'

Grigoris listened, and wrinkled his nose dismissively.

'You are a political man, Sig?'

'Isn't everyone?'

But *are* you, Zig? Looking at the herby lamb on his plate, he thought of a line from Brecht - first the belly, *then* moralising - and ate another forkful. A waiter danced a silver tray of Greek coffees to the adjacent table, and the rich smell drifted him to Zigland, to the little house in Leeds where Aunt Daze still lived. To take his mind off Derek Herring, he shared memories with Grigoris, as they ate....

The PC Kerr incident was months ago and Batten had only now found a spare weekend to paint the new back door and fit stronger locks on the windows. Dimi had agreed to help, so it could all be done in a day.

When Batten arrived, Mrs Yeadon from next door had dropped in for her weekly 'coffeh' with Aunt Daze. The pair of them were doing what they always did: drinking 'coffeh' and reminiscing. Both their houses sported 'Vote Labour' posters for the imminent council elections. Aunt Daze would be horrified that Batten rarely voted now - too swamped by criminals, and no longer certain who to vote for.

He accepted a 'coffeh' and waited for Dimi, listening all the while to the fond reminiscence of this compact woman - tiny, but able to be both aunt and mother at the same time.

On the journey north, he'd stopped at a motorway café and found himself sitting next to a young student, trawling back through the messages on his mobile phone, as if in a trance. The messages were in strings, by recipient, and seemed to go back years. C U in 10, logged for posterity. Is this how memory will be done, Zig, in future? Or will we forget how to do it all?

Aunt Daze and Mrs Yeadon hadn't forgotten. They had a photo album laid across their laps and were turning pages, giggling and remembering. He'd heard the stories before, but when someone gives up her life to raise you, you smile and listen. No sign of Dimi anyway.

He could recite by rote the story of the wet-behind-the-ears Tory candidate who door-stepped these two staunch Labourites, seeking their votes. A decade ago, but still fresh to Aunt Daze.

"Law and Order. Family Values. That's what we stand for,' the young man said. Well, I sat 'im down and showed 'im my photograph album, this one.'

She stroked it, a pet, a friend.

'That's my grandfather, I told him. He was killed in 1940, when the Germans bombed that tank factory over by....'

Batten smiled to himself; at least she can't remember *everything*. 'D'you mean Barnbow?' said Mrs Yeadon.

Aunt Daze raised a confirming finger and carried on.

'He was a fireman, you see, I explained. He was protecting the country from Hitler so *some* families could live in big houses and own dangerous quarries like the one that killed the man in this next photograph here. He was my father. He died when a rock-face collapsed. So they told us. No-one got prosecuted.'

She turned another page. Batten knew what was on it, every photo, every missing face.

'This young woman was my sister. Bright as a shiny brass button. She could have gone to university. Killed in a car crash, 24, with her 'usband. That's 'im there. He was only a postman. They didn't matter much. Driver who killed them was some sort of toff. He wasn't prosecuted neither. This one's a photograph of all their friends, family too, look, at the Labour Club. We held the wake there. Quite a nice club, in't it? That's me, see, by the piano, with little Zig on my lap? I was much younger of course, when it was taken.'

She paused. If she was looking back to what might have been, it was for the briefest moment.

'Tell me something, young man, I said. I was very polite.'

'Course you were,' said Mrs Yeadon. 'When are you not?'

'Tell me, I said, can you see anyone in this photograph, anyone at all, who might want to vote for *your* kind of Law and Order, for *your* Family Values? He left after that, the young man. Never came back.'

Batten finished his coffeh, picked up his paint-brush. Dimi had not turned up.

'This brother, *did* he turn up?'

'No. He'd....forgotten.'

Grigoris put his fork on the table, next to the still-silent phone.

'I am sad for you, Sig.'

'Why? No need to be.'

'Because here' - he flicked a hand at Greece - 'our family is very big, very long. Longer than the politics, yes? Many, many family. Advice, and help, and talk - and even paint your door!'

With each word his arms stretched further from his body till, fully extended, they brushed against a passing waiter, and over-loud Greek apologies broke the moment. Grigoris picked up his fork again.

'So now, you stop stare at my mobile, yes? And *eat!*'

They did, till the loudspeaker-van returned and a babel of politics drowned their laughter. They almost didn't hear the phone.

# Forty six

Rather than interview Baz in familiar environs, the police now requested his presence at the CID Centre - palatial surroundings compared to the Greek equivalent. Baz, though, received the usual cool reception and a long wait in an empty interview room, invisible eyes in the ceiling.

He guessed, correctly, that if he pretended to sleep, his head on the grubby table, they'd wait a few minutes, then wake him up and begin. It was the schoolboy cop's turn this time, with that big yokel copper, silent in the background. Baz sat up straight, filled himself with air, intimidating the speck of a youngster whose job it was to intimidate *him*.

Jon Lee pretended to flick knowingly through McRory's transport diary. The trouble is, Lee thought, when I look up from its brown pages, I really *do* look up.

'Your name's here three times,' he said, randomly tapping a dog-eared page. Baz made no response. 'And you only drive when 'Imp' - Import - is scribbled next to your name?'

'Or when my name's scribbled next to Imp.'

'Either way, when a shipment comes from overseas, it's you that's driving.'

'Except when it's somebody else.'

'Let's stick with you, shall we? Why *you*? Special kind of journey?'

He'd asked himself the same question, but only after the police found the hidden compartment in Manny's horse-box was he certain *how* 'special'. Lawrence had worked it out, though. Baz was ashamed, about the children. But he *was* there, three times over. Accountable, somehow.

'I'm a driver. I just do -'

'- What the boss tells you. Yes, you keep saying that.'

Baz couldn't think of anything else *to* say. Words were not his strong point. If Lawrence was here....But if Lawrence was here, they'd both be somewhere else, wouldn't they?

Ioannis Charalambos may have been taciturn to a fault but he was a supersized Greek policeman, well used to escorting prisoners. The fact that he had relatives not far from Bristol airport, where Batten's plane was heading, was a convenient arrangement with 'Grigoris' written all over it. Derek Herring sat between Batten and the silent Charalambos, firmly handcuffed to the latter, yet sighing with relief.

He had refused to make a statement until the fan in his cell was repaired, and he'd been allowed a shower and a change of clothes. The Greek detective dug his heels in, but Derek was experienced too. Once clean and cool, he efficiently traded destructive information about King Zog for a promise of extradition to England.

Having finally dealt with whatever is on the ground, here he was, in the air, squeezed between two policemen in Economy class, jetting off towards an English prison. The thought made him shudder, but knowing that Zog's hand could not touch him there brought relief. Once word reached Olly Rutter that his long-serving legal adviser, currently detained at Her Majesty's Pleasure, had said not a single Olly-damaging word to the police, prison would become a safer place. And his legal skills would be highly prized there.

Ignoring Batten's white knuckles clamped for take-off onto the arm-rest, Derek Herring stared through the window at the brown departing coast of Corfu, till it turned a deep blue-green and then all was wine-dark sea. A pity, they would confiscate his villa, his Mercedes, every asset they could find, to compensate the victims. *Victims?* Dolts – too stupid to leave even a mark on the world. Derek had other assets, ones the police would never find. When the prison system had finished with him he would emerge, and leave much more than a mark. He would rise again. Victorious. Instinctively, despite the handcuffs, he felt in his pocket for his inscribed gold pen. Gone.

Olly had sacked most of the staff at Wake Hall Horse - they knew not to argue - and was rapidly selling off every nag in sight. The fields behind the huge stable-block were almost empty, silent. He knew a thing or two about asset-stripping, did Olly, and a great deal more about revenge.

He watched the first Andalucian mare trot up the ramp and into the waiting horse-box. Just two more to load, and that was that. He'd found buyers for all three, at a whacking profit, though it wasn't the money that brought a smile to his face. He'd seen *her* stroke their long manes, whisper to them, sooth them, her hands brushing across their necks in that sensual, flowing way she had…. Well, go ahead, Lady Muck, pretend Wake Hall Horse never existed - it'll come as a nasty shock when you realise your beloved grey mares have all gone. To pastures new. Which is where Olly was heading.

Not before the police had driven up the road in numbers, though. Why don't they just bloody well move *in*? Plenty of room in the Hall - wipe their plod feet all over the Persian carpets, for all he cared. But it was not the main house that interested the police. It was Olly's office.

He could only assume it was genuine, the search warrant thrust into his hand by that northern plonker and his ginger humpty-dumpty. Never had to deal with crap like this when Del was around.

'We'll require keys to the office, zor, and to any locked cupboards and the like. If you please.'

'Baz! *Baz*! Brief-case - in the boot! Get this lot sorted!'

Olly couldn't give a toss; nothing left to find in the gutted office, or anywhere else where a plod's allowed to look. His remaining assets were safely offshore, and his ready cash and bonds were sitting in a very private vault. Not even Del knew about *that* one.

Batten was admiring an Andalucian mare, its head-collar tied to an iron ring, awaiting its turn to be loaded. The sudden arrival of so many cars had spooked it, and a lone stable lad was doing his best to calm it down.

'You're too late, Ziggy, it's already sold - and you'll never have a wallet big enough, not on *your* pay. What about a knackered Shetland pony?'

Batten ignored the sarcasm, gently soothed the grey neck of the soft-maned beauty.

'How old's this one, Rutter? Twelve? *Thirteen*?'

Olly shrugged. Once the pigs had gone, he'd be gone too. His instinct was to pop over to the drawing room for a large whisky with his feet up, but The Witch had put a stop to that. He strolled across to the over-polished Jaguar, flicked the passenger seat to 'recline', draped The Racing Times over his tanned face and took his afternoon nap. Alone.

Batten waited till Olly was fast asleep before loudly rapping his knuckles on the car window. They had found the wall safe.

'Your bruiser says he doesn't have the combination. I presume you *do*?'

Yes, I do - the combination to an empty shell, you tosser! Olly hated rude awakenings almost as much as he hated the police. He crumpled the Racing Times into an angry ball. With a vengeful glare he stomped out of the Jag and back to the office, through the now silent lines of stables, past gutted tack rooms and empty stores and across the vast, echoing yard that was once Wake Hall Horse. His £600 suit looked incongruous next to the grubby jacket and jodhpurs of the stable lad, struggling to coax the last Andalucian mare towards the ramp for yet another profitable horse-box journey - though a legal one, this time.

As Olly pounded past, the stable lad lost his grip on the horse's head-collar and it wrenched its glorious crown away from the box. Rearing up on its hind legs, whinnying and wheeling in a futile kick for freedom, its flank brushed against an already-seething Olly and its front leg clipped him on the side of his knee.

'*You bloody nag!*' Do you know how much this suit *cost*?' he screamed, and all the tension of his disastrous, vanity-pricking departure erupted into his pumped-up arm. He tore a riding crop from its hook on the stable wall, raised it high in the air and whipped it furiously down and across the animal's face with a skin-hacking slash. Fortunately for Olly, the shocked and wounded horse bolted away rather than *at* him, fleeing across the empty yard where it whinnied in hurt and pain, shaking its long-maned head as a vicious wheal began to swell across its face, an ugly red scar across pale-grey beauty.

*Un*fortunately for Olly, Sergeant Ball's alert hands instantly whipped Olly's mitts behind his back and clicked them into a set of cuffs. Batten's amazement found its way to his jaw which dropped and stayed dropped. What the *hell* was the ginger nut *doing*?

'What the fu -!'

'I am arresting you, zor, for malicious maltreatment of a horse, which is an offence - as your Mr Herring would doubtless tell you, were he not in a cell - under the Animal Welfare Act. You are not obliged to say anything but -'

'Get these bloody cuffs off me NOW!' screamed Olly.

To no avail. The handcuffs stayed in place, but Olly did not. Ball beckoned to Magnus and Hick. The pair of them, suppressing unprofessional smirks, bundled the struggling, cursing, expensively-suited Olly Rutter into a police car, ready for his final exit from Wake Hall.

PC Jon Lee was determined to *find* something this time. Batten had given him the lead role in searching Rutter's office, and he was going to show the Northern Fork that he wasn't totally useless. And find something he did, spotting how that weird painting of a lion and a horse stuck out from the wall at a funny angle. When he lifted it down: da-dah!

Baz Ballard said he didn't know the combination to the safe - not that Lee was surprised. Baz Ballard didn't seem to know that the muscles on his ugly mug were designed to *move*.

'Sit down there,' he ordered, pointing at Olly's throne of a chair, 'and keep your arse on the seat, or else!' In view of Baz Ballard's gym-honed physique, Lee chose not to specify what 'else' was on offer.

With a touch of puffed-up pride, he sent word that they'd need Olly Rutter to cough up the combination to a hidden wall-safe. He made sure to say 'hidden', to emphasise he'd *found* something. Mind you, if he had his way, fetch a crowbar and let's get on with it. He was thinking along those lines when the commotion began.

Stepping out of the open door, it was like watching a movie at home, cuddled up on the sofa with Luce. Villain lashes out - OK, at a *horse* - tough cop cuffs him, reads him his rights, clicks his fingers and more cops drag Mr Nasty into the back seat of a police car, pushing him down more firmly than required, in case he bumps his poor ickle head on the roof.

He found himself wandering over, wishing it wasn't Hick and Magnus doing the pushing, wishing it was him instead - or why not him making the arrest, something to surprise Luce with when he got home. *Justice Jon, superhero!*

Reverting to plain PC Lee, he tapped an amazed-looking Batten on the shoulder.

'Sorry, sir, but before Mr Rutter's driven off....'

Batten seemed to wake up, there and then. Olly Rutter, in *cuffs*, in a police car? How long could they detain him, under the terms of the Animal Welfare Act? It wasn't a law he'd had much use for in urban Leeds. Not long, he guessed. Would Olly Rutter ever coincide with a Serious Arrestable Offence?

'Er, Jonathon, yes, the combination. Just give us a moment to see if our Mr Rutter would like to cooperate.'

A crowbar'd be quicker, Lee thought but he did as he was told.

By contrast, Baz Ballard had disobeyed orders, and not kept his arse on the seat. He'd spent weeks trying to think like Lawrence Vann, but was no nearer to a scheme that would rid him of Olly - not without murdering himself. And how much longer could he hold on to his almost true mantra: I just drive. I just do what I'm told?

Not today. Today he did what he should have done long ago: he stopped trying to think like Lawrence Vann, and thought like Baz Ballard instead. Leaping, not planning.

Olly couldn't care less about the office or the safe anymore. Baz had clocked its new combination three times over when the Mammoth was gutting it. As soon as the wet-behind-the-ears little cop wandered out, and keeping an ex-con's eye on events beyond the office door, Baz stepped instinctively to the wall-safe and tapped in the numbers. It swung open with ease and he wiped any fingerprints from the small object that had been hidden in the lining of his chauffeur suit ever since Lady Wake had booted him out of his rooms. He swiftly dropped it into the emptiness of the safe, clicked the door shut, and gave it a final wipe.

Baz was almost smiling when he sat back down in his chair. Olly's initial response to the police was to tell them to shove the combination up their collective backsides, but when they offered to add various forms of obstruction to the charge of malicious maltreatment of a horse he took Del's advice. Deal with the issues on the ground. Plead guilty, pay the fine, walk free.

Even so, Baz was nodding off by the time he heard numbers being tapped into the wall-safe, and the now familiar click as it swung open. The young policeman's face was a picture. He'd actually *found* something, him and his scruffy sidekick - something the weird young cop said was small enough to hide in a sweaty sock. Baz knew exactly where it *had* been, because while packing away his much-loved model planes, he had covertly removed it from inside the fuselage of *Gypsy Moth,* its hiding place since the day Lawrence Vann was poisoned.

Before that, Lawrence had carefully concealed it inside the battery compartment of a broken mini-torch on a key ring, soldered shut, and replaced on Rhona Fiske's vast rack of spare keys. Baz wasn't sure what 'hiding in plain sight' meant, but that's what Lawrence called it. It wasn't the original memory stick stolen from Olly - that was in the furnace now.

'But don't worry, Baz. The new one contains no trace of *our* accounts. Perhaps you'd like to see what remains?'

And Lawrence had plugged in the stick, flashed private account numbers and multiple spreadsheets onto the screen. Once he'd got used to the columns and numbers, Baz saw how damning they were, and how riveting Her Majesty's Revenue and Customs would find them, particularly as not a single column was headed 'Tax Paid'. And there was the money laundering too. What would Olly get? Years - halleluiah - even with a lawyer twice as good as Del. So, Olly, memory stick it up your arse....

'*A sweaty sock?* What're you babbling about?' the scruffy cop jeered at his young oppo. 'Why should Lawrence Vann hide a memory stick in a sweaty sock? Are you daft? He could hide it *anywhere*, it's small enough!'

When he learns how big it really is, Baz thought, he'll turn cross-eyed with surprise. They all will.

It was a small cell for a mammoth, and barely big enough to contain his incandescent rage at being there. Olly's vanity, which ordinarily would have wormed through every pore in the concrete walls, had been forcibly shrunk. Not long ago he was living in a stately home, till Herself downgraded him to a sofa-bed in an office. Now he'd been downgraded *again*, to this shit-hole. He slapped the metal door, hard.

'Oi! Batten! Deaf-lugs! You can't keep me here! It was a bloody *horse*, a *nag*, that's all! You've got NOTHING!'

Nothing that would pin a *murder* on Olly, true enough. He slapped the door again, harder, but nobody came. They were far too busy having his secret data analysed, and deciding what else to charge him with.

# Forty seven

Both men felt the same thing, at the same time, but knew one another too well now for words to be needed. Batten's furniture was harmless enough; it had behaved impeccably throughout its slow journey from Leeds to the recently-purchased hamstone cottage on the edge of Ashtree. But when Batten and Ball climbed into the back of the hired van to unload it, unfortunate memories returned - of the last van they had entered together. They stood for a moment, hands on hips, in silent respect for four small trafficked children.

Respects paid, they set to work, effort and sweat somehow purifying them, and their sapped energy replaced by the goodies from the cool-box that Ball had placed reverentially on Batten's kitchen worktop. Vintage cider demanded reverence, and Chris Ball was its priest.

Batten had free-cycled the tired furniture that came with the house. They were the sticks of a dead man, and he didn't need such reminders.

'S'an impressive home, zor. No offence, but I hadn't got you down as, you know, domesticated.'

'No problem, Ballie. Your missus says the same about you.'

'And with damning evidence, zor, I'll admit. But this place is....*solid*, zor. A fine house.' He propped himself against the large oak chest he had struggled to ease through the hamstone porch. 'And some fine solid gear to dress it with.'

Ball was surprised to hear the furniture was mostly from auctions, even junk shops. He hadn't got Batten down as a handyman either, but he was wrong. The proof lay in the hand-restored pieces the two of them had carefully carried in, looking good now, looking right, against warm stone.

'Seems you're of a mind to stay, zor?'

Ball was fishing. He'd grown to like Batten's funny ways, even his occasional rages.

'He rages at the right things,' he'd told Di.

'*Will* he stay?' she'd asked. 'Now Jellicoe's turned up?' ACC Gribble was still wondering what to do with an oversized drunk who also happened to be a Chief Inspector.

Batten smiled. The only other place he'd be tempted to go was Greece, and that was a pipe-dream. He riffled his fingers along the books standing upright and proud on the shelves he'd built.

'Of a mind to stay? Looks like I am, Ballie.'

Of a heart, too.


Ashtree Lake was still as beautiful as he remembered, even if the fish were off their food. In between casting hopeful lines into the dark blue waters, Batten delved through case reports and summaries of interviews and background on everyone who might conceivably have the slightest connection to the murder of Lawrence Vann. The statement reader had already delved, but the stuff was bible-thick. Serves you right, Zig, for telling the team to dig till they reached Australia. Would Olly Rutter go down for Lawrence Vann's murder? Batten had his doubts, but.... Birdsong and the occasional flash of the birds themselves helped sugar the pill.

It was a relief though, to check in with Ball at Parminster, because he could talk instead of read, even if only for a minute. He sat in his car to use the phone, hating it when anglers yelled inanely into their mobiles, sending ear-destroying bollocks across the quiet waters, killing the sense of peace, killing the reason they were *here*, rather than at the office or at home, listening to yack from the telly.

'Hickie, is Sergeant Ball there?'

'Gone out, sir, 'bout half an hour ago.'

'OK, where's he gone?'

'Er, hang on, sir.'

The uncoordinated fleshy prongs which Hick used for hands failed miserably in their attempt to mute the phone or cover the receiver, so Batten heard every word of Hick's office conversation.

'Choirboy? Where's Crystal gone?'

'Message from PC Lee: does not respond to 'Choirboy'. Pratt.'

'OK, OK. Where's Crystal gone? Pratt yourself.'

'Crystal? How should I know?'

'I thought you were telegraphic?'

'Tele*pathic, pratt*. Just look on his desk. He always writes it down.'

'Your legs've come off, have they? I've got the Fork on the phone, Christ's sake. You've only got to reach an arm across.'

Batten heard grunting, scraping and paper-shuffling sounds.

'Um....says he's gone to Wake Hall.'

'Sir? Wake Hall, sir. Gone over to Wake Hall.'

'Yes, Hickie. And any particular reason?'

Hick's inept fingers again failed to mute the phone.

'What's he gone for?' he hissed at the invisible PC Lee.

'Keep your hair on, Hickie....Doesn't say. Getting forgetful, the geriatric ginger nut.'

'Sir? It doesn't say -'

'Yes, Hick. I heard. Thank PC Lee for his sensitive comments, will you?'

Batten could hear the reddening of cheeks in the CID office. Part of their learning process, he said to himself, punching the speed dial for Sergeant Ball. Nothing. Bloody phone reception. Ugly masts everywhere and barely a signal in the Wake Hall wastelands. He left a message, went back to not catching fish.


Batten's lunch was a local pasty and a beaker of metallic coffee from an old flask defying its 'stainless steel' description. He turned to a dull background report on Wake Hall's weird mix of misfits, optimistically referred to as 'staff.'

Sitting back in the padded carp chair he bit into a wrong pasty. He'd asked for steak, but the girl in the shop had given him chicken and mushroom instead. He began to pull out pieces of mushroom, the taste and texture of which he could never stomach. There were many pieces of mushroom, so he had a thin slow lunch of broken pastry and miniscule bits of meat. Essence of mushroom spread across his taste-buds anyway, despite a mouthwash of stained-steel coffee.

A mushroom-sticky finger turned to another section of the report. Oh great, 'Wake Hall Staff: External Links'. He ploughed on through interview summaries. Hay suppliers. Marquee suppliers. Feed suppliers. Butchers, bakers, but no candlestick-makers. Tractor mechanics. Staff Trainers. Dry-cleaners. A silversmith. Taxi firms. It was worse than eating mushrooms. If there's a fish supplier I'll give them a ring, ask them to top up this bloody lake with catchable carp.

What made him flick back to Staff Trainers? A name he actually recognised? Maddie Tyrrell? No, her little brochure was paper-clipped to the file and a white-haired head beamed out at him. He didn't recognise her name at all. But she bore a distinct likeness to Aunt Daze.

He skimmed through the information....she ran classes for Vito Valdano, it said, mostly at Wake Hall. The report mentioned the two most recent: *Food From The Forest,* and *The Hedgerows Are Your Larder.* Why not *Cooking and Eating your Sandals,* Zig? George Halfpenny had done the interview. Three Wake Hall staff had attended her courses: Debbie Farley and Jake Tuttle, the gardener - no surprise. But, more strangely, Rhona Fiske. Worth checking, he thought, lying to himself that his reasons were professional. He found Maddie Tyrrell's number, traipsed over to his car to make the call, then quickly wished he hadn't.

'Oh I *do* so believe in fate, Inspector, don't you? Or is it in fact serendipity? Or an invisible interpersonal connection perhaps?'

'Er, Mrs Tyrell - '

'I mean, that you should call, right at this very moment, when I was thinking of doing the *exact* same thing. Call Parminster at any time, that's what the nice-smelling young policeman said, and just as I was about to, you called *me*! Seren*dip*itous! And here you are, talking.'

No, *you're* talking, you batty old mushroom. I can't get a word in edgeways!

'Mrs Tyr - '

'It's my mailing list you see. *That*'s what I wanted to tell you about!'

Exciting.

'I'm not good with computers, Inspector. I'll admit it. Admit, admit. But we have a....a *thing* on ours, and do you know, it prints sticky address labels? At the touch of a key, straight from the database thing. So we don't have to painstakingly write them out by hand. Have you ever come across such a wonder?'

Oh yes. I've even got a device that grates cheese.

'Well, print print print it did, and I put the stickers on the envelopes and popped in the leaflets, ready for posting. Our new programme of events is *most* interesting, and I shall certainly send you a copy in the fullness of time.'

'Mrs Ty - '

'And then I spotted it! A *glitch*! I've been learning the jargon, you see, as I do so believe one must move with the times - '

'Mrs - '

' - bad though the times may be.'

' - Mrs Tyrell, I just wanted to ask if - '

'*Well*, there were three envelopes, Inspector, that was the puzzle, the *glitch*. And all three addressed to the same person, all containing an identical leaflet. Now, we can't condone such *waste*, can we? We champion re-cycling here, you know. Our envelopes and stationery, it's all made from paper which has been - well, perhaps I won't dwell on where it's been, Inspector - '

'- Mrs T- '

' - Suffice to say that the glitch has now been eradicated. *Zapped*, is the correct term, I am informed. You see, the....*thing* was printing labels based on course registers, *not* on a simple, sole, personal registration. You *do* see?'

Batten didn't see at all.

'Oh well, the *thing* was sending three identical leaflets in three identical envelopes to the same person simply because they'd attended three courses, yes? Wasteful, wasteful. And downright silly. But then I spotted the glitch! It was the courses! Oh, and I don't even mean *that*! It was three separate *attendances*, at three different times, but all on the *same* course. How strange!'

And so are you. Never watched the same DVD three times?

'Mrs Tyrell, I - '

'*Instantly* I said to Piers - that's my Mr Tyrell by the way - '*this could be highly significant!*' Oh, he wasn't interested, he has a model train, but I knew *you* would be. I mean, why would someone pay three times to attend an identical course?'

'Sorry, what course? What are you t - '

'Why, the *same* course - 'Plants Edible, Plants *Not*!' I thought immediately of your investigation, and that poor man, Lawrence Something. Well, *poisoned*, wasn't he? Aconite, the newspaper said? Definitely a Plant *Not*!'

A slimy-sharp, earthy, mushroom taste filled Batten's throat. He opened the car door, covered the phone and spat the taste onto the grass, a gob of phlegm the size and shape of George Halfpenny. You didn't do your *job*, George! 'Plants Edible, Plants *Not*' - and no mention in your report. Too slack to do the hard yards, weren't you? Didn't ask the batty woman some structured questions! Didn't follow up, didn't get beneath the surface, didn't *delve*. More than a rotten apple, George. A rotten bloody detective too!

'Mrs Tyrell, please, this person, who attended that course three times - do you have a name?'

And Mrs Tyrell told him.

Batten gave up trying to phone Sergeant Ball. No signal - No signal - No signal. Was it a mantra for the investigation? He rang Parminster instead.

'Hickie! You and Lee grab a car now, and get to Wake Hall, fast! And bring your cuffs.'

'Now, sir?'

"Now' and 'fast' - clear enough for you? I'll meet you there. If you arrive first, find Sergeant Ball and if he needs help, help him. Got it?'

'Right, sir. Oh, I remembered, he took the rest of the paraffin-ailey-o we removed from the Hall, to give back to the owners.'

'Paraffin-ailey-o? What the hell are you talking about?'

'You know, sir, all the bits and bobs, in case they were evidence. I think it was keys mostly. Anyway, he's returning 'em, to that Housekeeper woman.'

Crystal Ball almost sent Lee to Wake Hall, but at the last minute his inner voice told him to man up, confront his demons. Wake Hall is just limestone and glass. It stands on clay soil, and trees grow there - so what's to fear? He picked up the carton of miscellaneous belongings, and was reminded of the shoe-box full of car keys, a rather tipsy Batten's amongst them, at the village Christmas panto. Chuckling to himself, he started his car.

Was it fear for Sergeant Ball's safety or embarrassed boiling anger at his own inability to *see*, that caused Batten to drive like a demon, spinning his wheels at intersections and swerving and sliding down muddy lanes that were far too narrow for high-speed? Skidding to a halt in the Wake Hall car park, still in his old anorak and lumpy fishing boots, he sprinted across to the farmhouse kitchen, and flung open the door with neither knock nor ceremony. If Ball *had* dropped in, there was no trace of him now. The kitchen was occupied solely by Rhona Fiske, her paperwork on the big table, a cafetiere of fresh-smelling coffee at her elbow. Bizarrely, he remembered it tasting better than her tea.

When she looked up, shocked by his rudeness, he saw in her eyes what she perhaps saw in his: a brief flicker, a memory of sex, before the sharpness of the situation intervened.

'*Sergeant Ball!*' he yelled, much more loudly than intended.

'Good afternoon, Ins*pec*tor. Feel free to burst in.'

'*Sergeant B-*'

'Been and gone, having *politely* returned my spare sets of keys. Would you like to see the evidence, or is my word good enough for you?'

He knew there and then, she no more cared for him than….he did for her. If he had cared, he would have graced her with more words.

'*WHERE?*'

She flicked a slender, ringless finger, crisply. The gesture said 'get out', but also pointed to the door behind him, and at the distant line of staff cottages. Instead of turning round he moved swiftly towards her, frightening her, coffee spilling over newly-completed paperwork - but he swept past the table where she sat, heading not for the front door, but the back. He knew a short-cut. Neil Tapworthy, the giant farrier, had shown him, some time ago. Sprinting past Wake Hall Horse, he ducked across the lawn to a gap in the yew hedge, and raced down the track squashed into the soil by the giant farrier's feet.

Having returned what needed returning, Ball strolled over to the staff cottages and rang the bell - he'd do his duty, assure her that life could now return to normal. He'd had nothing to eat since an early breakfast, and the fresh curry smells embraced him when she opened the door. His reassurance was timely because it was a pale, almost trance-like figure who stepped back to allow him into the small kitchen-diner. The curtains were closed and candles flickered from glass-sided globes on the dresser and dining table. He'd forgotten, Debbie Farley was a Vito Valdano follower. But given all she's been through….

Without asking, Debbie Farley spooned spiced rice and a rich vegetable curry into an already-warmed Italian ceramic bowl. She placed the curry on the table, set for two. He noticed she had all but finished her own, so he made his excuses - half-heartedly, in the face of hypnotic scents of roasted spice wafting towards his nose. She sat back down and waved an inviting arm at the chair opposite. Oh, go on, Chris, keep her company. You can make reassuring noises, between mouthfuls.

*Abandoned me, didn't you? But I'm glad you've returned. Today, of all days.*

'I wish my wife could make curry like this. Don't suppose you give lessons?'

*I've prepared it just for you, Lawrence. It's not curry powder from a jar. I make my own, roast the spices myself. A touch of brown sugar.*

'Is it hard to make? Something special in the sauce?'

*Special, yes. For the two of us.*

'Wine? Is it wine you put in?'

*You like it with a tipple of brandy, don't you? That's what you can taste.*

She swallowed the last morsel, dropped her fork a little clumsily into the empty bowl and looked across the table, across the flickering candles, at her final companion. Shorter than she remembered - ah, but Lawrence is sitting down now, not walking, walking ahead, striding, always striding ahead, faster, faster than her.

*This is how it should have been, Lawrence. Not you alone, on that little hill. But the two of us. Together.*

The steam from Sergeant Ball's warm dish quivered in the candlelight, clouding his view of Debbie Farley. Why was she swaying slowly, from side to side, like withies waving in the wind on the Somerset Levels? *Was it the wind he could hear*, or the raspy tightening of his breath? Sly nausea crept from his stomach, up into his throat. His mouth and tongue were tingling - strong curry, this. Then spittle bubbled over his lips and chin and he wondered if what *seemed* to be was really so.

Debbie Farley's face dissolved into greyness, her hands clawing at the tablecloth, wrenching it towards her as she dipped and swayed in a primal attempt to remain straight and still. The attempt came to nothing; she quivered and collapsed, her clamped hands dragging the shroud-white cloth to the floor, snuffing out the hopeless candles and shattering two blue bowls, one of them empty, the other two-thirds-full of lethal home-made curry, rice, and aconite.

# Forty eight

A reluctant Nina Magnus was struggling with Missing Persons, phone glued yet again to her ear, yet again spelling out the impossible surname she could now almost pronounce. She was regretting her promise to Oksana Thing - 'don't worry, we'll find him, your brother.' Superwoman, are you, Nina?

Without Sergeant Ball, Parminster's CID Centre felt empty - more so since the hefty frame of Jess Foreman had returned to the 'fresh air and no writing' of his rural beat.

PC Lee was two desks down from Magnus, struggling to understand reasons, motives - struggling to understand Debbie Farley. The absence of a suicide note hadn't helped.

'Did she *want* to kill Sergeant Ball, sir? I mean, he's not exactly *Hitler.*'

Batten wondered if Lee was too sensitive for the CID. Not that the force couldn't use more sensitivity. Perhaps you should make a better fist of developing him, Zig?

'Maybe just bad luck, Jon. Wrong place, wrong time. She couldn't have known he'd turn up, could she?'

He'd seen such things before, on the Yorkshire force. Not easy to cease upon the midnight with no pain, in complete solitude.

'She'd lit candles, made a shrine for a suicide, set an extra place for Lawrence Vann. In the strangeness of her mind he was there in the room. And that would be that - if Ballie hadn't knocked on the door. Given a choice, people don't want to die alone.'

Or on a hill with just one lonely tree, brute agony hammered into every muscle on your face.

'The Sarge was a windfall, sir, is that what you're saying?'

'I hadn't thought of it like that. Yes, I suppose he was.'

An apple blown from the tree, dropping into Debbie Farley's hand. Batten was glad when a hiss of steam from Nina Magnus banished the thought.

'Well he's *not* called 'Dave *Smith*', is he? So just *live* with it!' she spat into the phone. 'How should *I* know why he's called what he's called? I'm not his *mother!*'

Batten drew PC Lee away from the noise.

'All the same, Jon, she *might* have deliberately dragged his bowl of poison onto the floor? In a moment of clarity? When she realised it wasn't Lawrence Vann sitting there?'

Lee was unconvinced.

'Or it might have been pure chance, sir.'

'Well, let's be thankful either way, eh, Jon?'

The slowly recovering Ball understood as little as Lee, but in the Sergeant's case the problem was memory loss. The doctors said it would return, by and by - for good or ill.

Magnus was on her feet now, throttling the phone.

'*NO! Not C! VEE!* Begins with *V, V* for Victor…. Yes, *ends* in S-I-C. *NO!* I said *C! - C* for *Charlie!*…The bit in between? A problem? *Is* it? *REALLY?*'

Two desks down, Lee was still shaking his head at an unjust world. Well, Zig, he'll either toughen up, or drift away. In truth, right at this moment, he couldn't decide which would be best.

Baz knew how long Olly would go down for, because the tall one, the black one, the scruffy one and the young one had all told him, at different times and in different voices, hoping it would frighten him into coughing up. He wasn't even sure what he was supposed to cough up *to*. At the start, as far as Batten was concerned, murder would have been acceptable, and conspiracy to murder almost as. Better still, put Olly in the frame for one or the other, and we'll go easy on *you*….

Where Olly, murder, conspiracy and trafficking were concerned, Baz had only what the police had - bits and pieces of evidence, but no *chain*, no clincher. To Baz's good fortune, circumstantial evidence was all the police had on *him*. When the crazy chef came out of the woodwork and the cops found the aconite she had painstakingly powdered in a spice-grinder, they had to let him go.

Even the cleaners at Parminster CID were bored senseless with his cracked record: I do what I'm told; I'm just a driver. Eddie 'Loft' Hick was so fed up of hearing it that when he let Baz out, for the final time, the corner of his mouth hissed, 'bugger off and effin' well drive, then!'

And drive he did, to Wake Hall in a hired van, big enough to hold his few personal belongings and his many model planes. While loading them he saw Lady Wake herself, with a short, well-dressed country-type trotting behind her. The pair wandered in and out of Wake Hall Horse, she flicking her suave, commanding fingers at various stables and tack-rooms and stores, he recording her every whim on a suede-leather clipboard. Baz noticed a large pale rectangle on the gates where the 'Wake Hall Horse' sign used to be. Good. He'd had his fill of equine. He slammed the van doors closed.

Given she'd said nary a word to him all the time he'd been there, he was surprised when she waved a commanding finger, not at clipboard man, but at him. Still attuned to taking orders, he lumped towards her.

'Ellory, do excuse me for one moment, mm?'

Baz waited. Lady Wake frowned, and gave the briefest shuffle of her pristine leather riding boots. Three hundred pounds a pair, according to Olly. Am *I* supposed to speak first, or what?

'I see you are finally leaving us?'

She'd either forgotten his name or didn't care to use it. He nodded, and she frowned again. Perhaps small talk with a minion was beyond her, because she pitched right in.

'It *was* definitely Debbie, who killed him? Not Olly?'

Sweet Jesus, I've had all this from the *police.*

'Killed Lawrence?'

He wasn't giving her any of that 'ma'am' stuff, not now.

'Of course.'

Looks like it. Though Olly *would* have, sooner or later. What do you want me to say? That it was *me* who got Lawrence killed? Baz just shrugged, and she flicked a disdainful chin at Olly's old office.

'The memory stick. In the safe. Was that you?'

'Olly thinks it was *you.*'

'And the odious Inspector thinks the same. But I know it wasn't. Scrupulously careful with his data, was Mr Rutter. I can't imagine who else it could have been.'

They'd grilled Baz too, wasting their time.

'Mebbe it was Lawrence.'

She thought about this for a moment, then gave the faintest sigh.

'Well. How fitting, were that the case.'

A rueful smile. He'd never liked her, so had never seen how beautiful she was. Beauty, land, power and money. Well, *he* had money now, whatever the source. And it's all tainted, isn't it?

'Where will you go?'

As if I'd tell *you*. Cardiff, where his cash was.

'Drive, someplace. It's what I know.'

She dipped her chin downwards this time. Was that Aristocracy for 'good luck'? Then without a second glance she was flicking her fingers at Ellory, and conjuring the new, expanded phoenix soon to be Wake Hall Equestrian.

Baz waited till they disappeared beyond the giant gates before nipping down to the furnace. With relief and a little trepidation, he dropped his chauffeur suit into the flames and watched it burn. His hat followed, but not before - from habit - he gave the leather peak one final buff with his sleeve.

Hospitals. Why so easy to dislike? Perhaps because he spent so much of his life in one kind of municipal building or another? Cop shops, courtrooms, prisons. Bloody hell, mortuaries too. Vinyl corridors and grey offices and heavy doors leading to cavernous stairwells, like the one that surrounded him now. He never used the lift in a hospital. Might as well inject yourself with bacteria and stand in a Petri dish.

If you hate hospitals, Zig, why waste your time in one? She can't *tell* you anything. Yeh, yeh - at least it's not Wake Hall.

The place was packed, and he struggled to make his way down the pale-green and disturbingly noisy corridor through a human obstacle-course of the bored, the concerned, the sick, the healers, past a coffee shop - closed - a flower shop, a newspaper stand and a long line of vending machines, queues of coin-jingling humanity at every one. No walk-in funeral parlour though. Yet.

Debbie Farley's room needed no police presence. Her adversaries - mistaken and malign - had neither reason nor power to harm her now. Stephanie Broke-Mondelle was the one remaining free agent with a motive, and her brief flirtation with law-breaking had been shock enough. She wouldn't be coming back for more. As for Debbie, her best chance of escape was in a coffin. The doctors phrased it differently, but Batten could read between the lines. Waving to the duty nurse, he went in, carrying a faint feeling of nausea instead of flowers.

*I did it for you, Lawrence. Make you stumble, 'stead of dancing through your orchard, plucking any apple that takes your fancy from any tree that takes your eye.*

Closing the door, he realised this was Debbie's third hospitalisation in a few short months. Third time lucky, Zig? For whom? He took in the familiar view: a clean white box with Debbie's bed, redundant TV, the little bathroom through a half-open door, the suck of the ventilator, breathing on her behalf. Put bars across the windows and it could be a clean white prison cell. A story he'd read popped into his thoughts. Hemingway, was it? A clean, well-lighted place? Is that what awaits you, Debbie, and nada-nada-nothing else?

*Till you dump the core in a ditch.*

Batten looked down at her eyes, willing them to open, to explain. Intermittent twitches, but nothing more. If Ged was here, he'd say 'park it, Zig. You'll never find out. Move on.' But Batten needed to know. Silent questions filled the white room. Why, Debbie? And poison? *Why?*

*Then a new apple comes along.*

He was struggling with the logic. Debbie knew Lawrence's style: hop-step-and-hump, in his search for Ms Right. And Debbie herself had padlocked the duvet. Yet they'd remained friends, went walking together.

*Neither of them saw me, but I saw them. Followed his car. Prince Lawrence Charming, sneaking into that beanpole's house. Her clothes, I bet they cost more than my cottage. Taller than me. Recognised her, from when I did the buffet, at that conference, at Wake Hall. She ate my food.*

He leaned closer. What if she *does* wake up, and learns of Lawrence's thwarted move to Cyprus? Small mercies, Zig. If she'd discovered what

Lawrence *and* Stephanie were planning, there might be an extra body in the morgue. He shuddered. Hospitals. Mortuaries. Must get out more.

*I was expecting a younger version. Of me. Posher, yes, but younger. I could've coped if she'd been younger. I suppose.*

Batten imagined Debbie dreaming, of fantasies fulfilled - a chic Mediterranean villa, Lawrence by her side. Randy nights, perhaps. But followed by what? Empty days? Poor Debbie. A good body - a good soul too, for a poisoner - but a good *mind*? Shake a plucked apple as much as you like, all you'll hear is the same rattle of the same pips, week after week. Lawrence would have drowned her, in the outdoor pool, after a month or two.

*But **older** than me? What were you thinking? I'm barely forty. She's sixty if she's a day. Sixty! Nothing's heading south on **me**....*

He glanced at his watch. Debbie had the advantage of dream-time, but he didn't. Miles to go before *you* sleep, Zig. And she showed no sign of waking, of signing a statement. He pushed back his chair. Then sat down again. Would it hurt to keep her company for a minute more? Solitude was fine for some - fine for him, if he was honest. But it wasn't solitude in here, it was loneliness.

*Leaving me, **me**, for someone ancient! I needed to make you....re-consider. That's why.*

Batten understood Lawrence Vann, post-mortem. He was beginning to understand Debbie Farley too. Even *with* Lawrence, she would have been lonely.

*I wanted to be with you, Lawrence. But you left me behind. We were meant to enjoy the sky, trees, birds. Sit down, drink our soup. I put some brandy in, the way you like it. Sit down and have our soup, together. Our special soup.*

Did Lawrence ever share his deepest thoughts with you, Debbie? Batten silently asked. You certainly lacked the vision to see them for yourself. When Lawrence breezed up Burrow Hill to enjoy the view, you saw no value. What did you say to Lonny Dalway, the milkman - I've seen that view so many times I could paint it, 'cept I can't paint? When all's said and done, you only bring your own eyes to the peepshow.

*Not her, Lawrence. Too thin, too old for you.*

Batten stared at the natural curves of Debbie's fine body, her breasts, flat stomach, shapely hips - plain to see beneath the hospital sheet. He felt a policeman's shame, nothing more. Where curves were concerned, Stephanie came second. But if Debbie had known it was a firmer, more rounded *brain* that Lawrence desired, what vengeance might she have wreaked on Stephanie Broke-Mondelle?

*Just the two of us. Get you away from that old bitch!*

The scrape of his chair became a shudder. Batten stood by the bed, staring down at the woman who had poisoned Lawrence Vann. Whether to kill, or to scare, they would likely never know.

*I found you, on the hill, slumped against that sycamore tree. Saw your face, pain all over it. Covered it with your hat. For you.*

She showed no sign of waking, so he left. Or was it because she might?

# Forty nine

He was surprised to find the Parminster CID office empty, apart from the cleaner, when he returned from a pre-breakfast check on his Sergeant, convalescing at home under the tender care of Di Ball. Where is everybody? The whole shift should be here. The only sound was the crinkle of plastic bags in his cubby-hole-office. He needed to attack the paperwork, but a large male cleaner was blocking his way. Was he new, this one? As Batten watched, the cleaner dragged items from the desk drawers and hurriedly stuffed them into a bin-liner.

'*Hey*! What the bloody hell are you *doing*?'

'What's it look like I'm doing?'

Thieves, Zig. Shameless.

'And just who the bloody hell *are* you?'

'I'm *ex*-Chief Inspector Jellicoe. Who the bloody hell are *you*?'

The empty office explained itself. His cowardly team had crawled away from the embarrassment of watching their old, bloated boss clear his desk for the final ignominious time. Or maybe he'd *told* them to bugger off. Batten introduced himself, loitered, unsure why.

'Am I keeping you from something? Inspector?'

He wanted to say 'yes, my office', but it still said Detective Chief Inspector K. Jellicoe on the door. At least his initial wasn't 'F'.

'Well, I....'

Two steel-pin eyes in Fat Jellicoe's face punched home their point: Batten's company - anybody's company - was superfluous to Jellicoe now.

Despite the paperwork on 'his' desk, Batten sloped away to the posh greasy spoon that served the coffee so highly prized by Hick. Through the glass door, he spotted Magnus, Lee and 'Loft', pretending to be in conference while chewing on bacon rolls. He felt a faint loyalty to the cashiered Jellicoe, felt a sadness for him, felt he somehow *knew* him, and almost returned to the office to impose an unwanted goodbye.

But, in truth, what he knew was a cop gone wrong - and it had been a bad year for such things.

He joined his depleted team, shrugged away their excuses, ordered a fresh round of bacon rolls and bang-on skinny lattes.

In response to Stephanie Broke-Mondelle's unusually quiet request, big Harry Teign removed Burrow Hill from the Scramblers' walking schedule. He chose not to tell her that Eth had already requested the same - demanded it, in fact - though for more embarrassing reasons. For the time being, Harry was leading the walks. Quiet, reflective walks. Walks unaccompanied by that constant plummy squeak the Scramblers had grown used to. And in a funny way, missed.

Gasping up an incline near West Coker, Harry remembered when he'd have heard the breathy wheeze of twenty Scramblers at this point. Today, only six tackled the gradient - five, and Stephanie.

'She moight jus' as well be back with them monks, shuffling down thar cloisters, soilent.'

Mick Baines still whinged in Stephanie's presence, but he'd stopped bothering to swear, because she'd stopped noticing.

'Mebbe not monks, then. Mebbe them zaambies.'

He had a point. Stephanie was tramping along, half in a dead daze, half on a pilgrimage - or a walking cure at least. Her minor crimes against the law were absolved by paying the hefty fine she could easily afford. As for silently disposing of Lawrence's little silver key - she saw this as a non-criminal way of preserving the name of a man she would never stop loving.

It was the crimes of others she struggled with. She refused to carry bitterness within her: bitterness at the car-wreck that used to be her life; bitterness at Debbie Farley, who had poisoned her future. Stephanie Broke-Mondelle would not let Debbie poison *her* as well. And so she walked, alone, daily, in any weather, slowly shedding the bitterness inside her, grain after grain, treading it right-foot-after-left into the hard ground. And whenever the Scramblers walked, she walked with them too - though they were no longer *her* Scramblers.

'Six,' Harry complained to Eth Buller. 'Hardly call it a walking *group*, would you?'

Numbers had dwindled since the day the Scramblers found a dead body by a living tree at the top of Burrow Hill. And without Stephanie, the process of recruitment - like many of the Scramblers - had fallen by the wayside.

'They'll come back,' said Eth. 'Most of 'em.'

'Huh.'

'She's sortin' herself, she'll get 'em back.'

'Sortin' herself? She can barely *speak*.'

'It's only grief, Harry.'

'*Only?*'

'People come *through* grief, Harry.'

'Huh.'

She threaded her gentle fingers into his big fist.

'*We* did.'


When was the last time he'd put his socks up on the evening sofa and listened to jazz? Greece was a world ago, and afterwards the push and shove of Olly's arrest was topped by almost losing Chris Ball to a suicidal poisoner. Bix Beiderbecke didn't care, as he tore into *Somebody Stole My Girl*. He could play a bit, could Bix. Sipping whisky, Batten was reminded that Bix didn't play for long, dead from drink and drugs at twenty eight. Dimi's face flashed into his head.

Beiderbecke's cornet soared above the clarinets, guitars, rock-solid drums and double-bass. Every track on the CD so far had been in a steady 4/4 time, and it was precisely what Batten needed, a regular underlying beat to settle him down, while the rest of life yelped and blared and syncopated around him.

'You listening to jazz again, you throwback?'

He'd barely heard the phone, his hand grabbing it automatically, assuming it was bad news from Parminster, or ACC Gribble after his skin.

'Ged? What a relief, I thought you were the police.'

'Hah-hah. Well, you're not the only one off-duty, as it happens. I'm escaping from the telly. Mandy's next door, watching a DVD with Brad Pitt.'

'Ah, he's dropped round again?'

'Funny.'

'Sorry, Ged, whacked.'

'Well, have a big yawn and listen to uncle. Serious.'

Ged rarely came to the point quickly, so Batten sat up. He was glad to hear a friend's voice anyway, Chris Ball's quirky protractions being much missed during his convalescence.

'D'you remember Arnie Goole? That chunky Sergeant from Tadcaster?'

' Arnie the Fish?'

'That's him.'

Because Arnie drank like one, and was a damn good competition angler.

'Well he's prison service now, down your way.'

'What, France?'

For Ged, 'down your way' meant south of Barnsley.

'Funny again. He works at Bristol Prison now. Seems they have prisons down there, dunno why, since you only get crime up north, so the tabloids tell me.'

'And?'

'*And*, there's a new guest at Arnie's hotel. Fetches tea and slippers for him every morning, does Arnie.'

'This guest have a name?'

'A very nasty name. Olly Rutter. For which, by the way, congratulations again. Never thought I'd see it.'

Ged had sent champagne. Merlot Marie too. Both bottles were in the fridge, waiting for someone to share them with. And Batten knew where Olly was. Bristol Prison was Category B, for inmates open-minded about escape.

'Upshot is, Zig, Arnie phones me this morning and gives me the goss.'

'Don't tell me, Olly's found religion?'

'Found *summat*. Found a dangerous dislike for Zig Batten.'

'I wasn't holding my breath for a Christmas card.'

'You might get one, so watch your back. That's the goss. Always was slap-happy, was Olly, and Arnie says he's got the itch right now. Your name comes up a *lot,* when they all sit down to pimms and a game o' bridge.'

Olly had already threatened vengeance, quietly, vaguely, once the tape machine stopped rolling. And Olly was Olly, so….

'You're a pal, Ged. I'll take extra-care.'

'You'd better, Zig. It's your round next.'

He had no idea if it was or not. But Ged's beer-memory was a legend. If he said it was, it was.

After a night of jazz and Speyside, Batten woke to a near-perfect sunrise over Ham Hill, and drank in coffee, sunlight and birdsong while sitting on the new bench in his partly-planted garden. He'd bought a bird book that came with a CD, to identify which bird was which. When he got round to opening it.

Intermittently, he'd been easing his Ford Focus past the thatcher's van whenever he drove up his lane towards the main road. Today it was Yeovil first, and Gribble's lair. His neighbours had run out of money half way through the re-roofing, and blue tarpaulin had been on display for weeks. When he turned his car into the lane, though, there was no tarpaulin, no ladder, no thatcher's van and no thatcher. All that was on display was - magnificence. He'd never seen new thatch before, never appreciated the intricacy, the craftsmanship. His neighbour's roof was double-covered in a geometric cloak, created from what seemed to Batten merely bits of twig and straw, thousands of them, which had once sprouted from the soil and were now carved into textured curves, delicate facings and an intricate patterned crown. He got out of his car to look more closely. Zig, this isn't craft, it's *art*. And you live next door to it.

The missing thatcher's van became bright red as Ozzie the postman pulled in, waving a parcel at Batten, who signed for a small package dotted with foreign stamps. Grigoris. I bet you ten euros, Zig, it's a false Greek moustache and some glue.

It was coffee, in a sealed pack, and with it an engraved, copper-bottomed pot, the kind he'd admired in Corfu Town, with a long handle jutting out from one side, so it could be removed from the stove and poured. He almost nipped back home to try it, but was already caffeined up and primed for work. Instead, he opened the envelope Grigoris had sent and drew out the folded card, home-made, a photograph glued on the front. It showed a flight of stairs up to the door of a pretty villa - the

Grigoris home, he assumed. Every step was crammed with people, two dozen or more, young and old, family resemblance yelling out at the camera, and on the top step a moustachioed, smiling Grigoris, one arm around a dark-haired, noble-faced woman, the other across the shoulders of three beautiful, olive-skinned young girls. The message on the card said, 'This is my family, Sig. When once more you come to Greece, they also will be yours.'


'Balance, sir, just as you say, sir.'

'And don't you dare imagine for an instant that I countenance tokenism, Batten. She's a good detective - full stop, rubber-stamp, file closed. Clear?'

'Clear, sir.'

'DC Hazel Timms' was printed on the buff folder marooned on Gribble's desk. She was George Halfpenny's replacement, and if the ACC was correct, had George's skill with sums and spreadsheets, along with guts and get-up-and-go. Batten welcomed the help. Gribble had misinterpreted his lukewarm reaction - it wouldn't be Gribble telling Jon Lee he was staying in uniform.

Magnus should be happy, though, not to be the only female. And new blood refreshed a tired team. Because they *were* tired, all of them, and Gribble knew it. Batten couldn't stop kicking at doors though.

'Any *other* changes, sir? While I'm in the building.'

Gribble chose not to bite.

'Changes, Batten?'

'Yes, sir. In view of Chief Inspector Jellicoe's....departure.'

Impasse. Gribble wasn't going to say so, but Batten's bad luck was being in the slot called 'Inspector', on the Force's over-worked middle rung. If only Batten had shown some interest in cricket. *Inspector grade, you see, it's the reliable chap who bats with gusto at six or seven, bowls a bit of spin. Well, doesn't open the innings, or get the new ball, does he?*

Gribble wished the Chief Constable had said that, instead of dictating that, for now, they 'luxuriate in the very large space *at long last* vacated by *your* Mr Jellicoe.'

But she had a point. PC Lee wasn't the only one not quite ready for the next step up. He looked across his desk of diplomas at Batten, liked him really, an experienced detective. Forthright. And we all have good days and bad. The Chief Constable had phrased it more precisely, mind. 'When he does have a bad day, *must* he turn into a rubber bullet?'

No, no other changes, yet.

Batten nodded at a smiling Mrs Pinch, breaking into a smile of his own when he reached the car park. Gribble had agreed to cut him a little slack from now on - out of superfluous guilt, it seemed. As if he *wanted* Jellicoe's job! He headed for Parminster, and a desk already plastered with Inspector-grade quantities of paper. Jesus, why want even *more*?

After a few miles, the smooth bump of Burrow Hill popped up through the roadside trees. He'd been wondering what to send Grigoris, as a thank-you for the Greek coffee pot now gracing his kitchen stove. Something that spoke of his new county - a water colour of herons on the Somerset Levels perhaps? Burrow Hill was forgiven now, and it decided for him.

Next day he was in the cider farm shop at the foot of the one-treed mound, in conversation with Erin Kemp, the green-eyed manageress. He had no trouble pulling his eyes from the shelves of tempting bottles to look at her instead.

'I didn't realise you had to serve in the shop too.'

He swallowed an acid memory of Rhona Fiske, whingeing about unpaid overtime at Wake Hall.

'I don't, as a rule, but Colin's slipped off somewhere.'

Erin Kemp was an honest woman but this was not the time to admit she had *told* Colin to slip off somewhere, when she saw the tall, moustached policeman park his car and approach the shop. Batten explained what he wanted. Oh yes, they sent vintage Somerset Cider Brandy all over the place. She'd be happy to package it for him if he liked? Did he have the address? Oh, Greece. I've never been.

'You'd like it.'

'Would I? How do you know?'

'Instinct.' And because I'm going to take you there, show you.

'Policeman need a bit of that, do they?'

Some more than others, he could have said. 'And I have an instinct about *you*.'

She returned his smile. Eyes, skin, warmth.

'An instinct?'

He was right. She loved springtime, loved walking. He suggested Saturday, his next day off. When she hesitated, he sank back down into his shoes.

'Oh, it's not a problem - I'm just thinking which grandparent to ask.'

'Grandparent?'

'To look after Sian - oh, you wouldn't know, of course. My daughter.'

'Ah. Right.'

He wasn't sure how he felt about that.

'How old is....?'

'Sian. She's just turned twelve.' Erin Kemp gave a golden laugh. 'I was young when I had her. 'She's lucky - *I'm* lucky - she has four grandparents still alive. More and more of us do, these days, don't we?'

Well, not him. A twelve year old, though. Thirteen before you know it.

# Fifty

Jess Foreman's duties 'assisting CID' now over, he made a pleasant return to his old haunt, The Lamb and Flag. He was finishing the sudoku puzzle in the evening paper when Lonny Dalway the milkman loped in for his pint of cider. He only ever had the one, and always said the same thing when he watched it being poured - 'it do look better'n milk, don' it, squirtin' into a glass?'

Lonny and Jess touched pints and shared gossip. Lonny's news was as much a surprise as it had been to Lonny.

'What, official, all above board? Not that you'd tell me if it weren't.'

'As I stands 'ere, Jess, s'all written down and signed. They's got a new Misser Vann up there, 'n he do it all.'

Jess had met the 'new Mr Vann'. His name was Ellory Waters, which to Jess sounded like a trout lake.

'Never thort I'd see the day, Jess. He tap me on the shoulder -'

'How'd he do that, Lonny? He's nine inch shorter'n you!'

' - he tap me on the shoulder, and says can I start deliverin' milk to that new 'orse place. Ev'ry day, six day a week. Aarh, course, says I. They wan' a *lot* o' milk, Jess. Place is even bigger'n before.'

Wake Hall Equestrian was well known to Jess Foreman. His daughter, now a stable-girl there, had shown him its new vastness. Most of the staff were young women, and local.

'She insist, see, do 'er Ladyship. Women get first crack, folk say.'

'Not at deliverin' milk, though, Lonny?'

'My good fortune, Jess.'

They touched glasses, then Lonny did something rare. He offered to buy a round, to celebrate - perhaps because he knew Jess was driving.

Draining his pint, Jess said his goodbyes and strolled out into the night. Seeing the note on his windscreen, he thought his car had been clipped while parked, but there was no obvious damage. The folded scrap, torn from a paper-bag, sported a few pencilled scrawls in block-capitals. There was an address, near Drayton, and a message: 'Pig, go see.'

Kids, probably, winding up the local copper. Sort of a welcome home, he decided, putting the note in his pocket for tomorrow. It was Friday night, and Jess Foreman headed for the chip shop.


Spring blossom hung like white marshmallow as she guided him through the geometric lines of apple orchard to the south of Over Stratton.

'It's pretty, isn't it?' she asked.

'It is,' he replied, looking at her, not the trees.

They'd eaten a fine beef and bacon pie in The Royal Oak, and were walking off the calories in sunshine and warmth. The stirrings of spring were welcome, but to Batten they held notes of warning too. How many 'first flush' relationships had he started, only for the buds to drop before fruit could form? He didn't want this to be another. Begin, and cease. And then again begin. A new place, a new life, Zig, and Erin Kemp is easy to be with. He hoped she felt the same about him.

As they emerged from the white-speckled orchard, an unwanted chirp from his mobile made him curse. He looked at the screen; it was Ball. Apologetically, he mouthed 'work' at Erin Kemp, tried to smile, moved a few paces away.

'No choice but to ring, zor.'

Saturday. He wanted to say 'spit it out, I'm on a promise!' But he knew Ball's tone too well.

''Fraid we've found a body, zor. By that, I mean a dead one, o' course.'

'Ah. OK.'

And now you'll see it, Zig. And smell it.

'Where?'

'It's in a barn, in an orchard, out Drayton way. Not pretty, zor. Not exactly fresh.'

Batten gulped down bile. A fine lunch, soon to be capped by decomposition and the stench of decay. He glanced at Erin Kemp, patiently sitting on a fallen tree, cheeks aglow, smiling expectantly back at him.

Ball was adding details - murder weapon left at the scene - a pair of bolt-cutters - heavy-duty - still embedded in the skull. When he said how long the body had likely been there, the timeframe clicked and Batten knew who it was.

Was it fair to send Nina Magnus to break the bad news to Oksana Unpronounceable? We've found your missing brother, but....Blast, he would have to go too. And what *was* Oksana's surname? Vossi-something? Vossi-Encyclopaedic? Well, it *ended* in 'ic', at least. He gave the white-speckled trees a final look.

'Is Magnus around?'

'On leave, from today, zor, if you recall.' Got a new bloke, Mike, they've gone walking in Turkey, the Lycian Way. Batten didn't need to know.

'It'll have to be you and me, then, Ballie, to break the news.'

'Break the news to who, zor?'

To whom, Ballie.

'To Oksana Vossi-Encyclopaedic, or whatever the family name is.'

'You've lost me, zor.'

'Well presumably it's Oksana's brother, Dave - the mis/per that Magnus was chasing. Timeframe fits like a glove.'

'Oh, no, zor, there's a wallet, photo driving licence, see. Enough left of the face to....well, to be who it says.'

'It's *not* Dave Thing, then?'

'It's a Tom, zor. A Tom Bowditch. Or it *was*.'

Batten turned to gaze at Erin Kemp. Golden skin, green expressive eyes - speaking volumes now. Is this a policeman's life, they asked? Does *life* get a look-in?

Give me time, his eyes said back. Please. I'll do whatever I can.

# Acknowledgements

A huge thanks to everyone who made suggestions and corrections after slogging through early drafts, especially Yvonne, Sam, Gwyneth, Pete, Moya, Brian, Tony, Albert, Alan, Susie, and Marielaine - and to Matt at Candescent Press for his prompt helpfulness.

Thanks also to the poor devils who put up with me nattering on about the damn thing.

Printed in Great Britain
by Amazon